Stones Corner

Light

Volume 3

Jane Buckley

ORLA KELLY
PUBLISHING

The Stones Corner Tetralogy

Volume 1: **Turmoil** (January 2021)

ISBN 9781912328710

Volume 2: **Darkness** (September 2021)

ISBN 9781914225598

Volume 3: **Light** (December 2022)

978-1-915502-16-2

Volume 4: **Hope** (To be confirmed)

STONES CORNER

Volume 3 Light first published in Ireland in 2022

Orla Kelly Publishing

27 Kilbrody Mount

Oval Village Cork,

IRELAND T12 E0XT

Warning:

This book contains scenes of violence and descriptions of a sexual nature. It also features graphic language in use in the 1980s. It is a work of fiction but the storyline is loosely based on actual events.

The views expressed in this book and the other volumes in the Stones Corner series are those of the author, and the characters are for the most part fictitious. In our efforts to move on from The Troubles in Northern Ireland, it is crucial first to understand how and why the turmoil occurred, then to acknowledge the hardships and sorrows that afflicted the country and its inhabitants, and finally to reflect upon the lessons learned. The Stones Corner series is written in the hope of facilitating this process.

Copyright © Jane Buckley 2022
Derrygirl.ie Ltd
All rights reserved.

No part of this publication should be reproduced, stored in a retrieval system, or transmitted in any form or by any means, electronic, mechanical, photocopying, recording, or otherwise, without the prior permission of both the copyright owner and the publisher of this book.

For further information on the Stones Corner tetralogy, please visit:

www.janebuckleywrites.com
Instagram @janebuckley_writes
Facebook jane buckley writes author
Twitter @janebuckley_sc

Contents

Jane Buckley	vii
Stones Corner Darkness	xi
The River's Tale	xiii
Stones Corner Light Chapters 1-54	1
The Importance of Book Reviews	427
Summary of Main Characters and Locations	429

Jane Buckley

Indie-Reader award winning author Jane Buckley was born in Derry, Northern Ireland, in the mid-1960s and has been asked many times when travelling the world, "*Why did the Troubles get so bad?*" Or "*What caused them to last so long?*" Or even, "*Why did they start!*"

Based on actual events, the Stones Corner Tetralogy (Turmoil, Darkness, Light and Hope (*to be confirmed*) will answer all these questions while taking you on a thrilling journey, a pilgrimage of heartache, bravery, treachery, and tragic love. From my own life experiences, I write about growing up during the Troubles, bringing with it sad, complicated and bleak memories.

Some readers may cringe when they come across a book about the Troubles, but I feel so passionate about helping others learn what life was like by telling a thrilling, fictional tale. So far, I've been overwhelmed by the fantastic response and feedback. It's surreal and has only fuelled my determination to get my stories to as broad an audience as possible. I moved back to Ireland a few short years ago, and I find it disheartening to hear the same language used in politics today as it was fifty years ago.

2023 is the 25th anniversary of the Good Friday Agreement, which enables us to live on a peaceful, fantastic island. Still, this stability is highly fragile, and we should never take it for granted.

In memory of Daddy, Charles, Brian, and Frank,
sorely missed and much loved, and for all the victims of The Troubles.

John, thank you for the endless cups of tea and loving support, Lynn Curtis for your infinite guidance, Orla Kelly for your absolute patience, and thank you to my bubble and grandchildren for just being you!

STONES CORNER

Volume 2

Darkness

"Having read the first book in this series of four, I couldn't wait to get my hands on this one and...it certainly did not disappoint! It's a cracking story with well written characters. The multiple threads of the story are crafted with such skill.

The last 20% of the book has sub-plots coming thick and fast and yet another cliff hanger ending which will keep us all coming back for more! I for one cannot wait to read the final two books!"

"The wait for this sequel was frustrating but very much worth it. Like I've read in other reviews it was hard to put it down. Absolutely riveting. The story moves from character to character, it's very easy to follow she has a knack of reminding you where you left off. Can't wait for the last two volumes. The books have got me back into reading again."

"Another absolutely brilliant book by Jane Buckley. I couldn't put this book down. It is so well written and goes into so much detail. It gives both sides of The Troubles in Ireland.

Living in the UK when they were going on, we only got information of what was happening from the tv and papers. I have now seen a completely different interpretation of what went on. Really looking forward to the next book in this series."

"Thank goodness to get the next instalment in the Stones Corner series - it was absolutely worth the wait!!! Once again, I could not put this book down as we find out what happens to our favourite characters after the explosive finale of Stones Corner- Turmoil.

The author weaves her magic by introducing new characters and plots without making the reader feel lost in the story line. The book has obviously been meticulously researched giving the reader an understanding of Derry's, and indeed Northern Ireland's, troubled past. Be prepared for another emotional rollercoaster as the storyline unfolds and you get caught up in the lives of the familiar (and new) characters.

Once again, I'm left wanting more and I cannot wait for Stones Corner- Hope. Another fabulous offering from the author whose passion and love for Derry and its people is clearly shown in this absolute page turner!! Well done!"

THE RIVER'S TALE

You took our sons and daughters in dark days gone by;
Fathers watch in silent dignity as mothers wail and cry.
They called it emigration, but we just called it pain,
As the river took our life's blood to a place without a name.

Why did you bring soldiers in their gunships from the war?
Stopping off in our town to take our girls to lands afar.
Just more emigration, dressed up in another name;
More blood ebbing from our land – different yet the same.

Somehow your magnetic forces draw troubled minds into the deep.
Keeping them there for so long, as families frantically search and worry and weep.
They're gone forever, yet you still flow from source to mouth and ebb from tide to tide.
Can you help us, can you warn us, to stop the scourge of suicide?

So, flow on wise old river, tell your tale to us someday,
About days when ones of our town were forced to go away.

And look how you divide us, nature's beauty but man's beast;
The east bank looking westward and the west bank looking east.
Bridges cross your troubled waters, but some hearts remain so cold;
Holding history in your depths, just like in days of old.

Looking out I see the changes, as you go to meet the sea;
Boats just messing on the river, not a threat to you or me.
Peaceful waters save our children from a future of exile;
Cooling waters, uniting people, seeing hatred reconcile.

Now a peace bridge spans your banks, reaching out to both sides;
Offering harmony to a city, instead of division and lost lives.
Still work to do but we will get there, and we will follow as you flow;
Telling your tale to future generations, because only you really know.

So, flow on wise old river, tell your tale to us some day;
About days when our sons and daughters stood up and had their say.

© Eamonn Lynch, Derry, 2022

Truth, Justice, Healing, Reconciliation

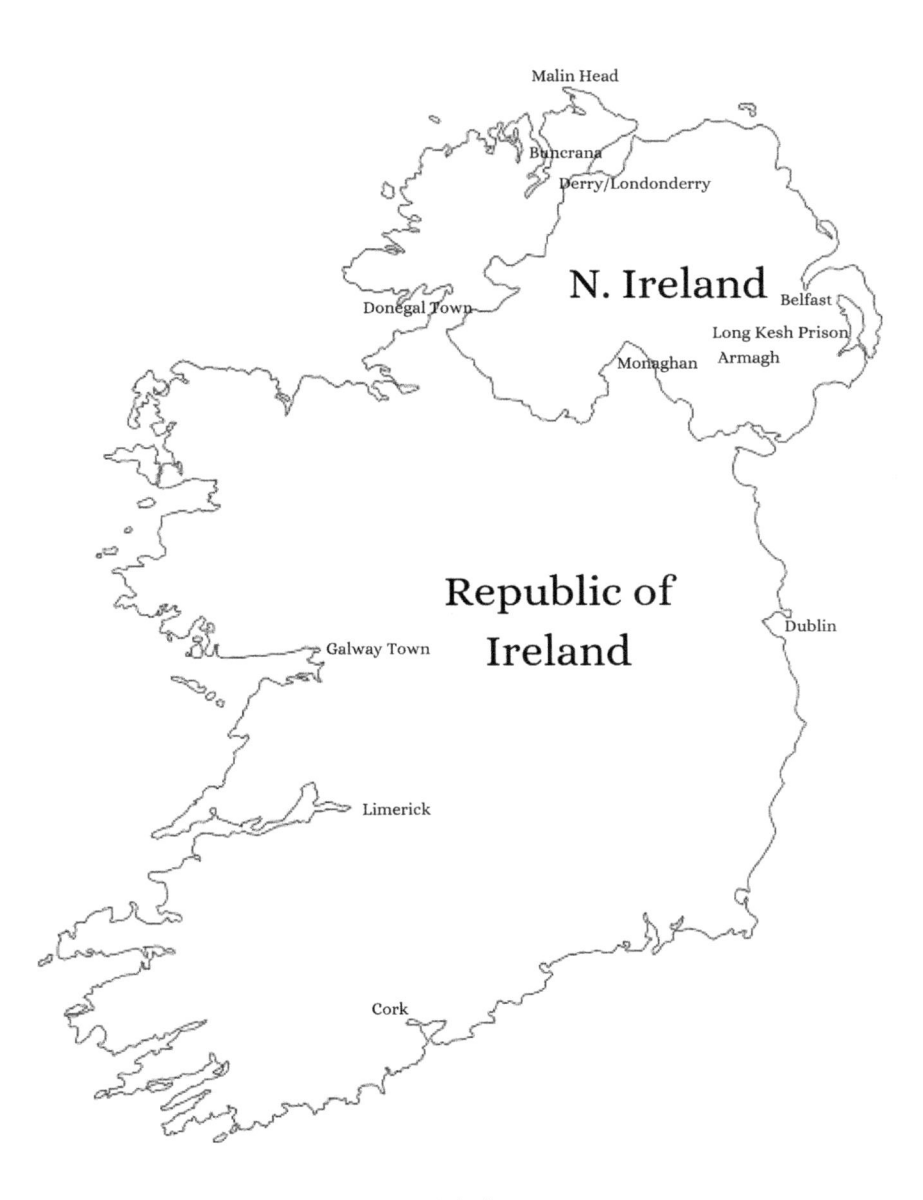

Ireland

- Malin Head
- Buncrana
- Derry/Londonderry
- Donegal Town
- N. Ireland
- Belfast
- Long Kesh Prison
- Monaghan
- Armagh
- Galway Town
- Republic of Ireland
- Dublin
- Limerick
- Cork

Chapter One

Christmas, London 1975

Never in her wildest dreams would Caitlin McLaughlin have imagined finding herself alone and friendless in a decaying London hostel one frosty Christmas morning. She felt hollow; all her foolish hopes and dreams ended forever. She thought she might go mad for a while, but even that escape eluded her.

Her gloomy accommodation consisted of a shared room that slept four in a pair of draped bunk beds on either side of a tall, murky Georgian window. It offered no view but for a couple of permanently drawn discoloured curtains that failed miserably to keep out the cold. Caitlin's head hung low as she gazed at her shabby suitcase on the mattress beside her. It contained the last of her worldly possessions. She'd paid little attention to her gloomy surroundings in the darkness last night, so grateful was she finally to rest her head on a pillow after her wrenching departure from Derry.

On the hour-long flight from Belfast, she'd kept her tear-stained, blotched face well hidden from the other passengers and did the same on the tube journey to the heart of London. Almost catatonic with grief and exhaustion, she'd purchased her tickets, read the Underground map and picked up a free Aussie backpacking guide to London, where she found details of the Victoria-based hostel. She couldn't remember much more about the journey, only a pestering male passenger on the train from Derry to Belfast and his futile attempts to flirt with her. Eventually, thank God, he took the hint, swore at her and likely went on to hound someone else.

She thought she'd better get a job quickly, but it was Christmas Day; everywhere was closed. Perhaps she'd been too hasty in leaving Derry. She'd lied to Kathy, her cousin, telling her she was going away for a few days, and poor uncle Tommy would be livid when he found out she'd left without so much as a goodbye to him.

James Henderson had failed to show up at the train station. Although she knew he loved her, deep down, Caitlin wasn't surprised. She should have realised he would never leave Derry with her, and now she felt like an absolute fool for daring to hope that he would. He wouldn't give up his well-respected position there, heading up the Rocola shirt factory, not in a million years. She cringed when she recalled how she'd urged him to run away with her. How naïve she'd been. But then, she'd heard love made people do crazy things.

On the endless, lonely journey away from the people and places dear to her, she wondered why so many awful things had to happen to her, her family and her friends. Her daddy died of his injuries after being wrongfully arrested by the British Army. Mammy, by her own hand, a poor ghost of herself in the aftermath of losing her husband and then their youngest child. Tina… at the age of fifteen, was seduced and led into darkness by a man who'd used her to further his murderous schemes. She had suffered a tragic ending, fading away and dying in Armagh Women's Gaol. And Anne Heaney, the liveliest and loveliest of Caitlin's friends, with her leg blown away when the girls were caught up in an explosion in Shipquay Street. What had Caitlin done to deserve all this doom and disaster when all she'd ever dreamed of was falling in love, having loads of babies and staying close to her family? Was that too much to ask? It appeared so. There wasn't only one gaping, painful hole in her heart. There'd been so many losses she doubted she would ever heal.

To stop herself from crying, she took a deep breath, retrieved the worn suitcase from the floor, opened it and took out her daddy's beloved Aran jumper. There was nothing of value in the case, but she tucked it behind the bunk bed anyway. She'd noticed a newsagent's shop on the corner and decided to buy a paper there so she could look for work. Her overcoat felt too tight on top of the Aran, but it didn't matter; she couldn't care less what she looked like so long as she was warm.

Exiting the hostel, which had all but emptied over the Christmas holiday, she walked toward the newsagent's, holding tightly to her purse with its last few remaining pounds. Fortunately, she'd enough money aside from her modelling work to pay for the single airfare and a bit more to live on while she found her feet. From the poor state of the hostel, she wasn't surprised it had proved to be mega-cheap. She'd been able to pay a week upfront, which was some consolation.

Outside, the air was crisp and dry, and there was barely any traffic. The wide streets were eerily quiet. Retailers had painstakingly decorated their shops for Christmas, but she paid no heed. She wanted to get a paper and something to eat, remembering that apart from the complimentary tea and snack on the plane, she hadn't eaten for a few days.

The pedestrians she passed kept their heads deliberately low and walked quickly on their way. As she stood on the threshold of the newsagent's, she saw that the middle-aged, red-headed woman behind the counter looked beleaguered and afraid as she stared fixedly at a blustering customer.

"'Ere, you're one o' them sneaky Irish bastards, ain't ya?" cried a short and burly boggle-eyed drunk, spitting out the hate-fuelled words through his rotting teeth. The shop assistant's rosy complexion drained as she felt the familiar rise of fear in her gut and the pounding of her heart.

Because of the IRA's London bombing campaign earlier in the summer, sadly for her and many other Irish people living in England, this type of tirade was happening more and more often. Nuala Mclean was tired of finding herself the butt of such abuse but knew it was best to keep her mouth shut or risk antagonising the ignorant gobshite even more. Just then, a pretty young woman entered the shop and picked her way past the sozzled tramp.

"Bloody carrot-topped micks… comin' over 'ere wiv yer bombs and yer bullets… we should 'ang the lotta yer!" The drunk ranted. He swung his arms back and forth menacingly.

He wore an oversized, dirty black coat with sleeves that were too long and had to be rolled up. The bottom hem of the coat practically swept the shop floor. A pair of worn brown boots were visible beneath, with only the right one laced and the other undone, trailing on the ground.

"I 'eard yer talkin' afore. So come on, answer me! You're an Irish bike, aren't yer? I can tell from that tarty red hair. Bet yer got the temper to go wiv it an' all!" the drunk laughed, turning to face Caitlin, who stepped back in horror from his rancid breath and sweet-sour odour.

"See her?" he spat, pointing one finger at the shop assistant. "She's only a flaming Paddy, a bombin' Mick! Fuckin' spud-pickers… I 'ate the fuckin' lot of yer!"

Caitlin said nothing but stared into space, visualising what would happen if he realised she was Irish too. She tried to formulate some response, but the frustrated tramp shook his head at her reticence.

"Ah, forget it!" he sighed, waving the hand in which he gripped a near-empty bottle of cheap whisky. Blinking numerous times and squinting his cloudy eyes, he belatedly noticed that the newcomer was a true beauty. Their eyes locked, and bizarrely, Caitlin noticed his were the loveliest shade of sapphire blue. Without thinking, she gave a soft, warm smile.

It seemed to unsettle him. He looked baffled, unsure of what to do next. "Fuck it, I'm off outta here!" he cried, grunting angrily and pushing Caitlin aside as he returned to the street.

She shook her head and looked enquiringly at the relieved shop assistant. "You okay?"

Straight away, Nuala relaxed. She'd recognised Caitlin's accent. "You've nothing to be sorry for, love; he's a drunken old tramp, but he right scares me at times." She smiled before she asked, "Derry, right?"

"Yeah. You?" Caitlin replied.

"Omagh."

There was a fleeting moment of awkwardness before Caitlin asked, "Does that kind of thing happen a lot over here?"

"You've no idea," Nuala sighed, "and it's got worse since the summer. All those bombings. People don't trouble to hide the hatred they feel for us... I've been in England nearly thirty years, and it's worse than ever now. You been here long?"

Caitlin half-smiled and shrugged. "Just arrived, and I'm looking for work. Which paper is best for jobs?" she asked, eyes wandering across the newspaper display.

Nuala looked more closely at the girl in the tight shabby coat and Aran jumper. Another lost soul from home, here to seek her fortune! She'd done the same and look where she'd ended up: working in a newsagent for Mr Patel, bless the old bugger.

"Best for work is the *Evening Standard*, but that one's from yesterday," Nuala replied, pointing to a few remaining copies of the London paper.

"That'll do," Caitlin muttered, opening her purse, "I want a sense of what's around. How much?"

"Don't worry about it, love, take it. I'll be throwing it out anyway. I'm closing in a while, heading home to cook the Christmas dinner," the woman replied kindly.

"Are you sure?" Caitlin asked, her eyes suddenly filling up.

Nuala saw and gave her a warm smile. "Yeah, go on." She folded the paper in two and handed it over. "Where are you staying?"

She'd seen too many naïve youngsters arrive in the big smoke, fall in with the wrong crowd, get hooked on drugs and end up living on the streets – especially around this area. She'd been lucky; she'd met a man who worked for Westminster Council, and in a matter of months, they were living together, just round the corner off Horseferry Road in a lovely little flat. They'd never got round to marrying, which suited Nuala fine. Tom was a kind man. He'd never change the world, but he was good to her. She couldn't complain.

Caitlin was pleasantly surprised by the woman's concern. "In the hostel over there, just a bit up the street. It's dead quiet. So far, I've only seen the man behind the desk."

"Aye, it would be; they've all gone home. All those Aussies and Kiwis were flocking back to their families and the sun. Lucky bastards!"

"I think I should have waited 'til the New Year to come over," Caitlin whispered. "I never realised..."

Nuala couldn't hear the girl's next words, but her face said it all. It was nearly lunchtime. Out of the blue, she decided to close the shop slightly early. Until that loudmouth walked in, she hadn't had a single customer all morning. "Tell you what, let's introduce ourselves: I'm Nuala. Nuala Mclean. What about you?"

"Caitlin. McLaughlin."

"Well, Caitlin, how about we have a cuppa together, and then we can get to know each other? Or do you have anywhere else in the world to be!" Nuala giggled.

"No. There's nowhere. And I'm dying for a cuppa," Caitlin replied appreciatively.

"Let me shut up this place, and we'll go out the back. I think I've got some sandwiches and bits here, too, if you're hungry?" She smiled at Caitlin, nodded and waved her through.

As Nuala poured the hot tea, she fired out question after question. She wasn't nosy; she wanted to hear this girl's story. Perhaps she could steer her right in some small way. Nuala had turned fifty and reminded Caitlin of an older version of Anne, her best friend in Derry. She seemed to possess an innate talent for taking the piss out of the worst thing that could happen and somehow making light of it.

"I bet you left because of a man? I know I did." Nuala's eyes twinkled.

Shame-faced, Caitlin nodded. "Mostly."

"Bastards," Nuala groaned. "Can't live with them, can't live without them."

They shared a smile and, by mutual consent, quickly changed the painful subject. Nuala added, "I love Derry, always have. It's changed, I'm sure since I was last there. It's an awful mess with these Troubles, especially for you youngsters. I suppose I don't blame you for getting out." She wasn't expecting an answer but slurped her tea and bit into an out-of-date orange Club biscuit.

"You want to talk about it?" she asked gently, looking at the girl with the pale, drawn face.

Caitlin's eyes dropped before she answered. She bit her lip and sighed, "Ah, Nuala, it's a very long story, and I'm so tired, I don't think I have the energy."

Nuala tutted and shook her head in commiseration. "Of course, you are, love. It must be sad being all on your own on Christmas Day. If you're around for the next week, I'll help you all I can. Together we'll get you sorted."

****

With Nuala's advice and support, a secure secretarial job was found. Caitlin felt newly determined to put everything behind her, to lock away all the pain, misery and heartache she'd lived through in Derry and learn to start her life afresh. Every day, she grew bolder about re-inventing herself. No one here knew her history, and she fully embraced the gift of anonymity that city life offers. For the first time, Caitlin McLaughlin could be and do whatever she wanted.

Nevertheless, memories would bear her back to Blamfield Street and Derry at unguarded moments like a mighty tidal wave. In these challenging, haunting flashbacks, she could almost see, touch, smell and hear the life that used to be hers: the sobbing of mothers and children and shrieks of resisting men, dragged from their beds by assailants in battledress—the deep reverberating sounds of the many bomb blasts and foul smell of burning, bloody flesh. Time was the best healer she knew, but sometimes, for Caitlin, it stood disturbingly still.

When she first looked for somewhere to rent on her own, she faced countless rejections from landlords who were vocal in their hatred of the Irish. Eventually, however, she found a bedsit in one of the many terraced houses off the High Street in Stoke Newington in northeast London. The house belonged to a short, bald, dark-eyed Turkish landlord who called himself Fred. Unlike far too many others in London, he welcomed her warmly.

He could only offer a small back room with a single bed, a two-ring electric stove, a small table and a lone chair, but it didn't matter. To Caitlin, it was perfect; it was hers alone, and she'd finally get out of shared accommodation at the hostel. As other tenants vacated rooms, Caitlin ended up in what Fred called his 'best' room on the ground floor. *Best* was certainly not the word she'd use for it, but it was way better than before, and he tried to make it as comfortable as he could for her.

Stoke Newington had turned out to be an area popular with squatters, artists and political activists – a far cry from the fabled glitz and glamour of the West End that had initially drawn her. But to Caitlin McLaughlin, the down-at-heel area was a home away from home. She was a Londoner now.

****

Chapter Two

London, England 1981

It was another clammy summer evening. The sun seemed reluctant to surrender its heat as Caitlin climbed down from the 73 bus and walked towards home. She felt sticky and tired. As she stepped onto the pavement, she heard a commotion. Looking to her left, she caught sight of the tail end of a group of black teenagers running like the wind along the high street, pursued by baton-wielding wooden tops who struggled to catch up with them while holding on to their Custodian helmets.

Like back home in Derry, riots and public unrest had become commonplace in England, politically or racially motivated, and the police presence in Stoke Newington had notably increased over the previous weeks. Although she'd been happy enough to live here for the past six years, she had seen more and more disorder on the streets lately. She walked past Johnson's Café, favoured by the kids in the area, black and white. The police conducted frequent drug busts there, harassing the young people but being especially tough on the black men.

This evening the atmosphere was tense; Caitlin grew nervous. She didn't have far to go before she reached her bedsit, but as she turned the corner, she heard behind her the familiar sound of breaking glass, the loud ringing of a burglar alarm and a screech of tyres followed by shrill yells and screams. Another raid on the café was in progress. She ran full pelt for the blue-painted front door of the multi-occupant house where she lived.

Over the years, she'd got to know quite a few of the boys and girls from Johnson's and was on good terms with them. Most had tried their best to find work but couldn't. Instead, many of the girls had babies; it guaranteed them dole payments and accommodation. The black youths were incessantly harassed by the Met police, who'd stop and question them on the flimsiest pretexts. For example, if they were driving a half-decent car or wore fashionable gold chains or heavy jewellery, it was assumed they were stolen. When the police stopped a black suspect, if they gave a wrong answer or else refused to give one at all, they'd be thrown in the back of a van and addressed as a *bunny* (short for *jungle bunny*).

"And once we're in the back of the van, they'll kick the shit out of us mob-handed and then bang us up, dragging their heels when it comes to bail. They treat us like animals. They treat their dogs better than they treat us!" Caitlin frequently heard.

Nothing in these stories surprised her; it all sounded depressingly familiar. Just like at home in Derry, prejudice and narrow-mindedness were permanently close at hand.

Safely inside the house, she hastily picked up the post from a hall table. She began searching through the ever-growing pile of assorted envelopes and advertising flyers – mostly from Pizza Hut. There'd been no letters from James Henderson, yet even after all this time and the awful, enduring pain of losing him, she still carried a tiny glimmer of hope that she'd hear from him one day. If he wanted to contact her, he could; Tommy had her address. Every morning as she left for work, she'd tell herself not to expect anything, but she did, searching through the post on her return, and it infuriated her. Although she'd not been back home to Derry for years, it felt like yesterday that she'd been waiting for James at the train station. He had become part of her DNA; she doubted she'd ever get over him. A confusing thought crossed her mind as she took off her coat. *What if he did contact her? What would she do – especially now?*

Sighing wearily, she threw her handbag and keys onto the double bed beneath the bay window and took in her decrepit surroundings. This place wasn't much, but it was at least a refuge. The walls were adorned with cheap black-and-white posters, including a shot of Audrey Hepburn in *Breakfast at Tiffany's*, a favourite of Caitlin's. They'd served their true purpose well, covering the spreading dampness and mould. An attempt at painting the room a comforting Irish green had proved futile, given that Caitlin had feared half the plaster would come off with each brush stroke. On top of a bedside cabinet stood a framed print of the only group picture of her fragmented family. It'd been taken one Christmas way before The Troubles and was now yellowed and faded with time. Before she slept every night, she'd kiss it and pray for her family, including her only surviving sibling, Martin.

Safe in the States and out of harm's way, the brother who'd once been an active volunteer with the PIRA had settled down with his employer Brian Meenan's sister, Sinead, and appeared to be doing well. They didn't correspond often, but he sounded happy and content when he wrote. Caitlin assumed any involvement with 'the boys' had been consigned to the past.

A scratched and battered chest of drawers supported a circular, brown-framed mirror alongside her mother's sterling silver hairbrush set. Her father's lovely Aran jumper was neatly folded and rested on a rickety chair in the corner. Apart from some clothes, these were the only things she'd taken from 30 Blamfield Street.

Picking up her mammy's hairbrush, Caitlin caught sight of her reflection in the mirror and smiled. She'd changed beyond all recognition. She'd swapped out her thick, long black hair for a shoulder-length, strawberry-blonde cut that cost her a small fortune to maintain. She wore it tied up for work and in a long bob outside the office. Her porcelain skin was enhanced by subtle makeup, and she wore dark navy mascara to heighten the blue of her eyes. Her clothes were unassuming but classic, showing off her willowy figure. Gone was the naïve young Derry girl. Here stood Caitlin McLaughlin reborn.

She was due to leave the bedsit for the last time this evening and had finished work earlier than usual. She'd given Fred notice weeks ago; her staying here was pointless.

Without warning, a loud, insistent banging startled her, and she heard her landlord cry in the hall, "Caitlin, quick! Open up!" She rushed over to find him with sweat on his forehead, his grimy face reminiscent of a coalman's and his clothes speckled with a fine powder of dust and dirt.

"Jesus, Fred, what is it? What's happened?"

In broken English, he told her she needed to leave and soon. The area was under siege.

"I don't understand!" Caitlin cried as she turned to grab her trusty suitcase, already packed, and gather up her remaining bits and bobs. Over the past weeks, she'd taken most of her clothes to her new home in Islington. Hurrying up and down the long hallway with her possessions, she heard Fred puffing, panting and gabbling to himself in a mixture of Turkish and incoherent English.

Taking one last look around, she felt a pang of nostalgia, but when Fred shouted for her to hurry, she quickly grabbed her coat and keys and shut the bedsit door behind her. He ran up and took the proffered keys.

"It is polis – they everywhere!" he cried. "Argos on fire, I inside but I okay! You must go to boyfriend. They come this way soon, lots of polis!"

"But I don't know if I can get there," Caitlin wailed. She imagined the buses would've stopped by now if there was trouble in the streets. Islington wasn't that far away, but how would she manage it?

"You take back way," Fred told her, answering her unspoken question while wiping his forehead with his sleeve. "Go out back. I stay here. You go!"

He pulled her down the corridor towards the rear door of the house. She had never had to go out this way before and found it led to a tiny yard filled with outdated electrical equipment, rubber tyres and yards of pipes – a natural dumping ground. She stopped in the doorway and, startling Fred, hugged him. Convinced he was blushing, he quickly waved her away. His warning was still ringing in her ears as she opened a rickety gate onto a long, rubbish-strewn, narrow lane: *"Go back way, not near street!"*

The last thing she needed was to step out into the middle of a riot. She held on tight to her suitcase and carefully made her way to the end of the lane. As she drew closer to the bottom, the racket grew louder, and she could see smoke billowing over the red-brick garden walls. Ear-splitting police sirens accompanied the overwhelming din of shop alarms, dogs barking, and men yelling and screaming, all illuminated by intermittent bursts of flashing blue light. Her heart raced as she stood frozen on the spot.

Youngsters threw firebombs at the police and shops. Like scavengers, looters of all ages, shapes and sizes ran in and out of Argos, grabbing whatever they could or teaming up to carry out more substantial electrical items. Others walked away in a casual, relaxed manner calculated to allay suspicion. Some carried clear plastic bags in which could be seen brand-new suits from Mr H's, a local menswear store that appeared to have been plundered to the last button and buckle. She saw a young man wearing a green, red and gold Rasta hat snatch a black sweatshirt and stuff it down the front of his jacket. Time and again, a few plunderers seemed to be returning to the electrical shop, consulting lists of items that were especially in demand.

Three lookouts in their late twenties stood on the opposite side of the street, watching on and smiling benevolently. Caitlin could hear their warning cries of *"Po–lice"*, with the accent on the first syllable, whenever the men in blue drew too close. An ageing ted dressed in a long drape jacket and brothel creepers, attracted to the Victoria Wine off-licence, wrapped a brick in a paper bag and hurled it with all his might at the window. It bounced back, leaving the glass intact, and

Caitlin almost giggled as she watched his red-faced attempts to smash the reinforced window – the only result being a dusting of powdered brick on the glass.

Meanwhile, brandishing riot shields, the police formed a line and charged down the street but were pushed back for a distance of forty metres before making a successful counter-charge. Bricks flew high in the air from behind the barrier railings outside the local Rio Cinema and landed, hard and nosily, on police Rovers, Escorts and vans.

Caitlin shook her head in despair. She had to get out of there. Walking as fast as she could in the opposite direction, she sought a safe phone box to call her fiancé, Christopher Pecaro, who was preparing dinner for them both not far away in his Islington townhouse.

****

Chapter Three

Derry/Londonderry, Northern Ireland 1981

"Daddy! Daddy, look! He did it again!" Four-year-old Charlotte Henderson stormed into the panelled study of Melrose, James Henderson's gracious nineteenth-century home in Prehen on the outskirts of Londonderry. Yelling at her father, who'd been quietly working, she pointed to a fierce red mark on the milk-white skin of her arm.

"I didn't! I didn't!" bawled Charlotte's twin PJ (Paul James), stomping after her until, coming within reach, he gave up the injured innocent act and viciously smacked his sibling on the very same spot. They were glorious-looking children with white-gold hair and green eyes, gifted with their father's enviably long lashes and relatively tall for their age. Charlotte wore her hair in two extra-long plaits, while PJ sported a bowl-shaped page boy cut. They both wore denim Oshkosh dungarees over blue-and-red checked shirts.

To the housekeeper's dismay, Charlotte's horrified screams rang through every inch of the old house and echoed from its solid walls. Mrs Moore had been frantically searching for the pair for the past ten minutes. Once the cook at Melrose, the middle-aged woman had filled the shoes of Henderson's beloved old housekeeper, Mrs Mac, following her retirement. James had convinced her mercifully to take Ned, uncle Roger's yelping dog, with her. For that, he was eternally grateful. He'd never liked the mutt, especially after his uncle's death when Ned had howled for hours.

The frustrated housekeeper struggled to steer the squabbling children out of the study by shooing them toward the kitchen. She hadn't agreed to this, child minding on top of everything else, yet more and more found herself babysitting, to the neglect of her other duties. As far as Mrs Moore was concerned, these two were spoilt, badly behaved brats, and you couldn't like them if you tried.

So far, their father couldn't keep a nanny for more than a month or two at the most, thanks to their surly behaviour and continual punching matches. As for Mrs Henderson's constant disappearances, well, there was another story altogether – *she was a sinner, that one, through and throug*h.

James Henderson finally lost patience and jumped to his feet. He caught his son by the scruff of the neck, grabbed his yowling, red-faced daughter by the elbow, and followed Mrs Moore in the direction of the stairs down to the cellar kitchen.

Sensing the grown-ups' anger – especially their father's – the twins quietened and sat forlornly at one end of the large central oak table. Mrs Moore got on with her chores, smiling inwardly to see the two limbs of Satan now looking more like a pair of cherubs, hands meekly folded in front of them, listening in silence while their father bollocked them.

****

A number of years before, under intense pressure to save Rocola, the family shirt-making business, James had agreed to a form of business arrangement – one he still bitterly regretted but, at the time, couldn't afford to refuse. It was far from ideal but suited both parties. With the active encouragement of his uncle Roger, James and Marleen Fry, one of his best and oldest friends, were to undertake an arranged marriage, pure and simple. Marleen would become Mrs James Henderson and acquire a veneer of married respectability that should, hopefully, hold at bay the lurid rumours floating around about her true sexual proclivities. In exchange, she would provide an heir for her family and his, and her trust fund could be raided to see Rocola through these troubled times.

The company by which his uncle and James set up such store was in severe financial difficulty, and they knew how vital it was to the city's economy. Its employees, predominantly women, were often sole breadwinners for their struggling families, most of whom resided in the Creggan Estate and Bogside area. The factory's closure would be a complete disaster for these hardworking people, the city's many independent businesses, and the Henderson's. James recalled his lack of interest in The Troubles when he first arrived in the city and felt embarrassed as he grew to understand how bad events really were in Northern Ireland.

He didn't love Marleen, at least not how a groom should love his bride. There was only one love for him, Caitlin McLaughlin, the raven-haired beauty he'd hurt so badly on two separate occasions. He'd been a fool to snub her after the City Hotel bombing, believing for a time that she was somehow involved. Her sister Tina had been implicated in the planned bomb attack and the previous gruesome murder of a young British soldier whom she'd lured into a honeytrap on the orders of her deranged seducer, Kieran Kelly. The whole sorry episode had been a mess, but luckily, the night before his wedding, he'd met Caitlin at the hospital by accident when he'd been visiting his uncle there, and she hers. They'd agreed to meet later that evening in a local café, where he'd told her how he felt and that she was still the only one for him.

She'd pleaded with him to run away with her, go to London and escape the Derry gossips, but he couldn't, and instead had left her waiting in vain for him at the train station on the morning that he married another woman. After failing to follow his heart, he was left permanently sad and filled with regret, with no love in his life other than that of his children.

Roger Henderson had been ecstatic at the prospect of his nephew marrying Marleen – it was the match he'd dreamt of for years – and, as a wedding gift, he formally handed Rocola over to his heir. Catherine, James's long-lost mother, attended the wedding but sat at the back of the small church and discreetly made herself scarce from the reception. Before James left for his honeymoon, mother and son found time to sit together in Melrose's rose garden. Unbeknownst to him, Catherine decided not to tell him the whole truth about what had happened between her and Roger while she was married to his brother, James Henderson Senior: her brother-in-law's violent abuse of her trust in him and her subsequent pregnancy. With James Senior recently dead in a car accident and Roger becoming a sick man, she decided that old wrongs no longer mattered. Hearing about them would only cause her son additional heartache.

She knew he'd married Marleen Fry for the wrong reasons, and no doubt that would come back to haunt him. Her account of her marital history seemed honest and straightforward.

It was a difficult time for her, she'd explained tactfully. She was unhappy with James Senior; Roger was miserable with his wife, Jocelyn. They'd given into their feelings only once...

It explained so much that had previously puzzled James and he felt almost relieved by this confession of adultery and his likely paternity. His relationship with his supposed father, James Henderson Senior, had been far from easy. After the wedding, he'd kept in touch with his mother, who had promised to revisit Prehen one day soon.

Roger's funeral was a massive affair where people from all denominations paid their respects. James gratefully recalled the kind words and letters of condolence he'd received from far and wide. However, the loss of James Senior in a road 'accident' that had been contrived, then Roger and Caitlin in such a short time, shook him to the core. To this very day, it still did if he allowed himself to examine his deepest feelings, which as a devoted family man, he fought hard not to.

Following their honeymoon, Marleen eventually got her choice of a Savoy wedding reception in London, where her parents and 250 other guests belatedly joined them. It was a grand, indulgent affair and undoubtedly cost the Frys a fortune. James found it pretentious and overblown and couldn't say he'd particularly enjoyed it, but for Marleen's sake, he tried.

Their Cancun honeymoon had been unnerving, with Marleen still grumbling about her husband's lateness at the church ceremony and the need for her to drive around the block. She'd given him a muttered reprimand when he eventually arrived, flustered and frantic after his inability to choose between the two women. James was painfully conscious throughout the service of Caitlin waiting for him. His fiancée noticed his tardiness and distracted mood as a bad omen; to top it off, her parent's delayed flight meant they missed the ceremony. The Fry's had prayed for such a match after discovering Marleen was unlikely to permanently fix her affection on any man. But by some miracle, their daughter's long-term friend, the highly personable James Henderson, was prepared – at a price - to make a go of the marriage.

The young couple eventually settled down and appeared happy. Not too long afterwards, Marleen announced she was pregnant, and James was delighted, especially at the prospect of twins. Marleen was not, though she revelled in the attention paid to her, mainly by her thoroughly mollified parents. The birth proved to be long and traumatic. Still, once she'd recovered, she snatched at any excuse to leave Derry, her husband, her colic-ridden, endlessly crying babies and stuffy old Melrose to head straight back to her girlfriend Penelope, aka Pen's loving arms. With relief that he'd performed his duty to the two families, James felt released from observing one aspect of their unwritten contract and quickly moved back into his old bedroom.

****

He continued scolding the twins in the kitchen until the inevitable happened, and his shocked kids began to weep uncontrollably. It was unusual for their father to lose his temper like this – he adored them. Still, he couldn't help it. Every day he grew increasingly frustrated by his wife's continued absence and blatant neglect of their young family.

He deliberately left the kids to stew for a bit. Charlotte spoke up first, softly and in a voice filled with regret. Most of the time, she knew how to get around her father but not today. Today was different. He'd scared her with his barking and scowling – she'd never seen him so cross before. She stood beside him at the end of the table and placed one chubby hand on the crook of his elbow. After pausing for a moment to be sure she had his attention, she asked shrewdly: "Daddy, when is Mum coming home? I miss her."

James sighed and quickly lifted the toddler onto his knee. He looked at the housekeeper and the woman's beady gaze softened with sympathy.

"I know, sweetheart. We all do, don't we, PJ?" James replied miserably. He reached for his son and pulled him in against his chest.

Mrs Moore thought it a sorry sight. James Henderson was a young, dynamic, handsome man with a hidden softness and kindness she'd come to admire, and by God, he loved those children with his very being. What a waste, she thought sadly; he should have a proper wife by his side, not that English floozy who – when she deigned to visit at all – flittered in and out, ignoring the wains, and all the time with her face as long as day! The lad reminded her of one of those Freeman catalogue models, sitting there in his open-necked shirt, corduroys and a tailored Donegal tweed jacket. His hair was no longer worn cropped but allowed to curl against his neck.

"Tell you what!" Mrs Moore suggested, clapping her hands in an attempt to distract them and lighten the atmosphere. "Enough of these tears. Why don't we have a go at making some Rice Crispy cakes and let your poor daddy get on?"

James looked at her with a smile of thanks.

As if the unfortunate event had never occurred, the children miraculously revived and jumped up and down with delight. They always found Mrs Moore a bit cranky and miserable, but they were thrilled at the prospect of cooking in *her* kitchen!

"Yippee!" they cried in unison.

Leaving the squealing children, James escaped to the study and sat down. He swivelled his black leather chair to look through two long sash doors at his Aunt Jocelyn's maturing rose garden. It'd been snowing heavily, and the garden looked magical and dreamlike in its mantle of crisp white snow. He promised himself he'd take the children outside to build a snowman as soon as he finished work.

****

Marleen Henderson, née Fry, was recovering from the most exotic massage she'd ever experienced, lolling in a chair in the foyer of London's May Fair Hotel. Guy, the masseur, had been recommended by Pen. He was a blond Australian with hands that dug deep into her flesh, mingling pain with ecstasy. She felt relaxed and carefree until she observed the time on the sizeable black and white clock above the hotel's reception desk. It was coming up to teatime, and Marleen realised she should phone Melrose though she didn't want to – calling her abandoned family would destroy her hard-won inner peace, and James would most likely be his usual grumpy self.

It'd been quite a few days since she'd last been in contact, and she felt the tiniest twinge of guilt. Her husband had become cold and aloof with her as soon as the twins were born. Roger's death further widened the gulf between them. Ghost-like, James would walk the floors of Melrose, silent and miserable. To her fury, he rarely allowed her to entertain, and it didn't take long before she grew weary, bored and apathetic, oblivious to her ever-crying babies. James would spend all the hours he could at the factory. Ultimately they'd become nothing more than ships that passed in the night.

The only reason Rocola was still an ongoing concern was her money – something her adoring papa had repeatedly attempted to remind her of, also expressing his horror at how her trust fund was rapidly diminishing.

She'd answered him repeatedly, "Papa, you've got your heirs now, haven't you? Isn't that what you and Mama wanted most? Besides, you've got zillions of your own. You can always help me out!" Usually, his response to this blatant rattling of the begging bowl would be to stomp off in a huff.

She watched Penelope walking in her direction. It could never be said that she was beautiful or even pretty. She'd too much of a 'horsey' look to her, tall and slightly unwieldy, with dyed dark hair she always kept back in a tight twist. But from day one at boarding school, something about her had intrigued Marleen; she'd grown to love and trust her old school friend, and from friends, they became lovers. Their relationship changed when, unfortunately for Marleen, who was stuck in the middle, she realised James and Pen detested each other. It was one of the many reasons she stayed in London, even though it soured relations with her husband.

Pen had returned from riding in Hyde Park and wore her usual attire of black jodhpurs, heeled boots and a fitted long-sleeved shirt under a tailored lightweight jacket. She carried her strapped riding helmet in one hand, looking every inch the equestrian, she was.

Marleen smiled as her lover slowly and casually kissed her cheek and then teasingly licked it. Pen chuckled as she stood back and stretched. Gratified, she exhaled loudly and threw herself down on a couch, causing it to bounce slightly, and with a giggle, excitedly asked Marleen about her massage.

"Wasn't he everything I told you? Those hands, Mar! Phew!"

Marleen couldn't disagree. She felt as if she was floating.

"He was divine, Pen. You've kept him a bit of a secret, haven't you?" she asked playfully.

"Yup. Don't you tell anyone – or else!" Pen replied, making her giggle again.

Moments later, the women sat together in peaceful silence, reclining in the velvet-covered seats. It was an easy atmosphere and one that lasted a few minutes more until Pen, disturbing Marleen's trance, asked cautiously, "Have you called?" Marleen knew what she was referring to and answered her in a miserable tone.

"No. Not yet. I've been putting it off. I feel so relaxed, Pen, and I know it'll ruin all this if I phone!" Pen understood but gave her advice anyway. "It's better you check in regularly, Mar, to keep the grouchy bastard and the little imps happy. Otherwise, he'll cause a scene again, and from what you told me, no one wants a repeat of that, do they?"

No, Marleen thought, *no, they don't*.

She recollected the night James was so rude while they'd been visiting her father's 2,000-acre estate in Buckinghamshire. He'd upset one of Papa's guests. Over a casual dinner with friends, an older man began questioning James about the ongoing upheaval in Northern Ireland.

"It's a sad situation. And all because of some Civil Rights march yonks ago," the retired academic commented.

"Not really," James replied stonily, about to add more when the other man rudely spoke over him.

"Pathetic! People getting bombed and shot at all over the place. I'll never understand it."

"No, not many English people do," James retaliated.

He wasn't prepared to discuss The Troubles, having witnessed the daily impact and the shock of so many deaths across all the communities. There was no way on God's earth he'd attempt to convey such a highly complicated and emotive situation to a dithering, opinionated old codger. And so, James remained quiet, his silence implying impatience and anger. Marleen cringed at her husband's open lack of respect for Papa's oldest and dearest friend and gave him a look of contempt.

Assuming James hadn't heard him, the scholar repeated himself, but this time in a more piercing voice. "They're talking now about a hunger strike of sorts. If those ridiculous men want to commit suicide, I say, let them!"

James remained deadly quiet. He was exasperated; it'd been a long day watching the local hunt since he'd refused to participate. He hated being away from the twins and disagreed with all blood sports. He quickly got to his feet, thanked his host and hostess for the delightful dinner and told them he was retiring. As he left the opulent dining room, he heard the curmudgeonly guest grunt, "Charming!"

****

After finishing his work, James fulfilled his promise. He insisted the twins wash the chocolate from their chubby cheeks before wrapping them up warmly so they could go out and make a snowman. There'd been a freak snowfall the previous evening – in October – and the children were over the moon when they woke up to find a Winter Wonderland.

The baking project proved to be an unbelievable success. The children hung on to Mrs Moore's every instruction. The novelty almost made her reconsider her opinion of the twins, but not quite. She could hear their laughter and screams coming from the garden as she made her way up the kitchen staircase to Melrose's black-and-white-tiled hallway.

Nearly reaching the top, she looked through the winding wrought-iron balusters, half expecting to see Roger Henderson dressed in elegant black-tie attire. She'd loved cooking for his numerous dinner parties and realised she missed him. It'd been such a long time since anyone had visited this unhappy house.

Opening Melrose's cumbersome mahogany front door, she watched the twins' efforts at building a snowman. The children weren't feeling the cold as happiness and love for their father warmed their hearts. They slipped and fell about, laughing loudly, and soon began throwing snowballs. James distracted them by getting down in the snow and teaching them how to form a snow angel.

The winter scene would have looked blissful to anyone other than their perceptive housekeeper. She thought Mr Henderson had the saddest eyes she'd ever seen, his broad shoulders perpetually weighed down by sorrow and regret.

****

Chapter Four

South Shields, England 1981

Few of his old friends would have recognised Robert Sallis, formerly a Private with the 2nd Battalion, Royal Regiment of Fusiliers, as he stood waiting to sign on in a never-ending queue in North Shields Labour Exchange.

In his army days, he'd been picked out of the ranks and trained in counter-espionage in Londonderry, or as he quickly learned to call it, while in Catholic company, Derry. Working covertly had been a gruelling challenge, and things worsened when he and the sulky woman partner known to him as IOWA had their cover blown by Charles Jones, a Unionist rabble-rouser. Their orders were to monitor the man, given that the security services were convinced he and his goons were behind several violent sectarian attacks. Swept along in his wake, Sallis and IOWA helped prevent the bombing of the City Hotel by a renegade ex-Provo, working to his own crazy agenda – but not before the Bishop of Derry and Jones's bodyguard had died before their eyes in an exchange of gunfire.

Violence at an event designed to foster mutual respect and tolerance between Protestant and Catholic business people, and to keep the Rocola factory from closing, had proved to be a disaster for the troubled city. Rob would never forget the stricken face of the beautiful black-haired girl who'd helped to organise the event when she realised she knew one of the people who had turned it into a blood bath – her young sister, dressed as a satchel-carrying schoolgirl to transport a bomb. Nor would Rob ever drive from his mind the second it dawned on him that it was this same sister, somehow transformed into a curvaceous blonde, who'd honey-trapped his own best mate, Private Val Holmes. Val had endured a cruel, drawn-out death, a degrading death, and to learn that young Tina McLaughlin had been instrumental in his execution and planning to bomb the City Hotel was mind-boggling.

Still traumatised by Val's slaying, it wasn't long before Rob came up against the full force of local hatred for the Brits – ironic, really, when his mam was Irish, and they still had many relatives living in the Old Country. Not that they'd been in contact since Rob went into the British Army.

He hated waiting in the dole queue. It was the same every week; like pigs to the slaughter, each man stood in a long snaking line-up, feeling hopeless and desperate. They wanted to work, regain some pride in themselves and bring home proper wages, not a few measly quid in handouts. But these days, with Margaret Thatcher and her government's hatchet, constantly cracking down on the unions and their mania for privatisation, the local shipbuilding and repair industry that had once employed sixty per cent of the men in the region was in rapid decline. Skilled men whose fathers and even grandfathers had been part of the 20,000-strong workforce in Swan Hunter or Austin & Pickersgill now found themselves superfluous – along with their sense of dignity and self-worth.

Finally signing on, getting out of the place as quickly as possible with the pitiful emergency cash advance he'd practically had to beg for, Rob decided to walk home. It was a fair hike, but so what? Some silly bugger had tried to set his local dole office on fire, leaving it temporarily closed. Why waste good money on a bus fare? He'd nothing better to do, had he? Although he had to dismiss the nagging feeling that there *was* something he was supposed to be doing if he could only remember...

Ignoring his misgivings, he decided he'd walk to the Shields Ferry, where the crew didn't take money from ex-squaddies, jump on, then make his way to the Dolly Peel in Commercial Street, where he'd treat himself to a quick pint.

As he steered towards the Old Town Hall marketplace, he passed Lloyds Bank on his left and then, seeing Carrick's Café, his heart lurched as he recalled Val and him as kids buying the best-minced beef pie with gravy in the world. Woolworths standing opposite was another place that brought back good memories of him and his mate buying pens and stuff for school. Happy days. Gone forever days.

In the years after Rob left the army on medical grounds, he'd walked the path of self-destruction, selfishly dragging everyone around down with him, including his mam and his young son. A sense of overwhelming sadness and shame dogged him perpetually. How had it ever come to this?

He struggled daily with headaches, ringing ears and a searing, blinding pain behind his eyes. However, it was his mental state that worried him most, how it played tricks with his thoughts and feelings. His life was a merry-go-round of emotions, from isolation and anxiety to withdrawal and sadness. But worse, much worse, where the waves of unrelenting anger. He hated what he'd become and sometimes contemplated ending it all to have some peace finally.

The journey across the Wear was dull, although he loved the smell of the salt air and the feeling of the wind on his face. In no time, Rob found himself propping up the bar in the Dolly Peel, using up his crisis fund on more than one pint. After that, the hefty barman refused to give him credit, sneering openly at the suggestion. Rob turned away to look up at a roman-faced clock. *Christ*, three o'clock already… and that was when it hit him. Hell, his mam was going to kill him – he'd been warned not to be late for his son's birthday party! He gulped down the last dregs of his pint, raced out of the pub and ran the half-mile back to Eglesfield Road.

When Rob had left home to join the army, his parents downsized and moved from their former home in Newcastle to a small, terraced house in South Shields. His father was one of many who chased but failed to find welding work in the rapidly dwindling shipbuilding industry. The shock of finding himself on the scrap heap had proved to be too much for him. He grew increasingly withdrawn and depressed, finally surrendering to kidney cancer.

This area had changed beyond recognition in just a few years. Where once it had been bustling with purposeful shoppers rushing in and out of quality independent stores, the numbers had dwindled. Most of the retail outlets were now shabby and on the verge of closing down or else already had. The long, narrow residential streets had become drab and dreary, and several houses close to Brigham & Cowan – the yard where Rob's dad had served his apprenticeship – stood unlit and empty.

The Sallis's now lived here in a dockworker's cramped terrace house. Rob missed their old home in the Toon dreadfully, but it couldn't be helped; needs must. He especially missed the comfort of his childhood bedroom since he found himself sleeping in a cramped box room. In a way, it was a good thing that they didn't need to accommodate his former fiancée, Tracey.

After the birth of their son, she had cleared off. The self-centred cow never fully forgave him for not returning for his twenty-first birthday celebration. The reason why was particularly horrific, but Tracey barely acknowledged the traumatic effects on Rob of his mate's appalling death. When, later on, their wedding had to be postponed because of his medical discharge, she'd told him she'd had enough of his unpredictable behaviour, and the last thing she wanted now was to be married and a mother; she was far too young. It hadn't taken long for Rob and his mam to realise there wasn't a maternal bone in Tracey's body. It seemed unnatural that any mother could abandon her baby, but then again, life had taught Rob that none of us will ever truly know what other people are capable of. Tracey couldn't hack the scarred, embittered man he had become and abandoned him, her baby and even her family – not that she was any significant loss.

He caught a glimpse of his dishevelled state in the window of a corner shop and quickly averted his eyes. He was certainly no advertisement for parenthood; unkempt, scraggly and dirty, not having shaved or bathed for several days. His clothes were wrinkled and stained, and he was pissed. With the best intentions in the world, he'd tell himself he'd have the one pint every time he walked into a pub, but while the money lasted, it always became two, three, four… and the rest.

Upon reaching the front door, breathing rapidly, Rob attempted to sort himself by brushing down his coat and running his hands through his long, wavy hair; he'd deliberately grown it on leaving the army. After several failed attempts with the key, his mother's friend and neighbour, Mrs Orr, opened up, hearing his fumbling efforts. She took one long look at him and frowned.

"Eeeh, lad, yer nivver going in looking like that? Gan upstairs and splash yer face, run a comb through that messy hair – and you a soldier once," she chuntered. Instead, Rob pushed past her and lurched into his mam's 'best' room, where earlier she'd set down the lovingly iced birthday cake on a gateleg table, ready for her grandson's return from school and his party.

Rob saw that the candy-striped candles had already been lit and blown out, the cake cut and distributed amongst the lad's schoolfriends and their mams, who were all clustered into the small space.

"Bloody hell!" he burst out without thinking, "could yez not have waited? Bliddy gannets, the lot of yer! Okay, I got held up… but I came as fast as I fucken could!"

He noticed Mrs Orr's raised eyebrows and the brief exchange of disapproving glances between two of the mams, who sat bare white legs covered in goose pimples beneath ridiculous skimpy puffball skirts. The scent of stale beer hung over him like a thick fog. His mam Bridie, ever the peacemaker, scrambled together a piece of cake, put it on a paper plate and offered it to him.

These days she barely knew her son. The kind, carefree, modest lad of his younger days had all but disappeared. Left was this shadow of a man who sometimes scared her severely, yet still, she loved him. After her husband's death, her son and grandson had become her world, and even with Rob's erratic mood swings, she wasn't about to give up on him.

Sickened with himself, he refused the cake and made a feeble excuse to leave, all too aware of the young lad clinging to his nan's pinny. Rob watched his son press his chubby freckled face against her legs: anything to hide the humiliation he felt as once again his da showed up the whole family.

Humiliation washed over Rob. He'd christened this lad with such sorrow and love, determined that his young life should be a testament to his namesake, the best man Rob had ever known: Val. So much for good intentions.

Now he was beginning to wonder if, like Tracey, he should leave rather than cast a pall over this place. He knew he was an embarrassment. Was it fair on the lad and Bridie to endure life with a wreck of a man who couldn't control his drinking and depression? As he shambled his way up to the box room, Rob could hear the women muttering in disapproval. He slammed the door behind him and held a pillow over his face to drown out the voices, but they would not be silenced. They were in his head, criticising him, condemning him. He wasn't sure how much longer he could stand to listen.

****

Chapter Five

Before washing her hands in an avocado-coloured sink, Caitlin removed her engagement ring and studied it. It was a stunning, timeless two-carat diamond solitaire in a four-claw setting. She was out for dinner in one of London's oldest restaurants, Rules of Covent Garden.

Christopher Pecaro had proposed to her months ago, and she'd accepted. He offered her everything a woman could want: financial security, a beautiful home, frequent holidays, and an exciting, fast-paced social life. He took her to places she could only have imagined previously and constantly bought her gifts. He was kind, generous, and cared deeply about her. There was nothing he wouldn't do for her. If in her heart, Caitlin knew that her feelings for him did not match the passion she'd felt for James Henderson, she was sure that some day she'd learn to love Chris as he deserved. How could she not?

Oddly, she occasionally thought about the Henderson's beautiful home, Melrose. With all her money, she imagined that by now, Marleen had probably gutted and refurbished it from its Victorian splendour to a much more contemporary style. She'd likely have gotten rid of Mrs McGinty, the old housekeeper. The latter had served Caitlin dinner in the fabulous dining room with its gleaming mahogany furniture, where Caitlin first met poor, long-gone RUC Chief Constable George Shalham. For a sliver of a second, she imagined what her life would've been like living there as Mrs James Henderson, but quickly nipped such a thought in the bud. After all, she was soon to become Mrs Christopher Pecaro, and unlike James, Chris offered her love, loyalty, and perfect security.

Caitlin had progressed as a secretary through the years she'd lived in London, from working at a small charity to becoming a highly paid PA in a large dynamic international management consultancy near

Victoria station. It was here that she'd met Chris, one of the Managing Partners.

He first glimpsed her as she stood waiting for a lift on the ground, and the sight left him almost speechless. She was simply exquisite. Her azure blue eyes twinkled when she smiled and said good morning to him. She was tall – which he liked – even in a pair of flat black pumps and wore a plain red A-line skirt complemented by a meticulously ironed white blouse and red cardigan. Like a mannequin, she was willowy, flat-chested, and could easily have graced the cover of *Vogue*.

"Morning," she'd said with a genuine smile.

"Morning," he replied, noting her soft Irish accent.

Afterwards, they'd met briefly in and around the office until they found themselves assigned to the same long-term project. Although Chris was considerably older, he was charming, fun and exceptionally brilliant. He'd repeatedly encouraged Caitlin to develop her skills and promote herself within the company. Working in this environment, she soon learnt she needed to slow down when she spoke and was extra careful with her pronunciation. More senior administrative positions were offered, and she became trusted and popular within the organisation.

She and Chris worked hard and then regularly visited a candle-lit cellar wine bar in Covent Garden, where they'd spend hours mulling over office politics. Chris was long divorced and resided in a splendid townhouse near Islington Green. When Caitlin first walked over the threshold, she'd been overwhelmed. He had offered to cook, jokingly telling her – or so she'd thought – that he was a master chef. It had proved to be true; dinner had been excellent, and she'd eaten every morsel, including oysters, which she'd never tried before. He'd gone to so much trouble with champagne on ice, soft lights and Phil Collins playing in the background. Chris Pecaro lived a life of absolute luxury, and soon Caitlin grew accustomed to accompanying him to the theatre, the races, and numerous meals in fancy restaurants such as Rules.

After that, she stayed at his place more and more until he suggested she bring some of her belongings and store them there. "To save you from scrambling back to your place to change before work!" It made perfect sense; being with Chris and sharing his luxurious home. In time, he asked her to marry him.

Caitlin fell into the opulent lifestyle so quickly that now it'd become second nature. She felt far removed from the young woman who'd linked arms with her friend Anne as they walked to work in Rocola. The girl who, with her mother, made her own clothes; scrambled and searched for coins under beds and down the back of sofas to top up the electric meter.

Life, she knew only too well, could take some unexpected twists and turns. Caitlin pouted her lips, put the top back on her Black Cherry lipstick, took a final approving glance in the mirror and fastened her quilted leather shoulder bag with its snazzy gilt chain.

****

Returning to their booth, surrounded by mirrors and numerous framed paintings, Caitlin smiled as she caught Chris's eye, who was looking particularly smart and sophisticated tonight. He wasn't a remarkably handsome man, but there was something about his confident, straightforward manner that made her feel safe. His black hair was thick and short, with a hint of grey at the temples. Tonight they were dining with a husband and wife who'd been friends of Chris and his ex, Sheila. At first, Caitlin was nervous about meeting them but instantly took to this couple she'd heard was extremely wealthy, having built up a multi-million-pound textile company from nothing.

They owned houses in London and Somerset and a substantial factory in Ballymena near Belfast, but not once over dinner did Maryann and Bill Fox ever act in a self-important way. They were good people – warm-hearted and fun to be with.

Caitlin listened as Bill told her how, in her absence, they'd been discussing the latest news about the first integrated secondary school to open in Northern Ireland, Lagan College.

"Multi-faith schools are pretty much the norm here. Why hasn't it happened over there before?" he asked with genuine interest. He seemed keen to learn more about Ulster and its turbulent history.

By now, Caitlin was well versed in explaining the complexities of The Troubles.

"It's still a big deal for us, I'm afraid, Bill. Up 'til now, Catholics and Protestants have been given little chance to mix. Ironically, most Churches are vehemently against integration. If you ask me, though, I think it's brilliant. Growing up, I knew very few Protestants." Her heart twinged a little at the thought of James Henderson, his uncle and friends – including RUC Chief Constable George Shalham, who had been a principled, well-meaning man.

Bill nodded. "Amazing, really, in this day and age." Smiling, he added, "Well, good for those parents and the twenty-eight pupils!"

"It's a start, I suppose," Caitlin replied with a polite smile. She wasn't in the mood to talk for longer about the state of things at home, not tonight. It was Friday, and she was looking forward to a carefree weekend.

Bill nodded and glanced over at his wife. Caitlin couldn't help but notice his adoring gaze as he took hold of Maryann's hand. She was pregnant and blooming, undoubtedly thrilled with being a mother-to-be; she'd often pat or rub her growing bump without seeming to realise what she was doing. She was pretty with shoulder-length dark hair, curly and shiny with a straight-cut fringe, and dark eyes against pale, translucent skin.

Bill was gorgeous-looking, with a genuine smile and eyes that would melt ice. She could easily imagine him in a gangster film; he looked so much the part with his Mediterranean-toned skin, dark eyes and thick, curling jet black hair. His frame was taut and sinewy from indulging in his favourite hobby, horse riding. When Caitlin first met him, she couldn't stop staring at him! She found she envied the couple's unmistakable aura of love.

Eventually, the convivial evening ended. Goodnights were said, and the couples agreed they'd catch up soon at Bill and Maryann's country home.

Chris suggested while driving them back to Islington that he and Caitlin should go away on a short break together. It'd been a particularly tough few weeks at work, and they could both do with a change of scene.

"I've been thinking about it – you've not been back home in years. Could we maybe go to Donegal Town and Londonderry after that? One of the guys at work recommended it. He was at a wedding there a few weeks back and says there's a fantastic hotel near Lough Eske."

For the second time that evening, Caitlin's heart lurched. Donegal Town! That was where James had taken her for their only weekend together.

"I don't think so. You'd hate Derry. And with your posh British accent, who knows what'd happen?" Caitlin replied, sounding much sharper than she usually did.

Chris was hurt at her choice of words and tone. He always felt he hit a brick wall with her whenever he tried to talk about Londonderry. She'd close up like a clam, and he was keen to understand why.

Caitlin felt bad but stared out silently at the shops on Upper Street. She paid particular attention to the expensive brick and stucco townhouses, thinking how distant they were from 30 Blamfield Street, her childhood home in Creggan.

She and her brother had given up the family house. They no longer needed it or to be reminded of the loss of their parents and sister. Martin was well established in America, and with Caitlin in London, their kindly neighbours, the McFaddens had packed the remaining personal belongings and held onto them; there wasn't much to keep.

The siblings donated everything else to St Vincent de Paul, a local charity.

While steering his sleek red Audi into the double garage, Chris told her, "It's your call about Londonderry, but I think it might do you some good."

"Derry," Caitlin replied softly, even though she knew he couldn't hear. The car came to a halt, and he patted her hand. "You look done in. Come on, let's get to bed."

After Caitlin finished in the bathroom, Chris quickly took a shower. He looked at the choice of aftershaves on a glass shelf and saw a bottle of the musky fragrance she had bought him for his birthday. He didn't particularly like it but, to please her, doused himself in it.

Caitlin lay back and watched him climb into bed. She felt his hand tenderly caress the birthmark on her hip. Although she'd been sharp with him, she couldn't stay angry for long. He hadn't known the significance of the trip he'd suggested to her. She turned to find him smiling at her, his face full of love and hope.

"You know you make me very happy, don't you?" he told her. "I love you so much."

"I know," she answered sheepishly, aware she couldn't repeat his words.

"Come here," Chris said, pulling her closer to him. He whispered, "One day, Caitlin McLaughlin, you'll say those three little words and mean them."

His tongue teasingly played with her lips. She felt his weight on her and the urgency growing in him. She wanted to love him; she wanted to say those three little words, but she couldn't. Their kisses grew more hungry. Chris's lovemaking was always like this, rushed and earnest as if he was afraid she'd evaporate.

He sought to contain himself for as long as he could but again found he was racing ahead of her. For all his years and sexual experience, there'd never been a woman who could affect him in such a way. He literally couldn't get enough of her; she looked so inviting, lying half-naked under one of his well-worn white Van Heusen shirts.

Her flawless skin was velvet to the touch, pert breasts perfect, lips opulent and still tasting slightly of the claret they'd had with dinner. He ran his fingers along the inside of one thigh and upwards, staring into her face. He was ready, but still, her eyes held a slight shadow of hesitation, confirming that he was rushing her. *Bugger*! He reluctantly pulled himself clear and propped himself up to one side.

"You okay?" she asked, anxious at his abrupt withdrawal; he must have sensed her reluctance.

"Fine," he told her before adding, "you, young lady, get me so aroused, I can't contain myself. I'll take it slower. Promise."

Remorse hit her. She smiled reassuringly before kissing him and murmuring, "Come here, you, we've got all night."

For Chris's sake, she'd try again. Inhaling the scent she associated with James Henderson, she closed her eyes and surrendered to her imagination.

****

The following morning, Caitlin woke to find their king-sized bed empty. Bright sunshine permeated the bedroom, and immediately her mood improved. She rarely slept well and couldn't remember the last time she'd gone through the night undisturbed. Nightmares about the raid on their house in Blamfield Street, when her innocent father had been seized and hustled from his home to be beaten and neglected until he died, were still frequent. And memories of her widowed mother's retreat from the world and ultimate suicide were still almost unbearable, always ready to creep into her mind at the most unexpected times.

Picking up her father's jumper, she folded it and sniffed at it in the hope of discerning a lingering trace of him – sadly, there was none. Next, she moistened her face and neck while thinking of her best friend.

After the nightmarish bombing of Shipquay Street, where she'd lost her leg, Anne had been depressed for months. She was finally coaxed into marriage with a wastrel who'd shown interest in her, mainly by the persuasion of her unsympathetic mother, who was tired of her moods and wanted the crippled girl off her hands. And so Anne had married Porkie, an unprepossessing lump of a man. After giving birth to their son Sean, she was abruptly widowed. Porkie had been dumb enough, along with his best friend Dickie, to spy for the British, and they'd both been murdered by the PIRA.

Following this, Anne was labelled a tout's wife and collaborator for a short time and found herself in potential danger. However, Caitlin asked for her brother Martin's help, and he intervened, assuring the Provo leadership that Anne had confessed to a local priest what Porkie and Dickie had been up to. Father Connolly had then 'hypothetically' pointed the finger at the touts, who were dealt with. Martin assured his fellow PIRA members that Anne had played her part, so she was safe, reverting to her unmarried name to sever any connection to Porkie Ballantyne.

It'd taken her some time to recover from this ordeal and meet Mr Right, but then one day, she had, purely by chance. "*On his bus!*" she'd squealed. In their regular phone calls, Anne would tell her, "*Caitlin, he's just gorgeous – and so good in the sack!*" Then her friend usually included too much detail before concluding, "*And he's great with baby Sean too. You'd think he was his own!*"

To Caitlin's delight, Anne's old vibrancy and humour had returned. Granted, she could tell her friend still had dark days when the pain from her missing leg would be excruciating. Her new beau Matt Friel was from Carrowreagh, a small farming village over the border in the Irish Republic. She'd met him on his bus after some hobo stole her pitiable purse, and she'd gone to Matt for help. He was a hardworking Ulsterbus driver and poles apart from layabout Porkie. Anne worried about him constantly and the threat of his vehicle being hijacked.

But with Matt being a strapping countryman, the young rioters of Derry had learnt the hard way to steer clear of his bus. Friel was well known as a tricky, obstinate bastard – and many had the scars to prove it! Not once had he surrendered his vehicle. Such bravery gained Matt respect, not only from his bosses at Ulsterbus but also from his grateful passengers and, grudgingly, the youth of Derry.

Caitlin searched for the matching charcoal-coloured silk robe to cover her sleek lacy nightgown – another gift from Chris. Picking it up, she stroked the soft material and sighed. Her memory strayed to the thin, poorly made floral cotton nighties her mother always wore. Poor mammy, Caitlin thought with regret; she'd never owned anything like this.

A mighty cry rang out from below, interrupting her thoughts, "Caitlin McLaughlin, are you up? Lazybones, breakfast is ready!"

She squealed, "I'm coming!" He was so good to her.

Later that morning, the telephone shrilled from Chris's study.

"I'll get it!" Caitlin cried as she ran into the bright, high-ceilinged room. Chris's house was always pristine. Each spacious room was decorated like something from a magazine. The walls were pale and adorned with oil paintings of country landscapes and iconic London sights; there were original cornices in every room and decorative plasterwork on the ceilings. Heavy cream-coloured satin curtains and sheer mesh blinds dressed the study windows, while antique furniture and bookcases added to the air of sleek opulence.

"Hello?" Caitlin said, immediately recognising the beeping of a payphone.

She waited until a male voice with a pronounced Derry accent said, "Hello! Is that you, Caitlin?"

Her mood soared. Uncle Tommy! It'd been so long since she'd talked to him, and she was thrilled to hear his voice.

"Yeah, it's me, Tommy! You got my postcard then?" she asked.

She'd recently sent him a card with Chris's home number.

"I did," Tommy said. His voice was full of emotion and cracked a little as he continued, "Ah, it's so good to hear you. How are you, love?"

"I'm good, Tommy. And you?"

"Manic, just manic. There isn't enough time in the day. Our Kathy has me tortured, forever nagging me about the fags and drink," he laughed affectionately, referring to his only daughter.

"And she's right, Tommy. You've had a few scares since. She's only doing it 'cos she loves you."

"I know, I know. But never mind that. I want to let you know – I'm coming to London in a few weeks, and I'd like to see you then."

A wave of joy filled her. It'd been so long since she'd last seen her uncle.

"That's brilliant, Tommy. I can't wait! When?"

He filled in his niece on the dates and explained the purpose of his visit – some nonsense about a second-hand car that was a world away from the truth.

****

They were saying their goodbyes when Chris wandered into the study and caught the tail end of the call. He caught sight of his fiancée's flushed face as she replaced the handset. She was clearly extremely fond of the 'big man', as she'd affectionately call him, and Chris looked forward to meeting him.

At times, Caitlin could behave oddly. It was evident that The Troubles would always have a damaging effect on her. He had witnessed her nightmares, tossing and turning in her sleep, mumbling, crying, and even, occasionally, screaming. She barely remembered them afterwards, nor did he talk to her about what he'd seen. *Best left alone.*

Chris was glad when Caitlin told him about her uncle's forthcoming visit. His fiancée rarely talked about her parents and sister, and when she did, he detected nothing but despair. Meeting her uncle, Tommy, might help Chris understand why – the man sounded like a good sort. Perhaps he'd even encourage Caitlin to go home for a visit? For all his worldwide travels, Chris had never been to Londonderry and was now more than ever intrigued by the place.

He loved Caitlin profoundly and would do anything for her. From day one, she'd been upfront with him, telling him she was damaged goods. He had always suspected that some prick had hurt her so badly they'd left her feeling like she'd never love again.

Nevertheless, Chris believed time healed all. He meant to protect her and trusted that, eventually, she'd learn to love him. With a wave of possessiveness, he studied her slender, upright figure. He swore to himself that he'd never again allow anyone to hurt this fantastic, beautiful woman of his.

****

Chapter Six

Belfast, Northern Ireland

Joe McFadden, the eldest son of Charlie and Maggie McFadden, closed his eyes as tightly as possible in the hope of returning to his dream. He'd been sprinting like the wind with a muddied ball towards the far end of a Gaelic football pitch. *Jesus wept!* He could hear the feral yells of the encouraging home supporters. His body and face relished the cleansing, fresh Irish air and welcoming, warm southerly wind. He was flying over the 130-metre pitch; his calves ached, and his breathing was hard and fast, but he was hyper with adrenaline; he had to score; there were mere seconds left of the thirty-five minutes of the second half. Each stride brought a burning sensation that almost killed him as opponents from every direction yanked at his shirt or tried to block his progress. Still, he held onto the ball as long as he could, almost as if his life depended on it. He looked up and saw the goalpost. With one clean, swift kick, the ball was up and over. He'd done it… they'd won! As the referee's whistle blew loudly, the roaring fans jumped to their feet, and their screams of victorious delight echoed through the stadium; the sound was deafening! Suddenly, body after body landed on him, his teammates all yelling congratulations for the win. *"You're a hero, Joe! You've done it!"*

But he could never return to that Gaelic pitch. In a sickening moment of realisation, he woke up to find himself crouched alone on the cold floor of a shit-smeared cell in *Long Kesh,* as the Republicans called it or aka *The Maze,* as the Loyalists called it, with only some coarse grubby blankets to cover his sinewy, foul-smelling body.

Interned in late 1972, Joe was convicted of possessing weapons and sentenced to fourteen years in jail. The men were caged in Nissen huts for the first four years, and it hadn't been *too* bad. But he'd got into a fight for no particular reason with one markedly obnoxious prison officer in H-block 6. This individual hated Joe due to their numerous sparring matches in the bathrooms. The PO's revenge on him had been to persuade a group of fellow officers to help him drag the cocky bastard into solitary confinement – after they'd administered yet another severe hiding. Later a niggling pain in Joe's jaw told him something wasn't right. He'd lost yet another brown and rotten tooth.

By now, after nearly five years *on the blanket* protesting against his non-political status and captivity, he was half the man he used to be; a skeletal, colourless wreck. Nonetheless, he was a proud Irish soldier, and it was his duty to support the protest and his fellow prisoners in their seven-by-eight-foot concrete boxes, with their bibles, a couple of single mattresses and a few blankets between them. A Republican song had become the unofficial anthem of the protest, and Joe sang it loud and proud, the gaps from his missing teeth adding a slight sibilance to his voice:

I'll wear no convict's uniform.
Nor meekly serve my time,
That England might brand Ireland's fight
Eight hundred years of crime…

Growing up, he had not learnt to speak Gaelic, but he quickly picked it up as his Irish-speaking comrades recited stories and poetry or sang rebel songs. It proved helpful when the men talked and joked between themselves. Few, if any, of the predominantly Protestant screws understood the ancient language. A number of them had close paramilitary connections. They revelled in their hatred of their Republican prisoners, seizing any opportunity for revenge on them, fuelled by their inborn sectarianism and revulsion against Catholics.

Between 250 and 300 determined Republican prisoners were on the blanket. Like all, Joe found the stench and filth in the cells overpowering. Everywhere there was the nauseating stench of human excrement deliberately spread thinly on the walls to suppress the smell. Long-dead maggots and flies carpeted the concrete floor.

Crushed to find himself awake and back in this squalor, he closed his eyes and imagined what his parents would say were they to see his hopeless state. He was undoubtedly a pitiful sight with his long, unkempt matted hair and straggling beard – a far cry from the ferocious, sturdy, unyielding young fella he once was.

He remembered his carefree boyhood, playing on Blamfield Street with his next-door neighbour, Martin McLaughlin. Joe's mother was best friends with Martin's ma Majella, and Charlie kept close to Martin's da Patrick. Unwell for years but a lovely, serene man, he'd died in custody after a severe beating following a house raid by the Brits. It was likely payback for his son's Provo involvement, but everyone knew Patrick was never involved. What a waste, Joe thought, another innocent man sacrificed to British oppression.

The two families had been close in every way, constantly in and out of each other's houses to borrow sugar, milk or money to feed the relentless gas and electric meters that frequently ran out at the worst possible time. Most, if not all, birthdays, Christmases and other holidays were shared, and they'd all eat, drink and relish the fun-filled, easy-going atmosphere.

Joe's main visitor in the Kesh until now had been Father Connolly, their parish priest, who tried to keep him up to date on his family's progress and told him about his ma losing her job as a catering supervisor in the City Hotel when Kieran Kelly, the two-faced backstabber, attempted to blow it up and involved young Tina McLaughlin in his evil plan. Once again, his family were there for their neighbours, Charlie as an unofficial taxi driver and Maggie helping out at the funeral and looking after Majella. Friendship was all about helping each other when necessary, and Joe was proud of the generosity his parents showed to others.

Liam, Joe's youngest brother and always the joker, was doing reasonably well at school. As for straight-laced Emmett, the middle son… well, that was another story. Emmett was soft through and through. Friendly with the Provos, thanks to his big brother's involvement, he had been drawn into working for them as a driver, making pick-ups and deliveries. But he hadn't had the mental toughness necessary to progress through the ranks or even to continue working in this menial way among the PIRA sympathisers referred to as the Unknowns. Joe was glad his parents never knew how Emmett had transported messages and supplies until his last experience when he'd driven a couple of touts across the border for the Provos' punishment squad to deal with. Joe was happy his bruv was out of it now; the horror of the Cause had become too much for Emmett. To his parents' delight, he was working hard to complete his apprenticeship and become a car mechanic.

*****

Charlie McFadden sat at the kitchen table at 29 Blamfield Street. He studied his wife as she washed the dinner dishes in silence. They'd both aged. Maggie's varicose veins played her up from years of standing on her feet. Today she wore her usual flowered wraparound pinafore tied tightly at her ample bust. Her bleached blonde hair, with a badger stripe of darker roots at the parting, was devoid of the customary multi-coloured rollers. Her looks were no longer a priority, given that she could not afford to bleach regularly, and she'd begun to neglect herself.
After leaving the City Hotel, she did menial housework, including bringing other people's ironing in to do at home, for a pittance. Charlie understood his wife still carried the guilt of having employed Kieran Kelly, who'd attempted but failed to blow up her place of work. Everyone knew it wasn't Maggie's fault and found it unjust that she'd

been punished harshly by instant dismissal. She was well-liked in the neighbourhood and known for her kindness and sense of fair play.

****

Maggie and their middle son Emmett continually and relentlessly nagged Charlie to find work. He'd tried everywhere but, given his lack of skill or trade, had failed miserably. Until he spotted an advertisement in the dole office for a well-paid kitchen help and cleaner position and applied. The interview went well. Although Charlie was very nervous, he was offered the job there and then, to his surprise. He was sent to an administrative office within minutes to sign the necessary paperwork and given numerous leaflets about work rules, regulations, and safety.

Much later, he was told to report promptly at 5 a.m. the following Monday. He was shitting himself; he knew this wasn't for him, but he had no choice. They were so broke. They were behind on Maggie's catalogue payments; he still owed on the Credit Union loan, and they religiously avoided the Pru man like clockwork every week, hiding behind the kitchen door when he knocked. Emmett wasn't bringing enough in, and Liam was getting as tall as a giraffe and shooting through his clothes. It was clear that Maggie was whacked from struggling to bring in money and look after the household. He read the disappointment in her tired eyes and loved her more for trying to hide it from him. In a pathetic, self-centred way, he was glad Joe wasn't home. It would've only added more worry; the boy used to eat like a pig. At such a notion, Charlie felt sick as he thought of Joe's gaunt face and thin arms when they'd been granted a rare visit to the Kesh and couldn't begin to imagine the poor lad's protest conditions for all the years since.

****

And so, decision made, Charlie accepted the job. He worked steadily for weeks, and the household soon began to benefit from the extra income. Surprisingly, he managed to stay away from the bookies and horses and drank very little; he was too tired from the early mornings. Emmett was working all hours at the garage, too, and when he was home, his parents worried about his quiet, sullen mood. They agreed they should take him out and check on him. The last thing they needed was for him to get involved with the Provos like his brother had – waste another young life. Charlie vaguely noticed his wife say something.

"Did you hear me!" Maggie bellowed, turning to face him, holding a dishcloth. "Emmett told me."

Charlie had no clue what his wife had been saying. "Sorry, love, I didn't. Emmett told you what?"

Maggie moaned and sat down wearily, studying her husband. He looked tired, with shoulders drooping and his eyes puffy and watery above a flat, broken nose. He'd lost a bit of weight, she noticed.

"Never mind," she told him, sighing. After taking a second, she asked, "Have you lost weight? Do you think?"

Charlie shrugged and felt under his belt. "Maybe a bit." He was secretly pleased.

She smirked. "Well, that's something! Whatever you're doing, keep doing it. You were turning into a pack of Cookeen," she teased, making her way back to the dish-laden sink and slapping him playfully on the shoulder with the cloth as she passed.

Charlie grinned and had risen to help when, without warning, he heard screaming and shouting coming through the kitchen's paper-thin party wall.

"Right on cue," Maggie said gloomily upon hearing the loud noise; she ran her hand through her neglected hair in exasperation. "What I'd give to have the McLaughlins back."

The newly formed Housing Executive had allocated 30 Blamfield Street to a young unmarried couple relocated for their safety from the

Waterside on the east bank of the Foyle – a predominantly Protestant area. When the young couple first arrived with their children, as good neighbours Maggie and Charlie made a point of introducing themselves.

Since then, they'd seen little of the pair, but they heard them, by Christ! Like clockwork, they could hear fighting and yelling break out every evening, plates and glasses being thrown and smashed. Maggie heard through the grapevine that the shaven-headed husband was a callous hood whom the Provos had already warned about his petty crimes, including burglary.

"This is getting on my tits!" Charlie cried in a fury, intending to go next door. With surprising speed, Maggie snatched his arm and held him back. She understood her husband's rage, but these neighbours frightened her, and she didn't want Charlie involved or, worse still, hurt.

"No, Charlie, leave it! Go watch the telly – I'll be in soon," she begged.

"You sure, love? 'Cos, honestly, it's no joke. Night after night, they're at it, yelling and f'in and blind'in. They'll be coming through the walls next!"

Maggie pushed her husband towards the living room and reassured him, "I'll talk to someone."

Charlie shook his head, "I don't know, love. It might make things worse."

"Trust me. The boys will deal with it, for our Joe's sake."

****

The following day Charlie waited patiently for the early bus to take him to work. Regretfully, he'd had to give up his pride and joy, a Ford Zephyr with lovely fleece-covered seats. They couldn't afford to run it anymore. It still pained him when he remembered watching his baby driven off by an over-enthusiastic boy racer.

Charlie quickly ran into the Stones Corner paper shop and bought a *Derry Journal*. He found the usual suspects standing at the bus stop, where they all said good morning. When the bus finally arrived and Charlie boarded it, he said a quick hello to Matt, their familiar driver, and took his customary seat, where he read the paper until it was his stop.

As he arrived, he changed into his work clothes in the staff locker room. One of his co-workers, Harry Shields, turned up late, looking agitated. Charlie was fond of Harry. He was a grafter who kept his head down and got on with the job. Charlie was worried about him: today, the lad appeared jumpy, frightened.

"You okay, son?" After craning his neck around, Charlie enquired to make sure no one else would hear. "You look a bit pale."

Harry Shields looked at him resignedly, not daring to tell him the truth.

"Same old shite, a row with the wife, Charlie. She does my head in, starting on me before I even get out of bed. Thanks anyway."

He tapped his friend's arm in appreciation and headed off. Charlie waited a moment and shook his head. He wasn't convinced. From the look on the boy's face, he was lying.

Hours later, while Charlie was washing the floor of a long corridor, it came to him in a flash of realisation. Suddenly he knew exactly what was wrong with Harry Shields.

****

Chapter Seven

Tommy O'Reilly knew he would never forget the day when an old friend of his, local businessman Gerard McFarland, first asked for his help. McFarland was a pacifist who fervently believed the only way to end the Irish conflict and bring peace to their small part of the world was to participate in discussions with the British Government. It all began when he was approached by Chief Constable George Shalham, who'd pleaded with him to persuade the Republicans to remove their weapons from the Bogside before Bloody Sunday. He did as requested, and the Republicans did too.

McFarland never told anyone of his involvement, including his wife and family, and regularly feared for his life. Still, he needed support and decided that Tommy would give it to him in his ever-expanding work as an intermediary between Britain's Secret Intelligence Service (MI6), the British Government and the Republican paramilitaries.

At first, Tommy had flat-out refused. He said he couldn't get involved, believing it'd be too risky for him and his family. On top of that, he was kept busy with his Sinn Féin community work. However, day by day, further innocent lives were being lost or destroyed, and Tommy grew more focussed on finding a solution. His gut told him this dirty war could go on for years, and the only hope for peace was – as McFarland believed – through some form of dialogue.

Inevitably, Tommy agreed after much contemplating and renewed prompting from his friend. During the first wave of hunger strikes in December 1980, because one of the strikers was so close to death, governments worldwide began to put severe pressure on the British. Tommy, McFarland and Father Connolly, an activist and local parish priest at St Mary's in Creggan, helped secretly negotiate a deal from McFarland's front room. The British agreed on a compromise, but controversy followed when not long afterwards, the prison authorities didn't honour the spirit of the deal. Everyone, especially the prisoners, felt tricked. The fallout from the rescinded offer led to an even more tenacious and unyielding second wave of hunger strikes in March 1981, led by Bobby Sands.

And yet there was no doubt now that engagement was the only way forward. Although they'd hit an impasse with the hunger strikes, McFarland and Tommy were determined somehow to reopen the lines of communication – no matter any risk to themselves.

After dealing with his sister Majella's suicide and the shattering death of his niece Tina in the abyss of Armagh gaol, Tommy was glad he'd said yes to McFarland. However, with his community work and now this, he was constantly living on his nerves. The weight of further responsibility bowed his already weary shoulders and was proving draining, mentally and physically.

He felt he'd lost his other niece Caitlin when she suddenly left Derry to begin a new life in London. Much later, she'd told him about her failed relationship with James Henderson, the young man's marriage to some hoity-toity Brit, and how hurt and humiliated Caitlin had been. He missed her and tried to persuade her to return many times, but she'd refused; the stubborn mare finally settled down in England and appeared happy.

Tommy and McFarland hadn't made it as far as London yet in their efforts to negotiate with the Brits, but a meeting there was in the pipeline for a few weeks ahead, and Tommy had made up some flimsy excuse that he was going to South London to look at a car. He loathed flying and planned to take the ferry; anyway, it was cheaper. Once his acquaintance, Belfast man Patrick Gillispie, had heard where Tommy was going, he'd suggested he and his mucker Brian Monaghan should join him since they had business there too – it'd be a gas, travelling together.

Tommy respected Paddy Gillispie but, at the same time, was wary of him. Paddy was a rock-hard, old-time Republican Provo who wouldn't hesitate to sacrifice his life for the Cause. In his efforts to broker peace, Tommy knew he'd be wasting his time trying to coax the likes of Paddy down the same path. Tommy knew for a fact that the Belfast man was brutal and determined. He and his twin Dolores were killers who'd never considered any way of solving a problem other than violence. Tommy knew it'd be unwise to challenge Paddy's offer to accompany him to England, though, and felt he'd no choice but to go along with it, massive inconvenience though it was. His involvement with McFarland was kept a closely guarded secret. Travelling in the company of two known Provos could put all their carefully laid plans at risk.

****

Tommy sat by the fireplace in the Blue Bell bar, a focal point of Republican activity in Derry, aka 'Maileys.' It wasn't far from the scene of carnage on Bloody Sunday and the infamous Rossville Street flats. As always, Hugh Mailey, the Blue Bell's proprietor, had lit a welcoming peat fire. No wonder he'd such a ruddy complexion. The heat and the smell relaxed the drinkers. After a while, Paddy leant closer to Tommy.

"All sorted for London?" he whispered, on the verge of tipsiness.

"I am," Tommy nodded, nursing a Guinness. He'd cut down on the hard stuff since his stint in the hospital and now lived with his daughter Kathy, a workaholic medic, who continually kept him on his toes about his diet and clean living.

"Good stuff. I always get anxy travelling to England. Between you and me, Brian and I are there scouting for one or two serious ops, and when I say serious, I mean *s-e-r-i-o-u-s*!"

"Ssshhhh! Ah, Jesus, Paddy, I don't want to know!" Tommy hissed. He was livid. "For fuck's sake, have you any idea what you're saying? Walls have ears, remember. Shut it!"

Tommy was right, and Paddy instantly apologised, raising his palms. "Sorry. You're right. Sorry."

Now that he knew that gem of information, Tommy was even more concerned about the risk of travelling with the two Provos.

From the look on Tommy's face, Paddy conceded he'd been wrong to say anything about London. He wasn't in the mood to take the big fella on in a political debate about the Leadership negotiating with the Brits again – not tonight; he didn't have the energy. Too many fine men and women had given up their lives in pursuit of a united Ireland, and he wasn't going to be one of the first to throw in the towel in favour of 'talks'.

At one time, Tommy would rant about the benefits of holding negotiations with the Brits. Still, Paddy had put a stop to that by reminding him pointedly that all the ceasefires in the seventies after bouts of '*talking*' hadn't worked – so why would they now? Thankfully, holding negotiations and the like hadn't been mentioned by Tommy recently. Grunting in frustration at the big man's glum mood, Paddy headed for the bar but first murmured against the side of Tommy's red-bristled head: "You know, you're too trusting. One day someone'll let you down badly. You mark my words."

Paddy raised his empty glass. "Another?"

"Nah, I'm good, thanks," Tommy replied, staring dejectedly into his pint. Paddy was likely correct. He was too trusting, but they had no option when it came to engaging in exploratory talks. There had to be a way to secure hope for the future. Someday this war had to end.

As Paddy chatted and laughed with Hugh behind the bar, Tommy stared into the stone fireplace and the pirouetting ruby-red flames at its heart. He wished things were different. He wished he was back in the kitchen at 30 Blamfield Street with Majella, Patrick and the girls. Even with all the gerrymandering, injustice and illegal stuff going on at the time, they'd been happy in their way, penniless though they were. The McLaughlins had been in blissful ignorance then of how soon all their lives would be turned upside down and inside out and that only two would survive the onslaught.

Stones Corner Light

****

From the bar, Paddy studied his companion. Tommy seemed unusually stressed tonight. Like most men and women involved in this conflict, he looked old well before his time. But was it any wonder? Living in a country under army occupation meant risking being shot by the security services or randomly blown to smithereens while going about your daily business.

For people like Paddy Gillispie, the risks were even higher. The pressure of being a volunteer was intense. Most of his PIRA associates died prematurely while imprisoned, on the run or from alcohol. Heart attacks, strokes and worse felled others. Such a lethal cocktail of different sources of stress also brought about numerous failed marriages and abandoned children.

Paddy had been ordered to Derry by the OC of the West Belfast Brigade, who believed the city and its brigades needed some support in rooting out informers. He'd then met Tommy O'Reilly, and they hit it off immediately. The prominent community worker was impressive and charismatic. He wasn't an active volunteer but stood on the sidelines, offering wise counsel, and was of great importance to the Provo Council, who respected his work for Sinn Féin. They trusted him.

Though it went undiscussed with his new friend, as part of the Provo Intelligence team, Paddy's primary objective was to round up the region's touting bastards and deal with the traitors accordingly. Depending on the severity of their treason, an internal enquiry or court-martial would follow, resulting in the appropriate punishment: kneecapping, exile or execution.

Paddy still vividly remembered one such operation. He and Brian often referred to it between themselves. They'd been suited and booted like two Donegal farmers when the Unknowns delivered two snivelling turncoats to them at Ned's Point near Buncrana. The sedatives used on them while the youngsters moved them were wearing off by then; the baffled fuckers, one of whom was notably obese, went crazy when they realised what was happening. One lay face down in the mud, crying like a three-year-old.

Following a brief interrogation, their own words only confirmed their guilt and to rid them of the infernal racket as soon as possible; the wailing man was ordered to kneel and raise his hands. Paddy promptly fired a clean shot into the back of his football-shaped head.

As for the other, the fat man, who'd witnessed his friend's demise in silence, knelt and raised his hands without being asked. He was ready – his last thoughts being of his young son Sean and wife Anne, followed by a desperate Act of Contrition. Remembering the man's calm acceptance of imminent death, Paddy felt a grudging sense of respect. Once he'd done the deed, their bodies were dealt with appropriately and thrown out to sea.

They were a duo of low-life cheapskates who, through either naïvety or greed, had passed on vital intel leading to the arrest of three of the Provos' finest bomb-makers. The Republicans sorely missed these talents, and someone needed punishing; hence the two eejits paid the price – anyone in their right mind knew what informants could expect.

Paddy smiled as he recalled a piece of street graffiti he'd witnessed earlier that day.

I knew Dickie and Porkie but thank fuck they didn't know me!

****

Derry suited Paddy. He liked the city, its people and the local brigade, especially its young, curly-haired Officer Commanding, Cahir O'Connell. The Provo leader was a fair-minded, profoundly religious man who attended Mass daily. More importantly, when it came to the crunch, he'd have the guts to make any tough but necessary decision.

Others had warned Paddy never to cross O'Connell. Pleasant as the man was in conversation, he could also be harsh and unforgiving.

Paddy loved fishing, as did O'Connell. They'd talk late into the night in his small office in one of the many candy-coloured terrace houses of Cable Street in the heart of the Bogside. In no time, Paddy became a trusted sounding board for the OC.

Loyal as ever, his old friend Brian Monaghan and his wife Teresa had followed Paddy to Derry. They loved being so close to the miles of wild beaches, especially the dunes of Tramore Strand near the small village of Dunfanaghy in County Donegal.

Lately, Brian, with his swanky Mensa membership, had joined the queue of people recommending Paddy to think about ending the conflict through dialogue with the Brits. Something in the air was changing, and the OC felt it too. A favourite street slogan read: *Let the people vote the ballot over the Armalite.*

Sinn Féin was no longer illegal and had won two by-elections in the Republic. Yet Paddy ardently believed any political path was too risky. There wasn't a cat in hell's chance it'd work. Nevertheless, Brian kept at him and, like Tommy, was beginning to get on Paddy's nerves.

"It's not hard to grasp… we simply put more candidates up for election!" On a roll, Brian would start lecturing his friend. "Fuckin' heck, Paddy, think about it! We're a legal democratic party now. Can you imagine what else we could do? We'll take them Orangemen on 'til we get enough votes to secure Stormont! And finally, Paddy, *finally*, it'll be ours for the keeping. We'll get our united Ireland!"

No matter how hard his comrades harked on at him, Paddy remained steadfastly unconvinced. He walked back through the pack of punters towards Tommy – between shaking hands and saying hello to a few he'd got to know. Holding tightly to his pint of Smithwick's, he surreptitiously downed a double Jameson. He relished the burning feeling of the golden liquid as it slithered to rest deep in his empty, growling stomach.

Tommy picked up on the sly manoeuvre. Christ, what he'd do for a decent drink! He sorely missed the taste of whiskey and the sense of well-being that strong alcohol gave him, but he feared his daughter's wrath more.

"Good?" He looked at Paddy with envy.

"Always good, Tommy. Always!" Paddy chuckled and smiled, slapping the big man's shoulder. The solidity of Tommy's broad back jarred his hand, and he hooted in surprise,

"You're still built like a brick shit house, I see!"

Tommy laughed as he watched Paddy inspect his reddened palm. "Aye, but I think I'm shrinking," he chuckled.

The barman had added more fuel to the fire earlier, and the sweet-smelling turf had begun to spark and glow. The men loved the atmosphere of the tiny bar, made even denser by the waft of tobacco from a smouldering pipe belonging to a pensioner in a cap, sitting alone but content in a far corner. This was a man's pub. Few of their wives or girlfriends visited. On the rare occasions when they called in, they sat in the partitioned-off women's snug.

"When's Brian back?" Tommy queried. He knew Paddy's right-hand man was away.

"Tomorrow."

Talking about their journey to London, Paddy warned: "I've been thinking about it, Tommy, and it might not be an easy ride for you, travelling with us like. They're likely watching us."

When operating from The Shamrock bar in West Belfast, Paddy had always remained guarded while attending crowded music events and fund-raising nights. He'd deliberately avoided the many high-profile Republican funerals or gatherings for fear the security services would take photographs or film him. He'd made it harder for them to track him by carefully keeping under the radar. However, his blow-in to Derry had put that anonymity at risk, and he regretted that.

Thinking of The Shamrock, Paddy could never understand how Brian had managed to pick up the body of Brona Doyle, as she'd called herself, and dispose of it with such lightning speed. Dolores, his twin, younger than him by four minutes, had assassinated the British spy with a double tap, and within seconds of her firing the shots, the security services were all over the place like a rash.

The remains of Brona Doyle, aka Alice Wallace, field name IOWA, were never recovered, no matter how many rewards and appeals the media, television, newspapers, and the undercover officer's devastated mother offered. Paddy felt no remorse; they were all combatants at war, and war cost lives.

The British Government remained furious. Following the infiltrator's murder and subsequent disappearance, most of the Belfast crew, including Paddy and Dolores, were lifted and interrogated for days. But with no witnesses to prove they'd murdered a soldier nor any evidence, they couldn't be charged and were reluctantly released after a few good hidings.

Later, Dolores was sent back to the women's gaol at Armagh, charged with the murder of two screws who'd regularly assaulted, abused and beaten the female prisoners there, including Tina McLaughlin, who died under the harsh regime. It wouldn't suit the prison services to have the truth of that leak out. Paddy strongly suspected he wouldn't see his sibling walk the West Belfast streets for some time.

He realised he should concentrate on his companion. Tommy was studying him, head tilted to one side.

"You're being watched, and you're surprised, are you? Remember, Paddy, I don't want any trouble," the big man said tactfully, hoping the PIRA pair would reconsider and decide to go it alone.

Paddy nodded and decided he needed another shot, so he quickly headed to the bar, where he soon had the whole place singing along with him. One after another, the punters took turns belting out rebel songs, embracing the convivial atmosphere.

Tommy felt he should go home, but, sweet Jesus, he loved this place. He pined for the light, warm, uninhibited feeling only a few slugs of Jameson's Red Breast offered. Stout was stout until it grew tedious, never kicking in, never offering the feeling of well-being only a real drink could provide. He felt like getting pissed and joining in as he listened to 'The Black Velvet Band' sung beautifully by the flat-capped, pipe-smoking pensioner perched at the bar. Tommy's eyes filled – he always cried a little upon hearing that song – and in exasperation, the devil on his shoulder whispered temptingly, *"Sure, you deserve it. Look how hard you've been working! Have a drink, Tommy, just the one, and then you can go home. No harm done!"*

He woke up the following morning at 4 a.m. feeling parched, lying on the sofa fully dressed – including his donkey jacket – with a throbbing headache. He was sure he was dying. As his sour stomach rolled, the only thing he could remember was nodding in agreement with Paddy when he'd told him, "Tommy, see about London, feck it, we'll travel together. You're squeaky clean and sure; we won't be carrying." Paddy laughed, "we'll have good craic, like tonight. It'll be grand!"

****

Chapter Eight

Three men sat talking earnestly in a 'specially adapted dark blue Ford Cortina, parked in a layby on the outskirts of Drumahoe, a small Presbyterian parish near Londonderry. Since some Provo-loving telecommunications engineers had compromised the 'special' phone line Londonderry 01504 232323 they had once used to communicate, they couldn't take any more risks but were forced by 'upstairs' to conduct face-to-face meetings.

Once upon a time, the regular Social Democratic Labour Party (SDLP) middle-class Nationalists remained neutral, but after the recent hunger strikes, they were swaying towards Sinn Féin. The British Government recognised that if they were to have any chance of winning this guerrilla war – so embarrassingly close to their doorstep – it was vital they procure reliable intel at any cost.

As Military Intelligence (MI5) handlers, the men in the front of the car had encountered their fair share of rough diamonds (from most paramilitary organisations), who'd greedily blabber and snitch on their comrades, friends, and sometimes even their own families, for money. For example, acting on their tip-offs, an MI5 team would clandestinely spend hours in an observation post opposite Londonderry's West Bank unemployment office to access vital intelligence. They'd photograph the hundreds of men and women signing on – it was a perfect place to spot them and an opportunity to ID and match for past or potential terrorist associations.

If they struck gold – which they often did – first, some civil servant would do an updated background check on the suspect. Then a little deeper digging where they'd most likely come across illegal activities they could use to blackmail the poor fuckers, giving them no choice but to cooperate with the security services.

Alternatively, covert operators could follow suspects for days, noting their every move. This practice proved highly successful too. They knew most people held secrets, and MI5 could easily find them out; soon afterwards, the blackmailing threats would start. Their ensnared victims knew they'd have no choice but to play the game for as long as needed. Their secrets were often surprisingly shocking, and the last thing they wanted was for their precious church, family, friends or neighbours to know.

Some would call the hotline, desperate to make easy money – others called purely for kicks. Another tactic used by the security services included innocents being told that if they didn't work for them, MI5 would sell them out to the Provos as snitches. This was the source of endless psychological torture for some but proved to be highly motivating for others.

The handlers had framed the individual sitting in the car's back seat, known by them as 'Cawley', for quite some time. He was a prized source now because he'd risen well within the Provo ranks and was trusted. Unfortunately, he now wanted out, and they refused to let him go. MI5 weren't prepared to lose him, not when they were getting such a good return on their investment. They'd given him the green light to do whatever was deemed 'operationally necessary,' to prove himself and stay close and well in with the Provos, but the pressure of the double life he lived was beginning to trouble him, and Cawley was becoming more anxious and scared by the day.

After murmuring a string of platitudes to reassure him, they only heard the slamming of a rear passenger door. They watched the hooded figure walk briskly away into the night, muttering and unmistakably pissed off.

"We need to find another surefire way of keeping that one onside, don't we?" the driver observed, starting the engine. "Time to dig deeper. Target his family."

****

Chapter Nine

Emmett McFadden completed his mechanic's apprenticeship and found himself practically running the small independent garage in upper William Street.

It'd taken him a long time to recover from the delivery of prisoners to Ned's Point that had resulted in the murder of two men. Afterwards, he was angry and upset with himself and his world. He didn't sign up for this when he joined the Unknowns. His recruiter Mickey Boyle hadn't listened when Emmett told him repeatedly that there was no way he could handle anyone getting hurt or dying.

He still suffered from recurring nightmares, waking up sweating like a pig, with his heart hammering. He'd replay the moment he and his Unknowns partner Liz McKenna had passed over their hooded and snivelling passengers. Condemned men, though the young lad had been slow to realise it. In his mind, he visualised Dickie's bloated purple body bobbing up and down in the waves of Lough Swilly, eyeless and nibbled at by the sea creatures. It terrified him beyond belief.

Not long after that fateful day, he'd tried to meet up with Mickey to tell him he wanted out and for good. It wasn't to be, however; Mickey was in gaol, charged with the murder of an RUC man in Derry. Someone had grassed. Coincidentally, he'd been sent to Long Kesh to share a cell with Emmett's brother Joe.

As for Liz, Emmett knew she'd been far from impressed by his reluctance to dirty his hands and wasn't surprised but somewhat relieved when she'd reported her concerns to the CO. Not long afterwards, a volunteer he didn't know told Emmett on the quiet that he was out – his contribution to the cause was over.

****

One Friday evening, he finished work later than usual and arrived home wearing a pair of dark blue, oil-stained overalls with Harrison's garage logo. His ma sat at the kitchen table sobbing, looking old, fragile and drained. Noticing him standing there and embarrassed by her show of emotion, she quickly wiped her eyes using a yellow-and-white-striped T-cloth and half-smiled at him. Emmett's gym-toned body filled the doorway, and a surge of love for her good, steady middle boy overwhelmed Maggie.

He was a sound individual but seemed to carry a burden constantly these days, no longer the happy-go-lucky teenager he'd once been.

"What is it, Ma?" he asked with concern. "What's up?"

"Ah, nothing, son, one of those days, that's all."

He wasn't sure he believed her and tried again. "You sure? Where's Da?"

Maggie sniffed and cleared her throat, rising to prepare dinner. With her back to her son, she replied in a soft voice, "At work. Should be back soon. Hungry?"

"Starving," Emmett replied gently.

An eternal cloud of sadness seemed to be suspended over the McFadden household. They'd been lurching from one disaster to another lately, and it wasn't just their family. Few in the city had been untouched or untarnished by the ongoing bloodshed.

Although his father eventually got some cleaning job, he seemed oddly quiet about it. He'd be up and out by dawn and was usually asleep or working a late shift when Emmett came home – he was proud of the change in the man who'd formerly preferred to run an unofficial taxi service to taking steady employment. The money he now brought in had taken the pressure off them all, especially for his ma, who once again could afford to buy the coloured stuff for her hair. Until tonight, she'd been looking more like her old self.

"I'll get a wash if that's okay?" Emmett asked. "Can I do anything? Are you sure you're okay?"

"No, love, it's fine. I'm fine. It's mince stew – nearly done."

Emmett nodded. "I won't be long," he said as he headed up the narrow staircase to their bathroom.

"Right, love," Maggie answered with a sigh. If she didn't have the Women's Peace Movement to keep her sane, she didn't think there was any way she could pull herself out of this dark, infernal hole she woke up in every morning.

The women's movement had snowballed since its inception in 1970 in Belfast. More so after three children died later when an IRA volunteer, whom the British Army had shot, ploughed his car into them. Peace rallies followed and spread to Derry. The women believed it could have been any of their kids mown down in the street, so when she could, Maggie became a volunteer.

The communities worked together to solve the issues that affected them, including poor housing, pitiable education and the increasing number of teenage pregnancies. Grannies, mothers, wives, sisters and aunts worked hard to maintain some semblance of normality for their working-class communities. These were the people – from both sides of the divide – who bore the brunt of The Troubles. The women of Northern Ireland were starting to make a real difference in their divided communities. They were determined to heal the conflict and division within their country.

****

Liz McKenna took delight in being a volunteer for the Provos. She'd studied the secret 1977 Green book several times back to front and learnt all she could about subjects from the political philosophy of the Provisionals (Provos) to techniques for resisting interrogation. At first, as a woman, she'd felt she had no choice but to work harder than most male volunteers. Her comrades didn't take her seriously from the outset, and her cell leader had given her the most menial jobs. These included cleaning well-rusted and dilapidated ammunition – leftovers from previous campaigns and unpredictable remnants from World War II.

By now, she was feeling disillusioned. The men treated her like a second-class citizen purely because she was a woman. Typical Derry, she thought. They probably expected her to marry and have loads of babies to increase the Catholic vote 'For Ireland'.

The many political prisoners expected the wives who weren't working to stay home all day. They believed they'd find things as they had been when they finally got out. However, with their men locked up, the women discovered a new taste for independence and not only liked it but fully embraced it for the first time. They welcomed the ties and friendships forged from their female solidarity plus a dollop of autonomy and self-belief. After years of prison visits and providing emotional support for their men, many of them knew they couldn't go back to an archaic and rigid patriarchal society. After their long confinements, the returning internees found adjusting to their women taking a political stand difficult. Numerous couples broke up under the strain.

If she wanted to be a success, Liz knew she'd have to prove her worth twice over. But surely securely delivering the two snivelling touts to Ned's Point must go in her favour? In her debrief, she reported that Emmett McFadden had almost compromised the reprisal operation and emphasised that it was entirely down to her that it hadn't failed. When others heard what happened, Volunteer Emmett McFadden was branded weak. *"He's a liability,"* Liz had said unflinchingly. After that, she'd never come across him again, which was a shame. Perhaps it could've been different between them in any other situation – after all; he was pretty cute.

She hurriedly made her way to the corner of Cable Street in Derry's Bogside for another operational briefing. Taking care not to be followed, she approached a small, grey-and-white-painted terraced house and knocked on the door. A tall, gangly, thin-faced man promptly answered, nodded, peeked out to check any activity on the street and, when satisfied, let her enter.

She walked into what would have been known years before as the 'good room' of the terraced house, adjacent to a short hallway that led to a kitchen the size of a phone box. Not so long ago, ten or twenty family members had lived together in such pocket-sized houses.

Two men sat quietly in a corner as they sucked the life out of their John Players' ciggies. One sat on a well-worn, multi-coloured crochet-covered chair, the other on a shabby floral sofa adjacent to a meagre, dying fire. They acknowledged her with apathetic nods.

Their leader Jon Healy, the tall, gangly man who'd answered the door to her, remained standing. He seemed to want to be literally on a different level from them. At their first meeting, Liz quickly decided he was a chauvinist. This father of ten children was a bit of a lad on the sly and liked women – to the dismay of his bedraggled, exhausted wife.

"I'll get straight to it," he said forcefully, "we need cash, and we need it fast."

Most volunteers were skint and merely living off their dole; others were on the run or in prison, and their families needed financial support. They also required cash for operational expenses after some substantial reconnaissance trips to England to plan bold future missions.

Healy's pointed chin jerked towards Liz as he continued, "Your woman here thinks she's come up with an idea." He winked sardonically at a man in the corner, who sneered at Liz in return.

She didn't see their exchange but jumped up to stand in front of the dying fire. She'd dressed casually, using little make-up, and wore a black shell suit over a greying, badly faded T-shirt adorned with a picture of Blondie. Scuffed trainers on her feet so she could move fast. There was a message in her choice of clothes. She wanted to be treated as an equal, not as some bimbo. But as much as it made sense to her, her comrades hadn't been particularly flattering about her practical look, continually joking that she should wear short skirts and low-cut blouses more often. They didn't warm to this dogged uncompromising woman who was way too boyish and unappealing to their mind.

Her heart was hammering as she began. "It's simple. I've met an HGV driver who takes a Currys lorry back and forward from Belfast to Europe, and I reckon we can hi-jack it! Just imagine the stuff in the back of a forty-footer: white goods, video players, TVs… a real Aladdin's cave. He's already got travellers set up in the Republic to take the load off us. A sixty/forty split." She allowed her audience to digest her words though their blank expressions gave her little confidence.

"Guys, for Christ's sake, it's simple!" It was a no-brainer. Why didn't they see it? "All we have to do is take the load, pass it over and hardly go near the border! I suggest the travellers break the load down into smaller lots to get it across in Free-State registered vans. We take the cash and get out." She waited, but the small, smoke-filled room remained silent as she added, "Don't you see? It's perfect. There's little risk to us other than jacking the lorry and driving it. We just need someone we can trust. Does anyone here know how to drive a lorry?"

The muted men remained still and stared blankly at her. Answering her question, she proclaimed nervously, "That's okay. We'll find someone." Taking a step back and opening her arms, she invited questions. "Well? What do you think!"

Liz looked about the room for gestures of approval, but the men only raised their eyebrows and looked at each other. Imagine a woman coming up with such a thought! All eyes in the room turned to Jon Healy, but not before Ronan Duffy, one of the youngest there, queried, "How much do you reckon we'd get?"

Everyone knew Ronan was sometimes a bit of a twat, but he was far from stupid. He was short, broad-waisted, and habitually wore the same clothes daily: a white T-shirt and blue jeans under a long green parka. It was a running joke whether Ronan had a wardrobe full of the same styles or if the boy washed his clothes every night. Either way, he was always meticulously clean, well-shaved and groomed. Sitting on a corner chair, he added, "I reckon it might be worth looking at." His voice faded under the glare on the boss's face.

Liz had worked it out already and was thrilled by his question. "We'd make anything from forty to sixty thousand," she told him, "it depends on what's in the container on the day, but one way or another, it'd be worth it."

The men sat like the living dead until the boss responded. He'd been against the idea from the beginning, not because he thought it was terrible; it was bloody good. It was because he didn't want some nip of a girl coming in full of fuckin' big ideas and showing him up. He didn't like her, but the OC wanted her on board for some reason. As far as Healy was concerned, with a few rare exceptions, women didn't belong in this war but at home looking after the house and wains. He'd deliberately not mentioned her plan to the OC in his determination to keep McKenna under his thumb.

"I think it's a shit idea," he told them matter-of-factly, "we should stick to what we know."

Liz's head fell forward. Her mind turned dry as a stone; she couldn't believe this.

"We do the usual and turn over a few bookies. Some big races are coming up next weekend. Job done."

Healy ignored Liz and looked to the nodding men for agreement. The boss was right – wasn't he always? Best stick to what you know. None of them paid attention to Liz's exasperated, shocked expression as she fell back into her chair. The rest of the cell, oblivious to her fuming anger, discussed the robberies in detail. Which bookies, when, and the many deathly boring details. She watched Healy bark out his orders until he turned to her and pointed a finger, instructing her what she was to do.

"You're to go to the safe house, stay there and make sure there's plenty of stodge and hot drinks ready for the boys. It'll be a long couple of days."

That was it? Unbelievable. But Liz carefully gave him nothing to pick up on; she wasn't for letting him see her fury and frustration. The guy was a dickless wimp with a severe lack of ambition. Bookie*s?* None of these plebs other than Ronan had even had the sense to ask her more about her plan. Didn't they hear how much the job was worth? They'd be lucky to get a couple of grand per bookie – and the risk of it all!

She'd do what Healy asked, but somehow she'd get the Currys job on the OC's radar. First things first, though, she'd say something personal and much more important to finish.

By the time they were ready to leave, it was dark outside, and they had to assume that, somewhere out there, the security services were monitoring the tiny house. Each wore a woollen hat, raised their collar and upped their hood. They left at intervals with heads lowered to walk speedily home.

As Liz reached her front door and was about to put the key in the lock, her stepfather, whom she loathed, swung it open. He wasn't slow to express his disappointment at her return.

"Ah, it's you. Where the fuck have you been?" the burly man asked rudely.

Liz didn't answer but pushed her way past his bulbous body and went towards the kitchen. She was hungry and in no mood to talk to the slimeball. For years, he'd come into her bedroom at night, whispering words a child should never hear or understand, then crawl into her tiny bed where he'd hurt her, leaving her sore and in pain for days. He'd repeatedly warned her that he'd kill her mother if she told anyone.

Eventually, he stopped when nature took charge, and her periods arrived. As an adult, she realised the paedo liked very young children. She'd never told a soul, her shame too intolerable, and she felt no one would believe her anyway. Most Catholics refused to swear allegiance to the Queen; thereby, they couldn't work in the Civil Service. But as a Loyalist, Edwards held a responsible administrative position, unbelievably overseeing several children's institutions throughout the province.

She never did tell her mother, whom she loved more than anything and, thank God, Liz was an only child. She still monitored him closely, subtly making it known to her close friends that he gave her the creeps. Pretending to be joking, she'd warn them: "Don't say anything about this to anyone... it's a weird feeling, but he gives me the creeps. He's never done anything to me like, but keep an eye out for him – especially around the kiddies."

She meant every word of it, but shame prevented her from sharing the whole truth about the man with whom she still shared a house.

****

George Edwards tutted at his stepdaughter's insolence and ignored the slut, returning to the living room. He hadn't expected her home so early. As soon as he'd heard her footsteps, he'd quickly taken the sacred VHS video tape out of its player and returned it safely inside a Walt Disney *Sleeping Beauty* cover.

He wished the girl would fuck off and leave him be, but she wouldn't. She was too stubborn and proud to let him have anything that belonged to her wretched, pathetic effort of a mother. He'd married the old bat years ago. Although she was a Taig, he'd needed somewhere to live after his last bit of fluff in Belfast, and her rancorous, sniffly kids, threatened to report him to the police and tossed him out.

After ensuring the headstrong young bitch was out of earshot, George recovered the video from the top shelf of a solid oak bookcase. He carefully removed the precious tape and placed it back into a top-of-the-range JVC video player that'd fallen off the back of a lorry.

It'd already proved its worth, he thought, smiling cunningly.

With a heavy sigh of satisfaction, he fell back and began to watch the film. On impulse, his grubby, long-nailed hand manoeuvred inside and down his off-white, sullied Y-fronts for the second time that night.

Upstairs, with her bedroom door double-locked and securely bolted, Liz suspected what George was up to. Unable to control herself, she'd recently opened one of his dubious VHS cases to find no *Sleeping Beauty, Cinderella,* or 'Happy Ever After' tale. Instead, there were videos of the horrific suffering and abuse of young children that she would've been unable to imagine without the evidence of her own eyes. In hindsight, she should have destroyed every one of them, but somehow George Edwards still managed to terrify her and probably always would.

The thought of his antics made her sick to the heart. She understood she should've been brave enough to report him long ago. Now she'd die of shame if anyone found out what he was and that she'd lived in the very same house People talked; she knew she could not face the fallout or their sympathetic 'Why didn't you say something?' looks. Telling the police would only add to the nightmare. And she certainly wasn't going to risk her standing with the Provos by tattling the whole sorry tale.

****

The boy pleaded continually with his mother, but in that disinterested tone he knew so well always meant no; she only replied, *"I'll think about it,"* and moved on to something else. She'd barely heard him, but Liam McFadden refused to give up. He'd do anything to get his parents to say yes if he was chosen for a Project Children trip. The idea of going to America in the summer holidays made his body quiver and his heart pound with excitement. As things were, the nearest he'd ever get to the US was watching the telly. Some other boys whom the scheme had chosen over the past few years still talked glowingly about their trips.

Today was the day when the names of the boys who'd receive an American holiday would be announced. Besides worrying about obtaining his parents' permission, he suspected he might be a bit too old. Nevertheless, as Mrs Mullin, the school principal, announced the winners in the assembly that morning, Liam still nursed a faint sense of hope and prayed to all the angels and saints as hard as he could!

He heard the woman's voice echoing across the vast St Peter's School gym in Creggan.

"Quieten down now, boys!" She waited, but their excitement didn't wane.

"If you don't shut up, lads, I won't bother naming the three lucky fellas!"

A miraculous silence washed through the gym at her threat, and 500 boys suddenly quietened, standing as still as statues.

The headmistress smiled as she looked around and saw their expressions; she chuckled as she tore open the A4 brown envelope and cast her eyes about the hall.

She already knew the identities of the three lucky boys and was delighted with the decision. It was a suitable choice; she understood precisely why the judges had chosen the trio and knew they needed this six-week break badly. She imagined them all under the American sun, feeling safe, secure and carefree. She'd visited the US herself and loved it. It'd been a chaotic year here with the awful hunger strikes, continuous bombings, shootings and maiming. Hardly an ideal childhood background.

For one reason or another, all three deserved this trip – she only wished the organisers could've taken more boys, but three was better than none.

****

Project Children was conceived after retired New York Police Officer Halloran and his colleagues came to Derry to repair some houses in Creggan a few years ago.

Upon their return to the States, the Americans came up with the idea as they sat around a table in Halloran's basement in a small village in New York state. They followed the news about events in Northern Ireland and, having seen the place for themselves, knew how young children were affected by the everyday horrors of life in a war zone. The men decided to do something about it. They'd offer underprivileged kids the chance to taste life away from The Troubles and experience a more expansive world where life could be full of opportunities.

The officers understood that Catholic children went to Catholic schools and only mixed with Catholics. It was the same for Protestants. Most schools were segregated, resulting in very few opportunities for these youngsters to mingle and socialise.

Taking this into account, the retired officers stipulated they'd introduce a 50/50 split amongst the children – half of them Catholic and half Protestant – creating equal opportunities for the kids to mix in a neutral, safe location. Where possible, a Catholic and a Protestant child would be paired off by the organisers, and to name a few activities, they'd play soccer, baseball, swim and hike together.

In the beginning, this stipulation proved difficult for the children. However, the sunny, cheery, safe environment they found themselves transported to soon tumbled the strongest sectarian walls, with their entrenched prejudices crumbling to dust. There was never any shortage of vetted host families, with offers coming in from New York and places farther afield, including Monroe, Middletown, Chicago and beyond.

****

Back at St Peter's, Mrs Mullin excitedly announced the names, "I'm delighted that Project Children chose Mallie O'Toole."

Her eyes searched until she spotted a group of lads congratulating a small, ginger-haired, freckled boy with crooked teeth, whose face broke out in a sea of blotchy red. Even from afar, she was sure she could see his eyes overflowing with joy. A few years ago, Mallie's younger sister, five-year-old Rosalin, was killed in a bomb blast in a tea shop. Soon after, his mother was sent to Grandsha, the local mental hospital, and never recovered from her loss. Delighted to see him so happy and giving him a warm smile, Mrs Mullin continued to speak.

"And next, Patrick Ryan!"

It didn't take her long to find Ryan, who jumped around like a frog, yelling and whooping with joy in front of the stage.

"Yes! Yes! Feck!" he yelled, punching his fist in the air. Slightly embarrassed at his reaction and fearing that he might well be overdoing it, he stopped.

His brother and a cousin had been on hunger strike. Ryan struggled with his depressed mother's moaning and crying and his father's drinking and anger. They fought all the time. The boy couldn't believe he would be getting away from this shithole. *Thank you, Jesus!*

By now, Liam's fear seemed justified, and he felt he'd no chance: Mallie O'Toole was in his first year and much younger than Liam and Patrick, the year above. Resigned in defeat, he picked up his brother's old school blazer with its poorly repaired pocket crest and prepared to leave. Words couldn't describe his disappointment.

"And last but not least…." Mrs Mullin piped up.

Once more, the gym buzzed in anticipation, but the headmistress quickly took control in a voice that could cut glass. "Now quiet, boys, let me finish!" Silence ensued.

"Thank you."

The bespectacled, grey-haired teacher deliberately kept the sea of anxious faces waiting. She eyed the final recipient and announced with a wide smile.

"And finally." She paused, "Liam McFadden!"

She had a soft spot for this lad she regarded as intelligent and promising. He could do great things if he kept his head down and stayed out of trouble. She'd been especially pleased to see his name on the list. He, too, deserved this opportunity, with his eldest brother Joe incarcerated in appalling conditions. His pitiful mother had never been the same after the City Hotel débâcle. The poor woman had lost her well-paid job, bless her, and it wasn't even her fault.

Liam came to a standstill, hypnotised and unable to move. Did he hear wrong? *No way*! Any uncertainty was set aside when one of his best friends, Phil Walsh, jumped on Liam's back and relentlessly thumped him, squealing in delight.

"Fuckin' brilliant, Liam! Fuckin' brilliant!"

Mrs Mullin duly gave him a look that would normally shake his very core, but not today!

Liam cried out and looked for his other best friend, Vinny Kelly, forgetting for a split second that he wasn't at St Pete's anymore. He was an only child who'd initially moved to Belfast to live with his uncle and aunt, but it wasn't too long before they got fed up with him. Vinny's father was in Long Kesh, and his English mother had a breakdown and left without a word to return to Nottingham. Last Liam heard, Vinny was in some boys' home in East Belfast, and there hadn't been a peep out of him since. The boys had been like brothers before that because Maggie McFadden practically brought the little lad up, and he'd spent most of his childhood at their kitchen table. *Poor Vinny*, Liam thought. *I wish he were here now.*

****

Getting through the rest of the school day was hell for Liam and the other winners. The clocks felt like they were going backwards until, finally, the bell rang out at 3.40 p.m. Liam couldn't remember the walk home, only that he had made it within minutes.

His heart was pounding as he ran like a scalded dog through the gaps between the concrete pyramids and barbed-wire barricades. He soared over the piled armoury of bottles, broken flagstones and missiles at Stones Corner before turning into Blamfield Street. He saw his mammy walking towards him, her head low and face hidden under the floral scarf that covered her rollered hair. She struggled to carry two laden Spar bags that caused her to wobble with their weight.

"Mammy! Mammy!" Liam shrieked as he ran towards her.

Maggie released both bags at her youngest's cries and manic waves. They exploded as they hit the path. Glass milk bottles smashed to smithereens with their creamy contents soaking the brown-paper-wrapped meat and vegetables. The rest splayed far and wide, covering the top of Maggie's scruffy black shoes.

With her heart suspended in her throat, she heard her son let out another wild cry, "Mammy… Ma!"

He ran towards her with a piece of paper held high. She had her hand to her throat as he drew closer and, oblivious to the ruined shopping, scurried as quickly as she could towards him. *Sweet Mother of God, what had happened?*

"Jesus, Liam. What is it, love? What's wrong now!" she screamed.

Blamfield Street came alive at such a clamour, and door after door – some still damaged from the many army raids – opened up.

"Ah, Mammy, you'll never believe it!"

Maggie began to cry as a sudden fear overtook her. She started to pat and frisk the boy.

"Are you hurt, Liam? Did someone hurt you, son!"

Now frantic, she pulled at his blazer, searching for any sign of injury, and cupped his head feverishly, checking his face and beyond. *What the feck?* Liam couldn't understand what the woman was doing! Stumbling back, he gently pushed her off. She was embarrassing him – the whole street was watching.

"Jesus, Ma, what are ye doing? I'm grand. What's up with you?"

Realising her son was unhurt and relieved, Maggie rested against a semi-broken fence for a moment. Then, with one hand on her wildly drumming heart, she shrieked and whipped him one across the head.

"Jesus, Mary and Joseph, Liam! You scared the bejesus outta me! What are you doing, yelling your head off in the middle of the street like that? You've nearly given me a heart attack!"

She was sure she could hear it hammering as she tried to understand what her youngest was saying. Even after a good hard whack that had gone virtually unnoticed, Liam's excitement only increased. "Ah, Mammy, sorry – but wait 'til you hear! I'm going to America. Ma, I'm going to America!"

Chapter Ten

Belfast, 1981

Time and the numerous medical procedures he'd endured from his many wounds, resulting from the Tullyvallen Orange Lodge bomb and gun attack, had certainly not been kind to Charles Jones. The short, rotund man glowered into the mirror, scrutinising his appearance before readjusting his blood orange-coloured tie. His surgeons had finished restoring his patchworked face, and he'd grown accustomed to his flat-ended nose, drooping cheekbone and bloodshot eyes. One remained particularly frustrating as it continued to discharge an endless flow of clear fluid.

He didn't give a rat's ass how he looked. He wasn't particularly interested in the fairer sex these days, but on the rare occasions he was tempted, he'd have no qualms about paying for a professional fuck.

At this time, however, his main concern about his well-being was a growing and uncontrollable dependency on non-prescription painkillers. He was downing them like sweets. The burning pain in his surgically reconstructed face was, at times, too overpowering and unmanageable otherwise.

It'd taken longer than he'd liked to get his finances back on track after the sham of the court case to which the good-for-nothing Yankee reporter William Barter had relentlessly pursued him. Jones felt it was only fitting that he should have been acquitted of murder amongst other things. However, his loyal sidekick, bodyguard Lemon, aka Mark Carroll, and the faithful band of supporting 'kids', ended up in jail for life, with no parole to be granted, for the numerous sectarian murders they'd been involved in, all urged on by Jones. He rarely thought of most of them again. Lemon, however, was beginning to piss him off. He'd been trying his damnedest to contact his former boss, and Jones either ignored his calls or tore up his many unopened prison letters.

Judge Dodds had proved to be worth his weight in gold, directing the trial entirely in Jones's favour despite some damning evidence against him having been found. Dodds continued to bask in his Boodles membership, the private London club where Jones was also a member. He had arranged for the judge's membership application to be passed. Later, much to Jones's displeasure, Dodds retired as a judge but continued using his membership. His departure left a worrying gap in the businessman's legal arsenal and one he was finding hard to fill. He needed to have a High Court Judge in his corner – nothing more, nothing less.

His funds were finally in the black again and having completed a few lucrative legal and not-so-legal financial deals, he was on a firmer footing. The next step in his strategy was to pair up with like-minded political acquaintances to go into front-line politics. He was also playing a significant and decisive role in his beloved UVF (Ulster Volunteer Force), though it'd been made clear they didn't want him involved in politics since that wasn't part of their long-term plan. The UVF was an impenetrable organisation that kept itself to itself and was particularly selective about who was allowed to join.

The egregious Republican blanket protests, hunger strikes and the outlandish behaviour of the Nationalists had caused Jones and his paramilitary acquaintances no end of trouble. The media continually hounded him for quotes on the matter. He'd been particularly vocal in condemning the Republicans' suicidal tactics, repeatedly telling the television channels that the men's bestial behaviour in spreading excrement over their cells was contemptible. When interviewed on camera, he willingly denounced them.

"These men are rendering themselves less than human by refusing to wash, cut their hair, shave, or wear prison uniforms. The whole exercise is shameful."

The thought that Fenians could vote in a self-starving prisoner to Westminster was almost too much for him to bear. However, the British Government subsequently changed the law so no UK prisoner could stand in future elections. Jones's initial consolation was that the Brits remained fixed in their opposition to reinstating Special Category Status (SCS) or meeting the prisoners' many demands following the second series of hunger strikes. However, much to his and his supporters' despair, the Brits eventually conceded to the Republican demands.

Another sore point for Jones and his infuriated comrades was that the Rome-ruled Irish Government were getting too close for comfort in arbitrating numerous meetings with the British Government to curtail the Unionists' power. The Irish Government had then dared to imply there would be a united Ireland within ten years, and Jones's blood curled at the thought.

****

Today he had been to lunch with Chief Constable Henry Bonner, who had replaced George Shalham after his assassination, accompanied by an ambitious Army Intelligence Officer (AIO) named Alan Hickey.

Hickey had undertaken several tours of Northern Ireland and other British territories worldwide, including Cyprus and Belize, as he progressed through the ranks. He was seen as someone who embraced the risks of covert and undercover operations. His latest secondment to the North had fired him to secretly undertake some solo clandestine and dangerous tasks.

As an AIO, Hickey collected collated and assessed intelligence to convey to the RUC Special Branch and Security Services. It was considered a means of determining in advance any threats to the province's security, particularly from the Republican paramilitaries, and of flagging up issues that might affect the political process in Northern Ireland. However, it also, unofficially and secretly, enabled Hickey to support several Loyalist groups and individuals, hopefully now including Charles Jones's armed offensive against the Republicans.

The intelligence officer wore a black leather jacket, a white open-necked shirt, well-pressed dark grey trousers and highly polished black shoes. He was an imposing presence. Non-regulation length curly black hair framed a firm-jawed face set off by a dark moustache.

Jones listened carefully to what the young officer had to say and soon recognised that this man was his golden goose and ready for the plucking. In any way possible, he'd use the officer's training and experience in his conquest to ruin Republicanism and destroy his enemies, the crusading nuisance of a journalist William Barter, and Brendan Doherty, a Londonderry solicitor revered amongst the Republican community. The two of them were comrades-in-arms who'd done nothing but pestered, bullied and stalk Jones in their efforts to send him down. As for James Henderson and Rocola, his long-time enemies, Jones had his plan for revenge there well in hand.

Bonner had managed to put on yet more weight, and Jones found the sight of him repugnant. He liked his food, he had to admit, but the other man was a positive embarrassment. Jones watched, appalled, as the top cop wolfed down his lunch. His RUC green uniform, always one size too small, did him no favours, only serving to emphasise his morbidly obese frame. Between regular bursts of chomping, he appeared pretty upbeat about local events.

"Reverend Paisley's ordered a Loyalist day of action. There'll be rallies all over, and the cream of Ulster will be there – they're planning to shut the whole place down!" he proudly told them.

Jones was well aware of Reverend Paisley's plan. The Unionists were frustrated at the increasing Republican violence and the improving relationship between the British and Irish Governments. Again, they felt betrayed by the British and especially by Prime Minister Margaret Thatcher, whom they'd once believed was on their side. Paisley planned to entice 4,000 or so Ulster Loyalists to strike in protest at the Iron Lady's betrayal.

They'd cut off rural villages and roads using cavalcades of tractors and other farm vehicles, believing they and they alone could control Ulster. Jones was to accompany him to speak at a rally in Newtownards the following month, and the very idea of sharing a platform with the great man was spine-tingling.

****

Jones listened with ill-concealed irritation as Bonner babbled on. "The Reverend isn't going to let all this talk with Dublin go down quietly. He's livid! Between you and me, the Brits are bringing in six hundred more troops. That's around eleven thousand stationed here now, and what use have they been, eh? They share nothing with us but fuck off and do their own thing." After reflection, he added a breezy apology to their young English guest.

"No offence!"

Hickey accepted the policeman's conciliatory gesture with a relaxed smile. "None taken." He wasn't partial to the wooden top. Having met him a few times, he thought the man a fool, totally unprofessional and plain stupid. It was hardly surprising that Det (the British Army's 14 Intelligence Company) remained aloof and didn't want to liaise with the RUC commander and his peers. They knew all about Bonner's shoddy leadership skills, poor decision-making and lack of authority.

However, he had at least introduced Hickey to Charles Jones, who felt the same way about the RUC man judging from his peeved expression. As for Jones, he was another story. What this man said, this man did, and he undoubtedly loathed the Republicans as much as

Hickey did. Jones rapidly picked up on the intelligence officer's disdain for Bonner and pointedly asked: "How are you finding your role here, Captain? I assume it's very different from your last tours?"

Jones was surprised when the Brit turned in his seat to look him full in the face. Most people found Jones's scars and watering eyes unnerving, but not Hickey, whose own eyes resembled a shark's, coal black and devoid of expression. Jones was secretly amused by the soldier's blatant attempt to psych him and grinned as he bit into a piece of baked salmon, waiting for an answer.

Hickey was keen to impress. Even with his chequered history, the businessman was a rising influencer in the province. It was a win-win for both of them if they found a way to collaborate.

"It's very different, Mr Jones. I'm sure you'll understand I've fingers in many pies as a liaison officer. My priority is to keep the lines of communication open between us and the security services about potential Provo and Loyalist plots. More importantly, it's primarily to ensure critical intel is quickly and easily available for M15 to pursue."

Hickey chuckled. "It appears we've got ourselves a real battle with the Provos and their sympathisers, and to win that battle, we need to understand how far the State will allow us to pursue peace and keep the Union." He took a moment and said, "If you know what I mean?" Jones listened. Hickey had his full attention now.

"I have to..."

Bonner was about to interrupt but was stunned when Jones reprimanded him with a loud hiss and a finger pressed to his lips. The CC fell back in disgust, his chest angrily puffed out and pushing against the table. Jones looked at Hickey like a mother disappointed in a disobedient child and waved a hand for him to continue. "You were saying, Captain Hickey?"

A hot flush of embarrassment flooded Bonner's face. "Charles! There's no need for unpleasantness," he whined, hoping the other patrons hadn't noticed his skirmish.

Jones's eyes grew cold, their message very clear, and Bonner cursed to himself. He was already walking a fine line with this man, who continually called him a failure and would demean him in whatever way possible.

To defuse the awkwardness of the moment, Hickey quickly interceded. "It's fine, Mr Jones, truly."

Time froze as Jones's watering eyes glowered at Bonner and eventually drifted back to regard the captain. He cleared his throat and wiped his mouth.

"Please, Captain. Continue what you were saying before the ill-mannered interruption."

For the remainder of the lunch, Bonner sat back in his seat, sulking and too upset to pay attention to the conversation. When lunch ended, Hickey finally stood up to say thank you and goodbye.

"Thank you, sir," he said, shaking Bonner's limp hand. The policeman grunted something unintelligible and turned away.

The captain shared a knowing smile with Jones. "Mr Jones. Thank you for such a delicious lunch. It was good to meet you finally. I believe you, and I have lots in common, and I hope we meet again… soon?" he hinted, emphasising the word.

Jones stood and offered his hand. "Don't thank me, young man. I believe it's the Chief Constable's treat today!" He laughed mirthlessly as Bonner's face radiated rage and affront. Once again, the other two men shared a smile at his expense.

"As for you, Captain, yes. You and I will be seeing each other again very soon," Jones concluded.

Hickey nodded and, as only a soldier could, left the room while looking proud and resolute. Jones found he was excited about the prospect of working with that young man. Folding his napkin, he looked at the Chief Constable and growled.

"For Christ's sake, Bonner! You have a face on you as long as a day. Quickly, pay up, man!"

Bonner grudgingly fumbled for his wallet as Jones continued, "That's one interesting young man we've got there, Bonner, don't you think?"

"If you say so," he replied petulantly, preparing to pay the exorbitant bill.

"I do say so, Bonner. Very interesting indeed."

****

A few weeks later, Jones watched the traffic below the sash windows of his Queen Anne office near Victoria Street in Belfast. Captain Hickey sat silently in one of two ox-blood leather-covered Chesterfield chairs facing the businessman's desk. Jones was contemplating a response to the officer's startling proposition. His idea was dangerous but could significantly increase Jones's influence within the UVF.

No one *alive* knew about his involvement in the assassination of Londonderry's Bishop Hegarty at the City Hotel. Only Lemon, his incarcerated bodyguard, was aware Jones sanctioned the double murder of James Henderson Senior and George Shalham. Whereas the bishop's murder was planned well in advance, Henderson and Shalham were removed from the wing once they were about to expose Jones for his involvement in the City Hotel massacre. Jones had done what any strategist would – he'd eliminated them.

Yet two similar menaces remained at the top of his hit list, William Barter and Brendan Doherty. This was where the captain's timely proposal came in very useful.

"Before I comment on your offer, may I ask why?" Jones asked, turning away from the window to sit in his chair. As ever, Hickey's eyes were unfathomable as he replied.

"It's simple, sir. These gentlemen have caused you nothing but grief since your trial, and I'm led to believe they're also meddling in sensitive matters that carry significant risks for you and us. They're interviewing witnesses and attempting to reopen cases we both know should remain closed. We also believe Barter has links with the CIA."

Such a revelation about the journalist surprised even Jones. Like a rabid dog, the American had pursued him since he'd hobbled down the courthouse steps in Londonderry, a free man against the odds. Jones laughed as he remembered the Yank's expression on hearing Judge Dodds's Not Guilty verdict – to see Barter's astonishment then had been as sweet as honey.

After that, he'd cursed Barter's many insinuations against him in the media, in print, as well as on the radio and TV. It was never-ending, Barter telling the whole world his suspicions about Jones's business dealings, including drug smuggling, bank robberies, and sectarian murders – all of which he repeatedly and categorically denied. He'd tried to get rid of Barter before by instructing his bodyguard to remove him but had missed the mark. This time, however, he wouldn't fail – not with Hickey taking the lead. Unlike Lemon, the big blubbery waste of space, Hickey was street-savvy, intelligent, and a trained assassin.

"Okay, go ahead," Jones agreed. "How will you handle it?"

Hickey beamed with delight and satisfaction. "It's relatively straightforward, sir. I'll deal with Barter first and then worry about Doherty later. I suggest you let it be known to the relevant parties that Barter is not only a high-level Provo sympathiser but a murderer and a double agent for the CIA."

Hickey took a moment to let Jones reflect on this before saying, "I mean, what are we in this for but to save lives?"

Saving lives had become a bit of a mantra over the weeks between the two men.

"Saving lives," Jones whispered, enjoying the irony. "Right, get to it. Have you an unmarked piece already?" Hickey shook his head. "Don't worry. Bonner will see to it." Jones had heard about RUC weapons utilised for such tasks. Time for the big man to show his worth.

"No need to get the CC involved," Hickey told him firmly. "I'm sure there'll be other occasions when he can be of use."

Jones grunted and murmured, "I'm not convinced about that, but if you say so. I'll leave it to you."

Hickey smiled. "Consider it done." He wouldn't need a firearm; he was versatile in killing.

****

Chapter Eleven

They'd told ex-Private Sallis the head injury he'd received during rioting in Belfast years ago would cause migraines and could, in time, affect his eyesight. Like many returning veterans, the British Army didn't tell him that it was probable he'd suffer significant trauma and anguish from his experiences on and off the streets of Northern Ireland.

After he'd lost control at Val's birthday party, Rob sought refuge in his room. He was ashamed, swigging forty-ounce bottles of Jack Daniels he purchased late at night when his ma and Val slept. He couldn't eat and, worryingly, night after night would leave his tray untouched outside his room.

Rob had always remembered the doctor's last words when he'd released him from the military wing of Musgrave Park Hospital, Belfast. The silver-haired man spoke to him like something stuck to the bottom of his shoe. In his harsh East Belfast accent, he exhorted Rob to: "Buckle up there, son! Maybe you shouldn't have joined the army. That way, you'd never have been here. Everyone's been affected by The Troubles, so shake the dust off your feet and go home. You're one of the lucky ones! Off with you and forget about this place. You'll be fine."

Rob felt far from lucky and wished with all his heart that he and his best marra, Val Holmes, had never joined up. What if they'd got their apprenticeships at Swan Hunter instead? Northern Ireland had been a fucken' waste and all for a piece of lousy tin – a so-called service medal – and a regimental beret.

After Val's murder, Rob had been the one to pack up his dead friend's kit and personal belongings. He'd never admit how deeply that had affected him, coming on top of the horror of learning how his mate had died, broken and burnt, his battered corpse abandoned on a dark country road, to be further violated by traffic. Rob spoke of it to no one, not even his mam.

Embarrassed and humiliated by his recent behaviour, he'd deliberately lost touch with his few friends. He no longer communicated with the regiment, not wanting them to learn of his sorry state. It seemed to him that the British Army and the government didn't want to know about returning vets and their mental health problems. These men were no longer of value, and it was left to the NHS to bear the burden.

It was all about money and politics. Rob heard about a veteran who'd approached a recruitment officer to tell him he was struggling. The indifferent officer retorted, "We all have to take a bite from the crap sandwich. So, deal with it."

In the depths of night, Rob suffered flashbacks to the trauma of an unyielding hammer cracking down against his skull. The final ignominious chapter in Private Robert Sallis's army career.

****

His unit was on foot patrol along the Falls Road, a predominantly Republican and Nationalist area of Belfast, coming up to teatime and dark. It was Halloween. In their briefing, they were warned that things could likely heat up following a recent spate of Republican arrests. They also needed to be extra vigilant as there'd probably be droves of children out trick or treating.

Rob found himself in a firing position on the doorstep of a two-up, two-down terrace house similar to those on the Lone Moor in Londonderry. Its blue front door suddenly opened, and a black-haired girl no more than twelve years of age stood. She looked fierce for such a young pup. Without warning, she spat at him and cried: "Get the fuck off our doorstep, you British bastard! I fuckin' hate yez!"

Rob was stunned by the ferocity of her words and quickly wiped her saliva off his face. He made to leave as the child scampered back inside and slammed the door. He'd never get used to the hatred that emanated from these people. This whole area was a hellhole of loathing in comparison with the Unionist and Loyalist Shankill streets, which for the soldiers, could be a much more pleasant experience.

Patrolling soldiers and police officers frequently found themselves jovially pestered by the children they encountered here, who would pester them ceaselessly, begging for blackjacks, fruit salad sweets or trinkets. Some even asked for their regimental badges! Inevitably, when Rob's unit heard they were to patrol the Falls Road, their spirits crashed.

He was still angry at the unfairness of being removed from covert ops. He knew that by not following protocol, he'd taken a risk chasing Jones's bodyguard Morris into the City Hotel. But Morris knew who'd murdered Val, and Rob had to find out. He failed when Morris was killed after opening fire on the Bishop of Londonderry. After a severe reprimand for insubordination, Rob was punished by being sent back on street patrol like every other know-nothing squaddie.

Unlike Londonderry, Belfast was vast and much more hazardous. Rioting, no matter what the weather, raged on night after night. Fortunately, Rob grew close to a Belfast man, Fred Chambers, who'd joined the British Army years before. Now a sergeant, he'd been deployed back home specifically for his local knowledge, acquainted with the city and its maze of narrow back lanes and streets. He'd share on numerous occasions – to those who'd listen – the fact that he'd been delivering newspapers to the locals here twenty years before.

"Lucky for you, lads, I know this city like the back of me hand!" he'd joke.

Rob felt better when assigned to Fred's patrol as, time and time again, the warren of terraced houses proved deadly to the security forces. That Halloween night, his mate whistled loudly to get Rob's attention from the opposite side of the street, then called and waved to him impatiently. "Oi, Sallis, get your arse over here pronto. There's fire and smoke up ahead!"

Rob didn't need to be told twice and ran over to Fred as if on hot coals. Hand signals were exchanged as the patrol slowly and carefully progressed towards the clamour.

They came across three RUC Land Rovers and two army Ferrets. A few RUC men and soldiers were cordoned in and surrounded by a volatile, jeering crowd of youths. Molotov cocktails were streaming overhead from all directions. It was chaos.

At least forty youths attacked the Ferrets, swaying and pushing to topple them. Three or more carefully held haemorrhaging lit petrol bombs while others jumped on top of the jeeps and drummed their feet against the roofs. Rob heard an unearthly boom as something blew up further along the street.

"Bugger!" Fred muttered. He looked at their Lance Jack and acknowledged his signal with a nod.

"Right, Sallis, with me. We need to help these poor buggers." He looked around for the rest of the unit and signalled for them to follow.

Fred Chambers was peeing himself. With no air or vehicle cover, they'd now become target practice. In a single file, they kept close to the street-facing walls of the last few remaining houses. Chambers stopped hearing a series of repetitive high-pitched pinging noises, and Rob ducked – *gunfire*!

"Incoming!" he screamed. "Back… go back!" he cried, half-crouching, half-running.

Chambers fell to his knees, his upper torso still and rigid. Most, if not all, of the man's face, had disintegrated, leaving a lone eye dangling over his exposed and bloodied cheekbones and jaw.

"Fuck! Fuck!" Rob yelled in horror.

Suddenly and from nowhere, a ghoulish figure wearing an all-white Halloween mask stood above him. The apparition held a large industrial claw hammer. Almost in slow motion, Rob, shocked and terrified, watched the spectre lift the tool and drive it down with such a crushing force that it cut into Rob's MK6 helmet and the side of his head.

****

These days Rob's only solace came from Jack Daniels, painkillers and weed. Under their influence, all his aches and pains would evaporate, sending him into a floating, untouchable sphere of peace and calm. But only for a short while.

Lying in bed, as usual, the heavy cotton curtains of his bedroom tightly closed against the day, he heard a soft, timid knock—his son's. Rob sighed and straightened up.

"Yeah," he replied hurriedly.

Val tentatively opened the door and stood hesitantly on the threshold. Rob waved him in and watched as the boy entered unsteadily, carrying a pink floral tray with a single mug set dead centre.

"Nan made you tea," he said quietly before coming to a halt near his father's tossed bed. Numerous framed Magpies posters adorned Rob's walls. He'd neatly stacked several Roald Dahl paperbacks and some old-school exercise books on a black bookshelf. A tape recorder rested on the floor, each cassette carefully labelled. Rob fell back against the bed's wooden headboard.

"Bring it here, mate," he said.

Val delivered the tray and held it out for his da to take the boiling tea. Relieved that he'd completed his task, he waited, the tray by his side.

"You okay?" Rob asked, supping the sweet tea.

"Yep," Val replied nervously. He looked about the room, noticing the football posters.

"You like them?" Rob asked with a tired smile.

"Yeah, they're great but well old!" Val risked a grin.

"Aye, they are that." Rob sighed. "From a long time ago, son. Maybe we'll get to a match one day, you and me. Would you like that?"

Val nodded enthusiastically. He loved football, and when he grew up, he was going to play at St James's Park.

"Leave that with me then," Rob said. "Here, jump up beside me."

"I can't, Da. Nan told me to come straight back," Val said nervously, turning to leave. He didn't want to be alone with his da; the room smelt awful.

"Right you are. You'd better get back then," Rob said, slightly wounded by his son's rebuff. Val slid the tray under his arm like a waiter, looked at his father wide-eyed and closed the door gently as he left.

****

Chapter Twelve

Predictably Caitlin spoke to Anne for too long on their weekly call and found herself running late. She hated being late for anything and hurried to backcomb and spray her blonde hair. After patting on a little Elizabeth Arden foundation and spreading slate blue eyeshadow over her upper eyelids, Caitlin added a sweep of blue mascara, finished with a deep pink blusher, and carefully applied rose-pink lipstick. The excellent news Anne had shared with her was rare these days.

"I think it's brilliant. You know yourself how many poor wee boys and girls have left Ireland 'cos they're gay, bless them. Now that the approval thingy has gone through, it's no longer illegal – and about time an' all."

Caitlin couldn't agree more. For too long, Northern Ireland had been left behind by the rest of the UK regarding the treatment of gay people. Their criminalising of homosexuality had been viewed with international disapproval. It violated the European Convention on Human Rights, and the legislation had had to be modified. However, the age of homosexual consent fixed by the revised order was still higher than the heterosexual age of consent in the rest of the UK. Still, Caitlin supposed, it was a start and hopefully would stop the haemorrhage of gay youngsters currently leaving the country. They talked and shared gossip before Anne switched to a troubling topic.

"It's all this shit going on here, Caitlin, day after day. It's wile upsetting... will it ever stop?" Her sadness vibrated down the line as Caitlin sat on her bed, listening.

"Jesus, I'm so fed up with it. Such a waste of life, and for what?"

Caitlin understood her friend's frustration and bitterness, remembering her suffering after the explosion.

"I know, Anne. I know. Sometimes it's hard being over here as well. People hear your accent, start going on about home, and blame you outright. Most of them don't have a clue, or worse still, think they know it all. I miss you and Sean like mad, honestly." A few moments passed before Caitlin mischievously changed the subject and asked with a grin, "Have you seen you know who?"

It'd become the norm for her to ask Anne about 'you know who' on their catch-up calls, but Anne had never before been in a position to say she'd seen James Henderson. That was until last week when, to her surprise, she'd recognised him across the glass-topped counters of Woolworths, standing with two young kids. She had to admit they were a gorgeous pair and noticeably adored the Adonis, as she liked to refer to him – standing on either side of James and holding his hands tightly.

Even from a distance, James Henderson didn't look great. Anne almost felt sorry for him as she drew closer and spotted the dark hollows under his eyes and cheeks. He seemed too old and vulnerable for someone of his comparatively young years. After a moment, James recognised Anne and gave her a fleeting smile as his little girl impatiently dragged him towards the cash desk.

Anne deliberated for days as to whether she should tell her friend about the incident, but in the end, after many debates with Matt, she decided not to. Caitlin had finally got her life together and was happier than she'd been for a long time. Anne wasn't going to upset that apple cart – not for anything.

Caitlin was getting married, and Anne couldn't wait for the wedding: to see her friend again and finally meet her fiancé. She liked Chris from how Caitlin described his constant kindness and open adoration of her.

****

Caitlin was to meet Tommy in a popular café in Upper Street, Islington. The Green contained a giant tree with decorations left over from

Christmas and myriad intermittently flashing coloured lights. The main streets leading from the Green were decorated with garlands of similar rainbow lights that gave the whole area a vibrant air. It was newly prosperous too. Numerous rundown houses were now being converted, turning the area into a popular yuppy stronghold. Sole families now occupied the four-floored homes where once several households had lived in crowded, unsanitary conditions.

Outside she passed a gang of builders swinging about on some scaffolding. She saw them nudge each other as she approached and heard a voice with what could only be a Derry accent cry out to her. A yellow-hatted lad shouted over the background laughter of his workmates, "Hello, love, you free the night?"

Caitlin stopped dead in her tracks and looked up at him. "Aye, right then. Where we going?" she answered in a deliberately strong Derry accent. The fresh-faced lad looked pleasantly surprised and slid down a series of ladders as his workmates stood by to watch. From above, he answered her with a broad smile brimming with tombstone teeth, "Anywhere you like, love. Just say the word."

Caitlin laughed and began to walk on, saying, "You're too young for me, son. What would your Mammy say, eh? Sure, you're still in nappies!"

The other workers broke out in applause and began to take the piss out of the poor lad who had only recently arrived in London. Caitlin smiled, it was good to hear some of the old banter, and she realised how much she had missed it.

She found Tommy waiting at a table near the window inside the café and viewed him for a moment as he concentrated on his newspaper. He'd arrived extra early, needing time to think. His trip on McFarland's business had been a disaster. The fallout from the hunger strike had put a spanner in the works, and he knew there was talk of another. This time, however, it'd be used as a tool to politicise the people of Ireland.

Whereas the Brits were once keen to discuss, in their own words, *eventual disengagement from Ireland,* this time, at the last minute,

Tommy and McFarland's mission in London stalled. The incumbent PM Margaret Thatcher, with her no-tolerance approach and determination to beat the Provos, had ordered there should be no further talks.

The Derry men found the establishment door firmly closed against them and had more chance of flying to the moon than a face-to-face with the Brits. Nevertheless, McFarland's MI6 contact, tasked with trawling for and neutralising external threats to the UK, insisted they keep in touch. He was old school, a professional spymaster who played by the rules. However, he knew it was imperative to have someone like McFarland on hand as a trusted and valuable Northern Irish arbitrator. McFarland vamoosed, sorely depressed, and took the first flight home. It'd been a washout. Tommy had never seen him so downcast, and it ripped at him.

He knew he'd been sidelined into travelling with his two Provo companions, which only added to his disillusion. He liked the pair but working with McFarland; he really couldn't afford to be near them, so he decided to hang on and make the most of London and travel back alone. Perhaps he'd catch up with some old acquaintances or even take in a museum. He chuckled; *Tommy O'Reilly in a museum*! Trying his best to keep off the booze might prove difficult if he met up with his old friends, but sadly, it was a necessity now. He'd have a word with Caitlin.

All the same, the pressure was getting too great. On the one hand, he was travelling in the company of terrorists and, on the other, secretly colluding in peace talks that one of them at least would undoubtedly violently disagree with.

Sneaking up from behind, Caitlin carefully slid her hands over her uncle's eyes and, in jest, whispered, "Got you!"

Tommy turned quickly and, playing the game, jokingly put his hands up in surrender, a huge beaming smile on his face. His eyes filled at the sight of her. He couldn't believe he was finally seeing his beloved niece again!

"Sweet Jesus, Caitlin, will you look at you? I wouldn't have recognised you, love! Sure, you're all grown up. And your hair is blonde as Marilyn's herself. If your Ma and Da could see you now, eh?"

He couldn't get over her transformation; she'd been a beauty before, but now she was a stunner. Her hair had changed entirely, and he liked the new look – it suited her. Her delicate features had matured but were still very alluring. She always was skinny as a rake, and now her fashionable clothes fitted her like a glove. She wore a red suit, and its substantial shoulder-padded jacket covered a black silk blouse, knee-length A-line skirt and matching high heels. Her stockings looked glossy and expensive. He had a brief mental flashback to noticing her bare legs at Patrick's funeral and how he'd bought her tights for her new job – boy, she'd come a long way since then. It all seemed a lifetime ago, but happily, his niece looked to have overcome all the early setbacks. He was thrilled to see her so prosperous – she deserved it.

"Ah, Tommy, I've missed you," she sang, happy to see him. There was so much to tell; she didn't know where to begin.

"Sit! Sit!" he suggested, keen to hear her news. "What'll you have, tea?"

"Just a coffee, Tommy, please," Caitlin replied. She no longer drank tea since Chris had introduced her to coffee, the only downside being that she'd fallen into the trap of staying only half-awake until she'd had that vital first shot of caffeine in the morning.

Tommy ordered her drink and another pot of tea for himself, accompanied by two iced buns. *Christ, London was expensive!* Once settled, he took another long look at his niece, pleased to see she was obviously on top of the world.

"You look amazing, Caitlin, friggin' amazing! My heart is racing at seeing you again. You were right to come here to London – it suits you. This whole place suits you."

He waved his arms and laughed. "Gone forever is that wee awkward Derry girl. You're a woman now, Caitlin. I'd better be careful what I say; you're all grown up!"

Her uncle's praise and the way he was so glad to see her filled Caitlin to the core with happiness. It was good to see him, too, albeit he'd aged much faster than she'd anticipated. He wore silver-framed glasses now, and his red hair had thinned, peppered with flecks of white.

Oblivious to the rest of the world, uncle and niece drank copious amounts of tea and coffee as they shared their news. The time flew by.

Then, to his utter horror and disbelief, Tommy looked over to see Paddy Gillispie and Brian Monaghan entering the café. *What the hell!* The two dorks looked so out of place here that it was almost comical, both possessing that unmistakably Irish look. He noted how guardedly the other customers viewed them upon hearing their Northern Irish accent. Tommy had not expected this, two known Provos and his niece so close. Hell!

Brian spotted him first and, tapping Paddy's elbow, nodded in Tommy's direction. They could only see the back view of the woman talking to him. Once they arrived at the table, she turned around. The sight of Caitlin in her full glory blew a hole through Paddy Gillispie's stony heart. He sank into a chair, struck dumb by the vision before him. The girl was exquisite, perfect. His cheeks flamed at his awkwardness when she offered him her hand. He feared that at his touch, it would shatter like glass.

"Hi," Caitlin said, secretly pissed at the interruption. Paddy laughed for no reason, only that he found himself speechless. Feeling self-conscious, he continued staring at her until she looked at Brian with a 'help-me' smile and raised her eyebrows. He smiled back at her and shook her hand enthusiastically.

"Pay no attention to yer man. I'm Brian. Brian Monaghan."

Brian understood Paddy losing his faculties. She was a doll, for sure. He sat down, noticing Tommy's appalled expression for the first time.

"You all right, Tommy?" he asked with concern. The big man bobbed his head.

"Jesus, there must be something in the air," Brian told no one in particular. "What's wrong with the pair of ye?" he tutted before rising to place an order.

"How'd you know where I was?" Tommy asked Paddy sternly.

He remained steeped in monkish silence, and Caitlin grew concerned by the shift in the atmosphere; something was wrong. She turned and studied Brian, waiting in the queue, talking to the server like he was a regular.

Tommy tried again. "Paddy. I said, how did you find me?" Sweat had formed on his brow, and his chest felt heavy. *Had they been following him? Had they found out about the meeting with MI6? What would happen to him if they had?*

But Paddy appeared unperturbed. Eyes still trained on the lovely blonde, he said: "The B&B. They told us you'd asked for directions to this address, so we thought we'd come and join ye… and, boy, I am so glad we did."

Brian returned with their tea. He asked Caitlin as he glanced about the café and its patrons, "Do you like it here, love, in the big smoke? Too many people for me."

He looked at Paddy intentionally. "Mind you, we'd a lovely morning lying in the sun in Hyde Park. That's some space there; you could be in the middle of the countryside. Just sitting there we were, watching the world go by. It was nice, Paddy, wasn't it? Lying back in those fancy deck chairs?"

"Yeah, lovely," Paddy mumbled.

"London's been good to me," Caitlin answered politely. Paddy's silent ogling of her grew borderline rude; she found the man crass. He was making no attempt at polite conversation, as his friend was at least trying to do. Tommy seemed miffed by the two men's unexpected appearance too, and Caitlin couldn't wait for them to leave. Hopefully soon. Although Brian Monaghan was warm and friendly, she found the dynamics between him and Gillispie bizarre – the two were such polar opposites.

Her internal warning voice grew louder as she scrutinised them closely. She finally took heed of it and intuitively knew. *Jesus, Mary and Joseph! They were fuckin' Provos, and they'd gate-crashed her and Tommy!* She looked across at Tommy and caught his eye; ashamed and embarrassed, he only affirmed her suspicions and quickly averted his gaze.

She was both startled and relieved when, without warning, she heard a high-pitched female voice sing out from the other end of the café.

"Caitlin! Yoo-hoo – Caitlin!"

It was Maryann Fox, waving frantically at her, all teeth and smiles. Laden with shopping, she tottered through the maze of occupied tables, repeatedly apologising as her growing baby bump bounced against the back of chairs.

Caitlin let an involuntary yelp of surprise on seeing her. The two women had met several times since the first time Chris introduced them. Tommy was bitterly disappointed at this second intrusion; he'd wanted his niece all to himself. Maryann lurched closer, and the three men jumped up to help her with her shopping. Tommy reluctantly pulled back a chair. Smiling her thanks, Maryann flopped down onto it, sighing, and said in her back-teeth English accent: "Thank you so much. It's not often you come across such proper gentlemen."

Caitlin hoped the two men wouldn't stay much longer. However, she felt she should introduce her friend to everybody.

"Tommy, this is my friend Maryann Fox. Maryann, this is my Uncle Tommy. And his friends Brian and Paddy," she added reluctantly.

Maryann smiled kindly at the three burly men with their old-fashioned clothes, stubbled chins and heavy sideburns. They looked so Irish. She giggled – it was too much; one of them was called Paddy! She immediately told them she loved Ireland, mentioning numerous trips to the factory she and her husband Bill owned in Ballymena. Caitlin grew more and more agitated by this ingenuous outpouring of personal information. She didn't want the two volunteers to know these things about her friend. There was nothing else for it. She hurriedly got to her feet.

"I'm sorry, Maryann, but it's time for us to go. I'll call you later."

Tommy sensed what his niece was doing and stood up to join her. Maryann was surprised by Caitlin's directness and faltered, "Ah, right, okay. Talk later then."

It hurt Caitlin to see the disappointment on her new friend's expressive face, but she had to get those two men out of there and as far away from Maryann as possible.

Once outside, Brian and Paddy said their goodbyes to her before inviting Tommy to join them for a jar up the street. He refused and remained with Caitlin as they watched the pair walk away. With a heavy sigh, he turned and gave her such a heartfelt hug that she didn't want him to let go. Feeling melancholy, he whispered into her hair, "I'll see you soon, love. I want to meet up with this fella of yours while I'm here. I'll ring you later. And remember, you're a survivor, Caitlin McLaughlin, and I'm glad about that. Maybe one day I'll explain to you about those two."

She looked at him in concern. "Be careful, Tommy. I don't know what you're involved in, but promise me you'll be careful. To me, that one Paddy is a mean bastard; my insides are telling me."

Meanwhile, walking towards Callaghan's pub, where they were to meet a compatriot for an intel exchange about what they'd discovered on reconnaissance in London, Paddy glanced at Brian quizzically. Their scouting had nothing to do with the idea that just hit Paddy, and he chuckled. What a very fortuitous meeting!

The spell Caitlin McLaughlin had cast over him was wholly forgotten now. It was another woman entirely who filled his thoughts.

****

Chapter Thirteen

James Henderson, Paul Doherty and Alfie McScott, Rocola's assistant manager and accountant, sat in James's office, trying not to give way to despair. They'd received a letter that morning from a Belfast-based company, FYJH & Sons Ltd, cancelling a vast order and were overwhelmed by shock.

Until now, Marleen's money had been a lifeline, but the men knew it was like putting a sticking plaster on a deep knife wound – Rocola was haemorrhaging cash, and a cure must be found.

James threw his fountain pen angrily across his desk. "Can't we sue them? I mean, we've got it ready to go out the door. How in God's name can they cancel just like that? What about the terms of the agreement!"

Paul Doherty was beyond reproach. From the start, he'd had a feeling there was something not right about the order. They were a new client, after all, and thus unproven. To his chagrin, McScott decided to process the order himself. Such a large order couldn't be sniffed at when they desperately needed to increase turnover.

And now, McScott was beyond distraught. He was in for it now, and he likely would be fired. In all his years at Rocola, and for the first time, he hadn't done the necessary due diligence for an order of this magnitude. Usually, it would take a few phone calls to local contacts and a credit check, but in this instance, he hadn't. Time was running out for Rocola, and they desperately needed new trade. As a result, he'd taken the risk upon himself and botched it.

James detected something was up when both his employees remained too quiet and very, very still. He jabbed a finger at the FYJH file on the desk.

"Well?" he cried, looking at the two of them for an answer or some comment, but none came. Then James noticed a heavy tear slide down McScott's withered cheek. *What the hell!*

"What is it, Alfie? What are you not telling me!" he cried. The accountant removed the glasses perched on his nose and bowed his head in shame. James was baffled. He swivelled Alfie's chair around, giving him little choice but to look up. The accountant slowly raised his smarting eyes to survey the young man of whom he'd grown fond. Any last vestige of colour drained from his face as he attempted to explain.

"It's my fault… All of it."

"What's your fault, Alfie? What the hell are you talking about!" James implored.

He looked to Paul for clarity, but the young man could only shrug. He wasn't sure what McScott was trying to say. "I don't know, boss. Honest." The assistant manager wished he was anywhere but in this meeting.

James narrowed his eyes. "You've got to explain, Alfie. What the hell is going on?"

Haltingly, McScott told them he hadn't carried out the standard credit checks, nor had he obtained the usual 50 per cent deposit on the £75,000 order. James's eyes grew colder the longer he listened. *No? No way!*

Forcing himself to remain as calm as possible, he sank into his chair and barked orders.

"Do that credit check NOW! I want to know everything about FYJH… and when I say everything, I mean *everything*! You too, Paul, go with him. Now, both of you, get out of my sight!"

The men were gone in seconds.

Mrs Parkes sat in the outer office. From a quick glimpse of the two men scurrying past, she thought it best to leave Mr Henderson alone for a while. Over the years, unspoken respect had developed between boss and secretary. Nevertheless, she felt he was fighting a losing battle. The poor man had done his best to keep this white elephant of a factory open, but they all knew it was doomed. She was counting down the days until her retirement, and by God, she was ready for it. She hoped Rocola had enough left in the kitty to pay her a decent pension.

****

Later that evening, in the dining room at Melrose, James sat beside William Barter and Brendan Doherty. Following Charles Jones's sensational farce of a court case when - with a list of charges as long as his arm, including murder - to everyone's fury, a corrupt Judge Dodds served Jones a ridiculously light suspended sentence. However, Jones's cronies, including Lemon, were sent down for a very long time. Subsequently, Barter formally introduced James to Brendan and they became good friends. All three were as one in their desire to seek justice and retribution for Jones's many misdeeds.

They believed young Tina McLaughlin's trial had been a bloody circus too and Dodds, Jones's pet judge, the ringmaster. There were extenuating circumstances in her case; the underage girl had been preyed upon by a ruthless manipulator who at first seduced, and then terrified, her into doing his bidding against her will. But none of that saw the light of day in court; the evidence was ruled inadmissible by the judge. Brendan had also done his best to secure an official inquiry into the circumstances of Patrick McLaughlin's death in custody and the involvement of another henchman of Jones's, Dr Harris. Still, for all the interest the authorities took, it was as if McLaughlin had never existed. He'd become yet another lost soul of The Troubles.

Over time, the three men recognised that besides their mutual antipathy to Charles Jones, they shared similar views on many issues, from politics to sports. It'd become a weekly ritual for them to get together for dinner.

Barter could hear the shrilling of a telephone in the hallway, but his attention was fixed on James, who'd been silent for most of the evening. Ordinarily, he was an affable host, so Barter asked him, wiggling his fingers in a *give-me-more* gesture, "You've been quiet as a mouse all night, James. C'mon, what's up?"

James shook his head despairingly. "You'd never believe it."

"Try us," Brendan replied.

"We'd a huge order from a new client, all ready for despatch. They cancelled at the last minute and Alfie McScott decided to take the order himself but didn't run a credit check. No due diligence. Not even a deposit."

"How much?" Brendan Doherty asked gently.

"Seventy-five K."

"Jeez!" Barter whistled. "And there's no comeback, none at all?"

"Doesn't look like it," James muttered. "McScott tried to speak to them all afternoon, but they weren't answering their phones – it's as if they've disappeared off the face of the earth. If he'd been doing his job properly, he should have spoken to Paul first. Paul wouldn't have touched it with a barge pole until all the searches were done – an accountant shouldn't even be taking orders. That's Paul's job!"

James felt partly to blame. His head was all over the place, what with trying to manage the twins, Rocola and his failing marriage. Marleen had yet to come home. It'd been months now, and the twins were getting worse. Another nanny was lost, and his housekeeper was close to walking out in frustration. She was growing snappier by the day and much more tetchy with the kids.

Speaking of his housekeeper, Mrs Moore knocked on the dining-room door to inform Barter there was a telephone call for him in the study. As he left, he apologised and explained that he was expecting an urgent message, so he had passed on James's number.

****

Marleen Henderson lay back in the warm depths of the lavender-scented bubble bath. She'd hastily put her hair up and tied it in a knot. Holding an antique gold-plated telephone, she listened to the engaged tone on the line. It was probably too late to talk to the twins, but at least she'd tried. She'd half-hoped no one would answer, especially that bitch of a housekeeper who was unremittingly rude to her. Marleen still felt the occasional pang of guilt for not seeing more of her children, but not very often and never for long. The twins were fine. James was fine. They didn't need her. Her remorse had lessened as the weeks and months flew by. Now she couldn't recall the last time she saw any of them and cursed her parents, who wouldn't let her forget it. They were increasingly annoyed and vocal about the fact that the twins had yet to visit them at Belmont Hall, their ancestral home. They'd no intention of going anywhere near Londonderry with all its violence and insisted that Marleen should fetch the children and bring them to England. Well, fat chance of that!

When there was still no answer from Melrose, she hung up in relief. Her musing was interrupted by a cry from an adjacent room.

"What are you doing in there? There'll be nothing left of you. I'm waiting!" a deep male voice crooned.

Marleen smiled. She couldn't help herself. She surveyed the opulent bathroom lined with Italian marble. It was most impressive, like the rest of this sumptuous apartment.

Her papa continually nagged her about the vast sums of her money handed over to shore up Rocola, so much so that she'd grown weary of his lecturing and finally told him it would stop. James could go it alone from now on. She'd done enough. Yet, given her extravagant habits, Marleen needed a financial fallback and luckily had found it in the form of Jack Edmonds, a retired politician and industrialist from New Zealand who was also divinely minted! After meeting Marleen at a party in Chelsea, he'd chased her so hard and spent such fortunes on gifts that she'd felt obliged to take up with him. Now she had formulated a plan: divorce joyless James, marry Jack – and keep Pen warm on the side.

"Hurry up! I'm waiting!" Jack yelled impatiently.

"I'm coming!" she laughed, stepping out of the deep bath onto the warmth of heated tiles. Drying herself with a huge fluffy white bath towel, she studied her nakedness in a floor-to-ceiling mirror and nodded appreciatively.

"That'll do," she whispered proudly. She looked good and, fortunately, through liberal applications of oil and yoga, had very few noticeable stretch marks on her once-huge stomach. Maybe her boobs could be lifted with discreet surgery, but that was another time. She liked how voluptuous motherhood had made them – and Jack certainly did!

Remaining naked, she headed confidently to the bedroom and posed seductively in the doorway.

Jack's mouth went dry. He couldn't take his eyes off her. This woman was something else. Unlike most of his previous girlfriends, he believed this one didn't want him for his vast wealth since she was already a woman of substance from a notable family. Consequently, he enjoyed spending serious money on Marleen, buying her gifts and spoiling her. Not only was she great fun and a born socialite, but she was also a goddess in bed. She'd do things he would never have dreamt of in his wildest imaginings. Boy, was she game!

"Come here!" he hollered.

Cat-like, Marleen prowled towards him and purred, "I'm coming."

"Not yet, you're not!" Jack replied mischievously.

Marleen crinkled her eyes in a smile, hoping it looked sincerely appreciative of his lame attempt at wit. God, he was predictable, she thought, as he yanked her down beside him. But he more than made up for what he lacked in subtlety with enthusiasm.

And, naturally, his enormous bank balance.

****

Chapter Fourteen

Joe McFadden knew his mother would be shocked by his condition when she saw him. It'd been five long years since they'd last seen each other. Apart from the odd visiting priest or bishop, he and his comrades had steadfastly refused the admission of visitors as part of their protest. Now that it was over, he prayed they'd return to some form of normality. If living behind bars could ever be considered normal.

During the protest, he'd been on his own a lot, and the isolation nearly killed him. He'd sought ways to keep his brain active. To counter the boredom, he'd tried to exercise but couldn't as there was so little room in his cell. He would pace six paces back and forth or walk in a figure of eight to break the monotony. Once he'd finished, he'd sit and study his bible, trying his best to concentrate on the messages within. Other times he'd recite the time's tables, count backwards from 500 or mentally revisit the numerous football games he'd been involved in and remember the players he'd known and loved.

There was little sense of time – day and night were only marginally apparent through the high windows partially blocked by a steel sheet. In their determination to break these proud men, the prison administrators had attempted to cut off the inmates from the natural world – further torturing the already tortured.

Neglect of his hygiene and poor nutrition had led Joe to lose more teeth. Bizarrely, considering where he was and what he was going through, he was strangely upset by losing one of his front molars. Perhaps a tiny fragment of long-lost vanity still existed deep inside him. He smiled at the thought.

He looked around his new cell in H-block 4. It'd had its final deep clean by alien-like screws dressed in heavy rubber suits, goggle-eyed protective headgear, thick black rubber gloves and big boots. They always seemed to struggle with the bulky industrial cleaning equipment laden with lengthy, serpent-like hoses that blasted out ice-cold water.

Cleaning a cell to eliminate the protesters' tapestry of rotting shit and decaying food could take hours; even with protective clothing, the sweet, overpowering stench clung to everything that came near. It was a job no one in their right mind would want.

Today, dead-eyed and near broken, Mickey Boyle, Joe's cellmate, was half asleep. To Joe, the freshness of the disinfected cell was a blessing. Anything was better than what they'd endured for so long. He climbed up on his bunk level with the narrow window to see if he could observe anything outside. He saw sweet fuck all but tried anyway and wondered why he even bothered when the result was always the same. He and Mickey were both due for their first family visit in years, but there was no sense of excitement, just a painful Sunday silence hanging over the small, grim space.

The prisoners waited patiently until a shouting screw opened the cell door and ordered them out. The worn men shuffled towards it but instinctively, after so many years of fearing beatings, stopped, wondering whether they were in for it again or if this was for real. Were they finally going to see their loved ones? The impatient screw repeated his order but louder. The prisoners eyed each other and smiled mischievously – *it was over, the protest was finally over.*

Others heard their footsteps and caterwauled along the narrow corridor lined with cells as Joe, taking the piss, cried out loudly in Irish, "*Am dom spa leaids!*" Or: "*Time for me spa ladies!*" He was promptly thumped on the lower back by the screw's baton.

"Move on, or you'll fuckin' go straight back!" he growled.

After his stint on the dirty protest, Maggie and Charlie McFadden would never forget their first sighting of Joe.

"Sweet Mother of God," Maggie gasped, her eyes tracking her eldest as he stumbled and faltered, reminding her of a homeless old bum trying to find the soup queue. And then, shockingly, he smiled at her: a broad, semi-toothless smile.

"He looks like the Lord Jesus himself… but his poor teeth, Charlie," she whispered beneath her breath. Maggie refused to blubber in front of her son, but by Christ, she couldn't breathe. She gasped and pressed both hands to her face. Her son's lovely thick sandy hair and bright green eyes had been drained of life and colour. His hair was much too long, limp and matted. It wasn't easy to believe this wizened face was that of a young man in his prime. She knew they couldn't touch or hug but was so desperate to hold him that she tentatively opened her arms.

"No touchin'!" she heard a voice bellow from the far end of the visitors' room.

In a quivering voice, desperately hoping to contain his pinballing emotions of happiness, sadness, fear and excitement, Joe asked: "Ma, Da, how are you?"

Jesus, the pair of them looked so old. His protesting had taken its toll on them, too. His ma's hair was a funny colour, blonde mixed with charcoal grey where she'd missed bits, not as pristine as usual. She'd never done that before, and it hurt him to admit she'd lost the best of her looks. She seemed weary and haggard, not helped by the old weight creeping up on her.

"Grand, son. We're grand, aren't we?" Charlie replied as loudly as was allowed while looking to his wife for agreement. "And yourself?"

Joe chuckled. He sniffed, cleared his throat and looked back at them, battling mixed emotions.

"I've never been better, Da. Five-star luxury it is in here, as you can tell. But it's great to see you both. It's been some time."

Charlie was at a loss for how to respond, so Maggie quickly intervened. She knew her son; she'd made him and sensed the conflict in his soul. Gazing down at his dry, parched hands, she noticed his fingernails were overgrown and caked red with dried blood. She shuddered. In a frantic, pleading voice, she asked naïvely: "Do you think they'll let you out now that it's over? We want you home, love. You should be home with us."

Joe smiled at his mother's innocence while his empty eyes told her – *no chance.*

This wasn't going anything as well as Charlie had hoped. He gently told his wife, "Ah, shush now, Maggie. One step at a time, eh, son?" he tutted, crossing his arms. "That's typical of your mother – you know what she's like!" he added quickly before changing the subject. "I have a job now, Joe. In a canteen like. It's hard work, but the money's good. You've no idea the flak I was getting from your woman here and our Emmett. Now they keep telling me I'm losing weight despite all the stodgy food at work."

Charlie glanced at Joe's emaciated frame and cringed at his thoughtlessness. *There he was, ranting like a moron about food when the poor lad looked like something from the missions.*

With one eyebrow raised, Joe asked, "And how's our Emmett? Behaving himself, I hope."

His cellmate Mickey Boyle had conveyed to him Emmett's recruitment to the Unknowns. Joe was proud that his brother had tried his best to support the cause; more importantly, he'd dared to stop. It was no easy feat getting out, but Joe wasn't surprised. Emmett didn't have it in him to hurt anyone – he was as soft as butter.

His parents were unaware of their middle son's shenanigans, and Joe certainly wasn't going to tell them.

"Sure, he's a qualified mechanic now!" they replied proudly.

"Ah! That's great. Good for him."

Joe began to ask about Liam and heard about his trip to America. They talked on about things outside, such as the price of petrol, what was number one in the charts, who'd died and who'd got married – the same old Derry talk. Too soon, the visit came to an end.

Joe rose, his heart breaking. Seeing the old pair face to face was way more challenging than he'd imagined. He thanked them for the much-needed food parcels and said a lingering goodbye.

"I'll see you again soon, okay? Send our Emmett and Liam me best and tell Liam to behave himself!"

"Will do, son, and for sure, we'll see you soon," Charlie replied tightly, with a tormented expression.

Maggie fumbled to put on her coat. She could hardly bear to look at her son for fear he'd see her tears but blew him a kiss and, with a stiff nod, turned to leave. Later, she couldn't remember putting one foot in front of the other as she walked past the glaring security personnel or as she was patted down again. The overwhelming pain of leaving her boy behind was cruel and unyielding. Time and time again, she remembered his condition, his tired, hopeless eyes.

Like the many other visitors, they waited for the special prison bus to take them back to Derry. Neither one of them knew what to say. As she clutched Charlie's hand, Maggie's tears flowed freely, fast and furious. Her legs felt like rubber. She could only manage the steep steps one by one as she climbed laboriously on board the coach.

Charlie recognised his wife's distress and felt unable to lessen it. His own heart was racing, pounding, almost thrashing against his ribcage. For so many years, he'd tried to reassure her repeatedly, telling her that Joe would be okay. However, having seen the mere shadow of him that was left, he knew poor Joe would never be the same again. Their happy-go-lucky lad had been stolen from them by war and politics.

Charlie felt a surge of white-hot anger. He hoped and prayed that all these young men who'd been on the blanket for so long, and those poor unfortunates who'd starved themselves to death, hadn't suffered in vain. Somehow their actions had to make a difference!

Maggie watched the bus fill up. None of the passengers spoke but took to their seats with nods to each other and sad smiles. Most, if not all, of the women, were sobbing. Maggie knew she was in trouble when her aching throat released a deep, uncontrollable groan. "*Joe, my baby… what've they done to my baby!*" she murmured.

Charlie grabbed her and pulled her into his loving arms, holding her as tightly as he could. God, he loved her, but this conflict made him and many others feel so powerless. *Would it ever end?*

****

Emmett McFadden knew it would be a tough visit and a difficult journey to Long Kesh for his parents, and he was worried sick. He'd bought his mother the best carnations he could find from Stewarts, the local supermarket. As he stepped over the doorstep, he smelt cabbage and bacon cooking. The homely, familiar smell made him feel hungrier than ever. The garage was doing well, and he hadn't stopped all day.

Removing a piece of paper from his pocket before he hung his coat beneath the stairs, he briskly made his way into the kitchen. Both his parents were sitting at the table, which was set for dinner. They looked like they'd been through the mill a few times, haggard, sad and worn out.

"Well?" Emmett asked tentatively. "How was he?"

Charlie wasn't going to worry the lad by telling him the unvarnished truth but answered as brightly as he could.

"Better than we hoped. Asking all sorts of questions, he was. How much was this and that, fags and all? He didn't look the best, but at least we've seen him now, eh, Mags?"

Still feeling crushingly sad, Maggie collected herself.

"Yeah, yeah, your Da's right. Not looking his best but yapping away." She turned aside so Emmett couldn't read her expression.

A mammoth wave of relief swept over him. *Thank fuck*! He knew that by now Joe would have heard about his stint with the Unknowns and had been terrified his brother would tell their ma and da. It seemed he hadn't.

Liam was at his friend Phil Walsh's house, and dinner was soon ready. Everyone sat down to eat until, after a while, Emmett excitedly held up the piece of paper and asked brightly, "Guess what this is?"

His parents shook their heads; they had no idea.

"It's my certificate, Mechanical Engineering, City & Guilds. It came this morning. I'm now a fully qualified mechanic. I can go anywhere."

This was his freedom pass, his get-out-of-jail card! If he was going to make anything of his life, he had to get away from Derry – everyone with any choice in the matter was leaving.

Chapter Fifteen

Christmas had been and gone since Tommy and Caitlin's catch-up in London. The big man had been thrilled to see her looking so happy, and when she'd telephoned him afterwards, his heart nearly jumped out of his skin when she asked if he'd act as father of the bride.

"Will you do it, Tommy? Stand up at the wedding ceremony and give me away?"

"Ah, Caitlin, I'm well chuffed. Thanks, I'd love to. Tell me what you need, and I'll be there. Anything… anything at all."

She was delighted and confirmed the date: Tuesday, 20th July 1982, at Islington Register Office in the Town Hall.

"That's a bit odd, having a wedding on a Tuesday," Tommy remarked – weddings at home inevitably occurred on a Saturday, allowing the necessary recovery time on Sunday.

"I know, Tommy, but it's the only date we could get the venue. I'm not bothered, but Chris's parents were married there, and since he isn't Catholic, we thought, why not go to a Register Office? It's not like Mammy or Daddy are around to give me a scolding – and I hope you won't!"

"Nah, love, we've all got more important things to think about. I'm chuffed to bits for you. What about Martin?"

"I've already spoken to him. It's not likely he'll be able to come, but that's okay. America's a long way. I don't want a big fuss anyway. The only people I want besides you are Anne and Kathy. Less is more. Chris is an only child, so there are no big numbers on his side either."

Her wedding day would be nothing like she'd imagined from an early age. She could remember her thoughts as she'd followed her father's coffin down the aisle of St Mary's Church in Creggan. Even though she'd known it could never happen, she'd envisaged them both on the day she married, their arms entwined, and then her daddy squeezing her hand reassuringly, so proud as he passed her across to her Prince Charming.

Brushing the pipe dream aside, she queried, "Kathy will come too, of course, Tommy?"

"Ah, bless you, love, but our Kathy's married to that job of hers. The chances of her making it over are slim, although I'll ask, thanks."

It wasn't news to Caitlin; she and Kathy talked regularly and shared their concerns about Tommy's neglect of himself.

****

Paddy Gillispie, Brian Monaghan and Tommy O'Reilly were in Belfast for a few days as part of Sinn Féin's Annual Ard Fheis (political conference). That day, a senior Republican speaker expressed the party's shifting mood.

"Who here believes we can win the war through the ballot box? But will anyone here object if, with a ballot paper in this hand and an Armalite in the other, we take power in Ireland?"

The hardened left-wingers of the old IRA and the Irish National Liberation Army (INLA) were keen to fight on, using any means of violence at their disposal. At the same time, the (PIRA) Provo volunteers wanted Sinn Féin to become more political and democratic.

Two H-block candidates were successful in the Republic of Ireland's general election following Bobby Sands' death. This convinced some Republicans that they should contest every election and put forward a Sinn Féin candidate in the North. Some called it 'The Armalite and Ballot Box Strategy'.

Brian and Tommy were all for the ballot box in their bid to gain peace and, God willing, a united Ireland, while Paddy remained violently opposed to the idea and couldn't be reasoned with. But he had at least come to the conference to hear and see what was being said.

Back in the old haunt of The Shamrock in West Belfast, Paddy, Tommy, and Brian gathered around the bar. Tommy was introduced to a few regulars, including the well-built, fit barman sporting his usual red and white Arsenal shirt. Paddy, who was particularly tired, had never seen the place so busy: it was packed with patrons, the air thick with the lingering smell of stale tobacco. It'd been a long day, and he could barely hear the TV News over the loud hubbub of background noise.

Signalling to the quiet back room, he led Tommy and Brian out there. As Paddy entered, a few comfortably seated punters promptly rose, grabbed their drinks and left with respectful nods to the newcomers.

"That's better," Paddy said gratefully, sitting down. "I couldn't hear myself think in there."

A satisfying lull followed until Tommy asked him earnestly, "From what you heard today, Paddy, would anything change your mind?"

He had been expecting the question.

"You mean, do we go down the political path or keep doing what we're doing, Tommy?"

Tommy nodded and cautioned the two, "We can't have another year like the last one. The hunger strikes escalated everything. The ball game is shifting now. People are finally behind Sinn Féin, not only here but in the States an' all."

Paddy was fed up to the teeth with this continual pacifist haranguing. For as long as he could remember, he'd fought for a united Ireland and strongly believed in defending the 1916 Proclamation of the Republic: "...*We declare the right of the people of Ireland to the ownership of Ireland...*" read out so bravely from the steps of Dublin's General Post Office. Yet Tommy and now Brian still rattled on and on about avoiding open conflict and were sorely getting on his nerves.

Recently he and Brian had been tasked by a seasoned Provo with considering new ways of raising cash quickly. Not the usual low-stakes stuff, like robbing banks or post offices, but something that would bring money in wads. Paddy was jubilant to suggest the idea he'd come up with in London and ecstatic when he got the green light after intense consultation with the Army Council. Forget politics and votes: getting their hands on that kind of cash could change the course of the war!

He pursed his lips and considered his words carefully before he spoke.

"Tommy, you're a good friend, but I'll not talk all this shite tonight. I'm too tired."

"But you're going again tomorrow?" Tommy asked, studying his half-pint of diluted orange. He still hadn't recovered from the night in Mailey's Bar when the devil on his shoulder led him astray. He couldn't get out of bed the next day and had sworn *never again*!

"Yip," Paddy replied, "Adams is parlaying."

"That'll be interesting, although I'm not sure I enjoy all this conference lark," Brian said sullenly. "I want to get out there and just do it."

"Do what!" Paddy scoffed, leaning forward. "Get the people's votes?" he asked sarcastically.

"Aye, Paddy, that's it!" Brian snapped. "I know you don't see what we're trying to do, but we've finally got a chance to change things the democratic way – lock, stock and barrel!" He hammered one fist against the table and went off, blustering away on his orange box. In annoyance, Paddy cursed him and fell back dejectedly against the wall. Frigging heck, he'd told them he was too tired to listen to them yammer.

"Ah, fuck this, Brian; I can't listen to any more of that old crap!" He rose to go and take a pee.

As Paddy disappeared, the other two exchanged quizzical looks and shrugged. Despite Tommy not knowing Brian particularly well, he trusted him and appreciated his support. Electoral politics was becoming increasingly essential, but the difficulty lay in convincing some seasoned Republican leadership to change course. That aside, he thought Brian looked like he bore the world's weight on his shoulders.

"How are you doing?" Tommy asked. "You look a bit done in."

"I'm okay, thanks. You know how it is," Brian said, closing him down.

Fair enough, if the man didn't want to talk.

Brian stifled a groan. He was so far from good that words couldn't explain his feelings and couldn't be bothered to try. He loathed being in this backroom with its evil bloody memories and wondered how he'd ever carried out all those killings. He was permanently beaten, and his friendship with Paddy seemed threatened. He was turning out to be a right stubborn pain in the hole.

Paddy re-emerged with another round on a Double Diamond tray. He carefully placed the glasses on the table and passed them around.

"*Slainte*," he said as they raised their glasses. "*Slainte*."

To lighten the tension, Tommy told them about Caitlin asking him to give her away at her wedding in the summer.

"Is that right?" Paddy asked, intrigued. "I bet your best pleased. Who's the lucky man?"

"An Englishman, for her sins," Tommy groaned, "but he sounds grand. Consultant of some sort… not medical like, something to do with business."

"Plenty of dough then?" Paddy queried.

"Suppose." Tommy had never thought to ask.

"Oh, I'd say there would be, from the cut of her. No offence. And remember that woman friend of hers? The hoity-toity one."

Tommy struggled to remember the woman who had joined them so inopportunely. After a short while, he suggested, "Mary something or other, wasn't it?"

Paddy's instantaneous response was chilling. "Maryann Fox, married to Bill Fox of Somerset and Ballymena."

Tommy sensed something sinister in these words and Brian's uptight expression.

"I've a good memory for names," Paddy told him reassuringly, shooting back a whiskey and winking at his friend. "Don't I, Brian?"

He nodded. "You do, Paddy."

Tommy picked up on the enigmatic wink but knew better than to ask.

Still, after all this time, Paddy couldn't forget how beautiful Caitlin McLaughlin was. He'd never come across a woman who'd had such an immediate effect on him, and he was still slightly mortified by his adolescent bashfulness with her. Something about her had made him feel highly uncomfortable but spellbound, all at the same time. It bothered him more than it should, and he forced the memory to the back of his mind.

"When's the wedding then?" he asked, feigning interest.

"July – a small one. She doesn't want a fuss. Mind you; I've got to put on one of those feckin' morning suit thingies. I'll look like a feckin' penguin or the like!" Tommy told them half-heartedly, still uneasy about what had just occurred.

He wasn't looking forward a bit to dressing up but was more worried about being in some posh banqueting hall with English strangers and, worse still, while sober. Unsurprisingly, Kathy couldn't come, but she'd warned him repeatedly that he wasn't to drink, and he'd sworn he wouldn't. Those people weren't Derry people, and there was no way he would let Caitlin down. It was her big day.

"July, eh? That'll be nice. Funnily enough, we're planning a weekend trip to London in July. Maybe we'll call in and have a few jars – toast the bride and groom!" Paddy joked, nudging Brian and winding Tommy up. It seemed to work when he saw a slight flicker of irritation sweep the big man's face.

"I'm only joking, mucker!" Paddy laughed, gently punching him on the arm.

Tommy's attempts to find this amusing failed. The idea of two Provos gate-crashing Caitlin's wedding was far from funny.

Brian saw his expression and quickly interjected. "Stop winding him up, Paddy. Leave it."

Paddy held up his hands in surrender. "Touchy! Sorry, Tommy. Sure, I'm joking."

Tommy accepted the apology curtly but gave him a doubtful look.

****

Chapter Sixteen

As ever, they were in the Cortina in their usual spot on the outskirts of Drumahoe. The two MI5 men sat in the front with the car engine running and Cawley, sullen and unresponsive, in the back. He sometimes wondered how he'd walked into this chaos. When he'd been arrested for the first time, he'd been sleep-deprived, hooded, beaten and interrogated at Castlereagh Holding Centre. Although he was innocent of involvement in the incidents they were investigating, the security services set him up beautifully, accusing him of multiple murders.

"Sign it!" they screamed as they threw down an unsigned statement. "Confess it was you who planted those bombs! You're the one responsible for the deaths of those mothers and children! Children, for fuck's sake. A three-year-old boy and a seven-year-old girl. Sign, 'cos, if you don't, we'll lock you up and throw away the fucking key. We can do whatever we like with you, you piece of Fenian shit!"

He refused, and the male interrogator, with gleaming excited eyes, smacked him hard across the face in a fury. Cawley's fear permeated the windowless room. He shook his head like a dog and sprayed them all with sweat. The other agent, a hard-faced woman with iron-grey hair shaved at the back, looked like she was made of marble. She was dressed in a black trouser suit over a creased white blouse sprinkled with coffee stains and a fine spray of blood.

Cawley's heart was pumping at such a ridiculous pace that he thought it'd explode. The male agent's angry voice seemed to bounce off the walls.

"Listen to me, you cunt, you've got two options!" He paused for effect. "One, you confess and join your comrades in the Kesh, as you Fenians call it for a long time; two, you work for us!"

At such a preposterous suggestion, Cawley shook his head violently.

"Then I'll go to the Kesh. But grass? No fuckin' way! I'd rather die. You can go to hell with your options!"

A hard-knuckled punch landed right on the bridge of his nose. Cawley screeched, more in annoyance than pain – not the nose again! He gently touched it and used a sleeve to wipe the blood off.

After that, the interrogation worsened until they eventually left him to sweat. Outside the interrogation cell, the female officer came up with an idea.

"He's got sisters, hasn't he?"

Her colleague nodded. "Yeah, two, I think. A nun or nurse, I think and a student."

He wasn't as well briefed as she was, she noted with satisfaction.

"Well then?" she said. "Think about it."

They shared a complicit smile. Back in the interrogation room, their idea began to evolve. Cawley swallowed and sat still, listening to the woman's detailed threats.

"You've got sisters… pretty too, I'm told. As it is, we'll charge you with multiple murders, but I have to say, we'll be sure to keep a wee eye on them for you. I hear they keep their noses nice and clean, but there's always a first time for everything. One's just started at uni– what's her name now?"

The woman looked up, struggling in pretence to remember. She pointed at the prisoner. "Ah, yes, Shannon. And there's the other one; she'll be a little harder to get at. But she won't miss out on all the fun, trust me."

The male agent looked miffed about something, but Cawley barely noticed. He sat perspiring, white-faced and dumbfounded. The woman looked over to her partner, who'd got over his pique at the way she'd demonstrated superior knowledge, now watching and listening with glee while swinging back and forth in his chair. His nicotine-stained buck teeth were on display in an unholy smile.

Without warning, the woman turned on Cawley. She was pissed off, tired and determined to reach an agreement with him tonight. She wanted to go home, take a bath and change out of the clothes she'd been wearing for two long days. Her frustration was rapidly mounting.

"Listen carefully, you fuck-faced Taig! Any other options for you are out the window now. You hear?"

The male interrogator unexpectedly reached across and dealt the side of Cawley's head a stinging slap, hissing menacingly into his throbbing ear.

"If you don't work with us, we'll send those sisters of yours to Armagh and let them rot. I hear it's packed, three bitches to a cell – hell on earth. Or heaven, depending on which way you roll." He sniggered wickedly.

Cawley's heart dropped like a stone. Mother of God, what was he going to do? He had to protect his sisters – they'd never survive, Armagh!

Once again, the pair informed him they'd charge him with multiple murders and convincingly maintained they'd an eye witness who was prepared to give damning evidence against him while screened from view, most likely in a calamitous kangaroo court. Or Cawley could always grass on other suspects in exchange for his freedom and his sisters'.

Looking back, he knew he should never have trusted the British bastards to leave it at that. Soon he found himself getting in deeper and deeper, scrabbling to meet their incessant demands for intel. They wanted juicy stuff, the meaty intelligence that would make them look like heroes to their superiors.

MI5 in London demanded more and more from the field, and Cawley's handlers were committed to delivering it. Much to their exasperation, he was proving particularly difficult at tonight's meet.

"I've got nothing for you. It's been quiet," was all they heard from him, over and over.

"You're talking rubbish. Quiet! What do you mean, quiet? The Provo bastards have blown half the fucking country up!"

"Nothing is doing." Cawley's weary voice cracked.

MI5 knew the PIRA had recently offered a temporary amnesty to informants who confessed to their crimes. They were then ordered to leave the country as an alternative to disappearing forever.

To the Provos and other paramilitary organisations, informants were the ultimate deviants, the most reviled people. Indeed, one potential tout had recently told an agent trying to recruit him: "I'd rather be called a paedo than a grass!"

They'd left that particular individual alone but wondered if Cawley might see this latest amnesty as his way out. No chance of that! He was a vital part of their armoury and had already proved his worth tenfold. Oddly, they admired his steadfast refusal to accept payment. This was a genuinely principled man. They had no intention of letting him out of their clutches.

****

Chapter Seventeen

Liz McKenna winced and groaned as she lay in her single bed in a semi-lit bedroom. It was early morning, and she hadn't slept particularly well. Liz was more than frustrated at the rejection of her plan for the Currys lorry hi-jacking. The cell she'd been assigned to by the OC was a boys' club, and no one there took her seriously even though she'd been right all along; the bookie robberies proved to be a waste of time, with very little cash return. Poor Ronan Duffy ended up in Long Kesh after comically tripping over and being collared by a brave and angry proprietor. A right cock-up! She'd heard the OC was far from happy with their efforts and decided she'd try to use his disappointment to her advantage.

Her life experiences to date had created an ambitious young woman who didn't know how to take no for an answer. At school, she wasn't popular; to the others, she was way too competitive and, at times, surly and only out for herself. They were right. Liz didn't want friends; she didn't want anyone to know what was happening to her behind closed doors. And to ensure that, she kept herself to herself and didn't give a flying fuck what other people thought of her. She only cared about being a top gun Provo; to do that, she needed to break down some of their chauvinistic prejudices against the fairer sex. Not all of the boys were like that, but there were enough of them to make it – for want of a better word – a *challenge*.

Since she hadn't slept, she'd passed the time coming up with some ideas for getting where she wanted to be. It wouldn't be easy, but as always, she was determined. First, she'd get rid of her stepfather for good. Secondly, somehow she'd get the Currys heist on the OC's radar. And finally, she'd arrange it, take part in it and get full credit.

Top of the list of her concerns: she'd recently noticed her cretin stepfather's sick addiction was worsening. Although she'd warned as many women as possible, he'd begun to sit in the local park to watch the kiddies play. Liz couldn't let him hurt the tots and decided she'd report him to the Provos without going into too much detail.

Later that morning in Cable Street, she did just that. In the office, Lady Luck stood next to her when she saw the OC, Cahir O'Connell, with Patrick Gillispie. Gillispie adopted a bemused expression when she asked to speak to the OC privately and remained standing in the corner of the room. The OC looked harassed, which only made Liz more nervous.

"Sir, I have to report someone."

"Who?" he asked, looking up. "What for?"

"It's my stepfather and little children. He watches those kiddie videos and stuff, and now he's sitting in the park when the wains are playing. He's a paedo." With this announcement, she got the OC's full attention. He dropped his pen on the desk and sat back, ready to listen.

"Your stepfather… doesn't he work for the Civil Service or something, a Proddy from Belfast?"

"Aye, that's him."

"Kids, eh?" the OC asked, his face darkening. "You've proof?"

"He's all the Disney video cases in a cupboard in the living room. All someone has to do is bash in, and then you'll see."

The OC looked at Paddy thoughtfully. The pressure here was mounting. The poor result of the robberies had mortified him, some fucking tout was out there babbling like a baby, and the Derry Brigade were well low in funds. As OC, he desperately needed to come up with something that would heft them right back up to the top of the brigades. It was a holy mess. But to have a paedo sitting on his ass in Creggan's heart – he wouldn't allow it.

"You get them," he ordered. Looking directly at Liz, he added, "You get the tapes, bring them here. Paddy there will deal with your man."

A huge smile spread across Liz's face.

"Is there anything else?" the CO asked as he stood and put his coat on. "I have to go. Just give me five minutes, will you, alone with Paddy, then I'll leave you two to it."

Liz nodded eagerly and left the office to wait outside.

Inside, the OC instructed, "Don't do anything terminal to the paedo, give him a right good warning, get him out of Derry – and soon. I don't need the heat of a murder inquiry. I'm getting it from all directions. Just get him out."

Paddy nodded; he was already looking forward to it. Cahir made to leave the room, but as if something had just occurred to him, he stopped and turned back. "I like that wee girl, Paddy. She's got brains. Keep her close."

"Will do, sir. You'd better be off," he answered, feeling slightly riled. Apart from his twin Dolores, he had no truck with women being allowed into the Provos. Additionally, the wee girl was just that, a little girl. Grunting, he called Liz back into the office and told her to sit.

Paddy casually threw himself into the OC's still-warm chair and asked for her address and a few other details about Edwards, her stepfather. Once he'd got what he needed, he rested with his hands behind his head and examined her.

"If I do this, what's in it for me?" he asked as if bartering.

"What d'ya mean?" Liz asked, astonished. "You heard the OC; you've got to sort it. I've nothing to offer."

"You must have something?"

"No, I don't."

"You're an ambitious little tease, aren't you, Liz McKenna?"

"I don't know what you're on about. I want to do my duty," she replied in a wave of mounting anger.

"Your duty, eh? Well, if you want to do your duty, how come that cell of yours fucked up so bad with those robberies? You got a comrade banged up and returned with just enough for a fish supper and a Coke."

"You're telling me! I knew that'd be a cock up from the beginning," Liz roared. "I told Jon my idea was better!" she cried in frustration, her face turning crimson.

Paddy's ears pricked up. "Your idea? You'd an idea, had you? And what was that then… the Brink's-Mat bullion heist?" He chuckled at the thought, then stopped; in fact, it wouldn't surprise him. Liz McKenna was one ballsy young woman. She stood staring defiantly at him, hands on her hips like a gossiping washerwoman.

He'd give her a chance and listen; she'd likely fall flat on her lovely arse. He leant forward. "Come on then; I want to hear it."

And so Liz told him. Every little detail.

****

George Edwards spotted his quarry in a leather-seated booth in the Rainbow Café in Derry. Before joining him, Edwards stared around at the other customers. He recognised Father Connolly, a local Catholic priest, sitting by the café's large window looking onto the street – probably writing his next sermon, though Edwards had heard the man was being moved on. The priest looked up and gave a quick, absent-looking smile when George passed by.

He tipped his hat. He knew a few of Connolly's colleagues particularly well, but that was for another time. Today he was here on business with that ever-worsening irritant, Dr Harris. After some big motherfucker of a Provo had cautioned Harris to get out of Derry, George – under duress from his associates and using his contacts in the Civil Service – managed to get the doctor a locum position in the women's prison at Armagh.

Now George's keen eyes studied Harris's emaciated and shambolic body, huddled into the booth; at the smell of stale alcohol wafting towards him, he shrank back. This pitiful figure looked so far removed from a typical pillar-of-the-community GP.

"What is it this time?" George asked him bitterly.

"I need your help again. I… I… need another job," Harris stuttered dejectedly. "I've tried, but no one'll touch me after Armagh."

George knew all about the good doctor's fuck ups. First, Patrick McLaughlin's death and Harris's wretched efforts to cover up his medical negligence there. Then his neglect of the women in Armagh gaol, resulting in the death of McLaughlin's youngest daughter – it was beyond ridiculous.

The Rainbow's ever-attentive waitress Siobhan, who'd almost become part of the café's furnishings, took their order. Harris couldn't eat but requested a black coffee, George a full Ulster fry with extra toast. He hissed at Harris across the table when the woman was out of earshot, "How the heck have you got yourself into such a mess? You're a walking disaster!"

Harris sat rigid in his seat, struggling to find an explanation. He'd done it again and broken one of the group's cardinal rules – *do not attract unwarranted attention of any kind.* Years ago, after some hard lessons, a cluster of men with similar illegal cravings for young boys and girls went underground, pledging to find ways of satisfying their tastes in secret. The price of membership was to undertake that they'd look out for each other, personally and professionally.

George, the group's current leader, wasn't prepared to let Harris fuck up again. They were all extraordinarily nervous and angry at the attention the doctor had already drawn and wanted something to be done about it. For the final time, George was prepared to give Harris the benefit of the doubt. He'd a job in mind for the man that would allow him to keep Harris close, and although he couldn't practise medicine, his medical skills would come in handy – very handy indeed.

Following a spate of graffiti threats around his Derry house, which he was sure his stepdaughter was behind, George had just successfully applied for promotion in East Belfast. In a way, the girl did him a favour as his new role included free accommodation and a cracking salary as Director Belfast Corporation Welfare Committee.

****

When he returned to his house in Creggan after the interview board and the meeting with Harris, George Edwards found a dark-haired man waiting by the garden gate. George didn't know him but felt the danger emanating from the man even at a distance. He kept walking but deliberately slowed his pace and stopped just a few feet away, enough to be heard if he'd to call for help. The stranger threw a cigarette butt in the gutter. With eyes like daggers, he stared at George before asking tersely, "You Edwards?"

George nodded and swallowed nervously. He'd been half expecting this for some time. *The bitch had finally snitched!*

Paddy Gillispie immediately saw that Edwards was a yellow-belly coward who wouldn't come to him, so he moved in closer. Sensing a few twitching net curtains, he knew he'd acquired an audience too.

"You know why I'm here?" Paddy asked gravely. George nodded but remained silent.

"Normally, I'd be here to kill you. Maybe take you away first, make you disappear. But today is your lucky day, and I'm only going to warn you. We want you out of that house by tomorrow morning." Paddy pointed at George's home.

"You are *n-e-v-e-r* to bring that fat arse of yours near Derry again. DO-YOU-HEAR-ME!" he concluded.

Paddy was livid that he hadn't been given a chance to do the bastard in, but the OC had expressly warned him to give the man a good hiding and get him out of Derry.

"You going to invite me in then?" Paddy asked before grabbing his victim by the arm and dragging him up his garden path. As much as he appreciated an audience, it'd be better to do this inside, with no witnesses.

****

Emmett McFadden was thrilled to hear Liam was off to America and generously withdrew some money from his Credit Union account to give to his excited sibling for the trip. Although the holiday was weeks away, Liam borrowed a suitcase from a kindly neighbour. What little he had was neatly folded and placed in the hardened red case that lay open and waiting at the foot of his bed. Night after night, he'd practise his American accent or watch American TV, wondering where he'd end up.

"I reckon it'll be New York!" he'd cry before changing his mind. "No! Boston, it'll be Boston! There are loads of Derry people in Boston!"

Emmett couldn't help but laugh. "Pipe down, will you? I'm trying to watch *Top of the Pops*." A new feeling of peacefulness had inched into the McFaddens' home. Its active ingredient was, without doubt, Liam's joy and excitement, but added to that, Charlie was working hard, and their money worries were slowly dwindling.

Surreptitiously, Emmett was beginning to make plans to leave for Australia, but he hadn't found the nerve to tell anyone yet. His ma was always busy working for the women's peace groups that were making significant progress, and the time never seemed right. The women were now promoting integrated education, and she'd even been on the news – they were well proud of her.

Liam settled into the sofa. It was a rare event, but his parents had gone to a local bar together. He felt relaxed and comfy as he sat beside his brother, watching Simon Bates's countdown. Emmett, however, found he couldn't concentrate on the TV any longer as his eyes kept straying to a black-and-white photograph above their empty fireplace.

It was of Joe in his Doire Colmcille football kit at Páirc Colmcille in Derry. His older brother looked handsome and carefree. Emmett shook his head, took a deep breath and heaved a despondent sigh. Even over the thumping music, Liam heard him and turned to see the sadness on his brother's face as he continued to stare at Joe's photo – it was their ma's favourite, and she polished the frame religiously every morning. Uncharacteristically, the boy squeezed Emmet's arm in reassurance.

"He'll be out before we know it."

Emmett smiled in return but said nothing. He couldn't find an answer and had no idea when or if he'd see Joe again. Liam broke the tension as he joked, "Maybe once I'm back from Amerikay, he'll be home! Yeeee-ha!" Emmett threw a heavy cushion at him and cried, "Jesus! Buzz off, will you? You'd think you were the only Derry man ever to get to America!"

Straightaway, Liam threw it back, and the fight began in earnest. The boys laughed themselves silly, forgetting all about *Top of the Pops* and the awful mess they were making as feathers burst out of the heavy cushion.

****

Chapter Eighteen

Charles Jones believed that, at long last, the red, white and blue Loyalists of Ulster were making significant progress. Ulster's paramilitary Third Force was up and running, supported by the Democratic Unionist Party (DUP). Paisley remained furious that Prime Minister Margaret Thatcher and her government had meetings with the Pope-loving, Irish Republican Taig, Charles Haughey.

To Loyalists, Thatcher was a traitor who'd been given a run for her money when they demonstrated and drove en masse to Hillsborough House, where she'd been staying. Akin to Southern states of America, preacher Paisley bellowed his fire and brimstone sermon from an elevated pulpit, hollering threats and warnings to his loyal followers. He was on a roll.

"If an IRA man comes to a Protestant home and my men are there, he will be killed."

The world's media watched on, as did the Loyalists, the British and Irish Governments and the Irish Nationalists and Republicans. They listened with growing unease and trepidation to the Reverend's language of war.

An opportunity for Jones to stand up in public next to his revolutionary idol still needed to occur. However, he was proud as punch when he and 500 of his compatriots responded to Paisley's call. They'd been summoned to the hills near Ballymena (Paisley's constituency) to demonstrate their militaristic power and show their capability to five waiting journalists.

Dressed in combat jackets and balaclavas, the armed men lined up like soldiers on parade and waited patiently in the dark. Each had a piece of paper, supposedly a legal firearm certificate held high above their head. These men believed themselves to be Paisley's army, waiting and ready for his orders.

It was the beginning of many such rallies, which Paisley self-reverentially dubbed the 'Carson Trail' after his hero Edward Carson, an early-nineteenth-century Scottish-Irish Unionist.

Jones watched the grey-haired titan at various rallies, with his jumble of teeth bellow and spat angry charges of hope berated into bouquets of microphones. He was captivated by the sight of the preacher, who commanded the fanatical devotion of his roaring, cheering followers. Paisley was forging an unbreakable bond with them, fuelled by their hatred and anger. The adoring mob furiously pounded out their approval of him on many oversized Lambeg drums.

A Loyalist Day of Action was planned in the hope of pressuring the British Government to take a more rigid stance against the Republicans.

****

Underhandedly and without telling Charles Jones, Chief Constable Bonner set a £5,000 bounty on William Barter's head, and news of it had just hit the streets. He'd met with a senior member of the Ulster Volunteer Force (UVF) in a quiet village just outside Newcastle, County Down. Although he was still peeved with Jones for the way he'd spoken to him at lunch with Hickey, he thought it a good idea to take it upon himself to get rid of Barter, hoping it'd earn him some brownie points. Getting the money for a hit wasn't a problem; he'd *borrowed* it from one of his many budget lines.

Nicknamed 'The Tank' for apparent reasons, the UVF man was colossal. He'd grown up a Loyalist in the Shankill Road, Belfast, and attended most, if not all, of Paisley's rallies. In 1971 he'd been charged with double murder in a Diplock Court, where he'd pleaded his innocence. Despite this, he was placed in the UVF quadrant of HMP Maze (aka Long Kesh), only to escape but be returned after recapture six months later. Hidden hands at work soon arranged an early reprieve for him, and he was back on the streets of East Belfast in June 1981.

Bonner discreetly passed over the payment package that included a small Browning handgun, recently confiscated as part of a vast Provo cache. The discovery of the armoury stemmed from a Republican supergrass; surprisingly, it was handed over to the RUC by MI5. Bonner thought it clever to use a recognisable Provo gun so that Fenian extremists would be blamed for Barter's murder. Without question, that was something the Republicans wouldn't want, as most of their funds stemmed from the loyalty and generosity of pro-IRA Irish Americans.

Bonner's career was spiralling downward fast. He was experiencing frequent panic attacks as long-time colleagues were either being shot, blown to smithereens, or committing suicide. He couldn't think straight and lashed out at the slightest mishap. His estranged wife and children were refusing to see him now, and even his mistress, whom he'd set up in a lovely stone cottage, threw him out yet still expected him to pay her rent; otherwise, she'd tell his wife!

He'd been sleeping at the barracks for weeks, and the station's wagging tongues were in overdrive as his peers bet on his imminent dismissal.

****

William Barter sat with Brendan Doherty in the solicitor's office, filled with legal files and boxes almost reaching the ceiling. Both men were ashen-faced, recently receiving a fax from Washington, DC. Barter's FBI contact, Dale Horn, confirmed what they'd been dreading.

"... *I have it on good authority, you and Mr Doherty need to get out of Northern Ireland as soon as....*" A spidery handwritten P.S. added: "*...especially you, William. There's a price on your head. You need to come back – and soon.*"

"Jeez, that's just great!" Barter strode back and forth where the clutter allowed. He sucked his teeth and yanked on his hair. "What the fuck! It's Jones at work again, the slimeball. I just know it!" He balled his fists. "I'm so close, Brendan, so fuckin' close to nailing him!"

Besides writing his regular contributions to the *Boston Globe*, Barter was still obsessed with researching Jones to write a piece that would see him adequately investigated and sent down for a long time. With all the evidence he was accumulating, he'd even considered writing a book. He'd expose Jones as a criminal mastermind and bigot, describe how he conducted his many illegal activities, including robbery and bribery, his involvement in sectarian murders, including that of a bishop, and his collusion with the RUC. But this tip-off from the States had thrown a mighty big spanner in the works. And there was no point in him going to the police to ask for protection – he knew Jones had the Chief Constable and others in his pocket.

As for Brendan Doherty, he shook his head and puffed out his cheeks. He'd heard these types of threats before, many times. Yes, it wasn't pleasant, but this news came as no real surprise; it was the name of the game he was in, and he wasn't afraid anymore. He'd made an enemy out of Jones when he'd first drawn attention to the unfairness of Tina McLaughlin's trial and the travesty and injustice of Jones's own trial. For that and many similar reasons, he now kept himself strictly to himself. There wasn't a girlfriend, wife or family for him to worry about, and as the adopted and only child of deceased parents, there was no one else in his life.

Doherty was alone, and alone he would remain. He wasn't going anywhere. But for Barter, it was a different ballgame altogether. The man was a US citizen. Suppose something did happen to him: his death would cause diplomatic mayhem.

Brendan told his friend matter-of-factly, "You've got to go back. It'd cause a political meltdown if something happened to you, especially now when Sinn Féin is trying to put on a political hat. No one wants a dead Yankee journalist on their doorstep."

Barter felt this was right but didn't want to leave. He'd grown to love this Godforsaken country, knowing many men and women – from both sides of the divide – who, at considerable risk to themselves, sought a peaceful solution. Their stories should be heard and reported, as well as all the gruesome tales of sectarian blood-letting, but now it seemed he was in no position to do either. White-hot anger flamed in him. He sighed with regret. Okay, he'd go back to the States for a spell until things died down here. But before that, there was one very promising lead he must follow up.

****

The rage of Lemon, aka Mark Carroll, intensified daily, weekly and year after year as his ex-boss Charles Jones, for whom he had taken the fall in court, failed to respond to Lemon's numerous letters and calls. He constantly re-envisaged Jones's look of contempt in the courtroom and his neglect at protecting Lemon and his 'kids' from being sent down. Unlike Lemon, Jones's private army had settled into the daily routine of HMP Maze. But Lemon hated it there, and his frustration projected itself in unhealthy ways, mainly at the expense of the screws and his fellow inmates.

He recalled the power he'd felt when he tortured and butchered pudden-headed Catholics that he and the kids, consumed by hatred, would grab off the West Belfast Streets, some while innocently walking out of Mass. They'd even posed as police officers once, and it'd worked beautifully when they successfully nabbed a couple of Taigs whom the gang hated beyond redemption. Lemon had relished the sense of power it gave him and desperately wanted that back.

The prison doctors tried to sedate him to keep the other staff and inmates safe. They'd even the gall to suggest he talk to a shrink. *A friggin' shrink*! The last thing he wanted was a pill-popping therapist. He wanted Jones to acknowledge him, respect him, visit occasionally – and work to get him out of this fuckin' hellhole! Lemon was growing increasingly restless and dangerous, hoping against hope that his former boss would pay him his dues. Eventually, he realised this would never happen and vowed that, somehow, he'd take Jones out for his treachery.

When the Yankee reporter suggested he spill the beans on Jones, Lemon couldn't believe it. He could kill two birds with one stone. If he sold Jones out, the crooked businessman would end up inside, and maybe, in exchange for Lemon's cooperation and testimony, his sentence would be reduced or, even better, he'd be released. With such deluded hope in his heart, he'd agreed to be interviewed by the American reporter.

Barter watched as Lemon and his fellow inmates were ushered into the cold, depressing HMP Maze visitors' room. He glanced around at the sea of depressed-looking visitors. As Lemon drew closer, he noted the reporter appeared nervous and pale, shifting his weight in his chair.

"You look like crap," he said, sitting opposite the Yank.

Barter nodded; the goon was right. He looked and felt like crap, on the edge of a precipice. If the thug were to tell him all before he left Ireland, it could change the course of his quest to bring Jones down.

As they talked, Barter realised Lemon was half-cracked. He gazed across the room and met the eye of a watchful PO, who tapped his head, meaning: *You're wasting your time, mate!*

Barter sagged in disappointment as the prisoner mumbled incoherently while manically pumping his left leg up and down. This was a man barely clinging to sanity. The journalist knew he needed to tread carefully to gain anything of value.

Beforehand he'd spoken briefly with the prison governor, who had warned him Lemon was becoming more dangerous and needed to be subdued by medication.

"He shouldn't even be here," the governor had said. "It's unlikely he'll ever be released into society."

Now Barter watched Lemon pick a scab off his arm and watch, like a fascinated child, as the blood began to flow.

"Are you okay?" Barter asked him when it was obvious he was not. He pulled a piece of tissue from his pocket and put it on the table.

"Grand. You gonna get me out of here, Yank?" Lemon replied, ignoring the tissue but continuing to pick his bloodied skin.

"I'll do my best," Barter replied politely.

"How! How are you going to get me outta here?" Lemon's leg was pumping faster.

"If you tell me everything you know about Jones, I'll do my best. I can't say more than that."

Lemon's tortured brain worked overtime. Sometimes his thoughts left him alone, but then the memory of how his former boss had stitched him up, the things he'd done on Jones's instructions, would pluck at him mercilessly, and he'd lose control. Mustn't do that now. Mustn't give way to them. The Yank was offering him a way out of this hellhole.

"What d'ya want to know?" he asked.

****

Chapter Nineteen

Opening his eyes with a start, Rob Sallis wasn't sure where he was. Once again, he'd had the nightmare about the Hallowe'en patrol and felt weak and out of sorts. It would be one of his bad days; he thought as he dragged himself out of bed to the distant sound of a radio playing.

Wearing a thin, beer-stained white cotton T-shirt and underpants, he couldn't be bothered to wash or clean his teeth but dragged himself down to the galley kitchen. He found his mam and son at the kitchen table, with Val eating cornflakes and his mam drinking tea.

"You want some breakfast?" she asked.

"Nah, I'm fine," Rob replied, sitting down next to the boy, who stared silently across the table at his nan.

"I feel lousy the day," she told Rob. "I'm gonna need you to help out. That okay?"

"Aye. Whatever," he told her reluctantly. The last thing he felt like doing was housework and running messages, but he couldn't say no to his mam. Her breathing was laboured, and her face looked flushed.

"I've got a cold comin' on; I could do with some quiet."

"Right you are."

"Could you mebbe take the bairn along and get me a few bits in Presto's? I'll make us a list. Maybe I'll put a stew on later."

"That'd be nice, Mam, class."

Rob and Val cleared the pots from the table, stacking them by the sink, and then the boy ran off to the shelter of his room.

Leaning against a cupboard door, Rob rubbed his aching head. Suddenly there was the foul metallic taste of stale alcohol in his throat, his mouth... Half-running, he made it to the bathroom just in time and violently threw up whatever vile combination he'd eaten and drunk the night before. His ribs hurt, he realised. He pulled up his T-shirt to find deep red scratches and purpling bruises on the left-hand side of his chest. *What the heck!* He couldn't remember anything.

"Do you want a cup of tea, Rob?" he heard his mother shout repeatedly.

"Nah. I'm fine."

A little later, he returned to the kitchen. On the table lay a shopping list. He noticed his mam's colour still wasn't good.

"You don't look the best, Mam," he told her.

She quickly replied, "A lot better than you do, son, but I won't ask."

"No, Mam. Don't. I'll go get dressed."

"There's not a lot on the list, but it's all essentials, everything we'll need for the next few days." With that, she took some notes and change from her housekeeping jar and counted what Rob would need to the nearest penny.

He knew why she was doing it and felt like shit. She didn't trust him anymore, and who could blame her? His drinking was well out of hand; all he had to do was look in the mirror to see that or put his hand to his ribs. He'd tried his utmost to remember what he'd done the night before and couldn't; must have been mortal.

Rob didn't take long to dress; washing could wait, and he returned downstairs. Val was back at the table playing with his football cards. He looked at his nan and asked if she was going out.

"Not the day, pet, your da will take you shopping. Give your nan a wee break."

Val's face dropped. He wasn't keen on going to the shops with his da; he never enjoyed being seen out with him. Though saddened by this, Rob tried to jolly him along. "It's a bonny morning, Val. We'll make the most of it. Go along the river, maybe? Best take your anorak; it's nippy by the water."

"Okay then," said his son, dragging out the words.

In silence, the pair of them walked to the supermarket. Usually, Val loved shopping here because his nan always treated him to a couple of massive, multi-coloured gobstoppers that lasted forever and turned his tongue different colours. And if he were really lucky, she'd buy him a wad of candy-coloured flying saucers that tasted like Holy Communion!

Rob quickly found a trolley inside the shop and made his way up the first aisle to the bakery. Val dutifully held onto its handle and waited while his da worked through the list. There were more items than he'd initially thought, and it would take some effort for the two to carry the bags the whole way home. He had no money for a bus or a taxi and was already knackered.

Queuing at the till, Rob saw Val longingly scanning the pic-n-mix display, but Rob knew that none of his mam's essentials could be swapped out for sweets. The dreaded question came.

"Da. Can I have some sweets and bubble gum? Nan buys me them all the time, never misses a day," Val said, eyes wide as he tugged his father's sleeve and tried his luck with the bubble gum. Rob felt completely powerless until...

"'Course you can, lad, but I'll need to swap something over. Stand there a minute."

Val didn't move an inch as Rob replaced a big box of washing powder and added the crucial sweets. He'd still a few regimental bits and pieces from his and his father's army days that he'd previously managed to pawn and reclaim. Once he got home, he'd grab them and take them down to the pop shop, hopefully, get a couple of quid, then off for the washing powder and maybe a nice, cold pint...

Pleased by his father's capitulation, Val struggled to speak around the gobstopper in his mouth. His plan had worked perfectly.

"Thanks, Da! Proper belta."

Rob laughed to see his son's bulging cheeks. He decided that to make it easy on his aching ribs, they'd hold on to the trolley, use it to take the shopping home, and later on, he'd return it when he got the washing powder.

But once outside, the irksome trolley seemed to have a mind of its own, proving challenging to push over the gravel at the far end of the car park. The two laughed heartily at their exertions, sharing a rare moment of mirth. It didn't last. Someone behind them started shouting and yelling. They looked back and stopped walking when they spotted a uniformed security guard running after them, waving his arms.

"You can't take that outta here!" bellowed the elderly man. He pointed a bony finger angrily at the large Presto's sign and hollered, "Didn't you read what it says! NO trolleys beyond this point!"

He was pissed off with chasing after people misappropriating the bliddy trolleys. Why didn't anyone read the signs? They were right there in front of them!

"And don't think you can keep it to store your junk in. I'm fed up to the teeth of you down-and-outs taking our trolleys! They're proper expensive they are. Why don't you go find a real job like the rest of us have to do?"

This acted like a red rag to a bull. Rob filled up with rage at the man's words, speaking to him like a tramp – and in front of Val too. It felt like an electric current was pulsing through him and wouldn't stop until he'd lashed out. He belted the guard in the face so violently that he knocked the old man's spectacles off and, worse still, dislodged his dentures!

Val let out a half-strangled scream when he spotted the guard's pale pink and white teeth flying through the air. The lad let go of the trolley. He dodged his da's outstretched hand before bobbing and weaving his way through the parked cars back to the safety of the supermarket.

Inside, he wailed aloud and pointed to the car park, declaring: "Quick, someone! Me da's killed some old man and knocked his teeth out!"

Rob let out a hollow groan and stood frozen to the spot, observing his son's flight. *No!* He watched the uniformed man retrieve and put on his glasses, then search for the teeth. Shamefaced, Rob offered to help but was rejected as the seething man searched in vain. Embarrassed to the hilt, Rob spotted them, dusted them off on his army pullover and passed them over. Then, to his horror, peering more closely at his victim's shockingly concave face, he realised he knew this man: it was Mr McClay, mam's neighbour and friend. In Rob's military days, the old soldier had taken an interest in him, passed the time of day, and talked about his service with the Desert Rats. No longer did, of course.

Christ, what had he done? Rob attempted to apologise, but McClay waved him away and staggered unsteadily across the parking lot. Some figures dashed out of the supermarket to intercept and help him inside. Among them was a lad in a familiar red anorak.

Rob hung his head in shame. This would finish his mam, shame her before the whole street. He didn't think she'd be able to handle any more. And Val… Better go and check that he was all right. He'd started to make his way back to the supermarket when he heard an ambulance siren wailing and spotted a police car speeding into the parking lot. A couple of figures flagged it down and then pointed to him. The next thing Rob knew, he was face to face with his mam, who'd stepped out of the cop car.

Bridie Sallis was beyond livid. She'd been told what had happened by the store manager, who'd telephoned when she was in the bath. Fortunately, he knew her and Val well. When they arrived, he'd reassured her that Mr McClay was just a bit shaken.

Rob went to speak, but she stopped him with a wave of her hand. She moved in so close that he could feel her breath upon his face. Her angry tone, one he'd never heard from her before, skewered his heart.

"You're a bloody disgrace, Robert Sallis. Your poor Da would be ashamed of you. I give up! Do you hear? You're no son of mine anymore. You deserve all you've got and all you'll get if you keep behaving this way. I want you out of the house! It's a sin what you've done, brawling with an old man and scaring your bairn half to death, leaving him with strangers. Well, that's it, Rob. I've had it with you."

Bridie began to cough and struggle for breath then. The store manager puffed up to them, followed by Val, who grabbed his nan's hand and clung to it. As the manager led them away with promises of hot tea, the lad glared back at his da. From the unforgiving set of his face, there was no way back for Rob.

One of the waiting police officers grabbed him then and read him his rights before roughly throwing him into the rear seat of the cop car.

"Back again, eh, Sallis? You're becoming a regular these days. We'll soon have to give you a B&B rate!"

But Rob didn't care about their gibes and piss-taking. He knew he deserved them all.

****

Bridie and Val sat at the cluttered kitchen table when they got back home. Bridie was feeling resolute. She loved Rob more than anything, but over her dead body, would she allow him to destroy her grandson's life as well.

"You want me to top the water up in the bath, love?" she asked. "It was scalding when I was in. You can bring your Action Man and wash him too. Mind, we'll have to cut that bubble gum off your hair first." Under the circumstances, she wouldn't reprimand him. He knew he was never allowed gum, but his father didn't. Val stared at her with a wounded expression, considering the offer.

He'd thought his heart would stop and was scared stiff when he saw the old guard's bloodied teeth flying towards him. He'd recognised the aura of anger surrounding his da only too well and wasn't stupid enough to hang around.

In reply to his nan's offer of a bath, he hugged her and prayed with all his heart and soul that his father wouldn't return. The prospect of a soak with his Action Man sounded nice, although he wasn't too sure about letting his nan loose on his hair.

"Okay," he said, squeezing her mottled hand.

Within seconds, he'd stripped down, grabbed his Action Man complete with a parachute and ran naked to his grandmother as only a child could. She ushered him upstairs and wrapped a towel around him while she added hot water to the bath from which she'd been summoned a short while before.

Bridie put the seat down and sat there on the pink toilet while Val splashed about in the soothing water. He seemed happy enough, playing with his military man. Unlike his father, the plastic soldier never drank too much, ran off at the mouth or lashed out in anger. At least for now, the fears and sadness of the day were set aside.

****

Chapter Twenty

Caitlin peered into the eyes of Maryann Fox's baby girl, 6 pounds 3 ounces of her. She'd never seen anything so perfect. The child's skin was like cashmere to the touch, complemented by a delicate, perfectly formed face and the tiniest button nose. As if saying hello, she opened her pale blue eyes and stared at Caitlin, gurgling happily, her chubby hands waving.

"Aaahhh, Maryann, she's just said hello to me! Oh my God, she's so gorgeous… beautiful!" Caitlin cried, grabbing the baby's soft hand and feeling a tad guilty at the thought of baby Sean, Anne's little boy, when he was born, he was perfect. But Caitlin knew deep down that this young lady was something special.

"I don't think I've ever seen such a beautiful baby," she told Maryann. "You must be well pleased!"

"I am, Caitlin. I really am. She's lovely, isn't she?"

"Have you decided on a name then?" Caitlin had noted a book of baby names on the tall side table next to Maryann's bed. The smell of flowers in the private hospital room was almost sickening, with so many massed on every surface, along with pink balloons and cards.

"We have. Ella. It means 'light' or 'beautiful fairy'."

"That's perfect. She's a perfect, beautiful fairy." Caitlin's fingers gently played with Ella's doll-sized hand.

"I wish Bill had been here," Maryann said sorrowfully.

Ella arrived a few weeks early, and Bill Fox was returning from Ballymena with Chris. They'd looked at new investment opportunities in the province for a while and, over the months, had come up with some exciting ones. Maryann and Caitlin's friendship strengthened as the men grew closer in their business dealings.

When Maryann's waters unexpectedly broke, Caitlin stayed with her. They'd been in Selfridges when Maryann grasped Caitlin's hand

and squeezed it while looking down at the water gathering in a puddle at her feet. The helpful staff promptly called an ambulance. They were no sooner off to Paddington Hospital than a nurse informed Maryann she still had some time to go. As planned, she was then admitted to the private Portland maternity hospital in the West End.

Caitlin never let go of Maryann's hand throughout the birth. She thought she had never seen anything more miraculous than Ella's tiny body being delivered and placed in Maryann's waiting arms.

Buzzing after the child's arrival, Caitlin found she couldn't wait to have a baby of her own. She'd do everything right; she vowed to give her child, or God willing children, the most beautiful and happy life possible. Being a mother was a must – there were so few left of her family, just her, Martin, Tommy and Kathy. Her granny on her mother's side had severed all ties after Majella's suicide.

It suddenly dawned on her that she and Chris had never discussed starting a family. And after what she'd experienced with Ella's birth, she knew she wanted to try as soon as they were married.

Reading Caitlin's mind, Maryanne cried, "Your turn next! Have you and Chris decided to go for it or wait a while?"

"Funnily enough, I was thinking that! You know, we've never really talked about it."

"I suggest you should – and soon, before the wedding!" Maryann declared.

For whatever reason, Caitlin's reply sounded anxious and unconvincing. "I better had, hadn't I?"

****

Arriving at Heathrow Airport terminal one and struggling to locate their driver in the crush, Bill Fox and Chris Pecaro were exhausted. They'd encountered a protest on their way to Aldergrove Airport to catch the flight. Swarms of people, both on foot and in cars, were waving flags and banging drums. Bill stopped a bored-looking policeman and explained why they needed to get through: his wife was in labour!

Moments later, an RUC jeep was escorting them like royalty through the bawling crowd and onto the A26 leading to the airport. The two men were surprised by such a show of compassion.

"Maybe they're not as bad as all that," Chris commented.

Driven by adrenalin, Bill was too excited to hear and nudged his friend. "What a way to end the week, eh?" he asked breathlessly. He'd been dying to become a father. Growing up in Hinton St George in Somerset's peaceful countryside, his childhood had been idyllic.

"It's exciting for sure. I think we've finally found what we're looking for," Chris replied, grinning with satisfaction. They'd had several successful meetings, and there were now many promising opportunities in the pipeline, especially since they could apply for the numerous government grants to help Northern Ireland out of the financial doldrums.

With a reproachful look at him, Bill cried, "I'm talking about the baby, Chris! Forget about work for once. This is my first child, for goodness' sake!"

Chris cringed. Feeling embarrassed, he nodded vigorously. "Sorry, Bill. You know me – all work, no play!"

As the executive car came off the M4 heading towards London, it hit the customary heavy traffic. They began to reflect on the exciting days and prospects ahead in silence.

Chris found the whole baby thing tedious and was already fed up with hearing about it. He'd listened to the women's excited yapping for months and Bill's never-ending daily bulletins on what stage of development the unborn baby had reached. You'd think Maryann was the first woman ever to give birth! And on top of that, he'd also been treated to running reports from Caitlin.

To Chris, there were more important things to focus on, and he needed Bill to be on top of his business game, not distracted by babies.

If they were to be successful, these investments would mean much hard work from them both and a great deal of time spent away from home.

The day's events reminded him that he and Caitlin had never discussed having children. Sheila, his ex-wife, made it clear from day one that she wouldn't give up her high-flying legal career for anything, that suited him entirely. There'd be no paternity risk, and he'd opted for the snip years ago.

****

Bill Fox was thrilled to have a daughter – and, fuck, she was a beauty! A man who rarely used expletives, now he found he couldn't stop. "Fuck me! She's gorgeous, isn't she!" he exclaimed, carefully picking up his bundled baby. "Shush!" Maryann hissed, outraged by her husband's language but laughing with everyone else. She'd never seen him so proud. He was ecstatic; stitches aside, she, too, couldn't be happier.

Caitlin grabbed Chris's hand, held it tight and giggled at Bill's attempt to look innocent. *"What!* What did I say?"

Chris had to admit the child was delightful, a natural beauty. Nonetheless, he felt troubled as he focused on his fiancée's captivated expression, the way she protectively took the pink-swathed child off Bill. *She wanted this. Caitlin wanted this for herself. Shit.*

Bill began to pour and pass round glasses of champagne. The proud parents welcomed more visitors who, in turn, cooed in awe at the new arrival. Caitlin sensed Chris becoming ever more quiet and subdued. Pulling him aside, she asked if he was good.

"You okay? Tired?"

He nodded. Yes, he was tired, but from what he'd just witnessed, he was more terrified than tired. How on God's earth would he tell Caitlin he'd had a vasectomy? Chris Pecaro had no intention of having children, not now, not ever.

"I am a little tired, I guess. Can we go? You've been here all night, and it's been a hell of a week. Come on; I can't wait to be home."

Disappointed and feeling admonished for no reason, Caitlin reluctantly agreed.

****

Outside they quickly hailed a black cab. Chris hadn't said a word from the moment he left the hospital. Caitlin had never seen him like this before and wasn't quite sure what to do.

"Are you sure you're okay?" she asked tenderly, taking his hand.

"I'm fine," he snapped. "Please, stop asking me every five minutes, will you?"

She looked at him aghast, quickly released his hand and inched as far away from him as possible on the leather seat. Her heart was racing, and her cheeks were burning. She continued to stare at him, hoping he'd say sorry, but the air between them seemed to have turned to ice. They climbed out of the cab together in a deafening silence before their pristine, empty townhouse.

****

Following a restless night spent in the guest room, Caitlin got dressed and, going without breakfast, took the tube to work. Heavy-hearted, she knew Chris wouldn't be in the office for the next few days but hoped he'd call her and apologise. He'd been up and gone before she rose.

In true London Underground fashion, the Victoria line was playing up. Complaining passengers were packed together like sardines. She'd hastily stepped into a smoking carriage and cursed her mistake. The air was thick with cigarette smoke and the stink of tobacco. So far, her morning could hardly have been worse.

Finally arriving at Victoria, she heard a station announcement from the speakers over the platform.

Ladies and gentlemen, this station is being evacuated. Please do not take the escalator but make your way to the stairs and use them carefully.

Moans and groans from the frustrated passengers rang out down the lengthy platform. Would this day ever improve? Diverging from her usual practice when travelling on the Underground, she made eye contact with others, who nodded back to her and rolled their eyes in a display of fellow feeling. They were surprisingly kind and polite to each other on the way up the endless circular staircases, waiting patiently and stopping should a fellow passenger need help. With a pounding heart, Caitlin eventually made her way to the top and gratefully stepped out into the ticket hall along with hundreds of others.

Glancing through the foyer on the forecourt, usually thronged by black cabs, she eyed numerous Metropolitan Police vans and three or four London Fire Brigade engines. Approaching a kindly-looking policeman who stood next to an empty newsstand, she asked him, "What's happening?"

The policeman grabbed the pretty young woman by the arm and propelled her towards the exit.

"It's those bastard Irish again, miss. A bomb scare! You'd better get that gorgeous head of yours out of here. Off you go now… step lively!"

Caitlin didn't need to hear it twice. Memories of the Shipquay Street bomb blast and Anne's injury filled her with dread. This couldn't be happening to her again, not here. Not in London!

On autopilot, she made it safely to the office, where small groups huddled together in the corridors discussing the ongoing terror incident. In all the time Caitlin had spent in this company so far, she'd never experienced prejudice against her for being Irish. Still, as she entered the kitchen to make herself a coffee, she felt a sudden change in the atmosphere.

With their rah-rah voices and velvet hairbands, these three women were Sloane Ranger types with whom she did not have much in common. They immediately halted their conversation on noticing her arrival and stared hard at her, cold eyes full of resentment.

"Morning," Caitlin said defiantly, ready for them.

Nothing.

The instigator, as thin as a knitting needle and just as sharp, was considered by most of her colleagues to be a bit of a bitch. She turned to the younger two and announced in an unbelievably stagey voice: "It's the bloody Irish, at it again."

After a pause for effect, she added, "Bloody bogtrotters – coming over to London where they're not wanted. Why don't they stay in their bloody fields and eat po-ta-toes!" With a cruel emphasis on the last word.

Bitterness in her heart, Caitlin threw a cup into the Belfast sink. It broke in two. She stepped across to confront the woman who'd insulted her. Caitlin stood straight-backed and defiant, perfectly calm. She craned close to the other woman's snooty face and told her, in a withering Derry accent, precisely what she should do.

"Why don't you go fuck yourself, you ugly racist hag? Because, fuck knows, missus, no one else wants to!"

The younger secretaries didn't know whether to laugh or cry. They giggled nervously when Caitlin turned on her heel and exited the kitchen. Her concerns about her fiancé's behaviour of yesterday were forgotten in the rush of calling out her colleagues' bigotry.

****

Chapter Twenty-one

James Henderson sat behind his desk and waited while the assistant manager led the next employee into the room. It'd been a nightmarish morning while James recited the exact words repeatedly – each time as painful to him as the first.

"I'm so sorry. We've no choice but to cut our workforce by thirty per cent for reasons beyond our control. Unfortunately, we've got to let you go."

Rumour was rife, and the media ceaselessly speculated about Rocola's potential demise. James did his utmost to dispel the rumours to reassure the remaining workforce that their jobs were safe for the time being.

Forty-nine-year-old Sharon McGill strode into the office, aware of what was coming. A Rocola employee for thirty-three years, she'd never set foot on this floor until now; she'd no reason to. She had six children and a husband, Andrew, whom she loved dearly and who loved her back. In many ways, she was blessed, but losing this job was a huge blow, not only financially. It was an emotional setback, too – she'd grown up at Rocola. The amazing friendships and memories she'd made here over the years were ones she'd never forget.

Last night the McGill's had talked into the wee hours and decided, sadly, they'd no choice. Andrew would have to leave home and go to Liverpool to find work.

James watched her enter with her head held high. Unlike most of the employees he'd spoken to that morning, this woman appeared as calm as a millpond. She'd done her hair 'specially and doused it in hairspray, pulling it back in a French plait she'd seen in *Woman's Own*. That morning she'd taken extra care when dressing and wore her best black 'funeral' frock with black tights and shoes.

"Morning, Mrs McGill," James said quietly, encouraging her to sit. He observed her pride in how smartly presented she was.

"Morning, Mr Henderson," she said, poised but at the same time holding back the lump rising involuntarily in her throat.

Paul Doherty skulked in a corner; he hated all this and admired how his boss handled it. Paul had known Sharon McGill most of his life. She was one of the site's most popular, loyal, strong-minded, hard-working women. He'd felt a wrench in his gut when he saw her name on the redundancy list produced by a penitent, Alfie McScott. She was one of the best workers they had, but she was one of the most expensive, too. Given her length of service and experience, she was fast and produced more products than most of the other women.

James picked up his prepared script and was about to start reading from it when he was stopped by the teary-eyed woman, who raised one hand to stall him.

"Mr Henderson, you really don't need to do that. I know why I'm here. And before you say any more, I have to tell you something."

Not taking her eyes off James for one second, she breathed deeply to contain herself.

"It's been a privilege to have worked for you and your Uncle, Mr Henderson. He was well-liked, and all of us downstairs know how hard you've tried to keep this place going since he passed away."

It wasn't the first time he'd heard this said today by the very people whose lives he was changing for the worse. How amazing his uncle Roger was, how they admired James for keeping the place open; Rocola had lasted much longer than they ever thought it could, and they were as sorry as he was that times were so hard. Upon hearing the generous comments, James's heart ached.

The women had remained stoic even when told of their diluted redundancy package. The factory couldn't pay them what they deserved, and James knew he couldn't ask Marleen for more money.

"You're very kind, Mrs McGill," he thanked her civilly. "You can imagine how difficult this is for everyone concerned. I can only say thank you." Though it was early in the afternoon, he'd have sold his soul for a drink.

The woman nodded. "So what happens now?"

James began to talk through her redundancy package and its timing. The darkly dressed woman sat silent, still and shocked. The offer was way less than she and Andrew had hoped, meaning he'd have to go to Liverpool sooner than they'd planned. Nevertheless, she remained calm and fought the hammering of her heart in its bid to escape from her chest.

"Any questions, Mrs McGill?" James asked sympathetically, knowing from the woman's perplexed expression that she was shaken and bitterly disappointed.

"No, Mr Henderson, I don't think so. That's fine," she replied.

James bowed his head. *Another one who was making it easy for him.*

"Right, Mrs McGill. And thank you again for everything."

Sharon McGill acknowledged his thanks with a quick nod. He stood as she was led out of the office by Paul, who gently closed the door. Mrs Parkes discreetly watched the pair leave and then, without being asked, quickly prepared some tea and placed a cup and saucer on James's desk. He looked haggard.

She recalled his swaggering, overconfident arrival at Rocola years before. He was all cocky and self-assured, and then the eejit got involved with Caitlin McLaughlin. At the time, she'd thought he deserved what he got, but after the bedlam at the City Hotel, his father's death, and then poor Roger Henderson's, she only felt pity for him.

James Junior changed after that; he'd grown contrite and sad, and to top it all, he'd had that runaway wife of his to deal with, who left him with twins to care for on his own. There was no trace in him of the man he'd once been; he looked worn out and beaten.

"Thank you, Mrs Parkes," he said appreciatively.

"Barely three more to go, Mr Henderson," she said, hoping to offer consolation.

"But plenty more tomorrow," he replied gloomily, hunching over the redundancy list. Mrs Parkes nodded to show she understood; it would be a long, sad week.

****

Three offices down from James's, Alfie McScott was still actively pursuing FYJH, trying to find some form of compensation for the lost order. However, he discovered that FYJH & Sons Ltd was closed by Companies House the day after the order was cancelled. The more McScott dug, the more he suspected something devious was at work.

He recoiled when he thought of the despondent expression on James Henderson's face these days, and McScott's recklessness had caused it – that fact was killing him. Nevertheless, he was determined to get to the bottom of it. A sudden knock on his office door alerted him to a visitor.

Paul half-smiled at the bespectacled man working away, surrounded by reams of papers and books. His puffy lids and heavy eye bags confirmed his remitting efforts to solve their problems. Paul felt a quiet respect for Alfie, who kept himself to himself, worked extremely hard and got on with the job. No one knew very much about his personal life and always thought him a bit of a dark horse but one who was very good at his job.

"Any luck?" Paul asked.

Alfie motioned his colleague in. "Nothing new. It's all very odd, Paul, and I'm trying to get my head around it. It's maddening. They've shut everything down without a trace the very next day after cancelling the order."

Paul was still learning about the ins and outs of limited companies, shares and partnerships. At times it was gobbledygook to him. Still, he felt for the older man and wanted to offer his support.

"This is what you're best at, Alfie. You'll sort it. We know you will."

Alfie kept quiet until Paul heedlessly piped up to fill the awkward silence.

"At least the women are taking it pretty well, though the boss is struggling." *Christ – not what Alfie needed to hear!*

He coughed self-consciously and quickly added, "It would've happened sooner or later, Alfie, you know that. It was a matter of time."

"I know, I know. It doesn't help me feel any better, though."

Paul patted his colleague's shoulder and left without another word, unsure whether he'd been a help or a hindrance.

Alfie groaned. It didn't matter how inevitable these redundancies were; he was the one who'd expedited the process, and for that, he'd never forgive himself. Somehow, he'd make it up to James Henderson and the incredible women of Rocola.

****

On a whim, Pen suspected Marleen was again two-timing her – with a man. She was devastated. She had been awake most of the night and now stood alone in her Sloane Square flat, looking down onto the street, feeling utterly heartbroken. It was raining heavily, very early in the dusky morning. Black-painted Victorian streetlamps shone brightly on the wet paving flags and parked cars. She wondered what they'd looked like in the old days, flickering with gas.

To ease the pain of Marleen's continual lies and evasions, Pen spent as much time as possible at the Hyde Park stables these days, riding out for hours. To her astonishment, she was beginning to find London life tiresome. Her body was telling her the party was over, and she wondered whether it was time for her to go back home to Somerset.

The previous evening the shit had indeed hit the fan when Marleen finally turned up after being MIA for days. Pen had received some upsetting news about one of her horses who'd been put down and had been desperate to find her lover but couldn't – no one seemed to know where she was.

In time, Marleen turned up, looking suitably contrite. Before she even had the chance to take her coat off or put her bag down, Pen had lost it. Black rage erupted. With blood pounding in her ears, she bawled: "I've been trying to get you for days, Mar! Where the fuck have you been?"

She threw the book she'd been trying to read at Marleen, who promptly ducked and sidled over to the far side of the room. She wasn't prepared for Pen's wrath and swiftly decided it was time to come clean. *No more lies.*

"I was with Jack."

Pen was aghast. Not Jack Edmonds? Though mega-rich, the man was a bore of the worst kind!

"What the fuck were you doing with him!"

"I might marry him, Pen," Marleen replied, knowing this would be a tricky conversation. Not only would she have to explain her infidelity to Pen, but she'd also concluded that she'd screwed James over for too long and cost her their friendship. As for the twins, she couldn't see a way of fixing things with them now; it was too late and probably right that she stay out of their life, though she did want her parents to have the chance to spend time with them.

She saw the hurt on Pen's face and knew she wasn't often lost for words. Her lover stood rigid in shock. Why on God's earth would Marleen want to marry… *Ah-ha!* And the answer hit her as a light went on in her brain; it was that obvious.

"This is about money. That's it – his money!" Pen jeered, shaking her head in disbelief.

Marleen wasn't going to deny it. Pen knew her too well.

Dropping heavily into a deep-seated Laura Ashley sofa, Pen grabbed a cushion and sat hugging it for comfort. She began to rock back and forth as the enormity of this news took hold. Her eyes glazed slightly, and she asked without looking up, "How long?"

"Not long. Not really," Marleen replied tersely.

Pen raised an eyebrow questioningly and stared, testing her. "How long is not long?"

"A while."

Pen repeated the question with a growing sense of frustration.

"How fucking long, Mar?"

"Six months, give or take," Marleen told her lamely, lying through her teeth.

Pen screwed up her eyes and released a painful sob as if she was at a funeral. Marleen sat beside her and tried to take her arm, but Pen wasn't having it and angrily pulled away.

"Please, Pen, let me explain. My trust fund is drying up, and I have to do something about money, but that doesn't mean we can't still see each other. I promise we will. Jack is besotted and generous and knows nothing about you and me. We can still go away together; he'll be back and forth to New Zealand half the time anyway. Please, I know I hurt you before by marrying James. But you must understand that was to secure two family lines. Now I need another marriage to survive. Please help me."

"Help you? Help you!" Pen cried, jumping up and away from Marleen as if she was contagious. "I don't bloody think so! Not this time. No more. Just go. You've clearly made your choice."

Marleen did as she asked and quietly left. She pressed the lift's call button in the hallway and waited. No sooner did it arrive when Marleen turned to hear Pen's howls of grief from the apartment.

****

Chapter Twenty-two

Liam McFadden was ready, steady, and so willing to go! The airport concourse was buzzing with excitement as the young boys and girls were given name badges on lanyards that they dutifully hung around their necks.

He felt like a millionaire! He wore a new pair of smart dark trousers, a green and blue plaid jacket and a V-neck dark green jumper over a clean white shirt finished off with one of his da's rarely used striped ties. He noticed the others were dressed in casual jeans and jumpers, and although he stood out like a sore thumb, dressed up to the nines, he couldn't care less. He'd seen all the business people on planes on the box and decided – much to Emmett's amusement – he'd look the same.

"Liam! Liam! Are you listening to me!" he heard his ma nag him. Waving a hand to stop her yelling, he mimicked her many warnings to him while simultaneously trying to take in the sight of the enormous green and white Aer Lingus jumbo on Dublin airport's sodden runway.

"*Don't forget to say please and thank you! Don't forget to say your prayers! Don't forget this! Don't forget that! Don't…* I know, Ma! I've been listening!"

He stopped when he saw her wounded expression. His face fell, and he grabbed her hand to comfort her.

"I've got it, Mammy. I know what to do. You've been at me for weeks. I promise I won't let you down. Anyway, I want them to ask me back!"

He'd it all worked out. He'd act so lovely and cute they couldn't resist but ask him back. His ma returned a half-smile, and he immediately felt better.

His da couldn't make the long journey with them to the airport. He was working an early shift. Maggie insisted she'd join the holidaymakers on the airport bus. She'd offered to help keep the excited children under control. Matt, the bus driver, was loving it – quite a change from his usual riot-threatened route. By the time he crossed Craigavon Bridge, the adults had lost all control, and the kids were running riot. Their shrieking, yelling and laughter couldn't be stopped, and the exhilaration of it was infectious.

If only you could bottle it. The sound of happy children was a tonic.

The order to board came, and it was time for Liam to leave. Maggie hugged him so tight and fussed over him so much that he blushed from embarrassment. She cupped his face and brushed back a few strands of his hair.

"Jeepers, Mammy, not in front of everyone!"

Maggie couldn't help but laugh even while her eyes filled with tears. She told him she loved him and warned him once more to be good. It was the first time he'd not sleep in his own bed. A small part of her was nervous at the thought of him going up in the sky on that jumbo jet. The bloody thing was huge.

Even when Liam was well out of sight, Maggie continued to wave. Finally, she removed a small white handkerchief from her well-worn fake leather handbag and carefully wiped her face with it. Patting the back of her freshly dyed hair to ensure it was in place, she sighed with satisfaction. *A son of hers with the chance to visit America*! It was a miracle!

****

When Maggie eventually made it home to Blamfield Street, she opened the front door to be met by unusual quietness. The house felt cold and eerily undisturbed. It was so still that she'd even welcome the customary yelling from number 30. She hated silence.

Fiddling to remove the stubborn key, she caught sight of some post lying on the mat. Picking up the assortment of mostly brown envelopes and sliding them under her arm, she made her way to her neat kitchen for a cuppa. She put her handbag and the unopened post on the table.

Before removing her coat, she lit the gas and put the kettle on. Next to the sink, she quickly switched on a Bush radio to drown out the house's unnerving silence, took her coat off and hung it in its usual spot under the stairs.

A BBC newscaster announced that the Falkland Islands had been recaptured by the British Forces, thus ending the war. *Who cares?* Maggie thought. *What about us? What about this war on their doorstep, not tens of bloody thousands of miles away!*

Once she'd made the tea, she dug deep in her handbag for her glasses and began to inspect the post. It was the usual stuff, bills, bills and more bills. She came across a small white envelope, well-worn and torn, and paused. Someone had written half their address in a childish scribble but addressed it to Liam – there was no house number. There wasn't a stamp either, and Maggie was pleasantly surprised the postie'd delivered it. But Liam wasn't here. Should she… filled with curiosity, she tore the envelope open.

Dear Liam

It's horrible here, and they're doing awful things to me. Tell your ma and da to come and get me. I mean it, Liam, please. Vinny x

"Sweet Mother of God!" Maggie cried, throwing the crumpled piece of paper onto the table as if it was toxic. *What the heck?* She didn't know what to think but steadied herself, drank some tea and picked it up to reread the short message. She could remember Vinny Kelly running in and out of their house for years. He was like a surrogate son and one of Liam's best friends. She'd been on to Social Services for ages trying to get the wee lad relocated back to Derry, even offering to foster him herself. She was fond of Vinny and knew what he meant to her son. Still, they weren't related, so the social workers didn't want to know. With their added workload, thanks to the frequent disruptions, they refused to listen.

Poor Vinny, Maggie thought, wait 'til her Charlie heard about this. He'd be up the social so fast! Maggie drank her tea and read the short note a third time. Her determination mounted to get the boy home. She'd an idea what 'awful things' meant! *The poor wee dote.*

****

Liam McFadden swore he'd never 'til the day he died forget the feeling of the jumbo jet taking off from Aldergrove Airport. One minute he was holding on for dear life to his seat. The next, the friggin' thing was up, up and away! The white-laden clouds reminded him of rolling waves as the plane sliced through the sky.

The well-groomed, Irish green-garbed Aer Lingus crew knew already what they were in for. Most opted for an early night before this trip – it was a never-ending workout. The first hour or two were the worst – chaos – as the over-enthusiastic kids' attention span lasted mere seconds. They murdered the call bells, continually crying, "*Miss! Miss! Miss!*" The kids pressed every button on the Aer Lingus Classic seats, sending tray tables tilting and seats falling back. It seemed that all the children would simultaneously have a sudden need for the bathroom – purely as an excuse to see what it looked like and where all the shit and pee went!

It would be a long flight, especially after the youngsters had had three or four glasses of sugary drinks, sending them extra hyper. However, their young passengers' contagious delight and excitement won over the crew.

Liam lay back in his seat next to the window and made himself comfortable. He wasn't quite confident enough to take off his seat belt yet. Out of the side of his eye, he scrutinised the boy beside him, who was extremely quiet and had not yet spoken a word. Perhaps the wee man was nervous or mega shy, and Liam wondered if he should try and talk to him. Feeling all grown up in his shirt and tie, he extended one hand and happily introduced himself.

"How ye doin'? I'm Liam. Liam McFadden from Derry."

"Henry Sharpe," the other boy answered sourly.

Liam took him in. Henry had squinty eyes with heavy dark shadows beneath them. Sharpe's severely cut, mousy brown hair had a jagged fringe. He wore a thin, off-white T-shirt under a light zipped-up polyester jacket and navy polyester trousers. For some reason, Liam felt sorry for him.

"Where you from?" he asked to make small talk.

"Belfast."

"Which part?"

"The Shankill."

"Where 'bouts is that then?" Liam probed. He'd heard of 'The Shankill' but had never been to Belfast.

"Belfast," the boy answered again in a sour voice.

"My best friend Vinny lives somewhere in East Belfast." Liam excitedly ignored Sharpe's lack of interest in him. "I'm hoping to get him back to Derry soon to live at ours."

At this, Liam's fellow passenger perked up a little. East Belfast? Hmm. "Where 'bouts?"

"Ah, poor Vinny, it's well sad. He's in some children's home."

Henry grunted and said nothing more to let the rambling prat next to him know he couldn't care less. Minutes passed until Henry casually asked, "What are you then?"

"What do you mean?" Liam replied, slightly confused.

The boy tutted in annoyance. "Are you a left-footer or a right-footer?"

"What do you mean?" Liam repeated. He had no idea what the lad was going on about and started to laugh, which seemed to antagonise Henry Sharpe more.

"Catch yourself on! Are you a Catholic – a Taig?" he bellowed in a robust East Belfast accent. Trust him to end up sitting next to a green sponger.

Liam suddenly understood. *What a twat!*

"In that case, I'm a Taig and proud of it," he said, continuing to laugh, but stopped when a scornful look spread over Henry's face and Liam heard his following harsh words.

"Ah, shit. Frig! I knew I'd get stuck with a Taig! Look at the shape of you – all dressed up like some old man going for a job!"

Liam was embarrassed and felt foolish after the boy's hateful outburst. *Emmett was right; the shirt, tie, and briefcase were way overboard.* All the same, anger bubbled in the pit of his stomach.

"I take it you're an orange Jaffa then!" he retorted in a bid to save face. He crossed his legs and began to remove his tie.

"Aye, and proud of it!"

Like clawing and screeching cats, the boys reached for each other, pulling on hair and scratching faces. Bemused young passengers watched in stunned silence until they began to shout and clap, "*Fight! Fight! Fight!*"

Liam immediately regretted keeping his seat belt on since it restricted him from getting a good run at his attacker, who had now jumped onto his lap to yank and tear at his hair. Crying at the top of his voice, Liam warned his assailant to stop.

"I'm warning you, ye Jaffa bastard! Get off me!"

"*Fight! Fight! Fight!*" yelled the other children until a lone hostess and a couple of Project Children supervisors rushed over in single file to break up the boys. Somehow a pretty stewardess eventually managed to get Liam's opponent off him. In a friendly but firm voice, she cried, "Boys! What on God's earth?"

The youngsters pointed at each other and cried, "He started it!"

The flight attendants had noticed Liam as soon as he climbed on board. *Bless him.* He'd stood out like a sore thumb in his jacket and tie, clearly in awe of the experience. He was even carrying an attaché case! For him to be fighting like this was surprising. In a pleasant but unwavering voice, she told the other adults who'd gathered around to leave her to it.

The hostess got down on her hunkers beside Liam, stared at the two rascals and declared in a stern, no-nonsense manner, "Now, tell me, what was that display all about?" She was met by stubborn silence and encouragingly asked them again, "Come on, boys. Tell me."

Catching Liam's eye, she told him warmly, "Look at you, all dressed up in your best. And you," she said quickly, turning to Henry, "you're hardly on the plane, and you're fighting. Why's that, then!"

Liam felt bad. The woman was so lovely and pretty, but he'd no choice – he had to stick up for himself.

"He called me a Taig and then went for me. I felt sorry for him and was just saying hello!" Liam told her in a slightly hurt tone.

The stewardess smiled; you couldn't but like the boy. He'd been blessed with one of those cheeky faces that you'd die to squeeze and kiss – he was so cute. Besides the suit, tie and attaché case, he reminded her of her boy at home.

Sadly the crew knew too well about incidents like this – it was inevitable. The plane was full of Catholic and Protestant children. Youngsters who'd been brainwashed to hate each other from birth and then suddenly put together offered some real challenges. Fortunately, it was a different experience on their return flight. After six weeks, they were well rested, fresh, carefree, tanned and happy – the hard-edged walls of hatred they'd built up over the years crumbled and forgotten.

With an amused smile, she explained excitedly, "Listen, boys, think about it. You're going to America. It's going to be hot, the sun shines all day, and you'll be swimming, playing baseball, canoeing… if you're lucky, horse riding! All the things you've ever dreamt about or seen on the telly. It doesn't matter where you're from. So please, for me, say sorry, shake hands and be friends."

The two reluctant schoolboys knew they'd no choice. They reluctantly mumbled a weak 'sorry' and shook each other's limp hands.

****

Chapter Twenty-three

Tommy O'Reilly stood in the middle of an eminent high-end men's shop, Grey Flannel Menswear in the Diamond, at the top of Shipquay Street. He gazed across the square to see that the city's only department store, Austins, had a summer sale. He reminded himself he should pop in after this to buy a decent shirt.

He was being measured for the morning suit he was renting for Caitlin's wedding. This sort of thing made him frustrated and edgy. He hated all the palaver and wasn't being cooperative with the patient old-timer attempting to determine his size with a well-worn tape measure.

"Sorry, I'm not very good at all this kinda stuff," Tommy said gruffly.

"Not a problem, sir, I understand," the elderly assistant replied soothingly. He'd come across all sorts in his day and dealt with much worse than this gentleman.

Tommy had chopped and changed the appointment for weeks until Caitlin snapped at him on the phone, "Get on with it. It's embarrassing. You've changed it too many times already!"

From her out-of-character snappish tone, he felt something was up, but as usual, she kept it to herself. When he'd asked after Chris, she'd been even more abrupt, and Tommy hoped she wasn't having second thoughts. She'd seemed so happy when they'd met in London. Although he'd met Chris Pecaro only briefly, Tommy had taken an immediate shine to him.

The man clearly adored Caitlin and Tommy believed it was a good thing he was a wee bit older and more mature. He'd looked after her well so far.

Tommy and Gerard McFarland had continued in their efforts to reopen talks with the Brits but hit a brick wall. Tommy had a strong suspicion they'd gone back to stage one. However, they were plugging away. One day…

The fitting was finally over, and he was back in his usual messy but comfortable garb of jeans, jumper and his ever-faithful, well-worn parka jacket. After finalising dates to pick up the altered morning suit, he thanked the shop assistant, gave him another apology and left. No sooner was he over the shop's threshold than he paused and lit up a badly needed John Player Special, sucking it almost dry.

Tommy was feeling scared. The weight was falling off him like no tomorrow, and it'd been the real reason he'd changed all the appointments. Feeling unwell terrified him so much that he wouldn't go to the doctor! At first, it'd only been at night, but now it was happening daily. He'd be up and down like a yoyo to pee and was spotting more blood in his urine, his lower body continually aching.

It didn't take a medical degree to know what this was, but he'd be fucked if he was going to go to the doctor over something so personal! He'd made his mind up and decided to hang on 'til after Caitlin's wedding; he'd see how he was by then. At the thought of it, a small knot tightened in his stomach.

The Diamond was quiet with few people about. Tommy pulled up his collar to make his way to his next appointment. Throwing the near-finished butt away and about to walk on, he came face to face with a person he hadn't seen in a very long time. He was shocked to see such a change in the other man's appearance.

****

Meanwhile, not too far away along the Strand Road, Paddy Gillispie and Brian Monaghan sat in the ever-popular Rainbow Café. Brian had finally given up on persuading Paddy to support Sinn Féin's new electoral strategy. He'd recognised his comrade was close to losing it with him on this topic. Paddy had made it abundantly clear he'd keep on fighting this dirty war by any means and at any price – subject over. They sat at the far end of the café in a secluded booth typically used by adulterous couples or love-struck teenagers.

Paddy was currently on a roll. Not only had he sold his big London idea to the Leadership, but he'd also managed to persuade the OC to agree to the Currys' hi-jacking. It was planned for the following night. Much to his irritation, O'Connell had suggested Liz McKenna be involved in it. Paddy had decided to keep her as close to him as possible. If the heist went well, he'd see who got all the credit.

As usual, Siobhan welcomed them warmly and dutifully served their order of tea, white toast and lots of potato bread, Paddy's favourite.

"So, what do we have?" he muttered as he doused the butter onto his bread.

Brian drank his hot tea, the veins in his neck swelling. They'd been talking intensely and for hours about their upcoming operation, and he wasn't happy about it – not one bit. Panic crept over his face; the London job was way out of his comfort zone. He preferred a 'get in, shoot and get the fuck out' process. But this idea, this idiotic notion, would not only take weeks to plan, but they'd also never done anything like it.

And demanding £1 million in ransom had to be madness, total insanity! Sweat broke out on Brian's neck as he fixed his eyes on Paddy. The unusual, feverish expression in his comrade's eyes concerned Brian, and he wondered if Paddy was thinking straight. For some time, he'd been behaving weird, all hyper-like, and Brian felt their long-term allegiance was shifting course – and not for the better. It hurt him no end, but he wasn't going to say anything about it nor rock the boat. If only this daft plan weren't taking up all of Paddy's time and attention…

"For the record, Paddy, I don't like it. Not one bit," Brian said with a steely gaze.

Paddy acknowledged his concerns with a nod. "I know. But listen, we've no choice. I've sold it to the Leadership already. That's why it's so *fucking* important we get it right from the very start!"

His voice rose as he emphasised his last few words; suddenly aware he might be overheard, he resorted to a whisper.

"So, tell me, where do we stand?"

With no choice in the matter, Brian, whom the OC had mandated to do the background checks and fact-finding on the Fox family, began to brief him. They would demand the payoff from young, self-made millionaire William Fox, married to Maryann and a new father to baby Ella.

Paddy had Maryann in his sight from the moment she breezed up to them in that crowded café. Hearing her snooty voice, seeing her mass of expensive jewellery and learning that they owned a factory in Northern Ireland, he knew the husband-and-wife duo would be worth their weight in gold to the cause. That was when the seed of this plan was sown – it was the perfect low-risk op for them.

Returning to Brian, who continued to read from his many notes, Paddy listened carefully and absorbed all the information.

"Fox was born in Somerset, has three sisters, Sarah, Penelope and Emma, but is the only son and heir of Spencer and Elizabeth Fox, who's loaded. We're talking zillions here. Old money, inherited, though Bill Fox has gone and made a pile of his own. Lucky us."

Paddy's excitement gauge went through the roof as he encouraged Brian to continue.

"His staff and locals like Fox. He's brought loads of jobs to Ballymena and is even talking about investing in Derry."

Paddy couldn't give a fuck about Ballymena; it was a solid Protestant district and one he'd made a point of never visiting. Derry wasn't particularly on his agenda either.

"Fuck that, Brian! I need to know more about where he lives. His daily routine. Who he works with? Who his friends are? What car he drives? Does he have a girlfriend, a favourite mistress, a boyfriend? I want everything to his feckin' shoe size…!"

Paddy ran his hand through his hair in exasperation. "I want *everything*, Brian. We need to know when the man shits! And not all about him but his wife too: where she goes, who her friends are other than Tommy's girl. Leave *her* out of this. I want to know everything and anything about the Foxes!"

Brian jerked backwards as if he'd been hit.

"Ssshhhh, Paddy. For fuck's sake, keep it down!" he hushed him, growing angry at such a tirade of frenzied questions.

Siobhan made her way over to their booth. The two men were evidently at odds, and she asked politely, "You gentlemen okay here? Do you need anything else?"

She watched as they sat back in the booth and politely told her, "No, thank you, Siobhan, we're grand."

With a look that told them to keep it down, Siobhan Devlin retreated to the back of the counter and began to wipe it down. Brian's eyes followed her thoughtfully and caught her watching him. He gave her a small half-wave before smacking Paddy like a child on his upper arm. "Jesus, listen to me; take it easy, okay? I've got all that. Give me a feckin' chance, will you!"

Feeling self-conscious about being told off, Paddy nodded. He was bang out of order. This was Brian, for fuck's sake. *Brian Mensa Monaghan*, wasn't he the one with the brains? If Brian couldn't make this op a success, then who could? *Shit*. Better not try that ecstasy stuff again; it was doing Paddy's head in, making him all hyper and paranoid. Taking drugs was hated by the Provos nearly as much as anyone who informed and taking MDMA meant Paddy Gillispie was walking on very thin ice.

****

James Henderson made his way across the Diamond, holding tightly to the twins' hands, Charlotte on his left and PJ on his right. They enjoyed a little shopping and were almost finished. They'd make one last call to make on a local tailor who'd been recommended to James. As he approached the shop, he was surprised and secretly pleased to see Tommy O'Reilly stepping out. He watched as the man, a little nervous and unsteady, quickly lit a cigarette and took an almighty but impressive drag to steady himself. Even from a short distance, James noticed Tommy's face had an unaccustomed pallor.

With a broad smile and still holding on to the twins, he rushed over and enthusiastically offered his hand.

"Ah, Tommy, it's so good to see you. It's been a long time."

He accepted the proffered hand and shook it with genuine delight.

"It has, James. It's good to see you too! Time goes by so fast these days; I must be getting old!" he replied heartily. "How've you been keeping?"

James pre-emptively grasped PJ and Charlotte's hands again and still holding them, raised them in the air and replied, "These two keep me busy, Tommy. It's never-ending!"

He chuckled. "You've certainly got your hands full there!" Crouching down, Tommy asked, "What's your name then, young lady?"

The child was beautiful, with the most amazing green eyes and white-blonde curly hair that flowed freely to her waist. She replied with great composure, "I'm Charlotte Henderson, and this is my twin brother PJ – or Peter James Henderson!"

She looked proudly at her sibling and continued to babble on, telling Tommy they'd been shopping and displaying their purchases.

What a joy, Tommy thought. He wasn't ordinarily patient with children, but this one was a real character, so he listened attentively to her. Once her feast of words was finished, he carefully stood up and gently patted the child's head while glancing at her father. James had aged badly for a naturally handsome fella. He reminded Tommy of a soldier returning from the front.

"How are you, James? You're looking a wee bit tired."

"It's been a tough time, Tommy, especially over the past few months, as you've no doubt heard?"

"I have, James, and I'm sorry. We all know you and Roger did everything you could. But, hey, you're still going!" Tommy said, attempting to end the conversation on an upbeat note.

James sighed, "I suppose so, Tommy, and we've a couple of things in the pipeline. They'll not solve all our problems but maybe offer us a glimpse of light at the end of a very dark tunnel."

"I wish you well with that. No one deserves it more." There wasn't much left to say until James enquired, "Been shopping too, Tommy?"

"Nah, not really, just getting round to sorting myself out with one of those fancy morning suits," he replied with a smile before whispering, "A total pain in the arse, to be honest. I can't say I'm looking forward to the thought of dressing meself up in one of those things!"

James understood.

"You'll be pleasantly surprised, Tommy. The whole dressing up a bit is fun when it happens. Is it for a wedding?" he asked without thinking.

Time stood still for Tommy. *Fuck!* What little colour was left in his face suddenly dissipated, and within seconds James knew. *Caitlin was getting married.*

Sensing the older man's embarrassment and not wanting to upset him, James added, "Ah, Tommy, I suppose it had to happen sooner or later."

"Suppose so, James. I've so much going on in this head that I didn't think properly. I'm sorry; you shouldn't have found out like this."

"Don't worry, Tommy. I hope she's happy and that he's a good man."

"She is, James, and he is good to her."

Intuitively, the twins sensed the uneasy atmosphere and began to drag their father towards the shop. Tommy was grateful to the youngsters. He pulled his parka more tightly around him and touched James's shoulder.

"Be seeing you, James. Good luck."

"And you, Tommy. Send my best to the happy couple," James countered. Taking the deepest of deep breaths, he held tight to the twins' hands and headed inside, pushing open the shop's glass door with one shoulder.

****

Henry Sharpe's prayers on the flight to New York's JFK remained unanswered – let alone heard – as one of the adults called out his name along with Liam McFadden's.

Sweat was pouring off him as he felt himself pushed towards the Taig and then in the direction of a middle-aged couple dressed like something from *Little House on the Prairie*. The woman's smile was open and welcoming. A giant of a fella with long greying hair tied back in a ponytail stood next to her. He was dressed in a red-and-black plaid shirt, blue jeans with predictable red braces and rugged black-nailed boots. He smiled lovingly at the petite woman next to him, his wife Maisie, a doll-like five foot one beside her husband's six foot five.

Mr and Mrs Frankie Campbell were of Irish descent. They had worked tirelessly in the background helping the Project Children organisers but until now had never considered volunteering themselves as hosts.

Months ago, the boys' appointed hosts had cancelled due to illness, and O'Halloran suggested the Campbells take them on instead, according to the standard guidelines of one Catholic, one Protestant. They certainly had the space and, with no children of their own, were excited at the prospect of having youngsters in the house. Their neighbour had two older boys the Campbells had known and loved from birth. They believed the Irish visitors would get along fine with Dale and Carter Matijasavich. Frankie promptly painted and refreshed their spare room and furnished it with two single beds, a desk between them and some other pieces of second-hand furniture. It was perfect.

Liam wasn't sure how he'd describe the feeling that overtook him when he realised the Jaffa was coming with them. Simply put, he was baffled, and the Jaffa was feeling the same from the expression of horror on his face.

"Well, hi, boys! I'm Frankie!" their host sang as he offered them his massive hand in welcome. Liam's was swallowed up and crushed in the man's eagerness. He did the same to the Jaffa as, without warning, the tiny woman snatched Liam into her stick-thin arms with enough force to make him groan aloud.

"Hello there," Maisie said in a Southern accent. She'd been preparing for weeks for their arrival and had arranged a short sabbatical from the local hospital, where she'd been a nurse for over thirty years, to spend the next six weeks with the kids.

"Hello," the two disgruntled boys replied, looking miserable but trying not to be rude.

Maisie instantaneously picked up on their expression and tone. The couple had been pre-warned that this could happen. Once some kids found out they would have to share with an enemy Catholic or Protestant, they went ballistic.

Frankie smiled as he swapped a look with his wife. Even after twenty-five years of marriage, it still made his insides go funny to think that she was his. He loved her with his whole being.

They'd been through so much together, having lost many beautiful full-term babies. He'd never understand how; she'd done everything she could to be healthy during each pregnancy, only to go through the birth trauma and then lose the baby after one or two days. After their sixth attempt, he'd finally convinced her to give up. Bridget first, then Christopher, Andrew, Mary, Anne and Christina – all treasured, if only for a short time.

"Let's get home, boys. I'm right sure you're exhausted after that long flight!" Frankie announced. "The truck isn't too far away."

The four of them began to walk through the terminal, took several lifts and then a series of endless passageways until they eventually reached their parking space in the ten-storey garage.

Neither Liam nor Henry spoke, the jetlag and tedium of the trip finally taking effect. Normally they'd be thrilled at seeing Frankie's yellow high-wheeled truck – it was huge – but they were knackered by now.

Frankie had hoped they'd comment on his wheels that he'd meticulously cleaned and polished and felt somewhat disappointed to receive no reaction from his guests. Again, he looked over at Maisie, who understood and explained.

"They're exhausted, Frankie; give them time. Wait 'til tomorrow – they'll love it."

By the time they exited the parking garage, Frankie had seen in his rear mirror that the boys were already out cold. He laughed when he noticed the bigger fella's head had fallen comfortably and peacefully onto the other's shoulder, drool oozing from the side of his mouth.

"Would you look at that?" Frankie whispered tenderly, stroking Maisie's arm. "They're only normal kids, but did you see their faces when they realised they'd been put together? It must be a hell of a mess over there in Ireland."

Maisie nodded. She knew many Irish nurses who'd left home because of The Troubles and had heard how chaotic, brutal, and fruitless it all was. That had only made her more determined to give these two the time of their lives. They now had a long drive ahead of them and hoped, with the boys out cold, they'd manage it with no hold-ups.

After three or so hours, they finally arrived at their eighteenth-century wooden-framed farmhouse, the exterior painted white and grey, with a welcoming ornate iron porch. Maisie had inherited the place from her grandmother. She adored its old-fashioned aura and the mature garden that contained everything from roses to magnolias, all overhung by a glorious weeping cherry that stood guard over the flower beds. An expansive sweeping lawn led to a wooden pier beside a moonlit lake.

The boys woke up when the truck stopped. Liam nearly jumped out of his skin when he discovered the Jaffa leaning on him. He growled, pushed the other boy off and wiped his mouth in confusion as he tried to make sense of where he was. As he took in the view, he rubbed his eyes and heard Frank say, "Come on, guys, let's get you something to eat."

Liam didn't need to be told twice. He jumped from the high-wheeled vehicle. The first thing that struck him was the warmth of the night air. It was comforting, and a giant full moon shone across an enchanting vista – Greenwood Lake. The noise of crickets added to the cacophony of other insects and animals. A dog began to bark somewhere close by and ran happily towards them.

Henry Sharpe didn't like dogs and instinctively stood behind Liam, who did, completely unafraid after befriending the many mongrels of Creggan Heights. He welcomed the big brute as it bounced across the lawn from the house next door. Liam knelt and opened his arms to embrace the dog. At first sight, he fell in love with the dark chocolate Labrador that pounced on him, wagging its tail with joy.

Maisie sensed Henry's fear and took his arm. "He's a kindly animal, Henry, just a pup. It's Toby, our neighbour's dog. He'll do ye' no harm."

Liam looked at Henry and smiled briefly. "Look, Jaffa! Sure he's a dote, drooling all over the joint!" Liam thought it funny that he was already using American jargon. He gripped the excited dog's collar tightly and then led him closer to Henry, who remained cautious and jumpy.

"He's a big softie, aren't you, Toby?" Liam commented, kneeling. He continued to pat the animal and scratch it hard under its chin. He then approached Henry and suggested he give it a try. "Come on, all dogs love a scratch right under the chin, have a go."

Maisie and Frankie watched as Henry's hand tentatively reached out to stroke Toby; it was as if the dog sensed the boy's uneasiness. Reassuringly, still slobbering, he licked Henry's hand.

He giggled and gave the other boy a brief nod of thanks but stepped away when Liam cried, "See, Jaffa? He likes you!"

"Jaffa! Will you stop calling me names?" Henry grunted, quickly distancing himself. He looked at Maisie imploringly. "Can we go in now, please?"

****

Chapter Twenty-four

MI5 identified and neutralised domestic security threats within the UK. These men and women played by a different rule book from M16, enjoying an arsenal of powers conferred on them by British law, which meant they could do whatever it took to safeguard the nation.

Left with no choice, they arrested his childlike younger sister Shannon when Cawley continued being recalcitrant with them.

They decided they'd interrogate the girl themselves. It'd be more effective if she passed on the message that they weren't prepared to keep up with Cawley's silence any longer. The terrified youngster was duly lifted from her home and taken by the RUC to Castlereagh Holding Centre.

As an additional tactic, they'd also arrested her boyfriend, Gavin White, a twenty-year-old Queen's University student. The plan was to play off one against the other. It was an approach that often paid dividends.

They recalled how she'd looked when they'd placed her in a cold, poorly cleaned interview room, with its lingering smells of vomit and piss. Shannon was a sorry sight, wearing a knee-length cotton nightdress under a bright yellow woollen cardigan along with a fluffy pair of babyish duck-faced slippers. Her blonde permed hair was worn long with a thick fringe that covered her frightened eyes. Without her usual headband, it was annoying her so much that she kept flicking it away, only for it to fall straight back. She was extremely nervous and fearful, but she shed no tears – they thought she likely didn't want to appear weak.

It was well known that female MI5 interrogators were more abrupt and unsympathetic when interviewing the fairer sex. Cawley's handler brought one with him and left her to her own devices. They'd nothing on the girl but could lawfully keep her here for up to seven days, and if necessary, they would. By now, Cawley had to know they were detaining her.

The interrogation lasted for hours, with the odd intermittent break when they'd place her in a windowless cell with a bed and a chair chained to the floor. Back in the interview room, there was a police statement on the table, ready for her attention.

"Read it!" they screamed at her repeatedly. "That's Gavin's signature! See… there?" The female agent pointed. "He's told us everything!"

But Cawley's sister didn't recognise her new boyfriend's signature, for fuck's sake! They'd only been going out for a couple of weeks.

"I hardly know him! I don't know if that's his signature," she cried.

With a half-leer, half-smile, the woman laughed and told her, "Let's talk sense here. You don't seem to understand: your boyfriend has told us you've been hiding guns for the Provos and letting the bastards use your place as a safe house."

The young student persistently denied it, screaming, "It's not even my house! I rent a room, for Christ's sake! I'm at Uni!"

Feeling terrified, Shannon had no comprehension of what was happening here. All she knew was that she'd done nothing wrong. Her older brother had brought up her and her sister after their parents died when a café was blown up in Belfast. He'd always told them not to get involved politically but to keep their noses clean. That's what she'd been doing. He'd also warned them: *Whatever you do if you're ever lifted – say nothing!*

Easier said than done. Feeling so tired and hungry, the young girl would do anything to escape the horror of this place – she'd heard about Castlereagh; everyone had.

As time went on, the female agent's tone began to soften.

"Listen, love, sign here, and we'll let you go. You could be home in your bed in half an hour, and all this will be over." She added craftily, "We have a car ready to take you back. You're tired; we're tired. Please sign there, and we'll sort this sorry mess out later. How about that?"

The frightened girl had had enough. As she signed the confession, the prospect of getting home was too alluring, and Shannon felt only relief, a vast life-changing relief.

Cawley always knew his younger sister wasn't hardball, that she'd break easily; he wasn't surprised when she called him and told him what'd happened.

They had him firmly by the balls with his sibling's confession and could send her away without notice – he'd no choice now but to deliver. Give them something worthwhile and concrete.

****

Chapter Twenty-five

Liz McKenna was nothing short of elated. After Paddy Gillispie heard the details of her heist plan, he'd passed them on to the OC and returned a few days later with the okay. He didn't look the best when he told her the OC wanted them to work closely on it. *Same old, same old*, she thought. Simply because she was a woman. But hadn't she done all the footwork and planned it down to the last detail? She didn't need Gillispie breathing down her neck. The plan wouldn't work without her, and she'd prove herself for sure this time.

A few weeks later, Liz and Paddy waited in a hired car near Belfast docks. They surveyed the laden Currys lorry drive onto the M2 motorway towards Derry with its precious load. They took off after the truck and followed it until it slowed down and pulled in next to some public toilets in the heart of Dungiven village, eighteen miles or so outside Derry.

On the far side of the road, the remainder of Liz's cell, Jon and Jim, sat waiting in a 'borrowed' Mother's Pride bread van. Next to Jim sat a somewhat nervous and recently qualified HGV driver, Donal Duggan.

As instructed, the Currys driver, Peter Rafferty, climbed down from his cab.

He'd first met Liz at the Stardust disco in the heart of the Bogside and fancied her like mad. He would've done anything to impress her at first. After he'd taken her out a few times, he discovered she was in the Provos. Desperately needing some cash – with hindsight, how fuckin' stupid of him – he'd shared his big idea, and she'd jumped at it.

The plan was for him to leave the keys in the lorry, go to the men's and wait. Someone would drive Peter around for a couple of hours, then bring him back. He'd go into Dungiven police station a few hundred metres away and report the lorry stolen. It was that easy.

The A6, usually manic and busy as the main artery to Derry, ran through the heart of the village but was luckily quiet at this time of night. As midnight approached, Jon and Jim stepped into the Gents to meet the driver.

"Hanging in there, Pete?" Jim asked as he took a piss.

"Aye," Peter responded. He listened as Jim went over the plan with him again.

"We'll nab you here and take a wee drive together, okay?" Jim told him, zipping up his Pepe jeans and pulling down his blue denim jacket. He didn't attempt to go near the only washbasin when without warning, he was suddenly grabbing Peter by the collar and head-butting him.

Shocked, Peter wailed, "What the fuck? What'd you do that for!" His eyes began to water.

Shit, it hurt!

"Don't be such a wuss!" Jim chuckled.

"We have to give you a wee bit of a hiding, don't we? Remember, you're hi-jacked, you stupid git. It makes it look more real like!" said Jon.

The men continued to laugh and take the piss as Peter was roughed up some more before they dragged and threw him into the back of the bread van. Paddy and Liz were too busy getting their replacement driver ready in the lorry to notice what was happening to Peter.

Liz's concern began when she saw their replacement driver, his apparent nervousness and jumpiness. She looked at Paddy, hoping for some reassurance, but saw him half-smile, likely in the hope she'd fuck it up. Well, she wouldn't.

From the moment Donal climbed into the cab, he'd appeared a bit of a wet week, and so far, she wasn't impressed. *Where the fuck did Paddy find him?* She did her best to calm the man by making small talk. Quiet and unmoving, Donal said little, using monosyllabic responses and frantically chewing his already chomped nails. Reciting the plan, she told him what to do.

"We'll be behind you the whole way. All you have to do is drive to Washing Bay." The small village on the banks of Lough Neagh was the prearranged meeting point where the goods would be exchanged for cash.

"Got it?" Liz asked Donal ominously. He nodded uneasily and answered in a gloomy voice, "Aye. I think so."

Fuck, he'd barely passed his HGV test and didn't like the idea of driving through dark narrow country roads boxed in by hedges. He had no choice though when Paddy Gillispie had *asked* him – you were a brave man if you said no to the Provos, especially someone like Paddy G – but the girl frightened him more. There was something clinical, cold and determined about her. It was her clear grey eyes; they said it all. She was the real McCoy, and he could see her efficiently finishing him off.

"Just take it slow; we're right behind you," Liz said, patting his shoulder to reassure him and herself.

Afterwards, she quietly voiced concern to Paddy. "Where the heck did you find Donal? He looks about twelve?"

Paddy didn't feel any necessity to answer. Under the circumstances, the lad was the best he could find, and he wasn't warming to McKenna's sarcasm either. The girl was too big for her boots.

Dismissing her query, he pulled her back to the hired car and remarked casually, "He's fine. Come on. We need to get outta here."

Donal sat alone and frightened inside the lorry's cab. On his fourth attempt, he managed to start the enormous truck.

It'd gone from slightly bad to worse after that. The other two lads had given Peter such a hiding; they'd left him with a sprained wrist, broken nose, black eye and a twisted ankle. Liz's misgivings about their replacement driver proved to be correct too.

As they drove along the dark country roads following the lorry, somehow Donal, the stupid bastard, managed to get it stuck in a storm drain. At first, it wouldn't budge. To avoid drawing attention from the security forces, Paddy told Liz through the driving rain that they'd have no choice but to abandon the op.

Liz was incensed and refused. "There's no way we're leaving this here! Do you have any idea how much that consignment's worth?"

Paddy knew, but he wasn't taking the risk of getting caught. He'd too many plans of his own to carry through. "I don't care. We're going!"

"No, we are not! Let's try again, one more time."

Paddy sighed and wiped the cold rain off his face. He had to admire the woman, despite himself. She had guts. In a way, she reminded him of Dolores, his twin.

"One more time," he replied. "I mean it, one more."

At that, Liz hopped up inside the lorry's cab and looked at Donal, sitting white-faced and terrified. She breathed in and patted his shoulder. Moving closer, she pleaded with him.

"Donal, please, I need you to think hard about this. We must get moving. Please, go check where the problem is and try one more time. I promise we'll take you straight home if it doesn't work."

Donal saw the desperation in the girl's face, sighed and turned up his eyes. He'd give it a final try, and if it didn't work, he'd be home in a hot bath in a couple of hours.

"Right you are, but one go." He pulled a waterproof jacket on and went to the back of the lorry to check it out. Paddy waited inside the car and watched while Liz stood getting soaked along with the driver. After Donal had finished inspecting the mud and storm drain, he pulled a piece of wood from the back of the lorry and placed it beside the hard-wearing wheels. He waved at Liz and climbed back up again to turn the engine on.

Paddy could hear the ratcheting noise of Donal's efforts as he struggled to get free. It wasn't working. As Paddy was about to climb out of the car and stop them, he heard Liz's screams.

"You've done it, Donal! You've only gone and feckin' done it!"

She looked over at Paddy and gave him a fuck-you-I-did-it look, her face alive with victory. Jumping up into the cab, she grabbed Donal and smothered his face in kisses.

"Thank you! Thank you, Donal, you're a star!"

When they eventually got to the meeting place, their waiting partners in crime, travellers, were excited to see such a valuable load and paid generously.

Paddy said very little in the car but was grudgingly pleased for the girl. He saw the thousands in cash stashed in plaid laundry bags and threw the money into the back of the car, feeling much happier. The OC would be more than pleased with that lot.

Days later, Peter Rafferty accepted an extra grand in compensation for his injuries and was warned to keep his mouth shut. With his lily-white record, the RUC promptly dismissed any suspicion of involvement on his part, concluding it couldn't have been an inside job – the poor bugger had been given such a hiding. As for Liz Mc Kenna, Peter made a point of keeping well clear of her after that, wanting nothing to do with the likes.

****

After the success of the hi-jacking, things in Derry became relatively quiet for Liz. She'd her house to herself since George had been bounced out of it and now, Paddy appeared to have vanished off the face of the earth. Nor had she managed to catch the eye of the OC to hear what he had to say about the successful swipe. She was feeling a little deflated about that.

As she went to grab some fish and chips one evening, she spotted a poster for a women's meeting at the Bogside Community Centre. With nothing else to do, she decided that after her fish supper, she'd pop in for a listen.

An hour later, as she rounded a corner at the bottom of William Street, she was met by a sea of headscarf-wearing women talking animatedly. Out of the blue, she heard someone call her name.

"Liz! Over here! Liz!"

Following the voice, she saw Maggie McFadden, Emmett's mum, waving to her like mad. *Shit.*

The word was that Mrs McFadden, who'd initially been involved in the Derry Housing Action Committee years ago to protest against unjust housing allocation for Catholics, was now helping many local women suffering from domestic abuse.

Breathless from chasing after her, Maggie drew up beside Liz, instinctively linked her arm and began to walk alongside the girl.

"Phew, my heart's racing!" Maggie laughed. "I'm glad I met you, Liz. Have you been talking to our Emmett of late? I know you, and he was pals there for a while."

Liz was surprised that Maggie knew of it. With a quick, bland smile, she replied, "No, Mrs Fadden, I haven't seen him for ages."

Maggie sighed. She'd been hoping the girl could tell her what was going on with Emmett. Although he was talkative and helpful, he was hiding something.

She'd half-hoped that Liz and he were now an item, and Emmett was being his usual private self. However, now that Liz hadn't seen him, she couldn't work it out, driving Maggie slightly mad. Liz read the distress in the older woman's puzzled expression, released her arm and stopped to ask, "Is he doing okay, Mrs McFadden? You seem worried."

"Ah, no, pet, it's one of those Mammy feelings, you know? He's up to something, so I thought maybe you and him like…" she explained, giggling softly.

"Ah, no, Mrs McFadden! No!" Liz laughed, linking her arm again and leading her into the hall. "If I hear anything about him, you'll be the first to know!" Liz told her with a smile.

Inside the smoke-filled hall, nearly full, they took up two empty but separate chairs.

"Hello, everyone!" a middle-aged woman cried from the front of the hall, where a table and two chairs were set up on a shallow stage. She was ordinary-looking, dressed in black trousers and a tight, black-and-white-striped top. A mane of long red hair had been twisted into place by what looked like a pencil. Her blue eyes were bright and kind, but sadly any potential for beauty was outweighed by a prominent nose and wide mouth.

"Can you hear me, okay?" she asked, looking around at the abundance of nodding heads.

"Ah, good." She paused, placing her notes on an empty chair beside her, then turned to regard her quietening audience.

"Thank you all for coming. We have an exceptional guest speaker tonight, whom I'm sure many of you already know!

"Born in Derry, Angela Sweeney, like many of us, was at one time a stitcher at Rocola. Sadly, she lost a baby son between various jobs and is now the single parent of a young daughter.

"Tonight, we've invited Angela to share her story by inspiring us *all* not to give up or give in. No need to doubt yourself or what you can become. The ability to achieve anything we choose is within us all. Ladies, I give you… the lovely Angela Sweeney!"

Liz knew women in the North of Ireland were way behind the rest of the United Kingdom regarding civil rights. Legislation on divorce was outdated, abortion was criminalised, and salary discrimination in the private sector and the education service was the norm. In the working-class districts of Derry, poverty and domestic violence worsened an already dim prospect for too many women.

Encouraged by this fulsome introduction, Angela rose to her feet and occupied the centre of the stage. She was unusually tall and skinny with unruly, frizzy, shoulder-length raven hair. She wore a knee-length, grey, woollen cardigan - that undoubtedly had seen better days - over an ankle-length black collarless dress. All in all, Angela Sweeny was an attractive woman with a forthright presence but one who harboured warm, chocolate-brown eyes that brimmed with enthusiasm and determination. The spectators cheered and burst into loud appreciative clapping – some whistled – while others stamped their feet on the wooden floor and laughed. Angela was well-liked and admired in the city for her fantastic work with its women.

With a smile that lit up the room, she waved her audience to silence and began to speak. She had a silky voice, musical and compelling. With her hands tightly interlaced before her, she introduced herself.

"My name is Angela Sweeney, and yes, I was born here in Derry. For as long as I can remember, I've always loved politics. Because of this love, I've been involved with the Civil Rights Movement as an activist and organiser. I've also worked with the Derry Labour Party and many more bodies.

"After graduating from a part-time degree in politics at the University of Ulster – which wasn't easy, thank God for grannies," she laughed and looked around to see the many nods of acknowledgement, "I managed to get myself and my youngest child a housing executive home in Lower Bennett Street. When I can, I work to help anyone, no matter *who* they are or *where* they're from, with benefit claims, tribunals and appeals. I now work with the Derry Socialist Women's Group, highlighting the vast number of homeless or battered women and children in this city and beyond. The initiative is aptly named 'Operation Desperation'!"

Most of the audience understood the problems of homelessness and the lack of funding for an independent, purpose-built, twenty-four-hour women's refuge. Most of Angela's listeners had experienced domestic violence in some form, though few would admit it.

"And so that's where I need your help!" she resumed enthusiastically.

Liz listened intently as Angela asked for support for a forthcoming project not dissimilar to the one that she, a couple of women and two men had started way back in 1976. At the risk of prosecution, the small group took over and squatted in an empty Social Services building in the city's heart, later opening it as the first Derry Women's Aid Centre.

Within months, it'd become home to some ninety women and three hundred children, proving domestic violence was endemic within the region. In the heart of the bloody carnage, and against all odds, women and children, both Catholic and Protestant, arrived at the aid centre with one common objective. To feel safe and protected.

No one had been turned away even when the centre was severely overcrowded. Since it'd originally been an office, there was a distinct lack of bathroom or cooking facilities for its many occupants.

Uninterrupted, Angela continued her talk for some time, describing the domestic and child abuse she'd encountered through her work. The audience called out their support and clapped her admiringly when she closed by telling them how an older cousin had abused her. They respected her honesty. She was fair and balanced – not one of those hard-liners, the bold feminist types, but a woman they could relate to with no hidden agenda. They'd back her all the way.

After a series of questions and a final round of applause, the murmuring crowd slowly made their way over for tea and biscuits. Liz tentatively approached Angela, whom a small group of fans surrounded. She waited patiently until the guest speaker was left alone and then, from behind, gently tapped her shoulder.

"Excuse me, but I'm Liz. Liz McKenna," she shared, feeling abnormally shy.

"Hey, Liz, I haven't seen you here before. First time?" Angela answered with a warm, open smile.

"Yeah. I spotted the poster."

Angela grinned and nodded. Almost immediately, she picked up on the young girl's nervousness and zero eye contact. Liz couldn't explain why she felt shaky and overtly nervous; it was very unlike her. But with Angela Sweeney... Looking intently at her, Liz thought she was being ripped wide open, her soul and all her dark, shameful secrets exposed. She shuddered, and it was then that Angela knew Liz was a fellow victim. It was the eyes that always gave that away—bleak, sad eyes like fathomless pools.

"How did you find it?" Angela asked carefully, aware she wouldn't get much out of the girl. *Slowly, slowly.*

Liz bobbed her head hesitantly. "It was good. No, I mean, it's awful all that stuff. Scary." She faltered again. "I'm not sure, but I think I might like to help?"

"That's wonderful! It'd be great to get some young blood in. We sure need it!" Angela said, secretly pleased. With another warm smile, she told Liz, "I can tell you, there's a few of us on our last legs. It's been a tough old journey."

"I can imagine. So, what can I do?" Liz asked sheepishly. "I hope I don't have to pay anything to join, 'cos I don't have much."

Aghast, Angela touched her wrist lightly. "Nope, nothing! Be back here tomorrow, say around three, and we'll have a good chat. How's that?"

"Three it is," Liz told her with a slight wave. "I'll see you then."

"Look forward to it. Don't forget now, three o'clock!" Angela cried enthusiastically to Liz's departing back, hoping against hope that she'd be able to help the poor girl.

****

The children's home was based in East Belfast and set up in the mid-1950s by the Eastern Health and Social Services Board to provide accommodation for reprobate teenage boys. Most were now long-term residents, having faced abusive or otherwise challenging home lives, and some didn't have any family.

The Victorian house was nothing exceptional. It was standard red brick with a couple of upper storeys plus a basement, finished off with bay windows and six concrete steps at ground level and a double rail leading up to a glassed-in porch.

When thirteen-year-old Vincent (Vinny) Kelly first stepped over its threshold, he sensed it was a bad place. There was the rotten smell, for one thing, a combination of fags, BO, pee and stuff he couldn't name. The whole place stank.

That'd been months before, and ever since, Vinny had tried to block out what'd been happening to him here. The way other lads scared and bullied him, and the House Father seemed to enjoy comforting him a tad too much. He'd found an envelope and scribbled a short note to his best friend, Liam McFadden, back in Derry. Luckily, that very same day, he and one of the other lads were sent to the shop for ciggies for their House Father. Vinny left the unstamped envelope on the newsagent's counter and prayed the old man, usually kind and welcoming, would stick a stamp on it and throw it in the post.

Day after day, he waited for a reply, but there'd been nothing yet, and he knew his cry for help was likely in some bin somewhere. Most nights, he tried to imagine Liam driving up with big Charlie in his flashy red car. They'd rush in like superheroes, beat the crap out of the House Father and take him back home to Derry.

Today at 2 p.m., he'd been summoned to the House Father's office. Vinny swiftly concluded that the man was a Proddy, taking in his surroundings again. A glass display cabinet held all sorts of prints and photographs of some Protestant group he'd never heard of. Like Aladdin's cave full of treasures, a display of archaic Union Jacks, Orange Order flags, shining shields, silver and gold medals and gleaming emblems adorned the walls.

This place and nearly everyone in it frightened the friggin' daylights out of him. He was the only Catholic and still couldn't understand why he'd been sent here. Although his home life in Derry had been far from perfect, this was much worse.

He never laughed, and his few remaining happy memories, the ones he clung onto like a life buoy, were disappearing, drowning in a dark, murky sea. He was in a bottomless pit of anguish and couldn't sleep. He'd had the scariest nightmares and had even begun to cut his arms and legs using sharp pens or anything he could find. Most of the other boys cut themselves, too; he'd seen them in the shared bathroom – at times, he'd even watched them doing it.

The only thing he could thank God for was his friend and roommate, Eddie Lafferty. Eddie was a bruiser, two years older than Vinny, and as soon as the young lad walked into their shared bedroom that very first day, Eddie took him under his wing. He'd protected Vinny from the many bullies in the home, and now no one troubled him anymore – all thanks to Eddie.

Today the House Father walked into the office with a huge grin, followed by a man Vinny had never seen before. He smiled, a mendacious smile, making Vinny shudder as fear suddenly gripped him. The room tilted as the man offered his hand and introduced himself.

"So, we've got ourselves a wee Londonderry man here! Well, well, well, that is *very* nice. I used to live there myself. Good to meet you, son. I'm George. George Edwards."

The House Father smiled at Edwards and quickly left the office, locking the door from the outside.

Over the weeks, Vinny had heard rumours of what had happened to some younger boys since Edwards's arrival. He couldn't believe the stories until now, but it seemed it was his turn today. His whole body froze, barely hearing Edwards's voice as he issued his orders.

"Come over here, wee Londonderry man, and take your clothes off. Your trousers and underpants first."

In the corner, Edwards pointed to a great big black leather wing chair and took Vinny's small, sweating hand.

"There's nothing to worry about. I promise; come on. There's no one else here, no more than me and you. Trust me; this won't hurt a bit."

****

Chapter Twenty-six

Everything was happening too fast for Chief Constable Bonner as he lay awake in the early hours of the biggest and most important day in the Loyalist calendar, 'The Twelfth'. Sleep eluded him as his anxiety mounted. He felt like shit, and his only comfort was food. For a man of forty-three, his body was shockingly obese, an embarrassment. But he couldn't contain himself. The exhilaration of his gluttonous eating was short-lived, though, before guilt seeped back in and sickened him.

After that, he'd run to a bathroom, stick his finger down his throat in the hope it would all come back up again – half the time it did, half the time it didn't. He was a hopeless case and knew it. The Chief Constable post wasn't what he'd expected or hoped for, and he was failing – miserably. All around him, in the offices and corridors of the barracks, secret mutinous conversations were taking place. Colleagues would suddenly quieten when he approached or walked into another room. Assistant CC Stephen Quinn slyly took it upon himself to make critical decisions without involving him. Bonner was at a loss for how to deal with his second-in-command.

Quinn reminded Bonner of himself many moons ago. Like him, he'd been an ambitious young bastard who would have sold his mother to get to the powerful position of Chief Constable. Younger than Bonner, Quinn was one of those athletic types who participated in all sorts of community social and sporting events. A devout Free Presbyterian, he was married to a nurse, and they had two children, a boy and a girl. Picture book-perfect stuff.

The Assistant Chief Constable believed success in life was about image and moral values, and his values were far superior to Bonner's. He considered himself a serious contender to fill the incumbent's shoes and was busy making powerful new friends to ensure their future support.

Bonner's boss had requested a meeting as soon as the tumultuous Orangemen's marching season was over. Intuitively, Bonner knew what the conference meant and decided he'd rather walk than be pushed. In consequence, he'd prepared a resignation letter.

Bonner had a problem, however. The two-faced snake had gone ballistic when he told Charles Jones of his decision. Bonner could still hear the small man's shrieks as he thundered out threat after threat.

"There's no *way you're resigning! You've still too much to do here. Do you hear? You owe me big time! I got rid of Shalham. Wasn't that what you wanted? Wasn't it?*

"And now, because you're a nightmare at the job and everyone knows it, you're taking the coward's way out! Well, **I do not think so!***"*

Bonner felt so alone; there was no one to ask for help, nowhere he could go. Jones was getting increasingly rattled at his failure to silence the Yankee reporter who had gone to ground, probably back in the States. Bonner's Red Hand of Ulster comrades had tried their utmost, but somehow Barter had been warned and quickly got out of Dodge. Bonner was furious, not only at their failure but that he still had to pay the £5,000 – otherwise, there'd be lethal consequences.

Brendan Doherty, the Catholic-loving Londonderry solicitor, was a work in progress. Doherty appeared unafraid of anything, and Bonner surreptitiously envied the man's courage.

Flustered after he'd met with his six Assistant Chief Constables to brainstorm the final preparations for 'The Twelfth' marches, Bonner sat alone in his office. Unsurprisingly, Quinn had done all the hard work and presented several strategies to the small group. They were expecting the usual trouble, fuelled by alcohol, and the inevitable riots to follow. Bonner remained deliberately quiet and left Quinn to it. Most, if not all, of the questions, were directed to him. *Why not let him do the extra work?*

The problem of Charles Jones continued to weigh on Bonner's mind. If he could get Jones out of his life, Bonner could resign and fuck off to England or as far away as possible. He knew where the many RUC skeletons were hidden. If he left, the Justice Minister would have no choice but to come up with a golden handshake, including a solid pension and a large lump sum.

Several possibilities played through his head. Mark Carroll, aka Lemon, had recently come up in conversation. The man was once fanatically loyal to Jones, but he'd been cast aside when his boss needed someone to carry the can for his misdeeds. Bonner sat up straighter in his chair and admonished himself for a fool. It had been right there in front of him all this time! He wasn't the only person with a grudge against Charles Jones, and Mark Carroll was an experienced killer. Bonner made some phone calls, set up a visit, and went home that evening feeling the first faint stirrings of hope.

****

Across Belfast city, Charles Jones was up bright and early. As for many of his Loyalist friends and family, 'The Twelfth' was even more important to him than Christmas Day. It was a day of pride, a day of remembrance, a day of: "*Fuck you, Rome-lovers, we're here now and here to stay!*" He laughed at his joke and wondered if he should use it in a speech. *Probably not!*

The annual Twelfth commemorates a centuries-old military victory over the last British Catholic monarch, King James II. The Protestant King William III of England, formerly the Prince of Orange, defeated the Catholic king and his army at the Battle of the Boyne, not far from Dublin. Ever afterwards, the Orange Order – named after the victorious king and founded in 1795 – would annually parade their banners and flags across the country in celebration, accompanied by numerous marching pipe and drum bands.

The Orangemen would wear dark suits, distinctive black bowler hats and white gloves – emphasising their 'Britishness'. Some carried black umbrellas and wore V-shaped bright orange collarettes over their jackets with numerous badges pinned on them from various Orange Lodges or Union flags.

Jones finished dressing and looked into the mirror that leaned against his bedroom wall. His made-to-measure Savile Row suit in charcoal worsted was the work of a master tailor, disguising his plumpness, worn over a Jermyn Street shirt and a plain black tie. His brightly coloured orange and white sash was new. It bore the number of his lodge and several awards he'd received within the institution. Other insignias announced his senior position within his lodge.

At last, he'd be sharing the platform with Reverend Paisley, appearing at the parade below Londonderry's legendary walls later that day. Busloads of bands and lodge members came to the city from all over the UK to parade and enjoy the festivities. As per the norm, the marching route would pass through the inner walls and end up by the Diamond square, the epicentre of the walled city. He'd been looking forward to this for weeks and was well prepared with a feisty vigorous speech. His thoughts were interrupted by a loud knock on the bedroom door.

"Yes!" Jones cried before letting out a grunt of irritation.

"Sir, it's Captain Hickey here to see you. He says it's urgent," his assistant cried through the solid mahogany door.

"Put him in the library. I'll be there when I'm ready." Jones wasn't prepared to rush this ritual.

He wondered what news Hickey had for him. He hadn't seen or heard from the good captain in weeks. Bonner was a zombie who'd had the gall to talk about resigning – the fool! He'd turned out to be a weaselling prick, nothing but a waste of space, but for the time being, Jones needed him, though hopefully not much longer.

He'd heard – through the grapevine – that James Prior, Secretary of State for Northern Ireland, would soon be announcing elections to the new Assembly at Stormont later in the year. Jones was thrilled.

No matter the cost or how he'd do it, he'd get himself set up as a DUP (Democratic Unionist Party) candidate. The idea of sitting high on Stormont hill beside the good Reverend aroused him beyond belief.

Ready to leave, he spared a thought for the semi-conscious woman who lay face down, naked and out cold, on his bed. A racy red bra, knickers, black stockings, suspenders, a red dress and matching high-heeled shoes were strewn haphazardly around the room.

At first, bitterly disappointed at her lack of effort and willingness to please, he'd done the necessary. Rohypnol's magic was still working. Prescribed by his doctor to help with his painful injuries, Jones had discovered it could be used in more beneficial ways than one. Anyway, the tart wouldn't remember a thing. As usual, his secretary would pay off the bruised woman appropriately, warn her to keep quiet and send her on her way. Singing softly, he went to the top drawer of a walnut dresser, fumbled around the plethora of medication and found what he needed. He swallowed four extra-strength codeine tablets, washed down with a slug of water, and smiled as he left the room singing.

"At the age of sixteen years,
he left his home in tears,
his mother watched
as he walked out the door…"

It was Jones's favourite, 'Shankill to the Somme', was written in tribute to the 2,000 men lost in a single day during WW1, all from the 36th Ulster Division. It would undoubtedly be sung constantly today, along with 'Build my Gallows', 'The Sash', and many more during the march. The thought of the celebrations ahead, and the cocktail of painkillers he'd downed in readiness, made him tingle.

By now, Captain Hickey had been waiting for some time and looked much less cheerful than on their last meeting. He'd nearly lost his cover after a few too many recently when he'd taken a massive risk and walked solo into a Republican bar, The Shamrock, in West Belfast. Having nearly perfected a West Belfast accent and learnt to sing their bloody Republican rebel songs over the past few months, he'd been trying to infiltrate the PIRA. So far, he'd done quite well, stepping in and out of the smaller Provo pubs across the city.

To his horror, in his inebriated state, he'd let his guard down and asked the wrong questions, like "How can I get over the border without going through a checkpoint?" He'd even the audacity to get up and sing solo. After one song, without warning, he was brutishly hauled into a back room where he'd been interrogated. After a bit of a hammering, including a few solid punches to his gut, he'd thought he was a goner until a new man walked in.

Without saying a word, he shook his head, ordering the three hooligans to stop. Confused, one of the Provos challenged him for a split second, only for the unknown man to strike him down with a single punch that produced a fearsome cracking sound.

"Out!" he'd barked at the confused thugs who disappeared at speed, carrying their downed friend. Hickey had no idea who his rescuer was but watched him carefully. The man came and stood close to him, bringing a haze of whiskey and cigarettes. The new arrival was pissed off. He knew this interloper was military, and with so much going on, the last thing they needed was The Shamrock to be raided.

"You're a cocky bastard, aren't you, coming here like this? I suggest you fuck off and never come back. There'll be no second chances," he told Hickey.

The young captain could smell his fear. Not needing to be told twice, he dived for the nearest exit and out into the relative safety of the Belfast streets.

Back in the ornate library, Hickey could hear Jones singing. He was a little bemused to see the portly, much-scarred man walk in, looking proud as a peacock. Jones was dressed in his best finery, including a bowler hat, gloves and an umbrella he held like a walking stick. Hickey thought the man looked almost comical. Before he could comment, Jones noticed the captain's battered face.

"Well, well, what happened to you?"

"You don't want to know."

"I don't?" Jones chortled.

"No. Not really, it's nothing," Hickey replied hurriedly. "Sorted now. You should see the other guy."

No one could ever find out about his drunken blunder. The very thought of it made him flinch. He'd been so foolish, drinking like that and then bearding the lion in its den. This time he'd been lucky. He still didn't know who had rescued him or why, though it would be useful to find out.

"I can imagine," Jones continued. "So, Captain, why this unexpected visit?"

****

Following his visit to Lemon in HMP Maze, Barter knew that whatever the man said, no court in the land would ever believe him. The irony was that he was most likely telling the truth. Still, Lemon's whole persona signalled 'Psycho alert!' The heavy drug regime the prison doctors had him on, and his fractured personality was sending him over the edge fast.

Nevertheless, there'd been enough lucid moments for Barter to record in shorthand – prison visitors were not allowed to bring in cassette recorders – and mull over once he was safely back in the States. Believable details about Charles Jones and the tasks he'd ordered his bodyguard and his '*kids*' to carry out. He'd described James Henderson Senior's murder, the assassination of Chief Constable George Shalham, and how Jones's previous bodyguard, the ex-soldier Morris, had managed to smuggle a gun into the City Hotel and murder Bishop Hegarty. He also described how he and the other Loyalists gang members would drive around Belfast and target Catholics to kill.

"It was him… Jones… who told me to do Henderson. They'd a fight when he found out Jones ordered the bishop killed and messed that hotel meeting thing up for his son. Henderson came over all Daddy-like and protective and was on his way to Londonderry to tell all. Didn't get a chance, though, did he? I went like a bat out of hell after him, and I did it! There wasn't another car on the road, though I heard Jones say one day there was a witness."

Lemon paused and creased up as his eyes and mind reeled back to that night. "It was sooooooooo easy. His car went straight off the road and… bang!"

He let out a savage cry of delight and threw up his arms, then pounded his fist on the visitor's table, sending their water-filled paper cups flying. As an afterthought, he moved closer to Barter and mouthed, "By the way, that judge was in on everything from the beginning. You know, the one who let Jones off."

Barter had sat throughout Lemon's tirade in stunned silence. It was all dynamite, but he wasn't sure what to do with what he'd learnt. Neither he nor Brendan Doherty trusted the security services, and no one was ever going to take Lemon's testimony seriously, now or ever. It was an appalling thought, but it looked as though Charles Jones would remain a free man.

****

Alfie McScott still hadn't given up on his search for FYJH & Sons Ltd, but although Brendan Doherty had done his utmost to help, it seemed to have stalled. Alfie asked his many business acquaintances, friends and family if they'd heard of the company, but with no luck. He'd even asked a local paramilitary organisation he secretly advised on occasion.

Purely by chance, the Yank had come into the factory to say goodbye on his way to the airport. It seemed he needed to get out of Ireland for a while, and Alfie wasn't too surprised about that. On his way out, Barter had popped his head around the accountant's office door.

"A quick goodbye, Alfie. Take care of yourself!"

"Ah, Mr Barter. You're off then?" Alfie asked, encouraging him to enter with a slight wave.

Predictably, the accountant's desk was laden with papers and forms in all shapes and sizes; Barter smiled at the sight. He never understood how people worked this way, but they did. He glimpsed a thick pile of invoices lying to one side, most of which bore a menacing red-ink FINAL DEMAND stamp.

"You've got a lot on from the looks of things?" he commented, grimacing at the paperwork.

"I do, Mr Barter, but we'll see it through," Alfie had told him, mustering as much conviction as he could. "I'm sorry to see you go. Mr Henderson is fond of you."

"I hate to leave too, but it can't be helped," Barter had answered with a smile of thanks. He felt particularly despondent about the whole affair especially having to leave Ireland like a frightened rabbit. However, seeing the fire, poor Alfie McScott was fighting made him count his blessings. At least he'd had the warning and would live to fight another day.

They shook hands, and Barter glanced fleetingly over the paper-strewn desk. By some miracle, out of the very corner of his eye, he read a name on a piece of paper, and an almighty alarm bell had rung in his head. *What the heck?*

****

Chapter Twenty-seven

The sour-faced policeman at the local cop shop observed Rob's every move as he passed him back his few belongings.

"No doubt we'll see you again soon," he said bitterly after giving him a formal caution.

Rob stood by the door of the police station with no coat and wearing a stained blue and white shell suit and a stinking T-shirt as his protection against the elements. To his astonishment, he looked across the road and saw Mr McClay leaning against a lamp post watching him. The veteran gave Rob a brief wave, inviting him over.

McClay hadn't been waiting too long. He knew the custody sergeant, who'd phoned him a quick warning that they were letting Robert Sallis out with a caution, thanks to McClay's refusal to press charges.

He watched as Rob crossed the road. The lad looked like shit, and McClay already knew that Bridie wasn't for having him back. She'd given him a letter to pass on.

McClay was kicking himself for his behaviour in the car park that day. He knew what PTSD was and saw the signs in Rob when he landed back from Belfast. The anger, depression, dead-eyed expression, and drinking on top. He'd done more or less the same himself for a few years on his return from WWII until he realised the damage he was doing to himself and his family.

As Rob reached his side, he held out one hand in apology, and McClay reciprocated the gesture. Rob could feel himself welling up.

"I'm so sorry, Mr McClay, something comes over me. I never meant to harm you."

"I know, son. I know." McClay nodded in understanding. "I'm sorry it happened, mind, especially for your Mam's sake. She's in a bit of a state."

Rob didn't know what to say to that. He looked up and down the street, searching for his family.

"Are they about, Mr McClay?"

Des McClay shook his head. "Sorry, lad, they're not. They're both back home."

"Ah, okay," Rob replied, disappointed, "better make me way there then, hadn't I?"

McClay pulled a crumpled envelope from his pocket with a pitying look at him. "Best not, son. Take a read of this."

Unaware he was rubbing his injured mouth, he stepped aside to let Rob read the letter unobserved. Rob's hands shook when he recognised his mam's writing, and he struggled to open the envelope. When he had, he had to re-read the letter several times.

Rob love,
This is probably the hardest thing I've ever had to write. After what happened at Presto's, I can't let you back home. Val is properly scared, and it's you that's scaring him. I have to look after him now, Rob. He needs me to make him feel safe. I love you, son. I love you so much it hurts, but I'm begging you to get help, sort out your head, and then we'll see.

Please don't come back until you do. I've given Mr McClay some money to give to you. It's not a lot, but all I have. Maybe it'll get you somewhere that'll help you. I'm sorry.
Mam x

Des McClay held out some cash, and reluctantly, Rob took it. He knew it was his mam's Christmas Club savings she'd set aside for a celebration meal and Val's presents. He was nonplussed and shocked when he saw Mr McClay reach into his pocket to add a few tenners. Horrified, Rob stepped back and cried, "Haddaway, Mr McClay, not after everything I did. Look at your gob. I can't take nowt off you!"

McClay wasn't having it. He knew the lad would need as much money as possible, and he could afford it anyway. He never went anywhere and had quite a stash under his bed. He grabbed Rob's wrist with a force that surprised them both and whispered fervently, close to his face.

"You take this, son, or you'll be the one with your teeth out!" Rob smiled a little. "I've been where you are now, and I nivver should have spoken to you like I did. I know what's going through that head of yours. Now do as your mam says and get yourself sorted, Rob. I'll look after her and Val. You'll not have to worry about them.

"Here, take this card: an old friend's son can mebbe help you out. He's in Glasgow. Why not thumb your way up there and meet him? He's an odd sort, but he works with fellas like you. I'll tell him you're coming. Will you do that for me?"

Rob nodded and took the card with a name and telephone number. McClay pressed the additional cash into his hand. Rob couldn't go home but appreciated McClay's kindness after everything. He knew he needed help; he'd known it for a long time. Glasgow, but… it was a long way to go.

****

Rob went from bad to worse, ending up in various homeless shelters all over Newcastle and South Shields. He lost interest in himself, rarely looked in the mirror and didn't want to. He'd become a stranger to himself, burdened with the guilt and shame of what had happened in the supermarket car park. His unemployment benefit he posted direct to his mam, getting by on cash-in-hand jobs filling pub cellars and occasionally helping out on building sites. It meant they'd some money coming in at least, which was good; it was the least he could do.

He eventually found himself travelling to Glasgow; the card McClay had given him was secure in his wallet. He wasn't sure what he was looking for, only knew that to keep his mam and Val right, it was better he stayed far away.

Rob had never been to Glasgow before. Stepping off the bus, he took in his surroundings. Bus stations all looked the same somehow: sad, decrepit, miserable. Some weary travellers – like him – were likely running away from their previous lives. He sat down in the long shelter by the exit. He didn't have much in his backpack, barely a few small items he'd picked up along the way from various charities. Aching and confused, his head fell forward. He would have slept but knew it was a bad idea here.

"Rob?" he heard a voice ask.

He raised his hand to shield his eyes from the early-morning sun and looked up. The figure before him had a short haircut, clean-shaven face, immaculately pressed T-shirt and jeans, complete with out-of-date, knife-edge creases.

"Aye. I'm Rob."

The man sat down next to him. Trying to hide a smile, he told him, "Des called me and described you. I have to admit, I expected you sooner." They shook hands. "I'm Michael – Michael Brooke."

Rob took a long, hard look at him. Along with a military bearing, the man had a strong, square jaw and brilliant brown eyes surrounded by a network of fine lines. His whole presence radiated confidence and contentment.

Lucky sod, Rob thought, shaking his head. He suddenly felt flat beat and answered in a crushed voice, "Hello."

For some reason, he suddenly felt he'd made a big mistake coming to Glasgow and was about to get up and leave when Michael took hold of his arm in a bid to stop him. In a soothing velvety voice, utterly unfazed by Rob's reaction, he suggested, "Come with me. We'll get you some tea and a wad, have a good chat."

It'd been some time since Rob had been shown such a welcome. Guardedly, he studied the man again. He could do with a cuppa and some scran, so he agreed with a tired nod.

The duo sat in the bus station's grimy café for almost an hour while Michael told Rob his story. Holding nothing back, he described how his wife left him after he abused her while living on bases in Germany and Northern Ireland. He'd stayed on in the army for a while but – like Rob – was injured in Belfast. Returning to civvy life, Michael couldn't hack it and had gone off the rails. *Yes, he knew where Rob Sallis was, and all he wanted to do was help him, and the many other lost souls like him that he met every week.*

****

Chapter Twenty-eight

Caitlin and Anne sat together in Chris's designer kitchen, finishing off a Chinese takeaway. Taking in the gleaming space around them, Anne squealed in delight.

"Jesus, Caitlin, I've never seen a kitchen so big and posh. Lucky cow!"

Caitlin had grown used to the perfect, sparkling, airy space but remembered feeling the same when she first saw it – it had seemed out of this world. Since then, she'd often watched Chris preparing dinner on the vast pristine stainless-steel worktops on either side of a chunky dark grey Aga. Numerous copper pots and pans of all sizes hung from hooks attached to a frame suspended from the high ceiling over a central island. The girls were sitting on comfortable, high-backed wine-red velvet stools.

"It is, isn't it? I suppose I've got used to it," Caitlin agreed. "Chris is so fussy, Anne. He loves cooking and insists everything's kept in its place. He's got all these gadgets… I'm not sure what half of them do."

"You've come a long way, love, haven't you?" Anne asked fondly, recalling the McLaughlins' kitchen in Blamfield Street. A touch of melancholy came over her as she recalled the family sitting around their table, forever laughing and joking. After her packed terraced home, she'd loved going to Caitlin's house, and the McLaughlins were always welcoming and fun.

The whole experience of travelling to London alone for the first time was nerve-wracking from when Anne had left Matt and Sean in Shantallow. Matt couldn't get time off work, and she'd found it taxing when she queued alone at the British Midland airlines desk. She wasn't sure what to do or where to go, but the lovely check-in clerk explained everything.

She'd never been on a plane before, and her heart was in her throat as it left the tarmac. Thank Jesus, she also got a lovely vodka and lime for free. Caitlin was waiting impatiently at Heathrow. As soon as they saw each other, and as fast as Anne's false leg allowed, they ran towards each other over the concourse, screaming like fishwives.

Although the townhouse was lovely, as was Chris, Caitlin's fiancée, Anne worried something was amiss here. It was the wedding soon, and though she was well excited at the whole 'big smoke' experience, a nagging voice told her to study her friend closely.

Caitlin looked even more gorgeous with her new London look and style, and this glorious lifestyle suited her, but…

The past few days had been jam-packed with final preparations. Until now, the friends hadn't had an opportunity to have one of those profound conversations that only true friends can share. Caitlin topped up Anne's wine glass.

Never a great one for wine, she'd felt it rude to refuse Chris's offer of a glass when they came in from the airport. At first, she found the taste somewhat bitter. Nevertheless, she grew to like it after another one or two large glasses – maybe a tad too much.

"I'm getting used to all this, Caitlin. You might not get rid of me that easy!" Anne giggled, referring to the wine and their luxurious surroundings.

Caitlin told her Chris was currently travelling to Ballymena, where his business partner had a textile factory, and spoke highly of Bill Fox. Bill had recently become a father and married the lovely Maryann, to whom Caitlin had grown close. Anne felt a slight twinge of envy. She missed seeing Caitlin at home but understood that she'd make new friends. Caitlin took a sip of wine, wanting to mention Chris's behaviour on their way home from the Portland but unable to broach the topic when Anne was so won over by everything around her.

Chris seemed to have forgotten entirely about whatever had been troubling him, but Caitlin couldn't, and it scared her a little. It made her realise she didn't know him as well as she'd thought. It could be her imagination, but it was enough to make her take stock and feel anxious and fretful for days afterwards – she still was.

Additionally, she'd been thrilled when she and Chris were asked to be Ella's godparents. But he wasn't, and she couldn't understand why. When she tried to get him to explain his reluctance, he still wasn't having it, and the tension between them mounted.

Placing her glass down and smacking the kitchen island with her hand, Anne turned to her friend and demanded to know what was up.

"Right, Caitlin McLaughlin, you've got a face on you like there's no tomorrow! What the fuck is going on? You should be dancin' round this kitchen, drinkin' all this in. You're getting married, and here's you, looking like it's the end of the fuckin' world. Tell Auntie Anne, what's up?"

Unsurprised by Anne's barrage of comments, Caitlin's eyes filled up. She'd been holding back, trying not to overthink Chris's mood swings. She'd hardly seen him of late. It was work, work and work with him. All the little niceties, the moments of kindness and small surprises he'd loved to spring on her when they first met, were over.

She was beginning to wonder if she was doing the right thing or perhaps was unworthy of happiness. When her friend challenged her to explain, she let out the weeks of hurt and cried.

Anne gasped. Her eyes widened in fear, and her mouth dropped upon hearing Caitlin's wailing sobs. She rushed over and gave her a soothing cuddle. She wasn't expecting this kind of reaction. *Bugger! Trust me. What've I caused now?* Sniffling and trying to wipe her own running, snotty nose, Anne quickly stuffed another tissue retrieved from an ornate box next to the Aga into Caitlin's hand.

"I know I should be happy, Anne, but I'm so not, and I don't know what the fuck to do!" Caitlin wailed, shaking her head. "He's gone all remote. He's not the same anymore and hardly talks to me. Probably doesn't help that he's never here!"

Raising her arms, she looked around the glossy kitchen. "I'm here on my own most of the time, Anne, and I've suddenly realised I'm lonely. He hasn't touched me in ages, and I'm going to marry him. What does that tell me, eh?"

Nothing good, Anne realised. Nothing good at all.

"Did anything happen? Did you have a row?" she asked, pulling Caitlin back onto her high barstool.

"I'm not sure, but when Maryann had Ella, he was fine at the hospital; then, as soon as we got into the taxi, he went deadly quiet with me, angry-like, and snapped my head off. I ended up in the spare room," Caitlin replied pensively.

"And when we were asked to be godparents, he went all funny again. I don't know what I've done, and he brushes me off whenever I try to talk to him about it. Maybe it's my imagination… maybe he's stressed out with work?"

Anne wasn't sure. Chris Pecaro was a nice guy, but he was nothing like the man she'd guessed Caitlin would end up with. To Anne, he seemed too old and set in his ways for her best friend, who was twelve years younger. And, yes, Chris was kind and loved Caitlin like mad, but he seemed more like a father figure than a husband. Worse still, if you were to put him next to the Adonis, well, there was your answer right there… talk about opposites!

Thinking about it, she couldn't imagine Chris as a father with a troop of wains running riot around this immaculate home. The house was flawless, and a great deal of thought and planning had gone into its design, from the carpet to the walls to the lighting and the bathrooms – it was perfection. He might have ACOD or OCD or whatever it was called – Anne was never any good at remembering stuff like that. However, she knew everything in this house was regimented; everything was in its proper place. Although stunning, it felt clinical and couldn't be described as a family home. *Oh, shit.* That was it! Didn't he want children?

Anne was appalled at such a thought. She gulped more wine before lowering her voice to try and explain her theory. "Jesus, Caitlin, I've got me a thought, though you might not like it." Anne was dying for a cigarette, but since her friend hated smoking in the house, she daren't even think about it.

God, how Caitlin missed her friend. Anne knew her like nobody else and always came up with an answer. However, from the look on her face, Caitlin wasn't sure she wanted to hear this.

"What is it, Anne? Be kind, please. I'm not sure I can cope otherwise!"

Clenching her teeth, she asked, "You know you said Chris went all funny when Ella was born and about the christening and godparenting?" She heaved a sigh. "Well… do you think he's got a thing about babies? I mean, maybe, only maybe like, he doesn't want any. Have you had the *I want lots of babies, Chris* talk?" As usual, she'd hit the nail on the head!

It was the exact thought that'd been going around and around the back of Caitlin's mind for ages. She never seemed to find the right time to bring the subject up with him, but Anne could be right. The thought of no babies was too much to bear, but what she'd said made so much sense.

Caitlin swallowed more wine. Her tears fell onto the marble worktop again. She quickly wiped them away with her tissue and looked at Anne, sniffling.

"God, I think you might be right. What am I going to do?" she asked, half-hoping for a rational answer.

"Jesus wept!" Anne surveyed the room, raised her arms and asked in despair, "I mean, look at this place, Caitlin! Can you see children running mad around here? You've got to talk to him, hen. You cannot get married if he doesn't want a family. You've always wanted one for as long as I can remember." She faltered an afterthought, "You do, don't you… you do want children?"

"I do, Anne, loads! I just never thought I'd end up with someone who didn't," Caitlin cried, startled at this notion.

The high-ceilinged kitchen grew quiet as the girls thought about this revelation. The only noises came from the persistent whining and barking of a neighbour's dog and the hum of traffic. Fuck, this wasn't going well, Anne thought. She'd better do something to save the day.

"You know what? Maybe we're jumping to conclusions here. It could be us eejits making a mountain out of a molehill."

"You think?" Caitlin asked hopefully.

"I do. I bet you a million pounds. You know what my imagination is like. Come on now. You know what me Father – wherever the old fucker is, and whomever he's shagging – used to say: '*If you panic, you're fucked!*'"

They both knew they'd come very close to explaining Chris's odd behaviour, but Caitlin knew only she could find out the truth.

Exaggeratedly playacting, pretending to be pissed, Anne giggled and dragged her heavy, braced leg across the extensive wooden floor towards the double-doored red Smeg fridge. Struggling, she opened one side and reached down to select a fresh bottle of wine. Recognising the label, she duly opened it and added a copious amount to Caitlin's glass. She hollered as she searched through the numerous kitchen drawers.

"Forget it all now, love. Let's have a laugh – we haven't danced for ages!" Pointing at her leg, she shrilled, "Even with this old peg, I can still boogie. Come on, missus, let's put some music on – where the fuck are the wooden spoons in this house!" she cried in frustration, continuing her search.

"Are you crazy!" Caitlin yelled, holding her sides and nearly spilling her brim-full glass. "If that man found we were using his specially bought wooden spoons for mics, he'd go feckin' ballistic. You have no idea, Anne!"

"Forget him!" her friend roared merrily, passing across a hand-carved Divertimenti wooden spoon she'd finally found in a side drawer by the Aga. "Now hurry up! Put on some Bagatelle!" she cried, swinging her hips suggestively.

As the evening went on and the drinks flowed, Bagatelle's well-known songs 'Second Violin' and 'Summer in Dublin' were sung repeatedly. The girls used wooden spoons as microphones and sang along at ever-increasing volume. The wine grew tastier, and the friends' laughter grew louder and boomed throughout the house, where they danced into the wee hours.

****

Earlier that day, sitting in a conference room in an upmarket Belfast hotel, James Henderson and Alfie McScott waited for their guests. It'd all been Alfie's idea. He'd read somewhere that a couple of financiers were nosing around the province in search of a potential merger or investment. Of his own accord, he'd contacted them and quickly arranged an informal introductory meeting.

As he waited, James re-read their profiles. The first was Christopher Pecaro, a London-based specialist in mergers and acquisitions at a large independent management consultancy. From what he read, Pecaro was very clever and had left a trail of lucrative corporate and commercial successes in his wake.

The second was William Fox, a dynamic young entrepreneur. He already owned a large textile site in Ballymena near Belfast, Fox Textiles, that employed around 900 staff and was on the verge of opening a new factory in Sri Lanka.

Until recently, Rocola was similar in size to Fox Textiles. James quailed inside as he recollected the recent layoffs.

Finally, the conference room door opened. Alfie and James glanced at each other for luck and reassurance before they rose. This was it, the Last Chance Saloon.

After a quick hello and brief introductions, along with the offer of soft drinks, the meeting began. Christopher Pecaro was drinking mineral water; from the outset, it was clear he would be leading the discussion.

He promptly gave James and Alfie an overview of his management company and its specialities. Bill then took a turn, explaining how he and his wife had built a thriving business from nothing and their plans for the future. Alfie followed with his introduction, and then it was James's shot.

"Well, gentlemen, I inherited Rocola from my uncle, who died some years ago." James gave details about himself, his time at Oxford and his work in Scotland before moving to Rocola. He then gave an overview and update on where Rocola sat in the industry.

"We've worked extremely hard and are looking to the future. However, for several reasons that I cannot explain until we sign a confidentiality agreement, we're looking for investment or a potential partnership."

Chris nodded. He'd done his homework and knew everything about Rocola, including the recently cancelled big order. He'd read about Roger Henderson's commitment to his factory, James Henderson Senior's death and the fatal incident at a hotel in the city. He'd even been told of wild rumours that James had an affair with his secretary, but didn't give a damn about those. Chris wasn't one to care about idle gossip but was impressed by what he'd read and been told about the young Scot. The man had the guts to take on the considerable task of managing a failing business, cutting the workforce by a third. So far, Chris liked what he was hearing.

The meeting finished much later than expected, and Chris and Bill rushed to leave. While Chris packed, he quickly announced that, by coincidence, he was marrying a girl from Londonderry and that it'd be nice if James and Alfie were to meet her.

"Congratulations, but be warned, you'll have your hands full!" James told him jokingly. "These Derry women are not only strong-minded, but they're also indomitable. I'm sure the lucky girl will make an amazing wife and mother!"

"Indeed," Chris answered solemnly as his heart hit the floor – all he wanted was a wife, nothing else.

Chapter Twenty-nine

Following the investor meeting in Belfast, James felt a glimmer of hope. He'd been more than satisfied with what he'd heard and seen; in particular, Chris Pecaro had made quite an impression. Within a matter of days, a confidentiality agreement was duly signed. In return, Alfie and James received a request for a disclosure agreement, outlining all the information Fox Textiles needed to take their discussions to the next stage.

****

"Mrs Moore," Marleen said to Melrose's scowling housekeeper, who held the front door open and stepped back.

"Mrs Henderson," she replied sharply.

Inside, Marleen dropped her case, looked around Melrose's impressive hallway with its winding staircase, and sighed. She had not expected to be back in Londonderry so soon. Still, following a terse telephone conversation with James, when he'd politely asked that she visit her children, she'd felt she had no choice. He'd also suggested they have a 'talk'. Jack was in New Zealand but was due to return to London in a few weeks, so Marleen decided it was now or never. It was time to sort out this sorry mess, and, like adults, she hoped she and James could agree on a plan to allow them both to move on with their lives.

She looked up when she heard the screams of excited children, followed by stumbling footsteps running along the landing and down the staircase.

"Mrs Moore! He's done it again!" Charlotte Henderson screamed. When she suddenly stopped at the top of the staircase, her furious sibling bumped into her. Both looked down at the stunningly beautiful woman watching them in bemusement. They knew their mother was visiting but hadn't expected her to arrive so early.

"Mother!" PJ cried, running frighteningly fast down the stairs to Marleen and hugging her. She felt slightly uncomfortable and awkwardly patted the boy's back, meanwhile looking at her daughter, who coyly remained at the top of the staircase.

Charlotte Henderson didn't want to see her mother, knowing the unhappiness she'd caused daddy. Charlotte had overheard numerous phone calls between her parents and certainly didn't like this woman. She always made daddy angry, and Charlotte couldn't care less about her visit. She watched her traitorous twin embracing the enemy and felt nothing but disappointment in him.

James heard the commotion and came out to the hallway to find Marleen, the housekeeper and the children. He'd forgotten how beautiful his wife was. She hadn't aged a bit, and her clothes were perfect and beautifully coordinated as usual. She dropped her matching handbag and, walking across the tiled hallway, her green and white silk floral dress sailed over her thin, tan legs, all complemented with a pair of spotless white huarache sandals. Like a catwalk model, she used a single finger to carry a dark green, shoulder-padded jacket across her shoulder.

Mrs Moore was definitely in Charlotte's camp on this one. Noting the child's angry expression and surly silence, she caught James's eye and took the girl's hand. Next, she pulled a reluctant PJ away from Marleen and suggested they all go to the kitchen.

"Come, children, let's go downstairs and have a snack. Give your Mammy and Daddy some time on their own. Would you like anything brought up, Mr Henderson?" she asked, looking at him directly and ignoring Marleen.

James looked at his wife questioningly. "Marleen?"

"Tea." To be seen as polite to the miserable old bat, she added, "*Please*."

James led her into the living room, where they sat opposite each other by a glowing fire. The atmosphere was awkward and tense, and neither knew where to begin after so long.

"This is rather awkward, isn't it?" Marleen asked.

"It is," James replied, "but it's good you're here, Mar. I appreciate it."

It was an opportunity for her to take a good look at her husband, and she was slightly shocked by the change in him. He appeared to be someone else altogether. He'd aged. Although his clothes were still immaculate, they didn't seem to suit or fit him anymore. He was far too thin, his cheekbones sharp under the skin of his face, but his eyes struck her most: dull and lifeless. She felt sad as she remembered how they'd partied and laughed as friends many years before. They'd been very close then and had trusted each other. Her heart plummeted. Her husband was noticeably hurting and extremely unhappy, which she had likely caused. She felt thoroughly selfish.

"I'm glad I came, James," she replied, speaking the truth, "and sorry it's been so long."

"It doesn't matter, Mar. You're here now. How long have you got?"

"A couple of days."

"That'll do."

Like strangers in a doctor's waiting room, they stared into the flames of the fire. James's mind was reeling. He had so many things to say, but by Christ, this wasn't easy, and he didn't know where to begin. He wanted a divorce, and he wanted this charade over.

Simultaneously, they began to speak. They each caught only one word, *divorce,* and laughed softly. The tension in the room dissipated almost immediately as Mrs Moore brought in a tray of hot drinks. Silent as a mouse, she placed it down and left. Marleen took it upon herself to pour. James relaxed and watched her. Mar had beaten him to it; she'd suggested they divorce.

"So we agree, Mar, we finally do the deed and call it a day?"

"Yeah, I think this has gone too far, don't you? Papa will deal with the financial side if that's okay. I've met someone who will give me what I need."

"And the children?" he asked cautiously.

"I think it's best if they stay here, don't you?"

A surge of relief overcame James. This was going exactly as he'd hoped. He took a cup from Marleen as she told him, "My parents, though, James, they want to spend some time with the twins."

He took a deep breath. He'd expected this.

"No problem, but I suggest they come here Mar. The twins have only started a new term at school."

"I'll have a word," she replied. "Although I don't think they'll want to come here, James, but I'll try."

After that, the visit proved to be even more straightforward than he had dared to hope. The children behaved reasonably well, albeit PJ clung to Marleen throughout, desperate that she shouldn't leave again. Charlotte stayed loyal and close to her father, though she spent most of her time in the kitchen with Mrs Moore.

****

James was delving into a ham and cheese sandwich delivered by his new secretary, Mrs Malloy, a middle-aged ex-teacher and spinster who wanted a career change. She was clever, business-like and reliable, and James liked her. Mrs Parkes had finally gone. Despite his initial dislike of her, the woman had proved her worth throughout the redundancy process and had been extra-supportive of him. She'd got her wish and returned to Bangor-by-the-Sea – alone. They gave her a fair enough send-off, and James was glad to have new blood in the office. The woman was enthusiastic and, thankfully, worked well with the team.

He found it a little easier now when he thought of Caitlin. His heartache had lessened a little but was still dependent on his mood.

He'd had the odd one-night stand but always far away from Derry, and still, he only saw Caitlin's eyes when he looked into those of other women. He even attempted to date a local girl from Prehen, whose father was a senior member of the Orange Lodge, but his heart wasn't in it and she gave up on him in time. It was only Caitlin's lips he wanted to taste, her skin he wanted to touch, her body he wanted to hold. When he was out for a run, his memories took him back to Donegal and that fantastic weekend together. Whenever he heard a Patsy Cline song, he remembered Caitlin's poor but fun attempt at singing in the bathtub. Most mornings, he woke feeling jaded, unfulfilled and depressed.

Barter had returned to the States, and James missed the Yank's enthusiasm and know-how. However, he kept in touch with Brendan Doherty – another workaholic though James was looking forward to having dinner with him soon.

The telephone rang, and he picked up. "Henderson."

On the other end, James heard a faint, inaudible voice. He listened hard.

"Good morning James – Thomas Fry here," Marleen's papa announced.

"I know," James replied – he'd recognise that voice anywhere and wasn't surprised to receive the call.

"Yes, well, I assume Mar has told you, but Mama and I would like to see the children."

"Yeah, she did mention that," James replied reluctantly.

"So, what do you suggest?" Thomas Fry asked, noting his son-in-law's lack of enthusiasm. He knew Marleen had visited Londonderry, though he hadn't managed to speak to her since.

"May I suggest you come here, Mr Fry? You'd both be very welcome," James answered, knowing full well the likely response. He and Marleen had spoken in depth about their children and the future. Ultimately, she'd agreed it was best if her parents came to Londonderry, allowing the children to stick to their routine. However, it appeared that she'd not told her father as much.

"Thank you, but that's impossible! Mama and I aren't fit enough for such a journey. And with what's going on over there, we'd like the children to come and stay here for as long as they want. It'd be for their own good, you understand. Much safer."

James struggled for control and swallowed hard before replying. *Stay for as long as they want!* He didn't think so. The Frys had missed their chance years ago. "I don't think them coming to you is a good idea, sir. As for staying at Belmont for as long as they want, well, frankly, no...." He drew breath and added pointedly, "They've got a great nanny proving her worth, and they've recently started a new school. I'm sorry, but the time just isn't right. As I say, I suggest you both come here. We'd be delighted to see you." Though he almost choked on the words.

"But James…"

He stopped Marleen's father outright. "No buts, sir. If you wish to see the twins, I insist you come to Derry. It's as simple as that. Now, if you don't mind, I have a meeting to attend. Goodbye."

James angrily replaced the receiver. Bloody old fool, did he think James was stupid? He knew if the twins were to go to Belmont Hall, he'd likely not get them back. As he went downstairs to the factory's ground floor, his whole body shook with reaction.

They'd cordoned off a large section of the cutting room, given it was no longer required, and were seeking ways to raise additional revenue from the space. Paul had suggested they rent it out to clothes designers or artists, which James thought was a great idea, leaving him to it. For James, the conversations with Fox Textiles had become a priority.

He stood at the back of the space and listened. The heart and soul of the factory, with its ever-running sewing machines, radios blasting from every corner, and the background hissing of industrial steam irons, had gone. The ghosts of bantering and laughing women lingered in the air. It was too damn' quiet now, and the resolute energy that was once Rocola and its women had been partially wiped out. It tore at his heart.

He sighed and made his way to the assistant manager's office to find Paul sitting with a look on his face that said it all. He held out the phone handset, shook his head and whispered,

"It's your wife."

Paul was aware of his boss's domestic crisis and made himself scarce with a smile.

"Hello," James said tentatively.

"Hello, James. I've had Papa on the telephone, and he's terribly upset," Marleen announced.

"What about?" he asked indignantly.

"Don't play games, James. You know what. They don't want to travel to Londonderry, and you can't stop them from seeing the twins, can you?" Marleen trod carefully, not wanting to turn this into a huge drama.

"I can stop them, Mar, but I won't. It's simple, Papa and Mama Bear must come here," he told her, unconcerned.

Marleen whined, "Ah, come on, James, please. I don't need this now. I had a good visit. We've agreed on lots, so please let the twins go to Belmont Hall for me?"

"I'm sorry, Mar; I know everything went well, but I can't let them go. I promise your parents will be well looked after here if they want to come. Listen, I have to go. Talk soon." At that, he replaced the receiver with a frustrated sigh.

"You can come in now," he cried to Paul, who stood waiting patiently outside.

Before his uncle died, he'd suggested Paul Doherty be promoted to assistant manager. Paul had quickly evolved into a natural leader with a flair for innovative ideas, and James had grown to trust and rely on him more and more.

Although McScott worked his damnedest to make up for his blunder with FYJH & Sons Ltd, James knew the old accountant's days were numbered.

"Tough call?" Paul asked with concern as he entered the office, noting his boss's flustered expression.

"Tough enough, Paul, same old shit," James sighed.

****

"He hung up on me!" Marleen cried in surprise at the dead phone she held in her hand. "Cheeky bastard!" She wasn't sure whether to laugh or cry. Although it was early afternoon, she wore a long red handmade silk negligee she'd bought using Jack's Harrods card.

She tip-toed over the lush, deep royal blue carpet of the panelled library and went to the bedroom to get dressed. She'd likely have to visit her parents and talk to them about going to Ireland, not to mention her divorce. She felt good, albeit her heart was sore at the thought of hurting Pen, and now she'd almost sorted out James by agreeing to a divorce; Marleen thought it was finally time to visit Pen and clear the air.

****

Pen was stunned and baffled to see Mar waiting for her at the entrance to Hyde Park stables. She was even more amazed that Mar knew where they were – in the past, she'd flatly refused to go anywhere near them.

"No, darling, please, I don't want anything to do with those great big filthy animals. Being forced to ride at school and clean up their mess… yuk! I'll leave that to you."

It'd been some time since Pen was left sobbing in her apartment, and it'd taken a while for her to move on too, but she felt she was doing better. Nevertheless, seeing Mar in the flesh, most of Pen's hard-earned resolve quickly disintegrated and vanished.

"Hello, Pen."

"Hello."

"How are you?" Marleen asked humbly.

Pen ignored her and strolled to a stable where Rochester waited. Her dark chestnut, Irish Draught cross stallion stood sixteen hands tall with a broad, powerful body. Pen grunted as she placed a recently polished leather saddle over the side of the stall. Her arms fell heavily to her sides as she leaned on the partition wall and stared hard at Marleen.

"I'm better now, no thanks to you."

Marleen knew she was taking the risk of being told to bugger off or worse, but she wanted to make things right and candidly shared her news.

"I'm divorcing James."

"And?" Pen replied with a grunt as she returned to her tasks. "You shouldn't have married him in the first place."

"Let's not go into all that again, Pen. You know why I did. I'd no choice."

In anger, Pen threw down a saddle and glared at Marleen. Pen's face was crimson with fury. "Choice! You had every chance to reconsider, Mar. I pleaded with you for so long. I even pleaded with you in the car to the fuckin' church not to marry him, but you did, Mar. You did! You weren't thinking about me or how I felt then, what it did to me! But so what? You're divorcing him, and now you're shagging that boring old Kiwi fart because he's as rich as a Pharoah!"

"Everything good in here?" Having heard raised voices, a teenage stable boy had come to see if there was any trouble.

"Fine. Fuck off!" Pen snapped to his disappearing head. A wave of guilt hit her then. Poor Ben, she'd apologise to him later.

"I'm sorry, Pen." That was all Marleen could say.

"It's too late, Mar. Too late. I'm tired of you thinking about yourself all the time. You fucked us up. We were so happy before your grand ideas of marrying James fucking Henderson and having screaming brats! Now you're on your own. I've nothing left to give you."

"Please don't, Pen," Marleen pleaded, moving closer. She gingerly placed her hand on her ex-lover's arm and said reassuringly, "I probably won't marry Jack. I don't love him the way I love you, Pen. I didn't love James that way, either. Please, let's try and sort this out. At least give me some time."

"*Probably*! What the hell does that mean? Either you want to marry him, or you don't!" Pen exclaimed.

Marleen looked at her and shrugged.

"We've been together for so long and been through so much, Mar," Pen whispered.

"I know."

"You've got to make a final choice."

"I know," Marleen repeated. "And I will."

****

Chapter Thirty

By now, Charlie McFadden was beginning to worry, really worry. He'd received two warnings already and knew he was playing a deadly game. Unsure what to do, he'd lost his appetite, couldn't sleep, and the stress of keeping it from Maggie was proving unbearable.

Nevertheless, seeing the difference his wages made and, more importantly, the new respect in his wife and sons' eyes meant he couldn't tell them. They no longer looked at him as the useless lump of a man who sat on his arse all day, drinking cans of beer and watching the telly. He couldn't tell Maggie, unduly worrying her. He'd no choice but to grin and bear it for as long as he could.

His fellow passengers on the bus saw an ordinary man reading the *Journal* on his way to work, yet Charlie McFadden wasn't capable of taking in the written words. His heart was racing, and his breathing ragged. Some clever bastard had placed a warning note inside his daily paper. In hindsight, the newsagent wasn't his usual cheery self this morning, grunting something inaudible to Charlie when handing over his purchases.

The bus stopped, and he watched as more passengers climbed onboard. An unknown man sat down beside him and gave him a stony stare. Suddenly Charlie was scared. He closed the paper with its menacing note and placed it carefully on his lap so he could look out of the window and avoid the man's scrutiny. Disappointingly, it was raining hard after a bout of lovely weather, and raindrops raced down the glass. Instinctively Charlie traced them with a forefinger until, without warning, he was callously elbowed by his fellow passenger.

"Oi, sarky Charlie. Did you get our wee note then?" the man whispered in a gravelly voice.

Charlie turned. Though he was middle-aged, unshaven, with a moon-shaped face and wire-rimmed glasses, his aggressor's expression told Charlie not to mess with him. He nodded as the bespectacled man issued his final warning.

"Enough is enough, Mr McFadden. You know what I'm talking about, so quit now while you can and don't think about ignoring us this time. You're so fuckin' lucky 'cos if it wasn't for your Joe, it'd be more than a warning, trust me. If I had my way…."

His face turned dreamy as if imagining what punishment he'd hand out. Seeming disappointed at the lack of opportunity, he added, "Well, anyway… quit now, today like comprendez?" A ripple of horror crossed Charlie's face, and he nodded.

"Fair enough," the man replied. Satisfied, he quickly got up and pressed the call bell.

Charlie watched him wait by the double doors and whistle like he didn't have a care in the world. He climbed down from the bus and, at the final moment, craned his neck to give Charlie a last warning glance, followed by a slow, sinister wink.

****

Joe McFadden sat in his cell writing a short letter to his mother. He wasn't sure what to say, remembering her shocked expression when she'd seen him for the first time in years. His mother was his rock, and he loved her to pieces. She was one of those strong Derry women who somehow coped by finding an answer to every problem.

Maggie would always keep going, work hard and protect her family, and he admired her for that. All the boys here felt the same about their mammies! He laughed inwardly. No matter what age, size or manner of fella his uncompromising hard-faced comrades were, they'd never have the courage to cross their mothers. These were the only women on the planet capable of scaring the shit out of them! He put the letter down to finish later.

For July, the cell was sweltering, but Joe relished the warmth on his thin bones. He thought of the many years he'd had only a few worn blankets to keep him warm. Hearing footsteps outside the cell, he walked out into the corridor. The prisoners were free to associate within their wings nowadays. He recognised the young Tyrone man staggering towards him. Sean Keenan had been one of the last hunger strikers until his mother intervened and sought medical care after thirty-two days. At first, he was furious with her, but what was worse, much worse for him, was the guilt he carried at his failure to follow the deaths of his comrades, his brothers-in-arms.

His heavily lined, grey-tinged skin hung loose on him. He believed he'd never regain his lost weight but would always be left unhealthily thin. One of the side effects of starvation was that his sense of smell had been weirdly accentuated. At his worst, he couldn't handle the scent of water. Until then, he'd never known it had an odour, but ever since starving himself, he found it so revoltingly hard to drink that sometimes it made him vomit.

His damaged teeth were stained a nutty brown colour, and his wide owlish eyes appeared staring and empty. For a man of twenty-three, his eyesight was extremely poor. He was bald as a coot, any lingering trace of youth and vitality forced out of him. What remained resembled an old-age pensioner but one with a stubborn, self-preserving heart.

Joe admired Sean for his courage even after everything that had happened and how he'd dealt with his sentence of fifteen years for handling explosives. As a fluent Gaelic speaker, he'd been a popular storyteller, poet and songwriter before the hunger strike. Joe did not doubt that Sean Keenan could've done anything at a different time – he could've been famous.

Sean smiled as he approached, and the two men stood side by side.

"Hi, how are you keeping?" Sean asked, shaking Joe's hand.

"Aye, not too bad. I've been trying to write me ma. Nothing to tell her, though, Sean. Nothing she'd want to hear anyway. It's been weirdly quiet round here."

"I suppose," he agreed. "Any news on you getting out?"

Joe smirked. *Keenan – ever the optimist!*

"Jesus, Sean, for the hundredth time, they've thrown the key away when it comes to me!"

"You've got to hope, though, eh, Joe?" Sean smiled, lifting his eyebrows.

He knew it'd be a long time 'til any of them got out, but he had to believe that someday they would – and sooner rather than later.

"I heard some changes are going on outside," he commented.

"How do you mean?" Joe asked.

"Since Bobby's election, Sinn Féin are going for votes. Politics over violence, they're calling it. The Brits built this fuckin' place to break us, but they haven't. Thatcher got it so wrong," Sean declared, staring down the long grey corridor.

The day Bobby Sands was victorious in winning a seat in the British Parliament for the Fermanagh/South Tyrone constituency was a day none would ever forget despite the bitter sadness that had followed close on its heels. The H-block prisoners had smuggled in enough parts to make a small crystal set. The OC gave the order that no one was to make a sound when they heard the result for fear the set would be seized and destroyed. There would be no roaring, screaming, shouting or clapping, nothing but the velvet silence of victory. When Joe and Mickey heard the result, soundless screams filled their cell as they jumped and danced for joy.

There was no way Thatcher would let a member of her Parliament starve themselves to death; they thought – not with the world's media watching. They hoped and prayed the hunger strike would end after such a win, but Bobby continued until he fell into a coma three weeks later, dying on 5th May 1981, aged twenty-seven.

"I think they might be on to something… political pressure might work," Joe suggested.

"You do?" Sean said. "You may be right, but plenty of the hardened old-timers don't want it."

It'd take a miracle to get *all* the Republican factions to agree on the way forward – even those with the same goal, a united Ireland. Nevertheless, Sean sensed something new in the air: a slight stirring that hopefully would one day become the wind of change.

****

Chapter Thirty-one

Paddy Gillispie lay flat out on his unmade bed. His glassy eyes were wide open as waves of rainbow colours zoomed in and expanded around his bedroom. He'd lost any sense of time. Flashes of pink, red and orange light pulsed around the ceiling before suddenly turning into an explosion of yellow and red – as if the sun had fallen from the sky. He was on a high, and a good one at that. Paddy loved this wonderful feeling of well-being, complemented by a Queen LP thudding at total volume in the background.

He examined his hands, subconsciously waving them back and forth. He smiled at his unhurried and deliberate movements, his twirling fingers causing a cascade of mirrored images that snaked through time and space in slow motion.

He felt he could fly if he wanted to and, in his dazed, deluded state, was oblivious to Brian Monaghan's frantic knocking on the front door. It wasn't the first time Brian had detected that something wasn't right with Paddy. He'd known for weeks. With his mood swings and irrational behaviour, Brian's comrade was turning into a loose cannon, and he was concerned. They'd been through so much together; he didn't want a fallout.

As ordered, Brian had researched the Fox family, which only confirmed that this op would be far from easy. Kidnapping was complicated, not clean and quick the way he liked things. And now Paddy was going off the rails! It was the last thing Brian needed, and his anger and frustration mounted by the day. Everyone knew how the OC felt about drugs.

Calling Paddy's name again more loudly, Brian stood back and looked up at the bedroom window. "Paddy, will ye, for Christ's sake, open up? It's me – Brian!" He detected curtains twitching in the adjacent houses and quietly cursed.

He heard loud pounding rock music, which had to be Paddy's choice. There was only one thing left to do. Stepping back, Brian stood sideways and ran at the door with his shoulder braced. Its thin, flimsy wood split easily and surrendered to his assault.

Inside the narrow house was a pit. Dirty dishes stacked in the kitchen sink, random items of clothing strewn across the sofa, and overflowing ashtrays with their contents half-spilt lay about the floor. An empty bottle of Jameson's and a half-filled glass lay beside some stale food on a glass-topped coffee table.

"Jesus, Paddy!" Brian cried in disgust. He ran upstairs to the bedroom and found his comrade dressed only in black underpants, lying back on his bed, without a doubt, away with the birdies.

"Ye fuckin' eejit!" Brian hissed.

He tried unsuccessfully to pull his friend up, but it was useless, and he let go. Paddy fell back onto the rumpled sheets and childishly squealed with delight as his head bounced off the pillow. He noticed Brian for the first time and reached out with open arms as if to hug him.

Brian pulled away and saw on the bedside table a couple of tiny multi-coloured tablets embossed with smiley faces. *Ecstasy*! That junk could kill. It certainly explained Paddy's fitful, bizarre behaviour recently. If it got out that he was taking MDMA, he'd be fucked. Although some Provo brigades taxed local dealers to bring in more funds for the cause, their OC would have none of it, despising the trade and anyone who used recreational drugs. He mustn't find out about Paddy's weakness.

From his friend's erratic movements and facial expressions, he was enjoying himself. Brian knew only time would return him to earth's orbit. He swore, slammed the bedroom door behind him and ran downstairs.

On impulse, he began to tidy up in the L-shaped living room. He and his wife kept their house spotless, and Brian suddenly missed her.

She'd returned to stay with her mother for a while in Andersonstown at the foot of the Black Mountains.

It took him some time to make the place look presentable then he checked on Paddy again. This time he found his friend in a deep sleep and decided he'd stay and keep an eye on him. Brian closed his eyes, throwing himself on the sofa he'd recently cleared of discarded clothes and takeaway trays.

He was very uneasy about the idea of the Fox kidnapping, it was majorly risky, and Paddy's insistence on taking the young baby, too, just wasn't right. Sleep took its sweet time as he raced through all the options.

****

Tommy felt rotten after telling James about Caitlin's wedding. Although the young man tried his best to hide his dismay, it was clear that James Henderson still cared deeply for her after so many years. Tommy told himself such a union would never have worked, but love moved in mysterious ways.

It wasn't often he reflected on his ex-wife Alison, but in his newly fragile state, she seemed to be creeping into his thoughts more recently. Kathy never knew the real reason her mother left, rarely mentioned her in fact, and so father and daughter got on with their lives. He supposed that one day they'd have to talk about his first love's desertion. He'd missed Alison when she first left, missed having someone to cuddle up to like spoons, and unsurprisingly, missed sex. Sadly there'd been no more of that for him. Alice had broken his heart, and the idea of such pain again kept him well away from women ever since.

Later that evening, Tommy planned to leave Derry for London by bus to attend Caitlin's wedding. He dreaded every second of the long crossing since he habitually ran back and forth to the loo countless times in the day, and being on a twelve-hour bus journey with a few toilet breaks would be a nightmare for him. Thankfully other than Kathy, who'd continually nagged him to go to the doctor, no one commented on his recent rapid weight loss and greyish pallor. He knew, however, that Caitlin would see it right away.

All day he'd kept off liquids in the hope he'd manage. The hired morning suit hung over the back of his kitchen door, pressed and pristine, ready to be packed in a suit carrier. He'd bought a shirt in the Austins sale, white as snow, to wear with it. His black patent shoes were packed along with the rest of his gear. Caitlin had sounded so excited when she told him over the phone that Anne had arrived a week or so before the ceremony. They'd been shopping, and Anne couldn't get over the size and splendour of Oxford Street, especially the Selfridges store. It was a far cry from Derry's bombed-out, semi-demolished depressing retail outlets, she said.

Unexpectedly, there was a rapid knock at the door. Tommy grunted and rose to answer it as another impatient knock followed. He swore quietly, opened up and was astonished to see that his visitor was James Henderson, looking awkward and out of place on the doorstep. *What on God's earth?*

"Hello, Tommy," he said with a sheepish smile.

"James." Tommy motioned him in. "Come on in, son."

James followed him into a living room that reminded him of Caitlin's front room, where they'd drunk tea together, and he'd first kissed her. A pang of pain and regret ran through him – this room was almost identical. Tommy had a low fire in the small grate; on the mantelpiece were numerous photographs of a young dark-haired woman, her First Communion image standing proudly in the middle. A familiar picture of Jesus with his hands spread and heart exposed hung at the centre of the back wall – James could never remember what it was called.

"Tea?" Tommy offered.

James nodded. "Yes, please."

Tommy disappeared to the kitchen, and James took a chair. He began to bite his nails and noticed how short and ragged they'd become. He'd once been so vain they'd been regularly manicured.

It wasn't long before Tommy returned, holding a tray with two mugs, milk and sugar, and a plateful of Wagon Wheels. He offered the steaming tea to James, who helped himself to sugar.

"Well, James, what can I do for you?" Tommy asked, making himself comfortable.

James coughed, feeling nervous. "Nothing, really. When do you leave for London? It's soon, isn't it?"

"Tonight, and to be honest, son, if it weren't for our Caitlin, I'd be going nowhere," Tommy sighed.

"You're not well, are you?" James asked with concern, noticing once more the older man's sweating pallor.

"A bit of man trouble is all. Sure, I'll be grand. The journey… it'll be a long haul on the bus. Overnight. Can't say I'm looking forward to it."

James didn't envy the sick man on such a trip but didn't feel he knew him well enough to pry further about his health. They drank their tea, and James told him about Rocola's redundancies and how amazing the women had been during the process. Tommy thought it was hurting the young man to talk about it. A short while later, he revealed the true purpose of his visit.

"Tommy, there is a reason I'm here. Would you give this to Caitlin for me?" He held out a sealed white envelope with her handwritten name in black ink.

"Ah, son. I don't know about that now," Tommy replied uncertainly.

"It's nothing, honestly. I felt I needed to explain something to her. You understand, don't you, Tommy? Why I couldn't follow her to England… It's been eating at me for so long. I want her to know, that's all. I'm happy for her. *I really am.* But I'll tell you one thing: not going after her that day was one of the worst decisions I've ever made."

Tommy began to feel even more uneasy. He didn't want to get involved in this stuff, Caitlin was happy, and this letter could bring back bitter memories for her. But the look on the young man's desperate face, his pleading green eyes, touched a nerve in kind-hearted Tommy.

"Please. There should be no unfinished business before a wedding."

Tommy reluctantly took the envelope and placed it along with some other papers on the sideboard.

"Right, James. But if there's any fallout from this, I'll be far from happy!" he warned.

"I know, I understand. Trust me."

"Fair enough." He topped up their tea, thirsty despite himself. Subject over. To lighten the mood, Tommy asked, "And how's that gorgeous wee girl of yours? What's her name again?"

"Charlotte. And she's a demon, Tommy, a right handful! Her grandparents are trying to get the pair to England for a visit, which'll be awkward, to say the least. They don't know the twins well, and I'm not sure how it'll work out!" James laughed. He didn't want to go deeper into the falling out with his in-laws. So far, he'd managed to keep the twins safely at Melrose.

After that, the men jabbered away about other events in the city before James rose to leave. They shook hands at the front door.

"I appreciate you passing my letter to Caitlin. You may think I'm selfish in writing to her, and you're probably right, but I have to settle a few things between us, and it's the best way to reach her."

Tommy watched James climb into his black Jensen and wave back to him. After returning the gesture, he closed the front door and returned to the living room. He picked up the letter and put it at the bottom of the stairs so he could remember to pack it away with his last-minute things.

****

Chapter Thirty-two

"He's gone, and frigging dumped me! The police an' all scared the bejesus out of him, and I really, really liked him!" Cawley's younger sister Shannon cried to him down the telephone line. It seemed her student boyfriend had been hateful to her ever since their arrest, so why she minded that the young prick had turned his back on her, Cawley had no idea.

"You're better without him!" he snapped. "Jesus, girl, you weren't even seeing him that long."

"A few weeks," she replied, her voice soft with disappointment. After taking a moment, she told him earnestly, "I genuinely liked him loads. Everyone was after him, and he chose me."

Cawley sighed, and his frustration evaporated. He could never stay angry with his youngest sister for long; she had him wrapped around her little finger.

"I know, love, but sure, there's plenty more fish in the sea."

"Sorry, but that doesn't help." Silence. Then: "What are we going to do?"

He knew she was referring to her signed confession. The gob-shites had dangled it like a carrot in front of him. They insisted that unless he gave them more good intel, they'd send her to Armagh. When he eventually told them a few unimportant pieces of information, it'd pained him beyond belief, but he'd no choice. For the time being, at least, they seemed satisfied.

"I can't do anything about that, love. Don't talk about it to anyone else, will you? And I mean *anyone*!"

Good advice, as always, but she was worried about him. He seemed so down.

"I won't. And I'm sorry for rattling on."

"Try not to worry. I get it about Gareth or whatever the feck his name is. He was a dickhead to hold it against you; in any case, remember what Da always used to say?"

Shannon smiled. Their da had been a fount of odd and soppy sayings; he'd like a phrase for everything.

"What's that then?" she asked playfully.

"'You don't find love… it finds you.' Or something of the like!"

It sounded such an old-fashioned way of putting it, and she laughed. "Do you still think about them a lot?" she asked, referring to their dead parents.

"All the time, love, all the time," Cawley answered, bursting with regret.

"It's sinful. The two of them went for a cuppa tea, and – boom! Gone forever, God rest them."

The day his parents were killed was embedded in Cawley's memory. One of the neighbours had come to their house in a state, sobbing that bombs were going off all over Belfast. In his position, he knew about it all in advance but had ensured there'd be plenty of the usual warning phone calls. But some were delivered carelessly or not correctly responded to by the security services. The Provos regretted the heavy loss of life that ensued. He'd had no idea his parents would be right in the city's heart then and had lived with the suffocating guilt of their deaths every day, hour, minute and second since. For too long, he'd been torn between his loyalty to his family and allegiance to the cause.

"Try not to think about it, love," he sighed to his sister. "They're gone, but they're together. The more we dwell on it, the harder it will be." He hated it when she brought this subject up.

The siblings talked a little longer, and the call ended on a happier note with loving goodbyes. Cawley placed the pay phone back on its cradle and opened the heavy pillar-box red door. He lit a half-used cigarette before taking a deep drag and holding in the smoke to savour its bitter taste.

He studied the darkened street. The rows of decrepit, two up, two down houses of the old Bogside were long gone. They had been flattened in 1966 and replaced by the high-rise, slab-constructed Rossville Street flats, with their row after row of primary-coloured doors, aka Derry's Rubik's Cube.

He heard a man call out and wave to him from the other side of the street. Cawley discarded his fag and jogged through burnt tyres, bricks, slivers of smashed glass and other debris – remnants of a recent riot.

"Everything okay?" he asked nervously. He was face-to-face with one of the most experienced Provos in the area.

"Not really." Cawley noticed the man was agitated and upset. "Same old fuckin' shit! Another grass at work but this one's in a league of his own," he declared.

"Why's that then?" Cawley queried. He lowered his eyes and poked about with his shoe, shuffling pieces of broken glass and stone. As he listened to the Provo's tirade, something shifted in his stomach.

"Whoever this fucker is, he's doing us severe damage. We've lost an M90, amongst other things. He's giving out name after name – and probably all for a few lousy quid. Selfish cunt! There's nothing worse than a fuckin' bigmouth. They're the bane of our lives! We'll get him, though, the bastard, you mark my words! Keep an eye out, will ye?"

Cawley felt his skin crawl with guilt. He didn't hesitate, but looked directly into the other man's eyes and told him with fake confidence, "I will. They always crawl out of their hole soon enough," he added.

The gunman nodded. "Aye, they do. Believe me; we'll get the bastard. They'd better make peace with God mind, 'cos they won't last long. You take it easy, mucker. G'night."

****

Chapter Thirty-three

Vinny Kelly sat on his neatly made bed in the bay-windowed room he shared with Eddie Lafferty in Hydebank boys' home. He was sobbing. There'd been no answer to his letter, and he doubted the McFaddens even got it. It'd given him a little hope to send it at the time, but now he felt stupid. It'd been a mad idea in the first place and had only added to his unhappiness.

After the past week, he'd decided to give up on everything. If nothing mattered to him anymore, he'd no longer be disappointed or hurt by thinking about different times and places. After what had happened in his House Father's room, he'd dug deep and managed to take his thoughts somewhere else. It'd been the only way to survive the revulsion and humiliation he'd felt in the aftermath of his encounter with the hulk of a man who'd treated him that way. Gone were his dreams of everyday life, a good life, which was all he'd ever wanted. The chances of that happening now were remote. He'd become a victim, an outsider, viewing the rest of the world from afar. He felt deprived, soiled, no longer an ordinary carefree boy – that vile man had sadistically stolen his innocence that day and afterwards, again and again, and there was no return for him now.

Eddie sat opposite, staying silent, staring at the broken boy before him. He looked at the bruises on Vinny's bony wrists, knowing marks on his ankles would likely match them, and his heart ached to think of how they'd been inflicted. He'd done all he could for Vinny but couldn't protect him from everything in this hellish place. He and a few younger boys had been taken to England a week ago by flaky Harris and that fiend Edwards, returning by ferry early this morning. The brutes always picked on the most vulnerable boys, with no family and no one outside to speak up for them. It was lads like Eddie who got abused. He'd been in and out of various homes from age two, with no family to raise the alarm. Way back, he'd tried to complain to the police, but they didn't believe him and sent him packing.

He'd never seen anyone change so much as his roommate Vinny in so short a time. The boy had walked back into their room this morning with his head hanging low in shame. Eddie ran over and hugged him tightly. As if he had turned on a tap, a wave of painful, heaving sobs and an unremitting stream of tears burst from Vinny's tiny, aching body. Shushing him like a baby, Eddie didn't let go of him while he cried, waiting patiently until no more tears were left.

Clearly in pain, Vinny squeezed his eyes shut as his trusted friend began gently to inspect his lower back, the top of his buttocks and beyond. Eddie understood what he was seeing. Sadly, the bruises and marks were no surprise to him. Nothing shocked him anymore, given what they had to do. With a weary sigh, he swore and looked at his friend with pity.

"Ah, fuck, Vinny. I've been there; I know how shit it is."

Downstairs, at the back of the old Victorian house, George Edwards settled in for the night. After the Provo wrecked his house in Londonderry, destroying all his electrical equipment and his step-daughter lifting his videos, he had to start from scratch. It hadn't taken long, and now a new twenty-eight-inch colour TV and video player sat ready and waiting; he'd even managed to get a deal on the never-never. George Edwards was enjoying his new responsibilities – *a lot*. They offered him and his old friend an umbrella of protection and some lucrative financial opportunities.

With Harris in tow for medical advice, they'd recently taken a party of youngsters to Liverpool, Manchester, and eventually London. It'd been a most worthwhile and profitable trip. In addition to making influential contacts, they took fresh photographs, some now out there earning money for them. Fortunately, the rich and powerful seemed more than satisfied with their efforts and were left wanting more.

He knew the House Father at Hydebank House reasonably well, including his connections with a mighty Loyalist group and a handful of high-ranking RUC officers. He also knew his colleague was extracting intelligence and money by blackmailing a few carefully targeted affluent clients.

Edwards's only concern was about Harris. He was beginning to recognise he'd made a colossal mistake in employing the doctor. Observing Harris at work over the past weeks, Edwards's distrust and dislike of the man had worsened. It could no longer be denied: Harris was a liability. Everyone seemed to recoil from seeing him wandering around zombie-like, with his broken, cracked skin, weedy body and permanently parched lips. The doctor was a runt, a useless link in their well-oiled chain. Something must be done.

****

It didn't take long for Liz McKenna to realise that women's community work wasn't for her, and she felt terrible. It was nothing to do with the work itself, more something in the way Angela Sweeney watched her as if waiting for Liz to bare her soul at any minute.

The last time they'd met was the final nail in the coffin. Angela caught her by the arm and steered her into a corner after a meeting in the community hall.

"Sorry, Liz, I've been meaning to catch up with you. How are you doing?"

"Grand," she replied non-committally.

"Really?" Angela asked in disbelief

"Yeah, fine. All good."

"Sit down a sec, will you?" Angela suggested, nodding to a couple of empty chairs.

Liz felt reluctant to, knowing what was coming. *Here we go*. Once seated, she stared around the hall, watching the other women busily chatting, sipping tea and eating homemade buns and cakes.

"*I know*," Angela said suddenly, out of the blue, in a deep, solemn voice. She was looking at Liz full-on.

Liz frowned. "Know what, Angela?"

"I can tell you've been party to some sort of abuse."

Liz liked Angela Sweeney and admired what she and the other women were trying to achieve, but if she thought Liz was going to discuss her personal life here and now, she'd another thing coming!

No one, absolutely no living soul, knew about what Edwards had done to her for all those years when, night after night, he'd slithered into her sparse bedroom and abused her while her mother slept. The very thought of it made Liz shiver. Although nowadays she enjoyed flirting with the men who asked her out, it hadn't gone beyond that. She feared they could tell immediately if it did, so she trusted no one. She was emotionally incapable of love and imagined that she would stay that way. The usual cycle of going steady, engagement, wedding and babies weren't for her; it was one reason she'd joined the Provos. Liz McKenna was shedding her protective skin and becoming more assured, decisive, and resilient rather than staying spineless, pathetic, weak, and ruled over by a fat pervert.

"I've no idea what you mean, Angela, honestly," she responded, looking straight back at the activist.

"You don't have to be afraid. You can trust me, I promise." Angela reached for Liz's hand. "It's a safe place here; you know that," she added, eyes skimming the crowded, buzzing hall. "All these women, at some time in their lives, have been through the mill, like you."

"Maybe, Angela, but I'm fine, really. There's nothing to tell," Liz insisted, trying to convince her.

Angela retreated. The girl wasn't ready, and she wasn't going to press her. "Okay. If you say so, but remember, Liz, I'm here – we're all here for you if you need to talk. Now come on, let's help tidy up."

Other than that embarrassing encounter, there was no question that these women were making a difference. Still, Liz felt she needed the adrenaline and excitement she only got as a Provo volunteer.

Slumped on the sofa, feeling bored and disappointed, she realised that in addition to delivering the touts and the massive success of the Currys haul, by fuck, she wanted more! At least for her, it'd been mega quiet ever since, and she felt there was no better time than now to get involved in another operation. Tension in the province was escalating, and the Brits had lifted loads of volunteers. More worryingly, there was talk of a supergrass at work, and the Leadership were getting well anxy, looking for the spy everywhere.

At the mere thought of it, she jumped up, gobbled the remainder of her Fry's chocolate bar and grabbed her coat. It was a lovely evening as she walked through the Bogside towards Cable Street. Children of all ages played happily – young girls swinging dangerously high on skipping ropes slung around lamp posts and others with pebbles playing hopscotch. It'd been a scorcher of a day, and many residents had moved kitchen or living-room chairs out onto their front paths to take full advantage of the late rays and lingering heat. The sun changed everything. Several women sighted Liz as she passed and waved to her. Unusually quiet, with no sign of the security forces – it could've been a typical summer's night in any city.

She stopped outside the white and grey-painted house and caught her breath before knocking. Paddy Gillispie answered. She'd forgotten how tall, powerfully built and broad-shouldered he was. Today, his eyes looked simultaneously sad and confident. With his curling, wispy dark hair and square jaw, he was a handsome bugger in a rugged, foreign-looking way. Slightly tanned, he wore a casual T-shirt and jeans.

He spoke in a Belfast accent with his customary sharp tone. "Well, lookie here. What d'ya want?"

Surprised by his tone and abruptness, Liz reddened. "Is the OC or one of the others here? I need to talk to someone."

Paddy looked at her, standing nervously on the doorstep. For the first time, the girl's appearance struck him. She looked old-fashioned but pretty. Her shoulder-length blonde hair was dead straight, centre-parted and tied into bunches that hung down over her red tight-fitting sleeveless jumper worn over an ankle-length black gypsy skirt. She had a delicate, soft-featured face. Her rebellious light grey eyes were bold, and her lips full.

Liz blushed at Paddy's gawking. The hairs on the nape of her neck tingled, and she felt an unsettling but pleasant feeling run down her back. *Bloody heck, the dirty git!* She knew what that look meant. Annoyed by her failure to remain calm, she snapped, "Is he in there?"

Paddy shrugged and, enjoying her obvious discomfiture, replied flirtatiously, "Maybe he is, maybe he isn't."

"Enough now, Paddy, let me in," Liz bellowed in an attempt to force her way inside.

"Ah, Liz McKenna, the lovely Liz," Paddy declared, taking the piss but stopping her from moving forward. He looked down and smirked at her. "Miss McKenna, if I tell you where he is, what's in it for me then?" he asked, biting his lower lip seductively.

Liz gave him a sour *fuck away off* look, and Paddy sneered as he stepped away from the doorway. Liz stumbled on the step, and Paddy caught her – he was so close, she could smell him.

"For Pete's sake, Paddy, I just want to know if the OC is around?"

As if deep in thought, he faked a teasing expression and took another long look at her. She found it hard to meet his probing gaze. Unexpectedly, he chuckled.

"No one else here, love. They're on a little holiday. It's you and me, honey."

Shit! Liz thought. She knew what a *wee holiday* meant, and her heart sank – her comrades were on an op without her. He noticed her disappointment.

"Maybe there's something I can help you with?"

Liz wasn't sure but said, "Let me in then. I don't want to stand here like an eejit!" She looked around the street for any security vehicles or foot patrols.

She was disappointed not to see the OC, primarily since after the Currys heist, she'd heard nothing from him. Not a word. There'd been no chance for her to tell him how close they'd come to aborting and how she'd been the one to salvage the heist.

"I don't think so, Liz. I was about to go out meself."

Paddy wasn't going to let this girl in, albeit she looked tasty. He'd already debriefed the OC on the Currys mission, and together they'd revelled in the glory and satisfaction that the influx of ready cash had brought them. As for young Liz here, Paddy had managed to keep her at bay, not wanting her to blabber on about the actual events of that night and how ill-prepared the driver he'd selected had been.

"I'll walk with you then," she suggested – at least that way, she could see if there was any way of insinuating herself into the current action.

"Don't think so," Paddy told her firmly. "Go home; I'll let you know when we need you."

Without warning, Cahir O'Connell chose that moment to pull back the front door. His face wore a scowling, impatient expression. "Jesus, Paddy, what's keeping ye!" he cried before noticing Liz. His eyes lit up at sight. "Ah, young Liz, where've you been? I thought you'd given up on us."

She stood frozen on the spot, dumbfounded. "I've not been anywhere," she replied.

"Well then, come in, come in, the pair of you!" Cahir smiled and hastily waved them in.

Liz practically jumped into the house, expecting to see the usual shabby living room, but it'd all changed. It was now an office, with a pair of battered filing cabinets stuffed with papers in one corner. A large red-framed steel desk stood at the far end of the room with some mismatching chairs set around it. Multiple posters highlighting marches and images of Republican leaders festooned the walls. A 1980 calendar with pictures of exotic fish lay in the waste paper basket.

"So where've you been hiding, lovely Liz?" the OC asked as he sat down behind his desk. He motioned for her to take a chair.

"I… I've been at home all this time," she stuttered nervously, glancing at him and then over her shoulder at Paddy, who stood directly behind her. "Have you been looking for me then?" she asked in surprise.

The OC looked up and stared hard at Paddy as he replied, "You have. Haven't you, Paddy?"

"You weren't in when I called by a few times, Liz."

She had been nowhere, knew he was blatantly lying but didn't know why.

"Ah, well, you're here now. That's all that matters," the OC said, clapping his hands.

He wasn't that keen on having women in the ranks, truth be told, but with the recent loss of some key players to a super grassing bastard, he'd no choice but to use all his assets.

"Right, Miss McKenna, that was some heist with the Currys load, wasn't it?" he asked light-heartedly.

Liz raised her head, looking almost defiant. "It was," she replied, blunt and direct. *This is it!* she thought—*my time to tell him what went on.*

"Paddy here tells me you did okay," the OC told her, amused by the girl's forthrightness. Liz's heart tripped.

"Okay… Just okay?" she stammered, craning around to locate Paddy again. She knew from his shifty countenance that the Belfast bastard had taken all the credit. *The fucke*r. Endeavouring to subdue a sense of outrage, she turned back to the OC.

"I want to do more."

He wasn't a fool, hadn't missed the animus between Paddy Gillispie and this girl. He liked Liz McKenna's style, admired her determination and grit, and would've welcomed more like her. But from Paddy's account of the Currys heist and the behaviour of the other volunteers, he knew something was being kept from him.

He'd get to the bottom of it sooner or later – he always did. For now, they'd bigger plans afoot, and with Liz here, everything was finally falling into place. He knew exactly where he needed her. The OC met Paddy's eye. They'd been talking about sourcing a female volunteer for the Fox kidnapping. It was karma; they needed a woman to look after the child, and Volunteer McKenna was right there. He felt that Liz McKenna could offer them much more in the future. She appeared intelligent and resourceful but, more importantly, was also keen, loyal and trustworthy.

Paddy wasn't so sure; he'd deliberately kept Liz on the back burner. However, he had no choice but to go along with the OC's express order.

"Well, Volunteer McKenna, if you want back in so much, how do you fancy a wee trip to London to do some babysitting?"

Liz felt as if her heart would burst. This was it! Bloody hell, she was going to London! Not for one moment did she contemplate, or even hear, the word 'babysitting'.

****

Chapter Thirty-four

At last! Thought Charles Jones as he stood proudly next to Reverend Ian Paisley. The clergyman had founded and was the leader of one of Ulster's main political parties, the Democratic Unionist Party (DUP). This was the organisation Jones wanted badly to be a part of. He listened in wonderment as the towering man zealously preached his message of Unionist solidarity, observing the spellbound audience that stretched back as far as the eye could see. This was Charles Jones's idea of heaven, and he was enraptured!

Many men and women stood at the top of Shipquay Street within the heart of the ancient walls of Londonderry. After the giant explosion there a few years before, the Council had finally restored the war memorial in the Diamond to its former glory. Union flags hung from every lamp post around the parade and down the steep hill. Bunting hung from building to building across the street, and the mood was celebratory and triumphant.

The media labelled Paisley 'a radical leader with a rabid following'. However, to Jones, he was a redeemer – a liberator – who would keep 'Protestant Ulster for the Protestant people!' Bellowing and hollering, Paisley's tirade continued as he voiced a warning to the British Government that they should: *"Quit the talks with Haughey! Stop the joint studies, and our campaign will be ended."*

Raising a clenched fist, he bellowed, *"But if you go on with these studies, you go on with your conspiracies with Haughey, then hundreds of thousands of Protestant men and women will bring it to an end!"*

The appreciative whooping and clapping of the crowd were ear-splitting, vibrations from their stamping feet almost shaking the high platform. Like a child who'd been bought a puppy for Christmas, Jones grinned and clapped his hands enthusiastically, nodding in agreement with his hero's declarations.

A short time later, Paisley shook his hand heartily and raised it high for the audience to see.

"Brothers and sisters, I have the pleasure of introducing a man who, like many others here, has personally suffered as a result of the IRA's unlawful campaign but, like every Protestant man, woman and child here in this beautiful square today, believes in the Union and Loyalism."

The Londonderry crowd cheered a welcome to Jones, recognising him from his many Free Derry Presbyterian church sermons. Paisley waved his arms to quieten them.

Jones was breathless with excitement. He took a deep breath and embarked on his speech.

"Thank you, Reverend, and thank you to everyone for being here today on this most special of days: 'The Twelfth'!" The crowd screamed in appreciation.

Jones had learnt from his previous speeches and, within minutes, had the many thousands hooked as he thundered out a tirade of anti-Catholic vilification.

"I have said this many, many times, brothers and sisters. There will be *no* surrender, not in my lifetime, not in yours, yours or yours!" Adding emphasis to his words, he pointed to several spectators randomly in the crowd. "We will never let the Fenians win! No Pope here!"

As if in affirmation, the sun suddenly appeared, and Jones looked at it crookedly. "Even the Good Lord says *no surrender!*" Along with his, thousands of voices rang out repeatedly, *"No surrender! No surrender!"*

A tsunami of laughter, applause and cheers ran through the square and beyond. Jones had never felt anything like it! As Paisley looped a long arm around him, he felt drunk on joy.

The Reverend leant down and whispered into his ear, "Good job, Charles, couldn't have done it better myself! You're a natural."

Eventually, after much patting of the backs and congratulations, Jones attended a dinner organised by the City of Londonderry Grand Orange Lodge. It was held in the impressive, oak-panelled Orange

Room of the Apprentice Boys of Derry Memorial Hall, not far from the Diamond square.

Paisley was ecstatic too at the day's events in Londonderry and was now on his way to Belfast. Before leaving, he'd promised Jones they'd talk soon about his interest in standing as a DUP candidate in the forthcoming elections.

****

Captain Hickey made his way to Londonderry. As soon as he arrived, he began to tail the pro-Republican solicitor, Brendan Doherty. The man appeared to have no social life, family, and few friends. He was a workaholic, arriving at his third-floor office on Great James's Street every morning at 7.30 a.m. after attending the gym and leaving only to attend the local courts or visit various prisons. Jones wanted Doherty eradicated. Like a true professional, Hickey would find the perfect opportunity to do just that.

A week or so into observing his target, he noticed him leave his workplace earlier than usual one day. The solicitor no longer wore his customary dark jacket but a light green Oxford shirt and khaki slacks. He was struggling to carry a brown two-handled Adidas sports bag in a hurry, tense and looking anxiously around. He opened the rear door of his white Ford Escort and carefully placed the large bag inside.

Once in the driver's seat, he took off. Hickey, who'd stolen a gold Mazda 323 in Belfast, shadowed the Escort along Strand Road, under the blue Craigavon Bridge and down Foyle Road. He'd no idea where his target was heading, not knowing this part of Londonderry particularly well. He was, however, aware from the graffiti that he was in a solidly Republican area. The Escort continued along the straight road until it abruptly stopped and pulled into a layby next to some woods.

To avoid detection, Hickey found he'd no alternative but to drive past Doherty. He swore, looked into his rear mirror and saw the solicitor sitting and waiting in his car. *What was going on?*

Driving ahead, Hickey found himself approaching a British Army border checkpoint. Hemmed in by cars front and back, he panicked a little. If he were to try and turn around, the soldiers would likely feel threatened and open fire. *Shit!*

Queuing impatiently and carefully going over the numerous speed ramps, he was eventually stopped by the wave of a soldier's hand. As he rolled down the window, he smiled at the young Private, who asked politely in a Yorkshire accent for his identification.

"Evening, sir. ID, please."

Hickey drew closer to the open window and, in his best Sandhurst accent, said softly, "Private, my name is Captain Hickey of the Royal Anglian Regiment. Please listen to me very carefully. I'm going to pass you my ID, but I need to turn this car around – and quickly, I'm in the middle of a covert op."

Against all regulations, Hickey always carried his military papers specifically for such occasions. He regarded this assignment as an 'off-duty' manoeuvre, which had nothing to do with his mandate from the army. But the squaddie he was trying to pull rank on had no idea about that.

Accepting Hickey's ID from him, the trusting soldier checked it out and nodded. Hickey raised his eyebrows questioningly.

"Are we good?"

The soldier nodded solemnly, retaining a deadpan expression.

"Fine. Now pull me over, use your common sense and somehow turn me around. Can you manage that?"

"Yes, sir."

"Good."

As promised, the soldier kept his cool. With a slight wave of his hand, he made Hickey pull into the side of the checkpoint. He then pretended to inspect the vehicle and its contents and finally pointed him in the opposite direction. Fortunately, no one paid much attention. It was a common enough sight. Hickey soon found himself heading back towards Londonderry. The Private watched him go and quickly ran to several colleagues to share his news.

Hickey made it back to the layby and couldn't believe his luck. The Ford was still there, but, frustratingly, there was no place for him to pull in or hide, and once again, he had no choice but to drive by. As soon as he could, Hickey parked the Mazda beside the road and headed back on foot. It was a warm evening, and he began to sweat as he made his way along a narrow woodland path. He could see Doherty talking to a tall, dark figure next to some trees a hundred or so metres from his car. The men were arguing, and as he drew closer, Hickey was astonished when he recognised the solicitor's companion. It was the man from the bar who'd saved him from a bad beating. Though he'd been unknown to Hickey then, the intelligence officer subsequently pulled in a favour and combed through MI5's library of active assets, identifying this one. What was he doing conducting a clandestine meeting with the solicitor?

Needing to get closer but remain unseen, Hickey cut his hands as he scrambled through the thorny gorse to keep undercover. Cars flew along the busy road, suppressing the sound of the man's argument. Hickey listened hard, barely managing to pick up the conversation.

"I've told you there's nothing I can do!" Doherty growled, dropping the sports bag onto the ground. "Take it! I won't have anything to do with it!"

"Jesus, there's got to be some way, with all your contacts? I have to get out of here!" the man with him yelled.

Brendan Doherty had had enough. He'd told this inconsolable, frightened man a dozen times before: he couldn't, no, wouldn't help him! If the Provos found out, Doherty and he would end up in a ditch with a bullet in the back of the head. Doherty couldn't understand why this man had even come to him in the first place, carrying such a burden. Ever since, he'd been to hell and back, torn between reporting what he knew to the Provos and trying to forget it. Still, ethically he couldn't be responsible for any man's death, and this one would undoubtedly be executed and made an example of if the truth leaked out.

"I've told you – I don't know why you've asked me. Now take the money back, please! I don't want it. You're lucky I'm not reporting you meself."

Doherty kicked the cash-filled bag and turned to leave but was abruptly pulled back. He felt truly afraid for the first time as he looked into the other man's tight, stony face. It was the look of a killer.

"I'll remember this. On my mother's grave, Doherty, I'll remember this," he warned before pushing the solicitor away roughly. "On my mother's fuckin' grave!"

Brendan Doherty was filled with sorrow and regret; he was torn but knew he couldn't help this despairing, hopeless man. *He couldn't.* He shook his head sadly and returned to his car to drive back to the city centre.

Left alone, the man grabbed the Adidas bag and effortlessly slid it over his shoulder before he turned for Derry. As he reached Hickey's hiding place, the British officer jumped out, scaring the living daylights out of him.

"What the fuck are you doing here!" the Provo cried, his face like thunder.

Hickey nodded in the direction taken by the solicitor. "Me! What the fuck do *you* think *you're* doing?"

****

Chapter Thirty-five

Rob Sallis suspected he'd never feel fully human again. No matter how many times he'd promised himself it would be his last time taking drugs, "*That's it, Rob, no more,*" it never was.

With little or no restraining himself, he found he'd inhale or smoke whatever he could find, whatever it took to evade the troubling memories and the heavy sense of guilt at how his life had turned out. Buying grass at fifty quid an ounce had proved difficult, but to his relief, he'd found a much cheaper way to get high: Evo-stick and a plastic bag, all for the bargain price of fifty pence.

At first, the quick high was brilliant and agreeably weird. Other times it was terrifying. He'd experience hallucinations, seeing cartoon characters running around frenziedly in circles.

He'd grown used to the chemical smells lingering on his clothes and breath and the contact rash around his mouth and lower face. Once, after losing consciousness, he woke up in an industrial dustbin. He couldn't remember how he'd got there or how long he'd been in it, and he panicked. He was covered in dried vomit, his hands and feet tingled, and he couldn't hear very well—a pathetic wreck of a man.

He found himself homeless with very few possessions, living under a tarpaulin tent beneath the M8 motorway, an area known as Kingston Bridge, outside Glasgow. The place teemed with an assortment of similar bums, mostly ex-mental patients, drunks or forgotten veterans. These fragmented leftovers of society kept themselves to themselves, each wandering around in their own living hell.

Though with the best intentions, Michael Brooke, McClay's contact, had proved too overbearing in his approach to 'saving' Rob. His militaristic rules and regulations at the halfway house he ran proved too much and got on Rob's nerves. He'd shared a room there with an ex-para who was some psycho. In the early hours, the hulk of a man was inconsolable, screaming and howling, though, by day, he never uttered a word: another statistic, another forgotten victim of war. Rob wasn't ready to stop drinking and sniffing, so he left without a word.

In the early hours of a July morning, after he came down from a particularly eerie trip, he realised he'd finished the last of his stash, and a wretched wave of panic and fear hit him. He'd run out of money, and the enormity of his physical deterioration began to sink in as he grew sober. His body began to shake violently as wild thoughts ran through his thumping head.

How could he have allowed himself to come to this? Living rough, sleeping under cardboard boxes and bin liners in a plastic tent, snorting fucken house glue! What had happened to him? It must stop. *He* had to stop. He imagined what his best friend Val would say about his pal's sorry state.

"*Fucken haddaway, man, and sort yersel out! Get a grip, marra. It's past time.*"

His shaking grew worse. His whole body vibrated. His eyes screwed up in pain as his familiar headache returned. Thump, thump, thump. His skin became itchy all over, and like a dog, he scratched at it, tearing it and feeling the stickiness of blood. He couldn't remember the last time he'd prayed but tried anyway: "*Hail Mary, Mother of God….*" The world tilted on its axis, and he passed out.

Hours later, from a short distance away, Carol Caffrey studied a trembling man's half-covered, curled body. She'd seen this sight so often, and it broke her heart each time. This guy was only in his mid-twenties. He had scruffy hair, a dirty, spotty face and soiled, overgrown fingernails. A can of wood glue lay empty by his outstretched hand. She angrily kicked it aside. Such a waste of a young man's life sickened her.

Once upon a time, she'd been a novice nun, but she hadn't lasted long in the Order. She'd kept her faith but couldn't hack the strict rule and left the order to work in Glasgow's Archdiocese Community Social Services department.

Their chief, Cardinal Winning, was an outspoken man who was unafraid to challenge the Catholic Church's encyclicals on matters such as abortion and homosexuality. He cared deeply about the poor of the Archdiocese, and one of his main aims was to help the homeless by working in partnership with local housing associations. Fortunately, he'd secured agreement from a few of them to help build a new all-male residential and respite facility in Pollokshields named Glengowan House.

The sound of a pair of loudly arguing tramps brought Rob around. He rubbed his eyes and, with a great effort, sat up. Predictably his head began to pulsate, and in an attempt to get rid of the pain, he shook it. He felt confused and numb. Looking up, he found a girl watching him, her pale blue eyes full of pity.

Embarrassed by her reaction to the sight of him, he felt anger swell in the pit of his stomach. He didn't want her pity. Who the feck was she anyway, and why was she staring at him like that? He tried to roll onto his knees and get up but fell over again. The girl put out her hand to help; Rob brushed it away.

His eyes met hers as he stuttered angrily, "What! What do you want?"

"Do you want some food?" the girl asked patiently in a soft, Scottish lilt.

He couldn't remember when he'd last eaten, and he was famished. Pride and stubbornness attempted to take hold, but his need was too great. He nodded.

"Don't go anywhere. I'll be back," she announced with a faint smile.

As if Rob *could*. "I'm going nowhere, pet," he muttered and watched as she hurried to the back of a parked white van.

Within minutes, she was back. Rob managed to heave himself up and lean against one of the many graffiti-covered concrete pillars. It was only then that he could see her properly. She was a big girl who wore what looked like a man's dark green V-neck jumper and a pair of loose green and black cheese-cloth trousers. Moses sandals on her bare feet. A scarf tied her blonde hair back. She had a round face and beautiful skin with no makeup. To him, she looked pure and clean as the moon.

In silence, she knelt and carefully placed a cup of hot tea and some hastily wrapped sandwiches by his side. Seeing the food made Rob even hungrier. He grabbed the pack greedily, tearing it open and cramming the food into his mouth. He munched at the tuna fish on thick-crusted white bread and butter. He'd never tasted anything so good.

For a woman, she said very little, Rob thought. He looked at her again, and she commented reflectively, "You'll feel better for eating. Good?"

"Aye, I was proper clemming," Rob told her, devouring another mouthful of sandwich.

You certainly were, she thought, wondering when he'd last eaten. But Carol found it best to say very little at first when dealing with street people. She needed to gain their trust, and most of the time, offering them food helped.

Satisfied, Rob picked up the tea but struggled with the violent tremors in his hands that sent the hot liquid flying. "Fuck!" he cried, looking at a red burn already emerging on the top of his hand.

Carol gently took the overfilled cup and emptied it halfway before returning it.

"Sorry," Rob apologised. He could feel the tuna sandwich sitting at the back of his throat and prayed he wouldn't throw up in front of her.

"I've heard worse. Believe me," Carol answered. She noted that beneath the dirt, he was quite a good-looking fella.

"What's your name?" she asked carefully.

"Robert Sallis. Rob."

"Can I sit down, Rob?" she asked, pointing to the ground nearby.

He moved some cardboard aside and offered her a spot.

"Aye, go ahead."

The air was warming up as the sun grew hotter. She looked into the sky, saying, "You're not local. How come you've ended up here?"

Rob wasn't sure how he should answer. "You wouldn't believe me if I told you."

"Try me," she challenged, making herself more comfortable.

Nothing about this woman was threatening. She'd a serenity about her he hadn't encountered before in such a young person.

"I don't think so, miss."

"My name's Carol."

He stared at her intently. Lonely, hopeless, and with the mother of all headaches hammering in his head, he felt like shite. He was even more sure he wanted to throw up, having gobbled his food too quickly and found himself swallowing hard to keep the sandwich down. He couldn't be sick in front of her; no way! Maybe she was here to be his guardian angel. He took a few moments before giving his reply.

"Well, Carol, you may not have spotted it, but I'm not really in the best condition to talk right now."

"Do you have somewhere better to be?" she asked lightly.

"Yeah, I should have been at the office an hour ago!" he quipped, looking at his battered Swatch.

His flippant reply surprised him. He was more than pleased to hear Carol suddenly burst out laughing. It was a sound full of happiness and hope. Rob couldn't help but smile along with her.

"That's a good 'un!"

"It wasn't *that* good!"

"Well, I thought it was!" Her wide, trusting smile reached her eyes and set them dancing.

Rob was captivated. This was a real woman who cared; he knew instinctively he'd not find a single self-seeking thing about her. He forgot about the sandwich, he forgot about the shakes, forgot about all his aches, pains and sorrows. There was magic in the air.

Carol settled down beside him. "I'm listening now, Rob. If you want to talk."

"You really want to know?" he asked tentatively.

"I really want to know," she replied.

She did, Rob thought and began his sorry tale. He told her everything, not leaving a thing out, especially his faulty behaviour. She asked very few questions but gasped as he described the tarring and feathering of a young woman he'd witnessed in Derry. Val's abduction and how he'd been tortured and murdered. Without giving away too much detail, he explained his undercover work with IOWA and the bomb scare at the City Hotel he'd been involved in before being reassigned to foot patrol in Belfast. He talked in depth about his injuries and recent behaviour towards his family after leaving the army. He wanted to make her understand that he was not bad deep down, though some of his recent actions might give that impression. As he finished, he sighed heavily but felt glad to have voiced it all.

"Nothing to be proud of, is it?" he asked.

"It wasn't your fault," Carol replied thoughtfully.

"Oh, it was! It was foolish of me to persuade Val to sign up for the army. He'd still be alive if I hadn't, and I'd never have ended up in this hellhole! As for Mam and young Val, I can't go near them. They're afraid of me. How sad is that?"

To hide the tears in his eyes, Rob gazed around at his decrepit, rank habitat as if noticing it for the first time. As far as he could see, there were multi-coloured, makeshift tarpaulins, canvas tents, sleeping bags and blankets on or next to numerous stained mattresses. He heard a kettle sing in the distance and a group of rough sleepers playing a game of horseshoes. Small groups of men and women huddled around tiny makeshift campfires while others with damaged shopping trolleys unloaded useless rubbish and tosh they'd picked up along the way. He remembered McClay's taunts and shuddered slightly.

A voice cried from the far side of the camp, "Carol! Come here; we've got to go!"

He watched as she picked up some rubbish. "Who's that calling you?"

"Geoff," she answered with a weak smile, "we work together."

She swallowed involuntarily and didn't know why. Despite her best intentions, she didn't want to leave this man, though she knew she had to. As she prepared to go, he put his hand on her elbow.

"Carol, will you come back?"

She nodded vigorously.

"Good. That's good," said Rob, feeling immeasurably relieved. He watched her go through the compound and out of sight before he finally liberated the tuna sandwich.

****

Back home in South Shields, Bridie Sallis sat on the floral-covered settee with her grandson, holding his hand. She'd got out her best cups and saucers for a visit from the social.

Val noticed the serious-looking visitor hadn't touched the digestive biscuits and longed to grab one himself but was too afraid of his nan to go anywhere near them. Until now, he hadn't been listening to the conversation, but his ears pricked up when he heard his mam and dad's names.

"It's only right the lad should be with his Mam," he heard the social worker say in a deceptively friendly tone. Next to his nan, she looked really chubby. She wore thick black tights, a grey skirt and a white blouse under an extra-large blue sweater. Val wondered if she ever shaved the wiry hairs off the mole on her chin and if it hurt.

He giggled and looked up at his nan, but she sat unnaturally still, staring into nothing. He squeezed her hand to bring her back, but she remained unmoving. What was going on?

Bridie Sallis was stunned by what she'd heard. Choked with fear and sadness, it took a moment before she could ask the woman to repeat herself. Sensing her strange mood, Val began to listen more carefully.

"It's quite simple, Mrs Sallis. The boy's Mam, Tracey, contacted us. She's set herself up with a new partner and life in Preston and wants the lad back."

This wasn't going as well as she'd hoped. The social worker contemplated the small shabby house and the stick-thin old woman. She would've thought Mrs Sallis would've been glad to see the lad go. It'd take a load off her and let her live her days out peacefully. At her age, who would want to be run off their feet caring for a youngster? As for the father, he was well off the scene. Rumour had it he'd done a runner to Scotland.

Bridie gripped Val's hand in hers. With a fierce look, she let rip at the interfering social worker.

"Not on your nelly will that useless article come anywhere near our Val!"

She stood up and pointed angrily towards the door. "Time you were leaving. And don't hurry back!"

****

Chapter Thirty-six

"Fuck me, Caitlin, you look amazing! Ab-so-lute-ly frigging gorgeous!" Anne howled in delight and clapped her hands.

"Shh, Anne, or the wicked witch'll hear you!"

It was a few days before the wedding and another scorcher in London. Every window in the house was open in an attempt to cool the place down.

Anne twisted her face at the thought of Chris's unpleasant mum. Otherwise, she was having a cracker of a trip and loved being back with Caitlin. Chris had recently returned from Ballymena and, to Caitlin's delight, was much more like his old self. He was extremely loving to her and had bought her a giant bottle of Chanel No. 5 at Belfast Airport.

She'd even managed to get a few words out of him about babies. It wasn't quite the conversation she'd hoped for, but it was enough to put her concerns to rest.

****

He'd only climbed into bed when he began to kiss her passionately. She rose to the occasion. His hands started slowly to caress the inside of her thighs. His mouth moved down in search of her nipples, temptingly licking and biting them, sending a wondrous sensation shooting through her.

She grew more aroused as he switched his attention lower and teased her gently using his tongue. Gasping in ecstasy and anticipation, she opened her legs a little – enticing him to continue.

Chris flattened his tongue and tenderly began to lick and suck. Flicking and tantalising, he sent her into oblivion. Moments later, her orgasm was so intense that her entire body shook and shivered. Chris raised himself and slipped deep inside. Riding her, he had no option but to release himself to the euphoria of their lovemaking. Their hearts raced to the same rhythm.

Later, lying contentedly in each other's arms, Caitlin began to stroke the dark hair on his chest. He felt pleased and relaxed, and she knew this was it. She'd not get such an opportunity again before the wedding, and the timing couldn't be better after such a lovemaking session. All or nothing, then.

"Can I ask you something?"

"Hmm, what's that?" he replied, toying with her freshly washed hair. The smell of Chanel and lascivious sex drifted in the air – he knew what was coming next.

"You've not been yourself since Bill and Maryann asked us to be Ella's godparents, have you?"

Tread very carefully, Chris thought before apologising. "I know, and I'm sorry. A lot is going on with work, but I'm fine now. Especially after that!" he replied, smirking.

She smiled warmly, then grew serious again, her eyebrows furrowed.

"There's something I must know, Chris, and it's important."

He didn't want to spoil this moment. *But too late.*

"Do you want babies?" she asked earnestly, pulling herself onto her side and leaning on her elbow. She stared fixedly at him.

Time stood still as he attempted to come up with an acceptable answer.

"I'd never really thought about it, my love."

Caitlin was afraid of what he might say next, but she kept her composure and waited.

"There's so much going on at work. I've Bill's new site in Sri Lanka and, on top of that, my newer clients." He regarded her for a moment, then gave her his best smile, lazy and confident, with warmth in his brown eyes.

"Tell you what – how about we talk about it on honeymoon? We'll both be relaxed then, loved up and happy. I promise I'll give it my full attention!" He grabbed her playfully, pulled her onto her back and sealed his promise with another long, loving kiss.

It wasn't ideal, but Caitlin supposed it was something. She didn't want to push him – the old Chris was back, and he hadn't said no. He was right. It could wait. Anyway, it wouldn't be long before they'd lie in the sun by the pool, drinking lovely, exotic cocktails. Her tummy rolled with excitement. Eventually, the lovers fell into a contented, deep slumber.

****

The following morning Chris announced a massive surprise. He announced he'd arranged for Anne to see a consultant prosthetist friend in Harley Street early that afternoon before the girls went to greet Tommy at Victoria Coach Station. He laughed as he watched the two dumbfounded women struggle to know what to say. Chris was busy meticulously preparing omelettes for them, with all the necessary kitchen utensils laid out neatly and in order, ready for him to use. Annoyingly, for the life of him, he couldn't find a wooden spoon missing from his set and asked Caitlin if she knew where it was, but it seemed she didn't.

As the girls arrived at the clinic later that day, they found it in a glorious, white stucco Georgian townhouse. Its waiting room could easily have been in *Homes & Gardens* with lush cream carpet and expensive lacquered furniture. It was bliss. They giggled as they waded through glossy magazines they'd never pay for themselves while showing each other photographs of famous entertainers.

Soon a tall, athletically built, suited, and booted consultant welcomed them with a genuine smile and led them into his consulting room, which was equally luxurious. After briefly explaining his specialism, he began examining Anne's artificial limb.

"Dear… dear, dear! What have we got here?" he asked, tutting and shaking his head. He looked at her with genuine sympathy.

"You, young lady, have certainly been through the wars, haven't you?"

"You could say that," she replied bleakly.

"And I bet you've had a lot of pain and messy infections?"

"You've no idea." Anne nodded, recalling the months and years of flare-ups and numerous courses of antibiotics. To top it all, she still found it challenging to look at her truncated limb, half-believing her leg was still there like the message hadn't reached her brain – it was gone for good. She'd get shooting, stabbing pains, pins and needles, and sometimes felt like it was on fire. She'd looked it all up in the library: Phantom Leg Syndrome.

"Well, we can get you sorted, I'm sure. Let me have a closer look," the doctor suggested soothingly.

Caitlin watched as he carefully removed Anne's prosthetic. She inwardly cringed at the sight of the stump. It was shiny, red and tender-looking. The skin appeared too tight from the healed but unsightly stitches. It was quite a daunting sight. Anne caught her staring, crossed her eyes and stuck out her tongue, making Caitlin smile.

The consultant discussed the latest prosthetic developments and displayed some brochures and samples for Anne to look at and feel. She was astonished at the wide variety available and how natural-looking they were. The women looked at each other worriedly, thinking the same thing. How much would this cost?

Afterwards, the specialist spent some time explaining Anne's best options until he opened the door for them with another sunny smile.

"Not long now until the wedding," he commented merrily, surprising them both. "My partner and I are looking forward to it. We hope it cools down first. It's lovely to meet you, Caitlin, finally!"

He gently placed one hand on her shoulder as he led them to the reception area. She'd had no idea Chris had invited the doctor! Much against her wishes, his PA was managing things from here on. "It'll make life easier if you leave it all to me. I want you to have fun with Anne while she's here!" Chris had said to appease her.

She wasn't happy at first that it seemed to be turning into a big affair over which she had little say, but now that Anne was here, it'd certainly given them much more time to enjoy themselves. Once more, Chris had turned out to be right.

"There is one small thing," the specialist said before clearing his throat with a slight cough and stopping mid-way along the corridor. "The cost."

The girls' hearts dropped in trepidation, and he immediately detected their worry.

He took Anne's hand and gently held it while he shared some fantastic news.

"Ms Heaney, we've got a special fund for victims of conflict here at the clinic – cases such as yours from all over the world. Without further ado, I have to tell you that we will cover your treatment cost. I hope to have you sorted out in the next few months. It'll mean coming back and forth between here and Ireland a few times, but I think you'll be satisfied with the result. Very satisfied indeed."

Anne tried to scream with delight but made no sound – she couldn't believe it! Caitlin had no problem vocalising her joy but exclaimed happily and hugged her friend as the specialist watched. He, too, was happy. This was what he loved about his job: he had the power to change lives for the better, and at moments like this, his gratification was immeasurable. The poor girl had undeniably been through a horrific experience, and he couldn't begin to imagine how uncomfortable she'd been ever since. Although the original surgery was well done, her poorly fitted limb had caused irreparable damage, but he had high hopes he could improve the quality of her life.

He clapped his hands and chuckled. "I take it that's a yes, then!"

"Oh, yes! Yes, please!" the women cried in unison.

With fluttering eyelashes, Anne chanced her arm and said, "I don't suppose it could be ready for the wedding if you got a special move on like? I am the one and only bridesmaid, remember."

"No chance of that, young lady. As I said, it'll take months. But good try! Bye now, see you at the wedding!"

****

As Tommy had foreseen, the never-ending overnight journey to London was an ordeal.

Much to the angst of the tired bus driver and his fellow passengers, Tommy had no choice but to insist on extra pit stops as the crammed bus made its way the hundreds of miles from Stranraer to London.

Eventually, the coach journey ended in London's Victoria, where the weary passengers gathered their belongings and disembarked. Embarrassed, Tommy deliberately waited until they'd all left, and he was the last onboard. He looked uncomfortably at the driver and shrugged an apology. "Sorry for that. I had to ask otherwise..."

The driver smiled sympathetically and offered some advice. "No worries, mate, but you're in a bit of trouble there. Best get it checked."

"Aye, I know," Tommy answered dejectedly. "Thanks anyway."

In disarray, he surveyed the busy station and soon found her – she was like a beautiful vision. Tears welled at such a sight, mingled with a pang of sadness. What would his sister and Patrick have felt, seeing their Caitlin looking like this? Wearing white-rimmed sunglasses, she stood there waiting for him with a welcoming smile. She looked stunning, dressed in a pale pink trouser suit over a white lace camisole – *she was pure class.*

At the sight of her uncle, Caitlin's face lit up. She'd been beginning to worry he wasn't on the bus, and she radiated happiness and joy when they finally found each other. As they walked towards each other across the concourse, though, she began to feel alarmed.

Tommy looked ghastly, she realised, and it struck a blow to her heart – her uncle was ill!

However, she kept her smile pinned in place and hugged his newly lean body. He looked dishevelled and rumpled. The familiar smell of Old Spice transported her back to Blamfield Street, where she'd watched her daddy douse himself in the same sharp, fresh aftershave. They hugged hard until Tommy pulled away and gently took her hand. Tears rolled down their faces.

"Ah, Tommy, it feels like forever!" she cried, grabbing him again and squeezing him tight.

"Caitlin, love, if your Mammy and Daddy could see you now... Let me look at you properly." He stood back and regarded her from top to toe.

The Derry girl had done good, really good, and made the right choice in leaving. Mind you, that Henderson boy was right – he'd dropped a right clanger by letting this exquisite woman go. *Oh, shit!* Tommy suddenly remembered. *Holy Mother of God, the letter! He'd gone and left the frigging' envelope behind!*

"Are you okay, Tommy? You've gone a funny colour," Caitlin asked. She was perturbed now and took his arm to lead the way.

"Come with me. We'll get you a cup of tea before we head back. Anne's waiting for us a bit round the corner on Buckingham Palace Road."

Tommy scolded himself for a fool and knew, one way or another, he'd have to deal with the issue of the letter later.

"Buckingham Palace, eh? I'm not sure I'm dressed for a palace!" he cackled.

Caitlin struck him playfully and linked her arm with his. Now that Anne and Tommy were with her, she couldn't be happier, although she'd sell her soul for the rest of the McLaughlins to be here too.

They made it to the coffee shop, once part of a church, where Tommy glimpsed Anne waiting patiently with a substantial stainless-steel pot of tea and an assortment of cakes on the table in front of her.

"Hello, you!" she said happily, hugging him. She'd known Tommy for years and loved him to bits.

"Hello, you, back!" he cried while instinctively looking for the Gents. "Just give me a minute, will you, girls?" he said. "Nature calls."

"Sure," Caitlin answered, her face filled with love and concern.

Tommy hastily went to the toilet, and Anne poured the tea. Making sure he was well out of earshot, Caitlin said, "He doesn't look well, does he?"

Anne was staggered by the change in the big man. He was almost unrecognisable with the massive weight loss he'd recently experienced, but his colour worried her the most: that grey-white, sickly pastiness. She recognised the death mask Tommy O'Reilly wore – she'd seen it before. Naturally, she decided to say nothing; it was too close to the wedding.

"Sure, he's lost a wee bit of weight, but don't forget he's done that long journey. He'll be grand when he gets a good night's sleep. You'll see."

But Caitlin wasn't convinced though she appreciated Anne's tact. Whatever it was, Tommy would tell her. She'd get him on his own as soon as she could.

Anne nervously cut the cakes into tiny pieces. She watched Tommy come back and sit down wearily. He was exhausted and just wanted to lie down.

****

The next day's pre-wedding dinner was meant for a few friends. However, as Caitlin looked around the beautifully dressed table in a private dining room at the Savoy, there were quite a few people present she didn't know. She thanked God Anne and Tommy were with her, already dreading their departure.

Chris had bought his fiancée a new evening dress from a recently opened ladies' shop, Hobbs. It was a classic Audrey Hepburn-style gown: long, black, strapless, with a circular skirt highlighted by a thick red waistband similar to a cummerbund. It complemented and emphasised her tiny waist, and its strapless top exposed her delicate shoulders – she felt fantastic!

Anne sat to Caitlin's left, displaying a brand-new hairstyle. She had straightened her wild locks till they were sleek and glossy and turned under slightly at the ends. She looked stunning in a 1950s full-petticoated New Look blue dress she'd found in a charity shop off Ebury Street. It'd been love at first sight. Now Caitlin watched her talking animatedly across the table to a gob-smacked guest about getting a new leg! Sitting close by, Tommy seemed happy enough to talk to some of the younger people from Chris's office with seemingly no difficulty adjusting to their metropolitan chat. He had never lost the ability to surprise her, Caitlin thought fondly.

"This is so un-fuckin'-believable," Anne whispered a short time later, leaning perilously across some tealights on the table. "Did you ever think Anne Heaney and Caitlin McLaughlin would be sitting in the fuckin' Savoy eating frass grass or whatever it's called?" She giggled. "It's friggin' delicious, by the way. What is it exactly?"

"You *really* don't want to know!"

Caitlin laughed, deciding not to tell Anne more about it; she'd been shocked when Chris first told her. He was sitting on her other side.

She felt him take her right hand and rub her palm the way she liked. He had a way of sensing her nervousness around strangers, especially in such grand surroundings. As usual, he looked very distinguished tonight in black tie, as did the other men. Wives and girlfriends wore cocktail dresses in satin, silk and velvet. Caitlin could hear the jazz band setting up for late-night dancing in an adjacent lounge.

She watched Chris's mother, Rebecca, and his father, Guido, talking enthusiastically to a group of Chris's school friends. He was an only child. Caitlin always sensed from Rebecca's reserved air that she didn't much like her. Caitlin's Irishness was perceived as an unsuitable match for Pecaro stock. Though Caitlin tried her best to win over her mother-in-law-to-be, it was a waste of energy.

As for Chris's daddy, he was lovely. An old-fashioned Italian gentleman, he was always beautifully dressed, and his manners were impeccable. He also had the twinkle in his dark eyes of a man who appreciated a beautiful woman when he saw one, and Caitlin felt sorry for him, having to put up with Rebecca, who always looked as if she had recently sucked a lemon.

Chris squeezed his fiancée's hand and whispered, "I hope you don't mind, darling, but I've invited a couple of these guys we're working with to join us for an after-dinner drink?"

Caitlin was so content and happy tonight that she'd have agreed to anything.

"Please, go ahead. I'm more than fine."

The gilded and mirrored walls of the dining room caught and reflected the sparkling light from many strategically placed candles. The atmosphere was dreamlike, almost magical. Caitlin felt she'd already been to hell and back in her short life, but now her life had turned into a fairy tale.

Soaking in the celebratory mood and watching Anne in full swing, she barely heard Chris tell her, "By the way, one of those guys is from your part of the world."

Before Caitlin could ask him where exactly, a circus of white-gloved servers arrived with covered dishes for their second course. They waited behind each chair in perfect unison before removing the shining silver domes to reveal honey roast duck with vegetables.

****

"Caitlin, I swear I'm going to burst out of this dress. I've never eaten so much in my whole life!" Anne cried as she struggled to rise after the delicious meal. Other guests began mingling or stepping onto the terrace to light up.

"Come with me. I need to pee!" she giggled, grabbing Caitlin's arm.

Chris watched them with an indulgent smile, enjoying Anne's antics. Anne Heaney was something else, the real McCoy, a gutsy young woman who was a true friend to Caitlin. He hoped she'd often visit once he and Caitlin were married.

He felt remarkably relaxed and happy, pleased with how he'd cleverly managed to deflect the baby conversation. He looked at his beautiful fiancée being dragged across the floor by Anne, and a surge of feeling went through him. He loved her so much. But other than with Anne and her kindly uncle, he wasn't prepared to share her with anyone, let alone a bald, bad-tempered, crying infant. There'd be time to think about all that later. Much later. Tonight he was too happy.

Making Caitlin giggle, Anne held her tummy and lurched towards the Ladies. Chris nearly choked on his drink at the sight and laughed heartily. Unfortunately for him, at that moment, his mother joined him. He caught her disapproving expression and half-smiled an apology. He loved her, but she was getting worse, constantly reiterating how unhappy she was with his choice of bride.

"She's much too young! I'm telling you, my boy, she'll be trouble and… and she's Irish, for goodness' sake! What will the neighbours think?" He'd refused to listen to her anymore on this subject. His mind was made up.

"Chris!" he heard Bill Fox call from behind him. "They're here."

"Coming!" he replied with relief, turning away from his mother and following Bill into the hotel's foyer with its mirrored walls and chequerboard marble floor.

****

James had decided to bring Paul Doherty, part treat, part business. After their last session, Chris and Bill suggested meeting up in London, and Chris kindly issued an invitation to after-dinner drinks at the Savoy. At one time, James had loved this hotel's Art Deco splendour. However, nowadays, it brought back memories of his and Marleen's

English wedding reception, and he wasn't keen to stay too long. He looked at Paul, who seemed wide-eyed and awkward in such elegant surroundings, and felt for him as a man out of his comfort zone.

"You look like a stunned mullet, Paul. Relax! They're good guys, so try and enjoy yourself!"

Paul had never been anywhere like it and was momentarily speechless. The sweet scent of the bountiful vases of flowers, the luxury of the deep pile carpet, the gilded furniture and the paintings on the silk-covered walls were out of this world. Then there were the women in evening gowns and jewellery and the men in dinner jackets, all smelling of money – serious money.

He trailed James until he saw two smiling men approaching them.

"Ah, James, delighted you could make it!" Chris exclaimed. They shook hands, and he enquiringly looked at Paul, waiting to be introduced.

"Chris, this is Paul Doherty, my assistant manager. I hope you don't mind if he joins us. Apologies, Mr McScott, couldn't make it this trip."

"Not at all! The more, the merrier. I hope Alfie is okay?" Chris didn't wait for an answer but introduced Bill Fox to Paul and, with the introductions over, suggested they head for the American Bar.

"We'll go and get a drink, have a quick chat, and then I'll introduce you to everyone else later," he explained.

Paul felt underdressed though he wore his best three-piece suit and a light blue shirt with his favourite candy-striped (Derry City FC) tie. Though he felt totally out of his depth, he couldn't believe he was standing here top-rated London hotel. What would the boys say back at Maileys?

****

Still, in the Ladies, Caitlin and Anne were refreshing their make-up. Anne felt slightly less bloated, and the wine she'd consumed was working its magic. She felt euphoric, especially after talking to Matt and telling him the fantastic news about her leg. He'd been ecstatic! Her voice slurred as she thanked Caitlin for the trip and Chris's unbelievable kindness in fixing up for her to see the consultant.

"I'll n'ver forget this, Caitlin, what you and Chris've done for me. I'll n'ver forget it for as long as I live. On our Sean's soul!"

She blessed herself twice, fast and furious. Caitlin looked at her in the mirror and smiled lovingly. She shook her head and touched Anne's arm.

"You'd do it for me if it was the other way round. And after everything that's happened, we both deserve a wee bit of happiness, don't we?"

Anne nodded tipsily. "We do, love. We most certainly do."

Wobbling slightly, she watched her friend apply her posh red glossy lipstick like a professional. Anne smiled crookedly. Caitlin belonged here in London; it suited her. By fuck, she'd come far, but at what cost? She knew too well how her friend had continually pined for the Adonis and why she was marrying Chris Pecaro.

Caitlin, oblivious to Anne's concern, began to search her evening bag, eventually asking, "Could you do me a wee favour? My blusher must've fallen out of my bag. It might be beneath my chair. You wouldn't hop along and grab it? I need to pee too."

Only Caitlin McLaughlin could get away with using such language – *feckin' hop along*! Anne wagged her finger and grinned drunkenly. "Only for you, Caitlin McLaughlin! Only you! I'll be two sticks of a lamb's bush!" she cried merrily tipsy, exaggeratedly hopping towards the door.

Caitlin's eyes shone with happiness as she headed to a cubicle to find actual goldfish swimming in the cistern; she shook her head. How the heck did that work?

Outside, Anne wasn't sure which direction to return to the private dining room, so she waited, hoping to find someone to help. She looked around and was relieved to see Chris and Bill standing by the hotel entrance. On her way over to them, she shuddered as if struck by lightning when she recognised the men standing with them.

Mother of God, it couldn't be! Wasn't that the Adonis himself, along with wee Paul Doherty talking to Chris and Bill? It couldn't be! *What was in that feckin' wine?*

****

Chapter Thirty-seven

Upon reflection, James felt something odd had happened to Paul as they made their way towards the main cocktail bar of the Savoy. His colleague's face turned deathly white, and he suddenly stopped and stood still, staring across the lavish foyer as if he'd seen a ghost.

"You okay?" James asked with concern, touching his elbow lightly.

"No. Sorry, boss, yeah, I'm fine," Paul stuttered. *Jesus Christ! Must be seeing things!*

He would've sworn he'd seen Caitlin McLaughlin's wacky, one-legged friend Anne Heaney all dolled up. He was convinced it was her, and from the look on her face, she was as surprised as he was! What were the likes of her doing at the Savoy?

Chris Pecaro sensed the young man's unease and looked across the foyer to see what was occurring. There was nothing much to see except the mingling guests, hotel staff and Anne standing by the Ladies. He looked at Paul enquiringly.

"Something wrong?"

He took stock and apologised again.

"Sorry, no. I thought I knew someone, but it couldn't be. Sorry."

The small group chuckled and were welcomed by a red-jacketed waiter in the bar, who swiftly took their order as they made their way to sit cosily in a quiet corner.

Bill Fox was feeling particularly tired. They were having a tough time with baby Ella and had been told by their doctor recently that she had severe asthma. Naturally, they were worried as Ella refused to sleep, and Bill felt responsible – the illness ran in his family, and from experience, he understood how frightening it was. They'd decided to keep it quiet, not wanting to worry the rest of his family and friends.

The good news was that he and Chris had positive vibes about investing in Rocola and were excited about working with James

Henderson. The partners had already decided to invest financially and in an advisory role in Rocola, but there were some stipulations, especially concerning the existing management team. Most notably, Alfie McScott would be the first casualty. His poor decision-making around FYJH had cost the factory dear, leaving them unhealthily cash-poor and vulnerable to takeover. They knew McScott was aware he'd screwed up, but they would've sacked the man on the spot if it'd been up to either Bill or Chris.

"Is this your first trip to London, Paul?" Bill enquired, making small talk as they waited for their drinks.

"It is, Mr Fox. I have to say, it's very different from back home, but that wouldn't be difficult!" Paul laughed nervously.

Bill turned to James and asked mischievously, "And are you going to allow Paul some time off to see the sights?"

James nodded. "Indeed I am. He's family here, and I hope to catch up with some old friends. We're going to hang on for a few more days."

James still wasn't sure what he was going to do. He had no way of contacting Caitlin but hoped she'd respond to his letter, which she must have had by now. He'd asked her to leave a contact number at the office or with his housekeeper. This was before he knew he would be in London himself at the meeting the investors had hastily called. Maybe, just maybe, if she had the time, they could get together.

Bill smiled. "Ah, that's good. It's been so hot here recently that you should take advantage of it! Is it still raining at home, or are you having some sort of summer?"

Everyone laughed and talked a little about the erratic Irish weather. The men's drinks promptly arrived, and the company sat back and relaxed. The party discussed very little business, the mood was light-hearted, and the conversation flowed easily. After the second round of drinks, Chris stood up, rubbed his hands together and cheerfully announced, "Time to get back to our guests! James, Paul, would you care to join us?"

James met his assistant's eye. They'd agreed to stay for two drinks, no more, not wanting to impose because they still had work to complete.

James shook his head, feigning disappointment. "I'm sorry, but I hope you don't mind if we leave. We've still got some final prep for tomorrow. We despatched a major order in the wee hours of this morning and left Derry later than expected. Another time perhaps?"

Bill was more than relieved by James's refusal – he desperately wanted to go home. Maryann hadn't joined them for dinner, and he was keen to get back to her and Ella; he was exhausted.

"We'll see you tomorrow," he replied hurriedly, bordering on rudeness.

Chris shook his head and looked at him, not understanding his apparent impatience. He felt a twinge of annoyance – he'd been looking forward to introducing and showing off Caitlin to his Irish visitors, especially James and now Paul, who lived in Londonderry. But no doubt, the trials and tribulations of looking after the new arrival had affected Bill and Maryann. Yet another good reason not to have a family, he thought.

"Let me walk you out then," said Chris, giving Bill a slightly sour look, then led his guests to the revolving doors where they shook hands and said goodnight.

****

The following day in his office, Alfie McScott put down the phone. He'd finished a rather informative call with William Barter in the States.

"I've been thinking a lot about that cancelled invoice from your mystery company since I left, and I've done a bit of digging. I guess it's been driving me a little crazy, but I have to ask – why were you guys dealing with FYJH & Sons?" he asked.

Alfie was flummoxed. After his late hours of fruitless research and probing, trust the Yank to steal a march. "You've heard something about them?" he asked excitedly.

"I have – at least, I think I have. One of my sources mentioned something 'bout them in passing—just the once. Don't go and get all excited, Alfie," Barter replied in his usual drawl.

"Who was it?" he cried, frantically rising from his chair while gripping the handset. "What do you know, Mr Barter?"

When Barter had observed that piece of FYJH-headed paper on the accountant's desk, he'd deliberately kept quiet. Before he said anything to Alfie, the poor wreck of a man, he needed to be sure. As soon as he returned to the States, he'd dug out the notes from his prison visit to Lemon. As Barter hoped, they confirmed the Loyalist had been privy to one of Jones's ranting phone calls when he'd talked about this company. Lemon was as mad as a box of frogs, but Barter had carefully and meticulously recorded everything he said – word for word.

He studied his yellow legal pad and smiled. There it was, in his scrawling handwriting.

Lemon talks about some company like SYJH or FYJH, and Henderson! Find out more… what is FYJH?

Barter knew the accountant wouldn't like what he was about to hear. "I'm sorry, Alfie, but FYJH *is* or *was* owned by Charles Jones."

"Damn it, no!" the man moaned. "Not him again!"

Barter heard Alfie's misery down the line and quickly revealed Jones had indisputably owned FYJH & Sons Ltd and very cleverly set it up as a dummy company, one of many hidden under three large umbrella or holding companies. But for CIA-sanctioned help from his friend Dale, they'd never have traced it. The sole purpose of FYJH & Sons Ltd had been to dupe Rocola into producing a vast and costly order and cause it irrevocable financial damage when the purchaser defaulted and disappeared.

Officially FYJH & Sons Ltd had now ceased trading and was dissolved. This time, it looked like Jones had scored a cracking goal, causing Rocola to lose a third of its workforce and be left with £75K worth of unsold stock.

"Is there nothing we can do? Is it even legal!" Alfie wailed, desperate and fearful.

"It's all legit. I'm sorry."

Barter was hoping to find a way back to Northern Ireland when it was deemed safe to finish off what he'd started with Jones. He thought maybe, with this titbit, there'd be enough to convince his editor to let him return. He doubted it, but heck, he'd try! They talked for a few more minutes before Alfie thanked him and hung up.

He remained shocked at how the wool had been pulled over his eyes. He'd given forty years of his life to Rocola and knew his time here was almost up. Anyone else would have shown him the front door by now; he knew James would have fired him but for his unblemished record and loyalty to date.

He decided that, no matter what, he'd find any opportunity he could to get his revenge on Mr Charles Jones.

****

Chapter Thirty-eight

Maggie McFadden could only stare at her husband in bewilderment. His face was virgin white; she had never seen such a colour. Shattered already from what he'd told her, she screeched at him like a banshee.

"I don't believe you, Charlie. How the fuck..." She stopped suddenly, not prepared to start swearing at her age. "How could you not have told me before? All this time, Charlie, you've kept this to yourself."

"I've told you, love. For the hundredth time, I was trying to please you! To keep you happy!"

"Please me? *Please* me! Don't blame *me* for *you* being such an eejit! You could be beaten to a pulp and that goblin body of yours thrown into the Foyle, like that other poor eejit-turned-fish-food they found in the Swilly!"

Charlie swallowed and nodded. Maggie was right. He'd had to tell her today, not because of the warnings, which so far he'd managed to shove to the back of his mind, but because another workmate didn't show up. The poor critter was found later in a country lane, kneecapped badly. He'd bled out and died after some stupo hit an artery instead of going through bone.

Charlie had to admit he was relieved that, at last, everything was out in the open. Good money or not, the job had taken its toll and, in hindsight, hadn't been worth it. He felt a thousand years old.

Maggie was livid; he could tell from how her fingers nervously twisted and played with her plain gold wedding ring. She sniffled and looked at him scornfully.

"All these months, Charlie, you've been carrying this around, lying to Emmett and me. I swear to Jesus, I don't know how you did it!"

She didn't know what to say, torn between incredulity and exasperation. The tension in the small kitchen was palpable; you could cut it with a knife.

Her arms went up in despair when she remembered her eldest boy. "You know, if our Joe hears about this, you'll be lucky if he ever speaks to you again! And Jesus, Charlie, think about how he'll feel after the nightmare he's only gone through with the Brits!"

She had to leave the kitchen to get away from him. She muttered as she stood in the doorway, "Come to think of it, that's probably why they didn't blow your knees out – or worse!"

Charlie moved to hold her back but sensed the tension in her body and retreated. She warned him in a stern voice, "Don't you dare come near me! I can't even bear to look at you."

She slammed the kitchen door with such force that their St Mary's Church calendar broke free and fell onto the vinyl flooring.

Charlie's crestfallen head dropped into his shovel-sized hands as he gave way to despair. He couldn't remember the last time he'd cried, but now it felt like his world was truly over.

****

Numerous seagulls squawking in chorus woke Joe McFadden from his customary dream of playing Gaelic. Reluctantly, he opened his eyes and found himself alone in his cell. *Fuck*!

He wanted to go back to sleep, to dream of Dunfanaghy in County Donegal, where he'd played numerous times. All he did these days was sleep. Being locked up like this was dehumanising. Hiding his mounting depression from his parents was especially tough – his ma could read him like a book, though he'd tried his best to pretend he was okay. He'd do anything to get out of this tomb, to breathe the sea air and be free to go wherever he wanted.

The Kesh was a very different place from what it'd been a year or so ago. Back then, an everyday clamour of men crying, "I…I…IRA!"

or "We're political prisoners. We want political status!" had been the norm. Now, however, it'd become quiet though there was a febrile buzz in the air at the changes in the political climate beyond these walls.

In time, the Brits had quietly conceded to the hunger strikers' five demands, if still with no formal recognition of the prisoners' return to political status. Now, though, they didn't have to wear a prison uniform or do prison work. They were free to associate among their wing. They had their educational and leisure facilities again, and their final demand of one visit, one letter and one parcel per week looked likely to materialise.

The weather had been stifling recently, and the cells were hot as a baker's oven.

Joe had been reading an out-of-date newspaper about some poor wanker breaking into the Queen's bedroom.

Alone still, he made his way slowly outside to the exercise yard. The sun was belting down on the hot tarmac. He looked around in search of the OC, who spotted him and quickly began to make his way over.

"You're getting your head together on what we need, McFadden?" he asked carefully.

"Yes, sir," Joe replied dutifully.

"Good. Stick at it, and don't forget to keep this to yourself." He looked at the inmates playing soccer in the yard, some of whom sported red Liverpool shorts, and added miserably: "We've enough grasses here to turf a football pitch."

The heat had encouraged most prisoners to remove their T-shirts while others were chatting and watching the game, wearing old-fashioned blue bell-bottomed jeans with tucked-in three-button granddad vests.

Joe had been told to make friends with several screws. The idea was to suss them out and prepare a psychological profile of each man. That way, it'd give the OC a grasp on how each PO would react if a gun was pointed at their head and they were ordered to hand over the keys. The Republicans planned to escape from the most notorious prison in Europe and were carefully and thoughtfully preparing for every scenario.

Joe spotted Sean Keenan at the yard's far end, leaning against a towering wall of steel topped with German razor-barbed wire. He was talking and laughing with one of the targeted screws. Joe smiled; good old Sean was able to speak affably to anyone.

"What's so funny?" Joe asked as he strode towards the two men. This particular screw hated McFadden, remembering his never-ending stubbornness and determination, the way he'd refused a bath during the blanket protest. He was never compliant and had always made wash time worse than the nightmare it already was. The PO blanked him completely and hurried away.

Out of earshot, Sean gleefully told Joe, "See that eejit there?"

"Aye, why? What's he done?"

"The daft fucker's no more than gone and told me where he feckin' lives!" Sean cried, fighting to get his T-shirt over his head before casually throwing it aside so he could bask in the sun.

"What the fuck? How'd you get him to do that!" Joe asked, flabbergasted. It was such a stupid thing for any PO to do. They were ordinarily paranoid and frightened of being attacked outside by connections of the prisoners.

"Ways and means, Joey boy, ways and means," Sean replied. He imitated, pointing a gun at the back of the disappearing screw. Nineteen PO's had already been targeted.

"Bang, bang! There goes number twenty!" Sean laughed and then pointed to the tarmac. "Friggin' heck, it's so fuckin' hot, you could fry an egg on that!"

Joe smirked. *Bang-bang,* number twenty indeed. He accompanied Sean and leaned against the wall to watch the game.

In time, his eyes began to roam the yard with its high breeze-block walls topped with razor wire. With no vegetation in sight, the men here inhabited a world of concrete, wire, bright lights, scrutinising guards and constant affliction. He recalled his childhood and the daisy fields that seemed to stretch for miles, where he and Martin McLaughlin would play until it got dark and they'd no choice but to go home. How carefree they'd been in childhood, and heedlessly they'd taken it for granted.

Then their lives changed almost overnight. He and many others like him would never forget 30th January 1972, Bloody Sunday. Like bees to honey, the teenagers of Derry weren't going to sit back and watch the carnage brought to their streets by the British invasion. Joe joined the IRA to become a soldier. He was still a soldier at war who would die for his country without question. He'd already suffered starvation, abuse, loneliness, isolation, bigotry and more for the cause. Yet he could hear his united comrades laughing, wisecracking and playing in this baking hot cesspool. The Brits would never break their camaraderie, no matter how brutal or demeaning the treatment they handed out.

Joe McFadden and many more like him were determined to win this fight until their island was ultimately united and free.

****

Chapter Thirty-nine

Shortly after Brian visited Paddy's house and found him in a stupor, he warned his colleague that the drugs had to stop.

"I'm telling you, Paddy, that junk you're taking is frying your brain! Look at yourself, man – you're rotten! If you don't fuckin' sort it, I'm outta here! I'm away back to Belfast!"

Paddy, who felt as sick as a dog, couldn't listen to any more of Brian's griping and told him viciously: "Fuck away off to Belfast then, I don't give a flying fuck!" Later, to Paddy's dismay, Brian did just that; he disappeared, and Paddy heard nothing from him, which was unusual and surprised him no end.

Brian wasn't typically one to hold a grudge, and Paddy felt quietly hurt – they'd had worse fights, but they'd always made up. Before he left, Brian handed over his work on the Foxes, their everyday movements, likes and dislikes, and more to Cahir O'Connell. The Derry CO had no jurisdiction over Brian and believed the big man had every right to go back home if he wanted to.

After that, Paddy knew he had to catch himself on and decided to go cold turkey and get clean. It was a task that proved to be way more complicated than he'd thought and took its toll on him, mentally and physically. He decided that as soon as the London op was complete, he'd find Brian and fix things between them; he loved him like a brother; they were kindred spirits.

Paddy and the Provo Leadership decided it'd be too risky to kidnap the couple but would target their baby instead. That way, it would reduce the number of operatives needed and leave the multi-millionaires at liberty to pay the £1 million ransom. The OC warned Paddy to be alert – kidnapping was a first for them. He and McKenna must be meticulous and stick to the plan.

So far, Liz knew very little about the operation besides that she had to go to London. When she'd asked about it, Mr Hunky, as she privately thought of Paddy, told her repeatedly, "It's purely on a need-to-know basis." Liz couldn't describe her excitement and didn't care who or what the op involved. She'd do whatever it took to prove herself in her determination to move up.

It'd been a rough ferry crossing from Belfast to Liverpool, and Mr Hunky remained quiet and aloof, but that suited her. She wasn't sure how she'd respond to him if he did show interest – her insides felt like jelly when he talked, he was so sexy, and she let her imagination run wild. He was one of those men who had 'it', and whatever 'it' was, it gave her palpitations! He'd given her cash for some onboard food and drink, but he ate nothing.

Although he appeared very laidback, he sometimes mumbled to himself, and she grew concerned when she watched him swallow a handful of painkillers.

"Are you okay? What are they for?" she asked with concern.

"I'm fine!" he snapped, dismissing her with a wave of a hand and giving her a *fuck off and mind your own business* look.

She got up in a huff and stalked off over the deck, finding herself an out-of-the-way seat where she sat with her face turned away, though she'd rather have been studying him.

Eventually, after the ferrymen shepherded the passengers to their vehicles, they were on their way down south. They'd been left a clean car to use at Belfast docks and had no problem going through security in Liverpool. Liz had never seen so many speeding vehicles as when their small Toyota veered its way down the network of motorways. After snapping her head off, she'd decided Paddy didn't deserve to be called Mr Hunky anymore. He remained quiet and aloof throughout the journey, and so did she.

Liz lay back on the headrest, closed her eyes to enjoy the sun's heat as it shone through the car window, and eventually slept. At her soft snoring, Patrick half-smiled. He felt like shite and didn't want to talk.

He respected the girl for not badgering him and knew they'd made the right choice in her. Not only did the security services not know her, but she was as sharp as a tack. She'd quickly picked up what he'd told her about the op and, when necessary, wasn't afraid to challenge him. Under that sweet shyness of hers was a cunning woman.

Sometime later, he heard her mumbling and whining. He watched in surprise as she woke and quickly swiped her eyes with her hands – she'd been crying in her sleep. He felt guilty for barking at her earlier; maybe it was his turn now to check on her.

"You good?" he asked, attempting to keep his eyes on the road.
"Yeah."
"Bad dream?"
"Yeah."
"Want to talk about it?"
"No."
"It might help."

She gave only monosyllabic responses, and his last remark went unanswered. Paddy made a whistling sound. *Okay, I was only trying to help.* He got the message.

Somehow Edwards's abuse and the awful things he'd made her do would float back into her mind's eye in her sleep. Checking her, Paddy watched as she regained her composure and licked her dry lips. He switched on the car radio to hear one of his favourite songs; John Cougar's 'Hurts So Good.' He loved it and increased the volume. He began to sing along to appease his passenger while beating the steering wheel to the rhythm.

'*When I was a young boy....*'

He glanced furtively at Liz, and she gave him an appreciative smile despite herself. Sensing it was a good time, he told her everything about the planned kidnapping and her role in it. She couldn't believe her ears, and her anticipation mounted. *Holy shit!*

****

Maryann Fox was at her wits' end as she looked around her baby's idyllic Peter Rabbit-themed nursery. On the top floor of their Holland Park home, it had everything and more that she or baby Ella could desire or need. All the same, she was truly miserable, and none of these luxuries afforded her any joy or contentment.

She was so exhausted she'd forget to eat, and her weight plummeted. It seemed that no matter what the couple tried, they couldn't get their baby to sleep for more than an hour or two. Ella's asthma had only worsened. Eventually, they took her to Great Ormond Street Children's Hospital; there was nothing more they could do, but they said Ella must continue with her prescribed medication. Maryann felt it wasn't working but was making her baby more ill and unsettled. The young mother was at a loss.

When Ella did sleep, she was a vision of beauty, a picture of perfection. When an attack came on, her delicate features suffused to a deep crimson colour, along with bouts of gasping and choking that terrified her parents beyond belief. As a mother with an instinctive desire to protect her child, Maryann tried her best to soothe her baby, but nothing worked, and she could only hope and pray that the attacks would stop in time.

****

The two volunteers settled into a small B&B in Kilburn. They'd been there for ten days, explaining to the landlady that they were visiting relatives and seeing the London sights. Liz was close to suggesting it would make more sense to share a room, it would look more natural, like an ordinary couple on holiday, but she wasn't sure how to broach it.

Instead, all they saw was the outside of the Foxes' Holland Park residence or the tail lights of whichever car the targets had chosen to use – one of them chauffeured. Today they were parked discreetly round the corner from the Foxes' double-fronted townhouse. They sat patiently in a dark-coloured van they'd stolen from a railway station in Mill Hill earlier that morning. They'd then swapped number plates with the Toyota, which they left in a large Tesco car park.

Liz had walked the park close to the house for the past week, which Maryann frequented on her daily walk with the baby. Liz was smiling hello to her in no time, and soon the young mother returned the greeting.

One day their paths crossed while Maryann sat dog-tired on a bench close to the Orangery and Liz asked if she could sit down. Maryann agreed, and the girl quickly introduced herself while complimenting her on the baby.

"Ah, she's such a lovely thing. I'm Michaela, by the way. Michaela McBride." She gave an easy smile.

"Maryann Fox," the mother replied wearily. "You're Irish?" she asked tiredly.

"I am indeed," Liz replied, "and who is this beautiful piece of God's creation?"

"That's Ella."

"She's certainly something else, isn't she? How old?" Liz asked, feigning interest.

The women continued to make small talk while Liz made a concerted effort to fuss over the baby, who, to her surprise, took an immediate shine to her. Liz had never been into babies; as an only child, she'd not been around many. Most of her young friends, now mothers, continually moaned and complained about the persistent sleepless nights, sore ears, sore throats, dirty nappies and the rest. They'd put her right off, but this was different; she was playing a role in which she was determined to excel.

Over the next few days, they'd meet, and Liz would fuss over Ella, eventually gaining Maryann's trust. Liz grew confident enough to pick up the baby as soon as she saw her, and Maryanne guiltily welcomed the diversion and opportunity for a break.

Back in the van this morning, Paddy rubbed his hands together and told Liz it was time. "Off you go then!" he said smugly. It had all gone amazingly well, and now it was D-Day! He'd grown to admire this young woman who'd proved to be dependable and quick-thinking. She displayed no signs of nerves or stress, and though he knew she fancied him rotten, she'd remained professional. The discipline of this critical assignment seemed to suit her; she was thriving.

"Today's the day, then?" Liz asked excitedly, staring at him.

"That it is!" Paddy laughed. "You know what to do. Stick to the plan."

In jest, he pretended to push her out of the van, and she childishly scrunched up her face and crossed her fingers. It was another scorching summer day, and she was wearing a flattering cotton red and white polka dot dress. Her hair was pulled back tightly into a high girlish ponytail with a matching red and white scarf tied in a bow. A pair of flat white sandals complemented the illusion of virtue and innocence.

Paddy watched the pale-faced mother with the pram step out from behind her sunny yellow front door and stroll down a tiled pathway towards a heavy iron gate. He surveyed Liz as she sauntered over to Maryann, who was struggling to open the gate with the pram in one hand.

"Hey!" Liz cried. "Let me help!"

Maryann was happy to see the familiar young Irish girl and accept her offer. She'd told Bill all about her, how they'd met in the park and how lovely and patient she was with Ella. Her name was Michaela McBride, and she was Irish and a part-time nanny for the summer. She described the reprieve of handing Ella over safely to someone, even for a few short minutes. When Ella was first born, Maryann was against getting a nanny as she wanted to do everything herself. Still, considering the continual sleepless nights and Ella's regular asthma attacks, they'd decided they needed help. Both grandparents lived far away, and perhaps Michaela McBride from Omagh might be interested in a full-time nanny position. Maryann was excited at the prospect and was going to ask her that day. The gate was soon opened, and, smiling, she suggested that Liz join her.

"Are you coming to the park today, or are you working?" she asked, dearly hoping the girl would come.

"I'll come along too if that's okay?" Liz replied, looking up at the deep blue, cloudless sky. "I've got the day off and wanted to do a bit of sunbathing anyway."

"You do? Come with me then, and I'll buy you an ice cream!"

"Lovely!" Liz giggled with a fleeting glance back at the waiting transit van parked by the entrance to the scorched park.

The women sat on their usual bench. Everything was going swimmingly, thought Liz as she spotted Maryann's heavy eyelids failing to stay open.

When they'd finished off their ice creams earlier, Liz had produced two small bottles of cold water from a Marks & Spencer bag.

"Want some?" she offered, holding one of the bottles out.

"Ah, yes, please," Maryann sighed, waving a hand to cool herself. "I hadn't realised it was this hot. That ice cream left me rather thirsty."

Liz said, "Help yourself then." She looked up again and basked in the sunshine and heat. "Oooohh… I love it here! This is tropical compared to home."

Maryann smiled and greedily gulped down the cool water. She quickly checked on Ella, who miraculously was lying contentedly in the pram, and shrugged. "I can't believe she's so good when you're around. She's been up half the night."

"You look tired – drawn-like," Liz commented.

"You've no idea, Michaela. I'm shattered."

Maryann had yet to mention Ella's asthma and the sleepless nights, fearing it might put Michaela off if she considered the job offer. She'd approach the girl later but not now; she was much more sleepy than usual.

"Tell you what, why don't you close your eyes for a minute, and I'll keep an eye on Ella? I promise we won't move from here," Maryann heard the lovely girl suggest from a foggy distance. Such a sweet offer was music to the new mother's ears. She nodded in thanks and closed her eyes, smiling.

Paddy had told Liz to give the sedative two or three minutes to work, so taking a few precious moments to enjoy the sun, she thought about how crucial the next few days would be. They'd gone through the plan meticulously, feeling confident they'd considered everything.

Somehow, she'd sensed a change in Paddy's attitude to her, giving her new faith in herself. He'd even asked her opinion a few times, albeit he'd laughed when she'd finally mentioned them sharing a room. "Not this time, pet!" he joked, chuckling. His rebuff hadn't embarrassed her as it would once have done. Instead, she flirtatiously returned, "Maybe next time, then!" More important than becoming his lover, she was beginning to feel like his equal and on the right path to proving her worth. She closed her eyes in satisfaction.

Moments later, Liz unexpectedly heard a loud thump and opened her eyes to find Maryann lying at her feet.

"Christ!" she cried as she scrambled off the bench to try and help her back up. It proved to be impossible; the woman was a dead weight! Liz put her hand under Maryann's head and felt something sticky. Liz held up her fingers and saw bright red blood that had already flowed onto the ground from Maryann's head injury.

"Everything okay, miss?" Liz heard a deep male voice ask. She glanced up to find a fucking uniformed, moustached policeman staring down at her!

Maryann began to moan as Liz's heart skipped a few beats. *Keep calm, sweet God, keep calm.* She took a deep breath and released it.

"I don't know… She fell off the bench," Liz told him in explanation.

"Here, let me help. Let's try and get her up on her feet first." The policeman then proposed, "I'll radio in for an ambulance."

He bent down and hefted Maryann's body under his arms but struggled to lift her. Liz heard him groaning, "Bloody heck, she's out cold."

She watched as he laid Maryann's head and upper body back down. He straightened up and looked about as he reached for his radio but stopped when he noted the pram.

"Is that baby hers?" he asked in concern.

"Yeah. Her name's Ella, and that's her mum, Maryann. I'm Michaela McBride, her friend. They live just over there." Liz pointed to the Foxes' townhouse. Thinking fast, she frantically suggested, "Shall I take the baby home? The nanny's there, and I'll bring her husband back!"

The policeman waved a hand for her to wait while he talked into the radio. Once finished, he looked at young Michaela, who appeared severely shaken. He glanced again at the townhouse and began to think. The girl looked kosher enough, and he'd noticed the two women talking earlier. "Why don't you do that? I'll stay here with her. Get the husband, leave the child and come straight back. The ambulance will only be a few minutes."

"I'll be as fast as I can!" Liz cried, grabbing Ella's pram and running towards the park's exit. As she sprinted towards the open gates, she looked back and saw that a small crowd had gathered around the policeman. *Shit! Shit!* The only good thing about it was that he couldn't see her; they blocked his view.

Sprinting past the iron gates at lightning speed with the pram, she caught sight of the parked van and headed straight towards it. Paddy saw her approach and quickly climbed out to open the back door. *Something was wrong!* Within seconds, he'd lifted the whole pram inside, pushed Liz in after it, slammed the door tight and driven off.

As soon as he thought it was safe, he screamed to her, "What the hell just happened?"

On cue, baby Ella began to wail, her cries reverberating in the empty, hollow space.

"Shut that fucking thing up, Liz! That's what you're fucking here for. *Sweet mother of Jesus, what a racket!*" Paddy yelled in a fury at the top of his voice. "And what the hell is that smell?"

****

Chapter Forty

"For Christ's sake, how many times do I have to fuckin' tell you? I don't know anything about anything!" Cawley raged from the back seat of his blackmailers' Cortina.

"I don't fuckin' believe you," the small man who was his primary British handler retorted as he looked back with a steely, cruel gaze. He kept his voice quiet and deliberate, making him seem even more threatening.

"Other than us grabbing that M90, you've given me sweet fuck all since. I warned you! You're becoming a liability to us now, Cawley, and believe me, I'll have no worries about sharing details of your collaboration with us with all and sundry. Your OC would be very interested, wouldn't he?"

Reaching for Cawley, the angry agent somehow managed to grab him by his jacket and yank him so close that Cawley could smell the man's garlic-fuelled breath. He recoiled in disgust and tried to free himself but again was surprised by the small man's strength. He heard his handler's callous words when they were eye to eye.

"I want something, Cawley, and before you even think about giving me any useless old crap, let me tell you something. You're not the only wanker we've got by the balls! You fools have no idea how many of your 'loyal' volunteers are turncoats!" Cawley knew he was right. "It's shameful. Pathetic traitors, the lot of you. You'd likely sell your mother for a few lousy bob."

The handler stared coldly at Cawley, allowing him to digest these words, but it didn't take long before his anger returned.

"We both know something big is planned, and now's the time for you to spill the beans. Otherwise, you'll be sorry, mate. You hear? Think of your fucking family!" The man's threat lingered in the cocooned space of the car. His partner, who'd been strictly instructed to drive and keep out of these negotiations, stared straight ahead.

In the blink of an eye, trepidation flashed across Cawley's face, and the handler recognised it in quick double time. He'd been right!

Without warning, he walloped the informant on the side of his head and cried triumphantly.

"You *do* know something. Get the fuck out of the car where I can see you!"

The short man climbed out first and stood waiting, leaving Cawley feeling sick and devastated. He'd given himself away. Slowly, he opened the rear door and started to get out but stopped when he found himself looking down the barrel of a Webley revolver.

Under normal circumstances, he would never flinch at finding himself in such a predicament; however, he'd seen his handler's manic eyes. This man was desperate and under intense pressure. To Cawley, desperation meant danger.

The handler stepped back, pointing the pistol, and Cawley watched him closely, unaware that the Brit had recently overstepped the mark with another informant. Because of his constant pestering for more information, one of his best touts had been exposed and subsequently kicked like a dog and badly beaten by a fucked-up Provo punishment team. His source was still in a comatose state and most likely brain-dead. The agent had been severely reprimanded and warned that he needed to get his act together and come up with something big to compensate for his bungling. From his experience of Cawley, he felt the hefty fucker had what he needed. And if it meant shooting the moron in the balls to find out what it was, then his handler would. His mind reeled back to his unwritten order from above. "Simply get the intel – fuck the consequences!"

The layby where they'd parked was next to a dense forest. With a flick of the gun, the agent steered Cawley towards some oak trees. They walked silently until they stopped at a picnic spot near scattered weather-beaten pine tables and benches.

"Sit."

Cawley carefully took the weight off his feet and slowly sat. He straightened his back and deliberately lifted his chin in defiance as he listened to his gun-wielding captor's threats.

"Needs must. If I have to kill you, Cawley, I will." The handler shook his head slowly and sighed. "You've turned out to be one motherfucker of a thorn in my side, an embarrassment, and I… am… so… fuckin'… angry right now; you'd better tell me what you know or else!"

Cawley balled his hands into fists. He hated this bastard but enjoyed seeing his desperation and felt it was well deserved. Other than the M90 and giving them the odd name of low-ranking veterans, he'd been feeding the Brits nothing but bogus, useless intelligence, and this was most likely why the agent appeared so wild and fraught. Out there, somewhere, was a real supergrass causing absolute mayhem for the Provos. It certainly wasn't Cawley.

The handgun was unexpectedly tucked away into the back of the handler's trousers, and as if in surrender, he raised his hands in the air.

"See. It's only you and me here, man to man. So let's talk."

"No," Cawley answered bitterly; he wasn't going to give this eejit the smell of his shite. It was over. "No. I'm finished. Done," he repeated, experiencing a flood of relief from being able to say it aloud.

"You think?" the other man replied, his words cloaked in sarcasm. He chortled, "Don't you fuckin get it, mate? Why can't I get it into that thick head of yours? Don't you see, this is your last chance!"

The only noise now was the rustling of the wind. Cawley waited.

"Fair enough. You're finished, you say? Well, before you piss off forever, Cawley, you need to know something. That pretty student sister of yours has been lifted again. Think about it: she's likely in some cell now with her lovely young legs open for the officers. I hear they take turns if you know what I mean." He waited, allowing his harsh words to sink in. And judging from Cawley's rabid expression, it was working!

"We thought we'd let the other one alone, at least for the time being," he added mercilessly.

The small man moved closer to Cawley and told him in a warning tone, "If you don't fuckin' tell me what you know, I swear I'll make sure that once the lads are rightly finished with her, she'll be the first on that meat wagon to Armagh gaol tomorrow morning." The agent laughed insultingly.

It hit Cawley that this had gone way too far. The girls would never cope or recover from being arrested and locked up in gaol. He'd heard about the abuse meted out there, especially the horrific neglect and death of that poor mite Tina McLaughlin. Against the urging of every molecule and particle in his body and at the risk of his own life, Cawley knew he had to spill some more details, though nothing about London. But only if this British cunt guaranteed they'd leave his sisters alone and get him the hell out of Ireland.

****

Chapter Forty-one

Vinny Kelly couldn't believe it as he held on tight to the small white envelope with its all-important postmark, 'Londonderry GPO'. It had to be from the McFaddens!

Thrusting the letter into his back pocket, he smiled happily at his protector. Eddie cautiously embraced Vinny's joy and smiled with him. He'd love to share his pal's happiness in another time and place, but his heart had dropped like a stone when Vinny got the envelope and flung him a glance of triumph as he waved it about. The poor critter was waiting for ages for an answer, and Eddie amazed that he'd got a response at all, was anxious about what the letter said.

Dear God, let this be good news.

Vinny mouthed to his friend to follow him upstairs.

Nodding inconspicuously, Eddie heard him seek permission from their semi-drunk House Father to leave the table. With a short wave, he agreed. Vinny tidied up and went to his room as quickly as was allowed.

The House Father watched the boy run up the broad staircase, taking the steps two at a time. Usually, he'd reprimand the scoundrel, but not tonight. Little did the lad know, his House Father had already viewed the pathetic contents of his correspondence. Over time and with practice, he'd become proficient at steaming open any out-of-the-ordinary post.

Eddie waited until he felt it was safe for him to leave the table. Picking up his empty plate, knife and fork, he carefully placed them on a stainless-steel tray and sought permission to leave. Returning his tray to the kitchen, he had to pass by the staff dining table. The House Master gripped his arm as he made his way past and viciously pulled it behind his back.

"You off to see your wee friend up there, are you? Sharin' his bit of news like!" the House Father spluttered nastily.

Eddie stood still as a statue.

"Do y'hear me, lad? I'm talking to ye!" the bearded man yelled, triggering the expulsion of saliva and food remnants.

Eddie didn't move or reply, calculatingly looking as contrite as he could manage. He wasn't going to antagonise the big fella, who was unquestionably on the verge of one of his hell-bent moods.

The House Father snorted, and his spiteful eyes flared as he pushed Eddie away, muttering, "Ah, piss off ye young twat! Get out of my sight!"

He then refilled his half-empty beer glass, looked at the gawking faces all observing them and cried, "You're useless, the whole lot of ye! Finish up and go!"

The terrified boys hung their heads low and scuttled off, hoping not to be chosen to become his afters.

Meanwhile, upstairs Vinny waited patiently. He'd heard the commotion but decided to stay put and was relieved to see Eddie arrive unscathed.

"He's in one of those moods again. That's happening a lot. I think he's getting worse."

"Aye. There's something up," Eddie answered. Maybe his complaints to the police were finally being listened to. He desperately hoped so. "Have you opened it!"

Vinny held up the envelope. "Naw. I was waiting for you!"

Now that the moment had arrived, he was petrified. He threw the letter onto Eddie's bed and cried, "You do it!"

Eddie didn't need to be told twice and quickly grabbed the envelope, tearing it open. Inside was a single sheet of paper, each line written in neat, blue-ink cursive handwriting. He scanned it over first to see what it said and then fixed his eyes on Vinny. Chuckling with relief and joy, he broke into a vast smile.

"What is it? Feck, Eddie! You're killing me! What does it say!" Vinny squealed.

"Shh, listen!" he cried.

"Dear Vinny. I'm sorry for not writing sooner, but there's been loads of things going on.'" Here Eddie looked at Vinny, who was beaming. *"'I can imagine how awful things are for you, Vinny, and we're doing our best to sort it out. Charlie is working all the hours God sends, and we've only talked to Social Services. They've been awful, and I've shown them your letter. We've told them we'd have you tomorrow...'"*

Like a court jester, Vinny jumped up and ran howling around the bedroom, no longer caring who heard him.

"Wait! Wait! There's more!" Eddie screeched anxiously, waving at Vinny to stop and listen. "Shut up, or you'll have him up the stairs!"

Eddie was right, and Vinny sat impatiently on the edge of his bed, fighting to control himself. He rocked back and forth in quiet disbelief. He was going back to Derry!

Eddie continued, *"...blah blah... 'Social Services. They wouldn't talk to us at first, but now they're telling us there's loads of paperwork and it might take some time. Mind you they're saying we might be able to foster you.'"*

Vinny began to snivel. He couldn't believe what he was hearing – neither could Eddie.

"'Hang on, love, we'll be in touch very soon. Love, Maggie, Charlie and Liam xxx'."

Rolling his eyes and pointing one bony finger at his roommate, Vinny cried with relief, "I told you, Eddie, didn't I? I told you!"

"You did, Vinny! You did!" Too choked to say any more, the boys hugged.

Downstairs, alone in the dining room, the House Father heard the commotion. He was surprised to learn how determined the McFaddens were to get Vinny Kelly back to Londonderry. Still, he'd studiously avoided the calls from Kelly's do-gooder of a social worker.

The pressure to provide attractively appealing new specimens had increased after their successful trip to England. However, the goalposts had changed –their clients wanted even younger than Kelly. With Social Services breathing down their necks, Kelly was no longer of use to them, though his photos and videos were still good little earners. His House Father wasn't too worried. Over the years, the paedophile ring had discovered plenty of unfailing ways to ensure that, once the little bastards left, they'd keep their traps shut. Vinny Kelly would be no different.

****

Chapter Forty-two

Bonner wasn't looking forward to the RUC Diamond Jubilee dinner at Belfast City Hall. They'd likely expect him to make a speech, and he hated standing up in front of so many people he despised.

"Fuck!" he hissed, knowing – for appearance's sake – he'd somehow have to convince his wife to attend. As he gazed down the list of acceptances prepared by the Justice Minister's office, there was nothing particularly unusual about it until he reached 'J' and spotted Charles Jones's acceptance. It wasn't that he was surprised Jones was coming, but he had hoped the man would show a little more discretion.

For years, Bonner's ego and the need to earn his stern father's approval had driven him on in his police career. George Shalham's fall from favour for espousing fair play for Catholics had provided an opportunity for Bonner to go for the top cop's job that came free when Shalham was mown down by a speeding car, the murderous driver never traced. At the time, Bonner reckoned Charles Jones was instrumental in bringing about the new Chief Constable's appointment.

Nevertheless, success came at a high price. In hindsight, Bonner would've preferred to have done a deal with the devil himself rather than with what turned out to be an egotistical, narcissistic, high-maintenance moron. Bonner's recent meeting with his superiors hadn't gone particularly well but better than he'd hoped. He'd received no more than a final warning. Once again, Jones had most likely intervened and blocked any chance of Bonner being fired on the spot. He was belatedly beginning to realise that the monomaniac had a surprising number of highly placed people on his payroll. Consequently, he found himself caught between a rock and a hard place. Somehow he must prove his worth to his superiors while at the same time finding a way to free himself from Jones's tenacles, which was where Lemon could come in very handy.

In secrecy and against medical advice, the Chief Constable had moved the Loyalist prisoner from HMP Maze to a low-security, high-dependency unit in Antrim not far from Belfast. Bonner recalled their many late-night conversations in an interview room, especially the initial one.

"Is it better here than in the Maze?" he had asked encouragingly.

Lemon sat still as a corpse and just as expressionless, staring up at a fluorescent light in the ceiling as if hypnotised. They were seated in a windowless, green-painted room with a table and two chairs screwed into the concrete floor. The place stank of strong-smelling disinfectant, and Bonner found it hard to breathe.

He carefully reached out to touch Lemon's arm, but the man jumped away like a startled rabbit and pulled back. He wore a blue-and-white-striped uniform reminiscent of a prison camp's, and although they'd only met a few times briefly before, Bonner was stunned by the transformation in him. Where Lemon's physique had once been taut and toned, any muscle was now gone to fat and blubber, his stomach swollen, and his face, which hadn't seen the sun for some time, colourless. He bore a wispy, unkempt beard hanging lifelessly below his chin. His dark eyes seemed unnaturally wide as if in wonderment. Bonner coughed and tried again; he couldn't give up his plan now.

"Lemon, it's me, Chief Constable Bonner. Do you remember me?"

Nothing.

"We met at Charles Jones's office?"

At the mention of Jones, Lemon growled, exposing a mouthful of large, threatening teeth, like a wild dog's.

"That's right! Charles – Charles Jones," Bonner hissed, hoping the old Lemon was still in there somewhere.

This time he grasped the prisoner's lower arm and hissed impatiently, "Listen, it was me who got you out of the Maze! It was me who got you out of there! Do you understand?"

Lemon looked straight at him without a flicker of recognition before rubbing his temples. His head was always muzzy these days, and he was so fuckin' tired. The lucid periods were growing less and less frequent, and he knew he was sinking deeper and deeper into a vacant, dark but welcoming hole – one in which he didn't want to be disturbed. And this prick was fucking bothering him!

Bonner wasn't giving up. He raised his voice this time. "Lemon, listen to me. Can you hear me?"

Lemon growled again. He didn't want to talk to anyone. The Yank had fucked off and left him high and dry, and he didn't care who this fat, sweating wanker was; he wanted to be left alone. He stood up to leave.

In desperation, Bonner smacked his arm, making a last attempt to convince him, "You've got to listen to me! I need your help. We can help each other. Please, Mark!"

At the use of his Christian name, he suddenly jerked his head and then slowly and carefully sat down again. Bonner dragged his chair closer and bent forward over the metal desk.

"I can get you out of here, Mark. I can get you home. But I was hoping you could work with me first. Can you do that?" He spoke rapidly to hold Lemon's attention.

The prisoner's head began to bob as he observed Bonner closely. The fat man looked like he might mean it.

"Charles Jones has let us down, Mark. Both of us. You're stuck inside, and I'm at his beck and call. He doesn't give a flying fuck about us; we're like shite on the bottom of his shoe to him. I can get you out of here for good, but I need you to do something for me first. Okay?"

Bonner talked on until he held even more of Lemon's attention. He knew he'd a long way to go to get this wreck of a man fit for purpose, but he'd no choice – he couldn't think of any better instrument of destruction.

****

Charles Jones was furious. If he wanted something done right, he had to do it himself! Standing in front of him, almost vibrating, was his red-faced and sweating accountant who – it appeared – had failed miserably in concealing Jones's involvement in FYJH & Sons Ltd. In a furious rage, Jones threw a copy of the *Derry Journal* onto his desk.

"You told me you had it covered, you prick!" he yelled ungraciously. "So why the fuck is it all over that rag?"

"I… I… did have it covered," the astonished man stammered. "I… I don't know! Someone must've told them…."

"WHO? Who could have told them? Only you and I know about it, and I haven't tattled to anyone," Jones said, his voice full of scorn. The accountant opened his mouth to speak again but was drowned out by his boss's accusation: "It has to be you!"

"No… no… not me, Mr Jones. I wouldn't," the accountant shrieked. "I'd never do that! I'm in this as deep as you are."

Jones knew the imbecile spoke the truth. The accountant was regularly rewarded for manipulating Jones's financial dealings, and if caught, he'd be in as much shit as his employer. But how did the *Journal* find out what no one else knew?

Crimson with rage, Jones spat, "Get the fuck out!" No sooner spoken than the terrified man dived for the door.

Jones idly studied his secretary through the glazed door. She was sitting at her desk, speedily typing the letters he'd dictated to her earlier. He took proper notice of her for the first time, reminding himself to pay her a little more attention. Unlike the numbers eejit who'd just let him down, she was tight-lipped and loyal and had often tidied up after his drug-fuelled nights with his favourite working girls. She was a pretty, petite girl with olive skin and dark, tempting eyes under thick, neatly plucked eyebrows. Her hair was tied back loosely and twirled around in a knot. She barely used make-up. She wore a neat, trim navy jacket and skirt with a modest white blouse. For a moment, it crossed his mind to give her a pay rise, but sensing he was watching her, she gave him a sideways look that could kill. *Cheeky wee bitch*. Any thought of a pay increase forgotten, he grunted to himself and quickly turned back to re-read the newspaper, still mystified as to how they'd got hold of the information about the dummy company.

He read on until his phone rang.

"Jones!" he yelled impatiently.

"Mr Charles Jones?" a quiet, controlled voice enquired.

"Speaking!"

"Mr Jones, hello. My name is Peter Breeze from HM Revenue and Customs here in Belfast. Is it a good time to talk?"

Jones's heart sank. *Bugger!*

"Actually, no. No, it isn't!"

"I see," the voice said. "Well, Mr Jones, I need to talk to you urgently regarding today's *Derry Journal* article." Breeze paused before adding quietly, "*Amongst other things.*"

"I can't see why," he barked.

"I'm sure you can't," Breeze replied impertinently. He'd been chasing Jones for years, and after reading the article over breakfast, he'd rushed to his office to retrieve Mr Jones's file – the jigsaw was finally coming together. What he'd read in the *Journal* was dynamite, and he'd already called the paper's editor in the unlikely hope they'd reveal their source to HMRC.

Jones knew he shouldn't rile this man; after all, he was a tax inspector. Inhaling deeply, he adopted a much more conciliatory tone.

"My apologies, Mr Breeze. Forgive me, it's… it's been a hell of a morning."

"I understand. Perhaps I can visit your office later this week?" Breeze suggested.

A date and time were duly set, and Breeze, with a self-satisfied smile, put down the phone. In an unusual gesture for him, he smacked his desk with the flat of his hand and, to the bemusement of his bewildered colleagues, cried, "Yes! Yes! Yes!"

****

Stones Corner Light

A few mornings later, before dawn, Captain Alan Hickey, intelligence officer turned vigilante, found himself standing on a street corner outside Brendan Doherty's usual gym. He watched the solicitor walk towards the entrance and disappear up a narrow staircase.

Hickey wore his usual running gear: a grey hooded sweat top and matching pants. He quickly tucked a lethal Queen Light Hunter deer knife into his waistband and crossed the street to stand at the bottom of the staircase. Before stepping up, he looked around the road to check that he was unobserved.

Running up the staircase, he opened the entrance door and looked around. The gym followed the usual layout, consisting of a central roped-in green and white boxing ring surrounded by exposed redbrick walls. These were adorned with a colossal tricolour flag and black-and-white photographs of boxers in their prize belts.

The gym felt stuffy; the smell of old sweat and the nauseating chemical stench of cleaning fluid filled the air. The large main room had four square mossy skylights. Weight machines had been scattered in and around the open space, along with black padded gym mats.

Brendan Doherty was singing in the locker room but stopped in surprise when he spotted Hickey walk in.

"Mornin'," Hickey said in his best Derry accent, followed by a brief hand wave.

"Yeah, mornin'," Doherty answered cautiously.

Hickey, in that same deceptively friendly tone, commented, "It's some gym, isn't it?"

Doherty nodded; he didn't know this guy whose voice was neutral, while his fathomless eyes told a different story. The solicitor slowly stepped away until the wall was at his back.

"You're here every morning, aren't you? How dedicated you must be," Hickey added in his normal English voice. He'd sensed Doherty was already onto him and couldn't be bothered to try anymore.

Doherty bobbed his head and slid along the wall, closer to the changing room exit, hoping to do a runner. He didn't have a chance. The blade was out and sliced left to right across his gullet as quickly as a flash. Like the pro he was, Hickey jumped back to avoid the wide arc of blood that gushed out.

Doherty stood and grabbed his throat, trying vainly to stem the flow. He gurgled and choked as his fresh crimson lifeblood pressed through his fingers, down his hands and onto his bare arms.

Hickey sneaked behind the boxing ring when Frank Ward arrived for his regular sparring session with the solicitor. Entering the locker room, Ward saw the mutilated body and cried out in surprise and horror.

Hickey was on fire; he relished up close killing over hardware any day. Pulling up his grey hood with a malicious smile, he carefully tiptoed down the staircase and began sprinting down the street like any other harmless early-morning runner.

****

Chapter Forty-three

It wasn't long before Carol Caffrey regularly visited Rob at the campsite. She encouraged him to clean up his act, and he now looked forward to her visits. She arrived one hot day, holding a sandwich and a drink for him; she smiled at the effort he had made, smiling at his attempt to achieve a shave and haircut. A local barber donated a few hours of his time to the homeless men every few weeks, and Rob had joined the queue.

"You're looking well," she said.

"It's a start," he answered shyly, aware that he was still a scruffy article compared to his army days. "I went to the YMCA and had a quick shower. I'm beginning to feel more human." He paused, then added, "Thanks to you."

Carol shrugged and dismissed his gratitude as she handed over the sandwich. She sat down on a rattan chair like something from the Far East that Rob had salvaged, telling him her news with a wide smile.

She was both excited about it and slightly fearful of Rob's reaction. Geoff, her colleague, had warned her she was getting too close to this case and should step back – it was becoming too personal. At night she'd worry about Rob sleeping in the cold under the M8 bridge. She ignored Geoff's warning.

As a novice, she'd worked in the bishop's office. She'd used her contacts there to make a case for Rob being offered sheltered accommodation.

"I've got you into Glengowan House," she announced.

"Glengowan House?" he quizzed.

"Aye, remember I told you about it? It's a new hostel for men. There's a place for you there if you want it."

Rob bit his lip. He wasn't sure how to answer; the offer was so unexpected. He'd grown used to living here, made a few friends, and was free from any responsibilities. Moving into a hostel would steer him back to real life, with all its worries and obligations, and he wasn't sure he'd match up to it. Carol picked up on his hesitation and touched his leg lightly.

"It's up to you, Rob."

As if reading his thoughts, she added, "I know you probably feel safe here, for want of a better word, but coming to the house could change everything for you. Maybe it'll help you get back to ordinary life. I think it'd be for the best. You don't belong here, Rob. You really don't."

He could only stare at her, wishing he felt as confident. She wouldn't let him allow this opportunity to slip through his fingers. "Think about it – it might help things with your family. You've told me about them so many times. They have to want better for you than living here."

Watching him slowly shake his head, she decided she wouldn't take no for an answer.

"Listen to me, Rob, please. I've spoken to the bishop himself about you. There wasn't enough space at the house, but somehow he's done this as a favour to me, so please – give it a try. I'll be able to see you there every day, and there are all sorts of support groups that'll help you too."

Rob's mind was in turmoil. Carol was right. He didn't belong here, but the prospect of starting all over again terrified him. His thoughts were interrupted when he heard a familiar voice greet him.

"Rob," Geoff Brady said gloomily.

"Geoff," he replied, watching the skinny, pock-marked, poorly-shaven man approaching them. He looked wizened, wearing a pair of faded, stained jeans that were much too big for him and an equally ill-fitting bomber jacket.

"You've heard then?" Geoff asked.

For months he'd been coaxing Carol to go out on a date with him; she was foxy, and he'd do anything to get into her knickers. Unfortunately, so far, her stock response was, "I like you but not in that way. Sorry."

For that reason, he'd disliked the ex-soldier intensely. The bawbag had nothing to offer Carol, yet she'd been fussing over the English bastard for an eternity. He'd warned her to step back as she was getting too involved, but she'd paid him no attention, and he desperately hoped Sallis would say no to the move – the thought of her seeing him there every day made Geoff want to vomit.

"Yeah, Carol told me," Rob replied drily. He couldn't stand gawking Geoff, especially after Carol had revealed he continued to beleaguer her for a date even after she turned him down.

"And?" Geoff asked darkly.

"And what?" he replied, looking him in the eye. From day one, this man had made it clear he didn't like Rob, not that he was bothered.

"You takin' it or what?" Geoff asked impatiently. "I don't know how she managed to do it. There's some waiting list."

He looked at Carol deliberately, knowing what she'd done – she'd bypassed him. She'd gone sucking up to the bishop. Geoff felt severely let down by her, it'd been mega embarrassing, and he'd lost face before the rest of the staff.

Carol put out her hand to stop Geoff from saying more; she knew she'd pissed him off, going direct to His Excellency like that. With a mock-playful expression, he added, "Not that I'm insinuating anything bad, Carol. I meant…."

Rob knew what Geoff was up to, undermining her confidence, and agreed to the proposal of a place at Glengowan without a second thought.

"Okay, I'll go."

A fire raged in Geoff when Carol grabbed Rob's hand and squeezed it triumphantly.

"Right," Geoff retorted. Smarting with anger, he turned to go. "Be seeing you then."

"Yeah, yeah, you will," Rob answered, fixing his eyes on Carol, who returned his smile. She knew why Rob had said yes. Poor Geoff. He had never stood a chance.

Jane Buckley

****

Following the social worker's visit, Bridie Sallis tried desperately to track Rob down but with no success. It seemed he'd disappeared off the face of the earth, and the police were about as helpful as a chocolate teapot.

That was until, out of the blue, her son called her. Or she thought it was him. Drying her hands after washing the dishes one night, she answered the phone after several rings.

"Hello."

She could only hear a crackling line and nothing else, but she talked anyway, hoping it was Rob. "Is that you, son? I need to talk to you, and it's well important! Just tell me it's you... please, we have to talk!"

Whomever it was hung up.

A few weeks later, it happened again, but this time she was ready. They were due to attend a custody hearing in court, and she needed Rob's help – this time, she was sure it was him calling. It was hard for her to believe that Tracey, of whom she'd been very fond at one time, now wanted her son after all the lost years, but it didn't seem as though she'd drop her claim on Val.

Once again, the line was silent, but she started talking as if this was a normal conversation. "Rob, if that's you, listen carefully. The social want Tracey to have Val, and she and her new boyfriend want to take him away to live in Preston."

At the other end of the line, Rob listened carefully. He'd only been in Glengowan House a short time and was already relishing the luxury of hot water, privacy and good food. His doubts about coming here were long gone, even though Geoff remained unwelcoming and aloof. Rob looked at Carol, who stood beside him, eagerly listening to the call. Earlier that morning, they'd talked about him trying to call Bridie again, and she'd encouraged him.

"Aye, Mam. It's me," he said slowly. "Say that again, will you?"

Bridie Sallis would never forget the relief that flooded her body then. Her eyes filled, and she let out a huge sigh, determined to stay calm and not spook him. "Ah, love, it's good to hear your voice. I've been worried sick about you and Val. They want to take him away. Give him to your Tracey."

"She's not my Tracey, Mam, and yeah, I gathered that. But there's no way she's having him. Given everything, I don't know what sort of weight my opinion carries, but I'll back you up, Mam, and you can reach me now to let me know what's happening. I'm in a hostel in Glasgow called Glengowan House, and I'm getting clean. No promises at the moment, but things are looking up for me."

"That's what I've been praying for, Rob! Oh, son, it's so good to hear from you. You will call me again, won't you?"

"I will. Love you, Mam, and give our lad a big hug from me, won't you?"

Bridie wiped her eyes and kept her voice steady when she replied.

"I will, son. And take care of yourself. We need you back with us."

"I'll try, Mam, I promise you. And I'll call one day again when I know Val's back from school. Maybe he'll speak to me. Let's give it a try. Call me here if Tracey kicks off at you or the social start to pester you again."

When they hung up, both crying but feeling lighter and more hopeful than they had done in years. Bridie had to trust their healing had finally begun and she'd have her son back soon where he belonged.

****

Chapter Forty-four

Tommy was gobsmacked when he hung up Chris Pecaro's phone – the shocking news from Derry made him feel like he'd collapse. Gerard McFarland had called him with the sad news about Brendan Doherty. So far, the RUC hadn't a clue who'd committed the murder as Loyalist paramilitaries had yet to claim responsibility.

Caitlin stepped into the room feeling bright and breezy. Her uncle's evident distress stopped her in her tracks.

"Dear God, Tommy, what is it!" she asked.

A light buzzing sensation whooshed inside his head, and his legs grew more unsteady. He reached out to his niece. "I'm okay, love. I've had a terrible shock, that's all. Brendan's been murdered."

"Ach, no!" Caitlin cried out in shock. "I can't believe it. Such a good man."

Brendan Doherty had been a rock for the people of Derry. He'd never shown a smidgeon of weakness or ceased pursuing justice for Caitlin's da and Tina. Doherty's never-ending tenacity, energy and love for the city's Nationalist community were widely respected. Ironically, as a warped form of respect, there'd already been serious rioting and protesting at his unjust murder. *What a fuckin' waste*, Tommy thought, filled with sorrow and anger, *what a bloody awful waste.*

"I'll get you some water," Caitlin offered, brushing tears from her eyes. She was frightened by how poorly Tommy looked and cried out for Anne to come and sit with him.

Anne heard the urgency in her voice and rushed to the study. Apart from missing Matt, the past week had been the best time she'd had in years, and she was looking forward to the wedding the next day. She'd decided she must've been either dreaming or plain drunk when she believed she'd spotted the Adonis and his office boy at the hotel and had already put the incident to the back of her mind without saying a word about it.

Caitlin went into the kitchen. As usual, Chris was reading *The Times*. He put it down as she came in.

"Everything okay?"

"Not really. Bad news from home. A friend's been killed, and Tommy's right upset."

"Shall I call a doctor?" Chris suggested.

Caitlin had been so right to say he'd get on with her uncle. Chris had grown extremely fond of the big man in a few days. They'd had a long talk where Tommy shared with him details about Caitlin's family history and their traumatic experiences. Chris was horrified but thanked him afterwards – the sorry tale explained a lot.

"No doctors, thanks, Chris. I think he'll come around. It was our family solicitor; he's been murdered. It's a big shock."

Caitlin took a sip of water, filled a glass tumbler, and returned rapidly to the study. Chris went with her. He watched Tommy shakily drink his water.

"He was a good man," Tommy told Chris, placing the half-filled tumbler on top of an eighteenth-century side table. Chris felt a twinge of horror at the thought of a ring mark on his precious antique. Having guests in his immaculate home was especially difficult for him, and Caitlin had warned him numerous times to be on his best behaviour with these particular visitors. However, Chris couldn't contain himself. He walked to a chest of drawers, removed a coaster, silently placed it on the table, and correctly positioned Tommy's glass. *There.*

Shrugging his shoulders and with a look of apology, he caught Caitlin's eye. She flinched at his untimely and unnecessary fussing and quickly returned her attention to her grieving uncle.

"Do they have any idea who did it?"

"Not yet, love. No one's claimed it."

The study fell silent. Not only had this awful thing happened, but shockingly Maryann and Bill Fox's baby Ella was still missing, and the female kidnapper was known to be Northern Irish. There was no escape from the tendrils of The Troubles.

"I don't know what's happening to the world!" Caitlin cried, and Chris took advantage of her distraction from the coaster incident to hug her. They were getting married tomorrow and should be celebrating, but he too was knocked for six by the recent kidnap of his friend and partner's baby.

****

Later, Chris said goodbye and left Tommy, Caitlin and Anne to fend for themselves in preparation for the celebration. The night before it, he was staying at a hotel not far from the venue, Islington Town Hall. Bill Fox – who should have been his best man – had been replaced by an old school friend.

A grandmother's clock ticked loudly as the two girls and Tommy sat quietly in the living room, each sunk in their gloomy thoughts.

Up to this morning, when they'd heard about Doherty's murder, they'd been busy going over last-minute stuff for the wedding. Ever since they'd all been feeling too flat and depressed, if it'd been any other evening, they'd have laughed and taken the piss out of Tommy's efforts to choose from an incomprehensible Indian menu. His attempts to eat the especially hot, spicy takeaway should've been enough to have them all in stitches – poor Tommy was a virgin to Indian spices, and the poor man was already suffering, given his frequent desertions to the loo.

Before Chris left, Bill Fox had called in at the house. Caitlin hugged him when he walked in; he looked worn-out and haggard. They took him into the kitchen, which was free from guests, dying to know if there was any news of the baby.

"Anything?" Caitlin asked first.

Bill fell into a chair.

"Nothing. Not a word and no trace of 'Michaela McBride', if that's even her fucking name! All we know is she had a Northern Irish accent, and it's likely she's with the Provisionals." He paused, staring listlessly at the floor.

Almost immediately, Caitlin's face burnt with shame and guilt. It was difficult being here in England when things like this happened. Although she'd tried to tone down her accent, people knew she was Irish and were always angry with Irish people of any affiliation when the Provos made the headline news. It didn't matter that she'd done nothing wrong; it was one size fits all.

"At least that's what the police think. Maryann is beside herself. I'm sorry, but with her constant crying and her parents sitting there doing nothing, I had to get out of the house. Pour me a drink, will you?"

Chris opened the fridge to pull out some cold wine. He looked at the bottle in surprise and shook it to check that it was empty. He glared at Caitlin, having told her numerous times to get Anne not to put her empties back in the fridge – it was another one of his hang-ups.

Caitlin glared back, and Chris grunted, "I'll go get another," and stomped off down a spiral staircase to his temperature-controlled wine cellar.

"Sorry," Bill said, eyes on his grumpy host.

"For what, Bill? You've absolutely nothing to be sorry for. Now take off your jacket. Chris won't be long."

Feeling drained and weary, he struggled to get it off until Caitlin helped him.

"Thanks. Have you spoken to Maryann? She's terrified about Ella having an attack. There was no asthma medication with her when she was snatched," he added miserably.

"I did, about an hour ago, and yeah, she told me." Maryann was right; if the baby were to have an episode, it could prove fatal. The whole thing was unspeakable.

"She's in a bad way. *Christ*, I feel so helpless, Caitlin! She blames herself for falling asleep and for being so fuckin' trusting!"

Caitlin felt uneasy. It was apparent the Provos had taken Ella from identifying passwords used by the kidnapper who'd telephoned the *Daily Mail* after the baby was taken. They'd demanded a million-pound ransom in used notes and mixed denominations. It'd even crossed her mind to wonder whether the men she'd met with Tommy in Islington might have been involved. After all, she'd introduced them to Maryann! Chris had told her in confidence that although poor Bill Fox was on paper financially sound, he was cash poor. Somehow, he and Maryann had to try and scrape the money together, probably from his family and the bank. They had seventy-two hours.

Caitlin wondered if she should say anything. She watched him huddle up on the navy velvet-covered chair. Eventually, he looked up at her and shook his head as an overwhelming surge of delayed reaction hit him. He began to sob. His mouth dropped open, snot hung from his nose, and hot wet tears flowed down his face.

She'd never seen a man cry so sore and watched helplessly as his shoulders shook. The pain in his heart had become almost unbearable. It'd been nearly a week since the bastards took Ella, and until now, he'd been unable to show any emotion, instead doing what was expected of him and keeping a stiff upper lip.

Caitlin held him tight, encouraging him to release his agony.

"You'll feel better for getting it all out, Bill."

Chris returned. He stood and watched, giving her a quick smile of apology for his fussing and seeing his friend so stricken saddened Chris beyond belief.

"How about a glass?" he offered, holding the bottle out to Caitlin.

"Not for me, thanks."

Chris opened it and took out two large Baccarat glasses. Filling one nearly to the brim, he passed it to Bill.

"Get that in you, partner. Then we'll call you a cab, and I'll bring your car back later."

Bill took the glass and drank greedily while Caitlin and Chris watched silently. When he appeared more relaxed and ready to talk,

Chris began: "Bill, we've said this before, but Caitlin and I can postpone tomorrow. We feel terrible about what's happened to Ella and what you guys are going through. It doesn't feel right for us to go on with our celebrations."

Caitlin nodded her head in agreement.

"Don't you dare start that again, Chris!" Bill snapped. "I've told you, it's your goddamn' wedding, and what's happened has nothing to do with you, so *please* stop saying that!"

Caitlin was startled by his intensity. From Chris's surprised and perplexed expression, he was too.

He raised his arms in defeat. "Okay! I won't say any more, not another word!"

"Good. Now please, may I have some more?" Bill requested, holding out his empty glass. He was determined to get obliterated before heading home. It seemed Maryann and her parents had already given up on Ella, assuming she was dead, but Bill refused to believe they'd never see her again.

****

The big day finally arrived. Caitlin had slept very little, tossing and turning with the reappearance of her old merciless nightmare, which still haunted her. She found herself in her bedroom in Blamfield Street, woken by a fierce searchlight and the noise of men and army vehicles outside the street. Shouts, heavy footsteps thundering up the stairs outside her room, and then her poor naked father being dragged from his bed and pushed into the back of an armoured vehicle. It was so vivid that she woke up sweating and in tears.

Next door, Anne was woken by Caitlin's sobbing and, as quickly as she could, hobbled her way to the adjacent bedroom, dressed only in one of Matt's old Donegal GAA T-shirts and a pair of purple lace knickers.

She craned her neck around the door and saw Caitlin sitting upright in bed. Anne shuddered when she saw how upset her friend was, climbed up beside her and drew her in.

"Same dream?" she asked.

"Yeah. It never goes away, Anne, ever, and I'm so tired of it. I'm back there. I can feel the cold, hear the noise, the screams, see the attack dogs, then poor Daddy and that cruel soldier... It's so real."

"I know, love, but look – look around you. This is all yours now, and you're safe and living far away. You'll be fine. It's your wedding day. Come on now."

Anne hadn't been able to check out Caitlin's bedroom before; she didn't want to intrude when Chris was around. Now, with him safely away in his bachelor room in a hotel, she looked around and whistled.

"Fuck me, Caitlin. Did you ever think..." she asked, without having to finish her question.

"No, I suppose not," Caitlin replied with a tiny smile of pride. Anne was right; it was very far remote from her old bedroom. She watched her friend dramatically open the bedroom's long, heavy, turquoise silk curtains. As if she'd switched on the daylight, yellow sunshine flooded the room.

"And it's going to be a beaut of a day out there too! Caitlin McLaughlin, you're getting married today. Oh – my – sweet – and – gentle – Jesus, Caitlin, *you're getting married!*"

"I know, I know!" the bride-to-be screamed back at her, feeling a sense of genuine excitement for the first time in days. For now, Caitlin forgot her nightmare. This was what her friend Anne did, now and always. She brought joy.

"Stop it. You're making me more nervous!" Caitlin yelled as she ran to the bathroom. "We need to eat, and then we'll get off to the hairdresser's!"

"Give me two secs!" Anne grinned, pleased she'd pulled her friend back from the darkness.

She awkwardly balanced her way back to her room and startled poor Tommy, who was walking across the landing. He sighted Anne's ravaged stump, but his eyes never flickered, nor did his expression change. He had no misplaced sympathy for this wee girl, only pride that she'd pulled herself back from her nightmarish injury and misbegotten marriage and now, like Caitlin, was happy again. With an enormous smile, he opened his arms, and she fell into them. He gave her the tightest hug he could and whispered tenderly in her ear, "You're a pal to her, Anne Heaney, and I love you for it."

Anne felt she would explode with happiness, Tommy was always a good hugger, but his words meant the world to her.

"She's a good girl, Tommy, the best, and I'm happy for her."

"Me too, love. Me too." He laughed, releasing her. "Did I hear someone mention the word *food?* I'm bloody starving!"

Anne giggled, not in the least embarrassed at being caught in her purple knickers with her limb exposed. She used her arm to balance against the wall before limping back to her room to put on her prosthetic leg. Anne hadn't told Caitlin that the pain had been excruciating over the past few days, and she couldn't wait for her next medical appointment. The consultant had taken measurements, and she'd have to come back in ten to twelve weeks to get the new leg fitted, which was great and one of the reasons she could put up with the pain – it was all so mother-feckin' exciting!

As soon as she'd dressed, Anne went down to the kitchen, singing at the top of her voice. Thinking about Chris's kindness to her, she felt slightly guilty. She liked him a lot, but by fuck she was enjoying him not being here – they were much more relaxed, not having to worry about his little quirks!

"*'I'm getting married in the mornin','*" she sang loudly, "*'ding dong the bells are gonna chime…'*"

Tommy shook his head and chuckled.

Chapter Forty-five

James had only returned from Brendan's funeral. It appeared the lawyer was well aware his life was at risk, and ever the professional, the order of service had been carefully typed up in advance and kept on file in his office. Like Brendan, the private ceremony at St Mary's Church in Creggan was modest and unassuming. Following a series of riots, the parish priest, Father Walsh, pleaded with the community far and wide to respect Doherty's wishes and to cause no more upset.

They heard the priest's pleas for calm and privacy during the ceremony and tranquillity in the area soon followed. Nevertheless, it didn't stop what felt like half the city coming out in respect to line the streets leading to the hillside city cemetery. The gathering deliberately and slowly applauded as the cortege made its way from the church to the vast graveyard.

Brendan had no family, so James said a few words during the service since there wasn't anyone else, and people knew that they had been good friends despite their faith differences. Barter had rung from America and was devastated, ranting and raving about Charles Jones and how he was to blame. The reporter couldn't make it over but sent a green, white and gold wreath. He said he would be back in Ireland soon, and James was looking forward to catching up with him, especially after today.

****

Later, sitting in the Rainbow Café for the first time in years, James nursed a cup of coffee in the same booth where, on the eve of his wedding to Marleen, he'd told Caitlin he loved her, and it'd always be her. His hurt still cut deep. Siobhan, the waitress of old, had aged but elegantly, and he imagined the woman over the years, probably witnessing and hearing all sorts in what was now her establishment.

Ever since he'd passed Tommy the letter, he'd hoped for an answer from Caitlin, but, unsurprisingly, perhaps, there'd been nothing so far. Attempting to reach her before her wedding was selfish, he knew. He could easily hurt her again by opening old wounds – that was the last thing he wanted.

He felt a bit of a prick for trying, but on the other hand, he needed to tell her how he felt. He let out an audible groan, oblivious to Siobhan, who waited patiently beside him, brandishing a substantial stainless steel teapot.

"Were you at the funeral?" she enquired while topping up his cup, being careful of James's spotless white shirt, black tie, and hand-tailored suit – she'd an eye for such details. Everyone knew Brendan Doherty's funeral was being held today.

"Yeah," James replied with a sad smile, "it was tough."

"Funerals always are, son, always. It's a sore one, mind. He was one of the few even-handed men in this city."

Brendan had helped her get her son Colm freed from Long Kesh in the early seventies. As soon as she could, she'd whisked him off to Australia and hadn't seen him since. He was now happy and safe, having married a lovely Aussie girl. Siobhan's first grandchild was on the way, although she doubted she'd see it any time soon, and her heart stung at the thought.

"Do you ever hear from that beautiful Caitlin McLaughlin anymore?" the waitress enquired. "I've not seen her in ages. Maybe she doesn't come home much. Somehow I always thought you two lovebirds would end up together." Sharp as a tack, Siobhan had recognised the lovelorn atmosphere that hung about him – oh, yes, she knew all about Mr James Henderson.

Besides a brief hello, goodbye and ordering food, this was the most extended conversation James had ever had with her, and he smiled at her words, enjoying the praise of Caitlin. Siobhan herself must've been some beauty in her day. Her silver hair was cut in a short bob, but softly curling strands framed her doll-like face. She had a diminutive nose and a pair of lovely dark-lashed twinkling eyes. Her skin was gently lined. She reminded him of a kindly Fairy Godmother, he realised.

"Ah, Siobhan, no, I don't. She left, sadly, and that was it for us." There was a bit more to it, but James didn't feel he needed to go into every detail.

"Well, that's a real shame. I watched you two together, you know. Always thought you had *it*!" Siobhan clicked her fingers and winked at him. She turned to leave then hesitated, adding, "And I suppose you can't blame her, you suddenly getting married to someone else an' all."

James was stunned by the waitress's candour. He opened his mouth to give her a dusty answer, but her warning smile told him he'd better not. After all, she spoke the truth. He'd no riposte to make other than a sheepish smile.

She giggled. "I'm winding you up, son. Mind you; I'm sorry 'cos you were mad about each other."

Another customer entered then. "Anyway, enough said. Take care of yourself, and don't be a stranger."

"I won't, thanks, Siobhan," James answered, watching her cut her way through the tables to take the next order.

****

Alfie McScott sat quietly at his desk. He'd quit before he was pushed, and now he was packing up a few personal items. Once he'd offered his resignation, he knew he'd done the right thing. The boss had accepted it without demur, knowing the likely scrutiny they'd be under when an investor was finalised. For the first time in years, Alfie was looking forward to the future, especially to more time working on his allotment.

He was proud that it'd been his idea for the boss to meet Christopher Pecaro and Bill Fox. These savvy businessmen could offer a lifeline to

Rocola now that Mrs Henderson's trust refused to release any more funds.

Alfie looked at the creased cutting from the *Derry Journal* on his desk and re-read it for the umpteenth time.

Barter's painstakingly researched piece outlined the many tax evasions that Jones's empire had conducted over the past fifteen years. The Yank had CIA research to back him up, but couldn't have done such a thoroughgoing hatchet job without the gift of the final nail in the coffin, passed back to him by the old accountant. McScott felt he would never forget the moment he'd answered an unexpected call in his office late one evening, long after everyone else had left for home.

"Hello?" a female voice had said.

"Yes, hello, Alfie McScott speaking,"

"Ah, good, Mr McScott, I've finally caught you," the voice said with relief. "You don't know me, but there's something I have to tell you."

McScott wasn't sure if this was a genuine business call.

"I'm sorry, miss, but it's late, and I'm swamped with work. Please, I'm not in the mood if this is a joke."

"Oh, God, no! No joke. This is important," the woman cried in alarm, adding quickly, "You see, I'm Charles Jones's secretary, Jill." She paused, "I know he's done Rocola some serious damage and I want to make it right."

McScott remained quiet as the girl nervously added, "You see, I can't stand the slimeball, and I've been thinking about it for ages. So just listen to me, please, Mr McScott."

McScott's heart raced as, for almost two hours, Jill spilled the beans on Jones's maliciousness and more. It seemed she'd taken copies of all the relevant papers and files and kept them safe. More importantly, she agreed she'd talk to Barter! McScott had told James Henderson nothing about his alliance with the Yank in case it didn't pay off. But it had. Charles Jones's business empire was now in disarray, and that thought was a considerable comfort to Alfie as he finished his packing and turned off the office light for the final time.

****

"Papa! Don't do this to me, please. You can't," Marleen Henderson whimpered. She'd met her beloved father off the train at Kings Cross, and they were having lunch at a local Italian restaurant, Albertini's, one of his favourites.

Marleen grasped Thomas Fry's hand, imploring him to listen to her. "I know lots has been spent on Rocola, but seriously, Papa, you can't expect me to come home like a naughty schoolgirl. I can't… I just can't!"

Thomas Fry was enraged. He'd warned her! She'd been spending too much on that damned business of her useless husband's, and it had bled her dry. They'd got their heirs for the Fry and Henderson families, but it'd come at a very high price. By now, Marleen's trust had transferred under half a million pounds to Henderson's white elephant of a factory, with no return other than a failed marriage and limited access to the grandchildren who were supposed to be her family's hope for the future.

Reluctantly, he'd had to leave the comfort of Belmont Hall that morning to get on a noisy, slow train and travel to London to tell his daughter face-to-face that he wasn't giving her another penny. He knew what a party animal Marleen was and all about her wild ways – he'd known for years. It'd been his idea for the couple to get married, not only in the hope of an heir for the Frys but as a means of discouraging his daughter from racketing around with that Penelope Fox female. His plan had failed.

He watched his daughter's beseeching eyes. It seemed she was finally listening and taking him seriously. For some reason, Marleen naively thought the Fry family were worth much more than they were. He sighed and took her hand.

"I'm sorry, Mar, but the party's over. Your trust is completely drained. Had you no idea?"

Marleen was speechless. She adored being wealthy and the privileged lifestyle it paid for. Until now, she'd never given a second thought to the price of things when she and Pen shopped in Harrods or Harvey Nic's, ate in restaurants like Rules or Simpsons, or attended the Royal Opera House or the West End theatre. Marleen Fry always got what Marleen Fry wanted. She'd had the money to pay for it. Now it seemed she did not.

Marleen's confused expression and silence told her father the answer. *She honestly didn't have a clue about her own money!*

"Half a million pounds, Mar. Half a million pounds *cash*."

Bloody hell! she thought. She knew Rocola had cost her a good chunk but not that much!

"How much is left?" she asked, attempting to release her hand and feeling somewhat overwhelmed. But he stopped her as she was about to lean back, fearing his answer. His fine-boned noble face softened. He squeezed her quivering hand and mouthed, "Nothing, Mar. There's nothing left."

She gasped. She couldn't believe it! She'd intended to meet Pen later, telling her what she had finally decided to do about Jack. She imagined her faithful lover's amazement when she heard Mar's choice. Forget Jack Edmonds. It was Pen she wanted.

"No! No, Papa! You're wrong!" she screeched to the bafflement of the other patrons. "I mean, you've still got money… You can help me out. You and Mama are loaded. We've got the hall, the land, and the tenants! You can't tell me I'm broke; I won't have it."

He felt responsible; this was his fault, he knew. He'd spoilt his daughter all her life, treasuring her. She'd been a beautiful, high-spirited child who'd grown up into this stunning woman, but she'd screwed up too many times, by God! Why couldn't she have been like most other county girls who married, had a family, ran the house and volunteered with the local church and charities? What was so tricky about looking after a husband, children and home? Women nowadays wanted it all, it seemed, unlike before when they did what their husbands told them.

Marleen shook her head and pursed her lips. She remained quiet and dismayed, hoping for any form of consolation. Slugging down her wine greedily, she waited for her father to resume speaking.

Thomas Fry did the same, slugged more wine himself, then prepared to share even more alarming news.

"I've never told you this before, Mar, because I thought you didn't need to know, but Belmont Hall is mortgaged to the hilt, as is the estate. Where else do you think Mama and I found the money to keep the place going – the roof, repairs for starters, the gardens, the constant bloody maintenance? Even though we opened it to the public, to our detriment, it cost us more than we'd expected. Your poor Mama is beside herself!"

This proved to be a revelation too far for Marleen, who began to cry genuine tears for the first time she could ever remember. What was she going to do? She'd had it all planned out, joining Pen's scheme to buy a farm, create a new ménage and breed show horses. This was a catastrophe!

"Oh, Papa, what have you done?" she cried. Fate had sat in judgment; she'd no choice now but to reverse her decision and marry Jack after all. She was sure her heart would break as she realised what she had to do next. *Pen... how the hell was she going to tell Pen?*

****

Later that evening, James was having dinner cooked by Mrs Moore, who'd cheered up considerably since the arrival of the twins' new and much-loved nanny Suzie. The children were joining him and were in perfect form. They were excited at the prospect of all going to Benone Strand for a picnic the following day. So far – fingers crossed – Suzie was a positive influence on the pair of them. It seemed the girl, who came from a prominent local family, was taking no shit.

"You both seem excited about the picnic?" James enquired as he cut into his lamb cutlet.

"We are!" they answered at the same time.

"Suzie's asked Mrs Moore to do a proper one for us," PJ shared.

"Oh, yes?" James commented warily. "And how was she about that – cheerful enough?"

Charlotte piped up first. "She was fine. Kept going on about getting the place to herself for once and having some proper peace!" The children giggled together naughtily.

James giggled along with them. "Well, that's good, isn't it? Maybe we'll get something special for dessert tomorrow night!"

The children snorted, knowing he was trying to be funny. They loved having dinner with him but correctly sensed he wasn't himself tonight. He wasn't like the other dads at school who'd smile and hug their children as they picked them up or, if lucky, dropped them off in the morning. He never took them to school; it'd always been Mrs Moore, but going with Suzie was way better. Daddy didn't even come to their sports day before they broke up for the summer term, although they'd told him about it many times.

In the background, James heard his study phone ringing and swore. "Bugger!" He didn't want to leave the table, loving that the duo were on excellent behaviour, but the phone rang.

The children chuckled at their father's flippant use of a bad word. "Sorry, guys!" He flung his napkin onto the table and told them quickly, "Don't move. Stay where you are and behave!"

They saluted and cried happily and loudly, "Yes, sir!"

James grinned and ran to the study and the trilling phone.

"Henderson," he answered snappishly.

The line was silent for a moment until, shocked to the core, he heard her voice – it was Caitlin calling him. At last! Smiling like an idiot, he breathed out a long sigh of relief.

"Hey, you, it's me."

"Hey."

"Can you talk?"

"Yeah, sure. Just wait a minute, don't go away!" he pleaded. "I'll close the door."

Caitlin waited, convinced she could hear her own heart pounding. She shivered. Her right hand, which held the phone receiver, shook as it edged towards the cradle. *Was she mad?*

"I'm back," James suddenly told her. "You got my letter then?"

Caitlin shook her head. "No, what letter?"

"I gave it to Tommy." No wonder there'd been no response, he thought with relief.

"No, James, he didn't pass it on. I'm sorry, I'll ask him about it. He's here."

"Oh, I see," he replied, filled with disappointment. Did Tommy not trust him enough to be his messenger? He supposed he couldn't blame the man if so, not after what had happened in the past.

The two of them had so much to express, but neither of them knew where to begin. The only sound was the crackling of the phone line.

"I hear congratulations are in order?" James said eventually.

"Yeah, thanks."

"He's a fortunate man."

"Yeah." *Awkward.*

James felt the need to fill the vacuum and nervously began to rattle out his news. "Marleen recently visited Melrose. We've finally agreed to a divorce. The visit went well, though the twins, PJ in particular, didn't want her to go. She's hardly been here since they were born; we never see her. And you, what about you? How have you been?"

Caitlin wasn't sure why he'd tell her about his divorce but sensed the note of hope in his voice. It was way too late for that; too much water under the bridge. She attempted to lift her flagging spirits and replied, "I'm good. I like it here. Life is better."

She was suddenly sorry she'd phoned. The defensive wall she'd taken so long to build around herself was crumbling at the sound of James's voice. The one that had whispered tenderly in her ear as they'd made love in Donegal. This was killing her; she was dying inside.

"I'm sorry, James, I need to go. I shouldn't have called."

"Caitlin – no! Wait, please," he exclaimed.

At that moment, his study door was thrown open. He turned and saw Charlotte standing with her hands on her hips, deliberately mimicking his stance when annoyed. "We're waiting! Come on, Daddy. Dinner's getting cold!"

On cue, Caitlin whispered goodbye and gently replaced the receiver. She closed her eyes and sighed. When she opened them, she discovered her uncle watching her, his face pale and body visibly shaking.

"Who was that?" he asked with concern.

"No one," Caitlin replied despondently.

"Don't lie to me!" Tommy declared. He was worried that she wasn't wholly in love with Chris Pecaro and suspected James Henderson still occupied the most important place in her heart. The colour left Caitlin's face. It was rare for her uncle to talk to her in such a manner.

"Honest, Tommy. A friend."

"It was James, wasn't it?" he asked crossly.

She didn't want to upset him. Caitlin walked over. Tenderly touching his hand, she smiled and replied, "Aye, Tommy, it was. He tells me you've something for me."

Tommy frowned. He didn't want to think about that bloody letter. What the hell was the silly girl up to on the eve of her wedding?

"I left it behind. You're playing a dangerous game here! Jesus, Caitlin, you're about to be married!"

"Please don't worry. I'm finished with all that now. The call was about ending things for good between James and me. I've thought about doing it many times but never called him, and now I do; I'm caught out by you straight away!" She attempted a small laugh to appease him.

"Please don't fuss, Tommy. Chris loves me and would do anything for me. That's all I want and need in a husband, so leave it now."

But his worry only increased when he noticed Caitlin still hadn't said *she* loved Chris Pecaro.

****

Chapter Forty-six

"Have you ANY idea what you've fucking done, Da! Seriously?" Joe McFadden was seething.

Sean Keenan had a quiet word with him a few days before his parents were due to visit, and Joe would never forget how his heart had plummeted like a stone when he received the warning. Recalling Sean's previous affable behaviour, Joe was surprised by his harshness – ever since then, they had abandoned their old camaraderie.

"Your da's a stupid bastard, Joey boy. We warned him three times. I'm telling you, if it weren't for you, he'd be pushing up the daisies by now. Many turncoat Brit lovers have, and many more will do. I don't know how the hell your ma never found out."

"Me, ma! What about fuckin' *me*? No one fuckin' told me a dicky bird. I don't know what to say, and I'm so ashamed! I'll kill him when I get my hands on him. He's an embarrassment…."

Sean's affable, whimsical storyteller persona had been shrugged aside, and the dangerous man beneath became apparent with shocking suddenness.

"So you should be ashamed. It's a disgrace, is what it is. But there you go. I've been told to order you to sort it out once and for all. It's a final warning. Otherwise…" Joe knew what 'otherwise' meant, and he'd have none of it.

When he met his parents on their next visit, he looked at his mam's haggard, worn-out face, full of humiliation. Most, if not all, Republicans knew it was an unwritten rule that any loyal Republican man or woman wouldn't work for the military in any capacity. But that was precisely what big Charlie McFadden had been doing for several months, working for the British Army, for fuck's sake, as a cleaner.

"How, Da? How the hell did you get away with it for all that time? And you, Ma, what the heck – how could you not have known?"

Once again, Maggie McFadden was at her wit's end. Charlie had belatedly told her everything, but she still couldn't believe it. She'd heard of men like him being beaten up badly, knee-capped or executed. Some men and their families were exiled from Ireland for contravening the code. She was inconsolable about how her husband had fooled them all and put them at terrible risk. A little part of her felt slightly guilty, too – after all, she and Emmett had nagged Charlie to get off his fat arse and find a job, bring some money in. Well, he'd found a job – of the worst possible kind.

"I know, son. I know. With so much going on, I never thought to ask. I just assumed he was working in the kitchen at Rocola. We've hardly seen each other, and when I did try to talk about it, he'd complain he was too tired. In my mind's eye, I see it all now, so clearly."

Charlie McFadden felt as if his pulsating head was about to blow. He'd been dreading this visit and wasn't surprised by Joe's reaction. He thought it best to keep quiet, not challenge his exasperated son.

"You understand what you've got to do now, Da? They've laid it on the line for me. You've to get the fuck out of Derry – all of you!" Joe declared as he smacked the visitor's table. A screw shouted for him to back down.

Maggie grasped her son's hand and cried, "No, Joe, we can't! We can't leave here. It's our home!"

He held on to her roughened fingers. With tears in his eyes, he shook his head sorrowfully. "I asked them to reconsider, but they want to use Da as an example. Even the relatives of trusted volunteers are not beyond punishment. And since he's offended them, the rest of us must suffer too. I can't forgive him for that."

Charlie might as well not have been in the room while this uncomfortable conversation was conducted between mother and son. The big man was dying inside at the thought of leaving his lovely Derry – it was crushing him. He noticed a sharp pain in his left arm and began to sweat profusely.

Maggie and Joe's once clear voices suddenly became muffled and distant as Charlie's breathing grew ragged. He quickly reached for Joe's arm and tried to apologise. "I… and I'm… son…" Charlie knew he was blacking out.

Joe screamed, "Da! Da!" His chair fell back as he jumped to his feet. Before he had time to think, Joe was seized by a couple of screws, who roared at him to step away. He could only watch his father collapse onto the grey lino, his head cracking on impact.

Maggie was on her feet in seconds and kneeling beside her gasping husband. Commotion and turmoil overtook the visitors' room as she screamed at the top of her voice, "Charlie! Charlie love, it's okay! Someone, call an ambulance!"

A young ashen-faced PO seemed unsure what to do and stood uselessly at her side as she roared again, "For Christ's sake, call an ambulance NOW!"

Maggie whispered reassuringly, stroking her husband's brow, "It's okay, Charlie. It's okay. Everything's going to be okay." Her husband's frightened eyes told her he loved her as she cupped his face and stroked his hair. If this was how he would go, that was okay with him; in a way, he was glad. It'd be easier for Maggie and the boys without the shame of living with him. Charlie fought to wheeze out his words. "Mags, I… I'm so sorry, love."

****

In Greenwood Lake, Liam McFadden, oblivious to the pain and sorrow of his family back home, was having a ball.

When he'd woken up that first morning in the freshly painted bedroom of the Campbells' house, bright sunlight filled the room. He lay on a cuddly feather pillow, and a wave of happiness gripped him – one he'd never be able to describe or to forget. Jaffa appeared to be still in a deep sleep, so Liam hopped out of bed wearing the red check pyjamas, bought specially for the trip.

He opened the bedroom door, and a delicious wafting smell of bacon hit him like a hurricane, tempting his gurgling stomach. Without an ounce of shyness, he stormed into the kitchen as his hosts worked away. Maisie was cooking something in the most giant frying pan he'd ever seen.

"That's the hugest pan I've ever seen!" he told her excitedly. "And what's that smell? I'm starvin'!"

Maisie giggled at the boy's strange accent. She wasn't sure what he'd said, but his face and eyes told her everything, and her heart softened. He was so cute – she could eat him!

"Well, young fella, that's for the pancakes! You ever had pancakes?" she asked, turning to the stove and theatrically flipping a row of flat cakes up and over.

"Nope, but I'll sure try one!" Liam cried.

"When they're ready, I'll call y'all," Maisie teased, ushering him towards the front door and pointing a spatula at her husband while she called, "Why don't you take Liam outside? Let him look around."

Frankie was keen to do just that; once Maisie got into her cooking, she hated being interrupted. Liam stood on the porch, whistling as he took in the view. A white bandstand was visible at the end of a glistening lake, and everything seemed shining as if only polished. The grass was purest green, the trees so tall they almost touched the sky. By the lake was a small shingle beach with a jetty. Flagpoles proudly displayed the Stars and Stripes at the end of many gardens enclosed by white picket fences. The sun was fierce, trying its best to shine through the dense tree canopy overhead.

"Brilliant!" Liam squealed. "This is amazing… and look, a roundabout and swings!" He could see a playground in the far distance.

Frankie looked at the boy, seeing he was on cloud nine, and his heart soared. Project Children was about bringing these tired kids over and giving them a taste of what life could be like. There were no guns, no soldiers, no random bombs going off, no inequality or prejudice, just clean, fresh air, peace, great food, fun and lots of laughter. He looked forward to their shared summer.

"I can't believe this," Liam whispered as if entering Wonderland, "it's beautiful, Mr Campbell."

"Frankie. Call me Frankie."

Liam surprised himself by taking the stranger's hand. "Thanks, Mr Campbell... no, sorry, Frankie... for all this and for bringing me here. I'll never, ever forget it." Man and boy shared a magical moment until Maisie cried to them from inside.

"Henry's up!"

"Ah-ha, the Jaffa's up," Liam announced, the special moment broken.

Before they headed indoors, Frankie knelt. He looked at the young boy and asked, "Why d'ya call him Jaffa, son? It's right clear he doesn't like it."

A flood of guilt rose in him as he tried to explain. "I know, Frankie, but he was horrible to me the whole way here on the plane and called me a name first. Don't you know what it means?"

Frankie shook his head.

"It means he's a Proddy-like. You know, a Protestant, an Orange man... Jaffa, as in oranges?" Now Frankie understood and attempted to contain a smile.

"I see. Well, son, why don't you do me a favour and stop using that name? You're not in Derry anymore but in America, in our house. Your faith nor Henry's has any bearing here. So we'll call him Henry – no more Jaffa or the like, okay? We got a deal?"

Liam knew Frankie was right. If he'd ever called a Proddy a Jaffa in front of his mammy, she'd have given him a good clip around the ear.

"Okay, deal," he replied. Frankie offered his hand, and Liam shook it enthusiastically.

He shouted as he ran towards the open door, "Hey, Henry, get out here quick! It's gorgeous, and we've got six whole weeks of it. Come and see!"

In time, Liam and Henry drew close to living the American Dream. At first, the Campbells' surrogate sons and neighbours, the Matijasaviches, welcomed the two Irish boys. Still, they grew to resent the attention lavished on the visitors by the couple they regarded as their surrogate parents. Hostilities broke out, though not in front of Frankie and Maisie: the Matijasaviches versus Liam and Henry.

On occasion, Liam spoke briefly to his mother by phone. The poor woman barely got a word in as he told her about all his adventures. The only downside was another close call when one of the Matijasavich boys started to pick on Henry, taking the mickey out of his accent. Liam, bold and unafraid, immediately stepped in and forced the Yankee back with a hard kick to the groin and a stunning whack on his face.

"You leave him alone, you hear me? Or I'll tell Frankie how you've been winding us up. Now piss off!"

The smarting boy couldn't afford to let the Campbells know of his bullying, so he and his brother reluctantly stepped back. But they kept a close eye on the neighbouring house from a distance, counting down the days until the two interlopers left.

Liam's instinctive defence of Henry changed things between them. Soon their friendship blossomed, and they became inseparable. Neither of them ever referred to their religion or home background again. They sometimes felt a little homesick for their families but nothing more. This miraculous sun-drenched summer was life-changing and proved to be an experience that would influence them forever, allowing them some hope that they need not return to the old ways.

****

Chapter Forty-seven

Cawley's two sisters sat in The Teashop in Royal Avenue, Belfast. The eldest, Sister Monica, had opted for a two-hour train journey from Derry to Belfast, taking in the stunning Antrim coast and marvelling at the beauty of the seven-mile Benone Strand. They were desperately worried about their brother, neither having heard from him in ages. He was missing, and both knew this was likely bad news for a long-serving Provo.

Cawley had insisted that his younger sibling tell no one about her long nightmare in detention for a second time before, without warning or explanation, she was released from the back of a police jeep and thrown out onto a back street. She felt guilty about the whole experience; she'd been a coward for confessing in the first place to something she didn't do to get out of jail quickly. Now she and her brother were being blackmailed by M15. Living with the constant awful fear of being picked up again by the police was terrifying; she wasn't sleeping and couldn't contain her unease any longer.

She was going mad and had to tell someone. Sitting right across the table from her, was the one member of the family who always kept calm, thought things through logically, and came up with a solution to everything – her elder sister, Monica.

A Nazareth nun, she first trained as a nurse and currently worked at Altnagelvin Hospital in Derry. Looking after battered victims of The Troubles was becoming more and more of a struggle for her, and a recent offer she'd received to move overseas and do mission work was tempting. Day after day, night after night, she'd witnessed first-hand the awful carnage, dealing with shocked, broken or burnt patients, some with missing limbs or eyes. Then there were the dead bodies blown to smithereens that had to be recorded and reassembled after a fashion. Some were only identifiable by their dental records.

Worse still, many innocent children had been shot dead with rubber bullets, and countless others suffered lethal or life-changing gunshot wounds. One of the saddest things she'd dealt with was a pregnant woman who'd been tarred and feathered, tied to a lamp post for hours, and later tossed onto the hospital's doorstep like a piece of litter.

The difficulty of working long hours under abysmal conditions meant that Monica now relished the thought of the train journey instead of driving, a chance to sit back undisturbed and read her bible. She didn't want to take a day away but had had no break for months. Mother Superior had agreed to the trip so she could visit her sister.

Shannon seemed to have aged far beyond what a first-year, happy-go-lucky student should look like. Her blue eyes were heavy-lidded, red-rimmed and bleak. The girl's expression revealed only indifference as if nightmares had forced all the joy out of her. They hugged warmly. Sister Monica sat there without taking her coat off. Her voice sharpened with concern as she tried to understand why her sibling looked so desperately unhappy.

"What's happened to you, love? You look awful. Tell me."

A woebegone face stared back at her. Shannon's eyes glimmered with affection for the briefest of moments. She adored her sister and brother, but she'd been numb with fear since her arrest, interrogation, and forced confession. She couldn't concentrate. Her ex-, Gavin White was spreading malicious rumours that she was a Provo volunteer, and she'd been called into her tutor's office, where he'd asked her outright what the hell was going on. It'd taken forever to convince him it was all lies until he eventually accepted her version of events. But then, later, she was arrested in the middle of a lecture, and all hell broke out.

Of late, she was finding it physically difficult to get out of bed in the morning. Precisely where she'd be if she didn't have Monica's help in finding their brother, she did not know.

"It's nothing; I'm fine. Have you heard anything about him?"

"No, love, nothing. It would be best if you told me everything, Shannon. Something is happening with you two. That's all I know, and that's why I'm here."

The younger girl began to sob. "I'm sorry to drag you over here. You look mega tired, too, working all the hours God sends in that hospital. You might not like what I tell you either, Monica."

Not prepared to pay attention to her sister's warning, Sister Monica asked another question with a wave of her hand. "Have you spoken to her yet?" referring to their missing brother's wife, who'd always been bossy and overly possessive. She begrudged the closeness between her husband and his family. It was a mixed marriage; she was Church of Ireland, which didn't help. Eventually, after many petty arguments, the siblings had agreed – for the sake of peace – to keep her off limits.

"No. You?"

"Nothing. Although it might be worth calling to see if she's heard anything?"

The nun rolled her eyes. "Let's not. We'll find him ourselves."

Upon seeing how exhausted her sister was, the student was even more worried about explaining what had happened to her but knew she must. She needed it out in the open, hoping they could devise a plan to find their brother together since there was no chance in hell they'd go to the RUC. He was, after all, a Provo and they'd a feeling he was high up.

Taking off her dark coat and growing impatient, the nun petulantly asked, "So tell me – I want it all, word for word!"

Their waitress arrived with their order, including a couple of jam turnovers, which the women hungrily ate in between small talk. As soon as they'd finished, Sister Monica took charge.

"Go on then, Shannon," she commanded.

She listened as her sister told her every detail of her double arrest, interrogation, forced confession, and verbal and physical abuse by security and police officers. She shared the difficulties at uni, her now ex's rejection of her, the tutor and the police pulling her out of a lecture. Finally, she got to the crux and described the blackmail she had been subjected to, her genuine concern for their brother's life, and the continued threat of her being rearrested and sent to Armagh women's gaol – no detail was omitted.

As she listened, Sister Monica fumed. For pity's sake, why hadn't they told her this before now?

"That's it! That's everything. What are we going to do now?" Shannon asked imploringly.

"I don't know what to do, love. All I know is that this is bad, really bad. Give me a sec, and let me think."

****

Cawley couldn't believe he was still holed up on a decrepit, abandoned farm even though his handler had assured him it wouldn't be for long and was solely for his protection.

"It's in your best interest until we act on the information you've given us. You'll be free as a bird and long gone soon, starting all over somewhere else with the missus."

That was ages ago, yet here he was, sitting in a straw-filled, pig-shitty, damp and cold barn. By day they kept him hidden away in here, and by night he'd get a camp bed in an old, cockroach-infested pantry next to a cobwebbed scullery. Fucking hell, he thought, this wasn't what they'd agreed! When he'd first arrived, in an attempt to win him over, they'd burnt his sister's confession before him to seal their agreement. They were lying through their bastard teeth. He knew they'd have a copy up their sleeve or even, by sleight of hand, the original.

His butt hurt like hell from lying all day on a bed of rough straw, and with no washing facilities, he reeked. The midges were rife in the air and under his clothes; never-ending raised red bites studded his arms and legs. They wouldn't allow him to make a phone call, and he knew his family would be worried sick. He'd stupidly boxed himself into a corner and couldn't see a way out, so left with no choice, he'd told them what he could to protect his precious girls from the nightmare of the women's gaol in Armagh.

He looked up at the barn's timeworn rickety roof and wondered about its past, who'd built it and when. He'd always loved reading about olden times, especially Irish history, and read any history books he could get his hands on. Politics had always held a particular fascination for him too, and once, he'd spent hours debating the rights and wrongs of the world. He groaned and swore aloud. "What the fuck have you done, ye eejit?"

He heard his handler's cheerful voice and footsteps approaching the entrance to the barn. "It's a sign of madness when you start talking to yourself; you know that?"

Cawley ignored the flippant comment but asked in frustration, "When the fuck are you going to let me outta here?"

The handler surveyed the old barn and looked back at him with a wicked smile.

"That's precisely why I'm here: to tell you that your revelations have proved to be of use, and we've contained the situation. Thanks to that, you can leave of your own accord and go wherever the fuck you want."

He supposed that three low- to middle-ranking volunteers were now in custody. Like chess pieces sacrificed on the board. He hated himself for what he'd been forced to do.

"Leave? And go where? I can't go back! You promised that me and the wife would be set up in Canada!"

"Did I?" the handler answered cynically, faking surprise. "Did I really? I can't say I recall." He laughed disdainfully and grudgingly threw a sealed white envelope at Cawley, who reached out and caught it.

"Take it. It's yours to do with as you will. Cheerio and good luck!" the handler called before waving goodbye and exiting the barn.

Cawley feverishly tore the envelope open. *Fuck... fuck... fuck!* There wasn't even enough there to get them to England!

He'd been tasked with delivering a good chunk of cash to Derry from a post office raid in Belfast. But in a desperate bid to escape, he'd wrongly believed that Brendan Doherty could help him get to Canada. It'd been a waste of time. Once he'd explained what he needed and why, the solicitor steadfastly refused even after Cawley left the sports bag full of cash at his office as an inducement. If it'd worked, he'd planned to keep what was left to bankroll his new life, but in the end, he'd no choice but to hand it into the OC.

Coincidentally, it was after that his handler had told him that if he gave them worthwhile, substantiated intel, not only would they get rid of Shannon's confession, but under witness protection, they'd get him and the wife to Canada. Cawley felt like a dick forever believing the British bastards! They'd thrown him to the lions, and there was no escape for him now; he knew he'd no choice but to go back and resume his life with the volunteers. He'd been MIA for way too long.

****

Chapter Forty-eight

Paddy and Liz, in haste, dumped the transit van and took off in the Toyota, still parked unnoticed in the Tesco car park. Baby Ella's constant wailing was irritating Paddy; she hadn't stopped for the entire forty-minute journey from Central London, and Liz had run out of ideas to soothe the child. She'd done everything she could think of: held her, endeavoured to give her a bottle, and when that didn't work, her dummy, but Ella's piercing cries persisted.

"Are we nearly there?" Liz cried over the din from the back seat of the car. Her head was pounding, and this was going so wrong!

They were on their way to Harlow New Town to hide in a low-rise block of flats the Provos occasionally used as a safe house. It was owned by a sympathiser who normally sub-let it. The kid's endless crying was doing Paddy's head in, but much as he wanted to, he couldn't put his foot down and speed up. He didn't want to attract unwanted attention from the police.

"Can't you get that fuckin' wain to shut up!" he yelled. "You're a woman, for Christ's sake; sort it out!"

Liz might be a woman, but she'd no understanding of babies and, until now, hadn't given it a second thought. They were in for a nightmare if this was how it continued to be. She grabbed the baby's bottle she'd brought with her, and in horror, a sudden thought entered her mind. *No!*

In their urgency to get out of the van, she'd left behind a bag containing nappies, baby food and some of her belongings. Like a caged bird, her heart fluttered. How the hell was she going to tell Paddy when he was in such a foul mood?

Ella refused to take the bottle and screamed once more. Liz was close to tears and started to rock back and forth, comforting herself and the baby. In seconds, she began to sing softly, and Ella's cries finally faded.

"Thank fuck for that!" Paddy whispered; he was ready to kill. The girl had a pleasant voice, and he began to relax as he listened to her sing 'She Moved Through the Fair':

> *My young love said to me:*
> *'My mother won't mind.*
> *And my father won't slight you.*
> *For your lack of kine....'*

****

As Liz had feared, everything became a nightmare on their second day. When they came through the door to the flat, they walked into a pit of hell. Leftovers from the previous occupants, including maggot-infested food, stinking beer cans and cigarette butts, were strewn everywhere. Liz couldn't begin to describe the toilet and the kitchen stank from discarded rubbish. The icing on the cake was the bedroom with its soiled bedding and heavily stained mattress. This was no place Liz wanted to be, no matter a tiny baby.

"You'd better clean up – it's a bit of a mess," Paddy suggested, casually throwing himself onto a battered brown sofa. He lit a cigarette and flicked the match across a sticky coffee table to land on the floor.

Liz stood by the doorway, holding Ella, who'd finally settled. She still hadn't told Paddy about leaving the shopping bag behind. However, she was livid at his suggestion that she *alone* should tidy up.

"What? You expect me to straighten this trough up *and* look after the baby, all on my own!" she hissed, aware she shouldn't make too much noise.

Paddy looked at her in surprise and laughed. "Yeah, why not? I'm certainly not doing it! You're the fucking woman." It was incredible that she'd have the cheek to ask him for help!

Liz shook her head and grunted, "We need food."

"We've got food," Paddy stabbed back. "It's in the bag."

"We didn't pick it up."

"What do you mean *we* didn't pick it up?" He was sure he'd told her to double-check that they'd left nothing behind.

"The bag, it's still in the back of the van," Liz muttered nervously.

"I told you to check everything!" Paddy barked, rising to his feet to confront her. His blaring voice set Ella off again.

"Ah, shit, look what you've done now!" Liz cried angrily. "Jesus, Paddy!"

"For fuck's sake, I'm gone. I've got that call to make!" He grabbed his coat and disappeared, leaving Ella screaming and Liz crying. He was already wound up about making the ransom call, and the kid's constant bawling was getting under his skin.

After ringing the *Daily Mail* and issuing the ransom demand, he'd walked for hours by the canal, returning later with a bag of cheap food. He'd picked the wrong nappies but, fortunately, suitable powdered milk. Liz thanked God that Maryann Fox had prepared a baby bag and tucked it on the shelf underneath the pram; it proved a lifesaver.

She attempted to tidy up the flat but was constantly distracted by Ella, and her labours were perfunctory; they'd have to put up with it.

"Three more days of this, then?" Liz asked Paddy bitterly. He'd reverted to lying on the sofa reading the back-page sports section of the *Sun*. She read the front cover and saw that Ella's disappearance was still headline news and that a famous comedian had been caught having an affair with some posh model Liz had never heard of.

"Yeah," Paddy replied crossly, "three more fucking days with the pair of ye whining and that one howling like a banshee!" He signalled to Ella.

"I have to go out!" Liz said brusquely, ignoring him. "I need a chemist."

Paddy scrutinised her. "Are you off your rocker? You can't go anywhere near that front door."

"You want to go for me then?"

Throwing his newspaper aside, Paddy sat up and asked, "For the wain?"

Liz blushed; she couldn't meet his eye. She'd been dreading this from early morning when her period had started. "Yes and no."

"Yes and no?" Paddy repeated, his voice brimming with irony. "What kind of answer is that? It's either yes or no!"

Their fractious relationship had disintegrated further over the past few days, and now neither wanted to be in the same room.

"I need sanitary towels for me and nappy cream for Ella," Liz stated as matter-of-factly as she could.

It was Paddy's turn to redden; he could feel the heat rising from his neck upwards. If that woman thought for one second he was going to walk into a chemist and ask for a packet of women's thingies… she'd another thing coming!

He laughed. "No, no, no, no!" He chuckled again at the very idea.

Liz didn't find it funny. "It's nothing to laugh at, Paddy. I need them. And if you're not going to get them, then I will. It's bad enough having to stay in this dump. I *need* them!"

"Didn't you pack some?" he blurted, almost embarrassed to be having such an intimate conversation. "Oh, yes, I suppose they were in the bag, too!" he added angrily.

Liz didn't respond, and Paddy knew then he'd no choice. "Write down what you need; I'll go."

Under any other circumstances, Liz McKenna would've relished this moment and taken great joy in the bastard's defeat, but today she couldn't. Her back ached, her stomach was wringing, and she felt grungy. Liz had cleaned the bathroom as much as she could, enough so she could step into the shower, but using the dirty towels had proved to be another moment of abject misery. Her eyes welled up as she searched for a pen and paper.

Paddy left the flat and waited for the erratic lift. He had to make a phone call to the OC to find out what to do next. Inside the lift, the smell of pee bored into everything and reminded him of the maze of long corridors and lifts of the notorious Divis flats in Belfast, where he'd spent most of his youth.

The chemist wasn't far away, and Paddy, mortified, handed the small shopping list to a stunningly attractive blonde assistant. She read the note, looked deliberately at him and beamed. *Poor man, he was all flustered. She'd enjoy this!*

"What size?" she queried, raising an eyebrow.

"Sorry?" Paddy asked uncertainly. *Sweet Mother of God, was she asking what size of pads?*

"The jar of cream for the baby's rash. What size jar?" the girl replied with a mischievous twinkle in her eyes.

"Ah! Small is fine," Paddy replied in relief. He saw what she'd been doing, shook his head, pointed a finger and laughed. "Ah, right, I see!"

The girl put everything into a brown bag, and he paid her while giving her a flirtatious grin.

Back in the flat, he passed the bag to Liz, who looked inside. He'd gotten everything right, but she noted the miniature jar of baby cream; it wouldn't last long, though she decided to say nothing. She'd seen his wallet, full of tenners and fifties; stingy bastard.

Later that afternoon, Paddy called the OC from a public pay phone. Their conversation was brief and vague, but Paddy understood it. Although Cable Street was swept regularly for listening devices, the Provos remained ultra-cautious.

Outside, the temperature was rising, and the flat was suffocating. He'd tried unsuccessfully to open some windows, but no dice. He left Liz and the baby to it. The call went well, and he was relieved to hear they'd be picked up earlier than planned and driven to Scotland, where – eventually – they'd travel on the ferry as a married couple going across to Larne.

Meanwhile, Liz McKenna stood wide-eyed at Ella, who lay on the living room floor. Liz's shrill cries of desperation went unheeded as she watched the mite choke and gasp for air. Ella's round face was no longer rosy and healthy-looking. Her nose and fingertips were blue-tinged and her lips white as she huffed, whistled and coughed, her little lungs labouring for fresh air.

Paddy heard Liz's anguished cries from the hallway and ran in on a hellish scene. He glanced at the baby on the floor and thought she was having a fit. *Ah, shit!*

The atmosphere felt sinister and surreal. Liz's panicked cries filled the small living room.

"I don't know what to do! What do I do? Paddy!"

"Sweet fuck, Liz, I don't know, do I?" he shrieked back at her.

How the heck would he know – he'd no experience with children. This was catastrophic!

Immobilised, he watched Liz pick up the child and hold it at arm's length. Its little legs dangled as she turned it onto its tummy and gave it a wallop. Liz had seen someone do the same on the box. Her actions made little difference. The babe-in-arms gulped and panted even more.

"She could die, Paddy! We've got to do something! Call an ambulance!" Liz cried. She was practically hyperventilating.

Paddy stood in the middle of the room, stunned and uncertain about what to do next. They couldn't call an ambulance, daft bitch! This was beyond his understanding, far from the guerrilla warfare in which he was skilled.

"If she dies, we can carry on with the ransom," he announced insensitively.

"What?" Liz screamed, running towards him, carrying the baby. "No, Paddy! We need help. Call an ambulance."

There was no chance of him calling for help, and Paddy made that known to Liz by backhanding her across the face.

"We *cannot* call an ambulance!" he roared.

Ella's gasping suddenly stopped, and her natural colour slowly returned. Feeling shaken and unsteady, Liz held onto the baby protectively, revolted by Paddy's cold-heartedness. She walked out of the room.

For days, her comrade had treated her like a skivvy; he was demanding, selfish, arrogant and full of self-importance. She could handle that, but he'd taken matters to a new level by revealing his indifference to a child's welfare. Until now, she'd never felt any maternal impulse, but something had stirred in her today.

She was no baby killer. Ella tossed and turned. As Liz began to sing to her, she turned over the next move in her mind:

> *He came in so sweetly.*
> *His feet made no din.*
> *He came close beside me.*
> *And this he did say:*
> *'It will not be long, love....'*

****

The following morning, Liz woke from nightmares of her blighted childhood and, looking at Ella, contrasted it with the gilded life this child was born into. Seeming surprisingly peaceful, the baby lay wide awake, staring at the ceiling. She gurgled, and Liz took her little finger. Ella batted at her with a wide-open, toothless grin that made Liz melt.

The sound of a flushing toilet interrupted her planning. Paddy. In a matter of minutes, she heard him shout from the bathroom: "I'm starving! We're off today."

He hadn't told her the latest plan and noticed her look of surprise as she entered the kitchen holding the child.

"Yeah, we're being picked up tonight. I've got a few more calls to make, setting things up for the exchange. While you were feeling sorry for yourself last night, I got us some more food. There's enough there for a good Irish breakfast first. On you go then," he snapped.

Liz saw the ingredients sliding out of a shopping bag on the corner of the kitchen surface she'd cleaned and sanitised. She felt so poorly and depressed that cooking was the last thing she'd do. After yesterday, she'd had enough; this man was an old-fashioned, primal pain in the hole.

"You cook it. I'm sick," she told him cuttingly, walking back to the bedroom.

Paddy shook his head in despair. *Cheeky bitch! Wait 'til he got her back to Derry.*

****

"It's been announced earlier today that kidnapped baby Ella Fox has life-threatening asthma. Her distraught parents have pleaded with the kidnappers that Ella be taken immediately to the nearest hospital where she can get the critical medical attention she needs..."

Liz nearly hit the roof when she listened to the headline news on the radio after Paddy had gone out to make his calls. When she heard the announcement about Ella, her mind raced back to the baby's seizure. *Jesus Christ, no way!* Ella could have another attack at any moment, it seemed. It was past time for Liz to act.

She packed the few items she and Ella possessed. Paddy had thrown his old newspapers around the place, and Liz had seen in one a dedicated police telephone number for anyone with information on Ella. She quickly wrote it down on a piece of paper.

Gripping this in her fist, she left the flat, waited on tenterhooks for the lift and pushed the pram inside. She felt sick with tension as she counted down the floors.

Outside, after being shut up in the flat for days, she was overwhelmed by the usual sounds. Booming reggae music from a building site. Intermittent cries of laughter and cheerful shouting from a bunch of kids on school holidays. Car horns blared in the distance. Life had all but stopped for Liz, who was locked up for days in that hovel. Well, it would never be the same again after what she was about to do.

From the murky windows of the flat, she'd spotted a playground and, next to it, a red phone box. Walking as fast as she could, she strode towards the swings and saw several women chatting and overseeing their playing children. Placing the pram and Ella next to one of the benches, she asked an older woman to mind the baby as she had to make a call.

"Excuse me, would you mind keeping an eye on her? I have to phone the doctor for a prescription," Liz said, tilting her head towards the phone box. "I'll be two seconds."

"'course, love. I'm not going anywhere," the woman replied warmly.

"Thanks, missus, thank you," Liz replied with a quiver in her voice. *This was it.* She looked into the pram, kissed Ella under the stranger's watchful eye, and whispered, "'bye, darlin', be happy."

She quickly dialled the hotline number, and a man's voice answered.

"DC Pollock."

She hesitated, her hands shaking, and, finding herself wordless, began to cry.

"Hello?" the calm voice said. The man waited a moment before suggesting, "If you're still there, please, take your time. When you're ready."

Liz sniffled and wiped her nose with the sleeve of her cardigan; she turned to look out of the phone box and take in her surroundings.

"I don't know where I am, somewhere in Harlow New Town, some estate with three big blocks of flats. Ella's in her pram beside a black woman by the kiddies' park."

"Sorry, wait, please! Can you repeat that?" the policeman shouted, but Liz McKenna hung up. The only sign of her recent presence was the phone's handset swinging back and forth.

****

It didn't take long for the Metropolitan police to find Ella Fox, supported by the local constabulary. The mum watching Ella had noticed Liz running in the opposite direction and shouted after her. She'd then quickly asked for help from the other mothers, one of whom ran to the phone box and called the police.

All of this was unbeknown to Paddy Gillispie, who was merrily making his way back to the flat when he heard the frantic sound of police sirens. He thought it'd likely have nothing to do with them, so he entered the lift, but once inside the flat, he understood straight away – the place was empty.

"Fuck! Fuck! Fuck!" he screamed, throwing down a soft toy he'd picked up along the way for the baby. The sirens grew louder and closer. He ran for the lift.

****

Once he reached the ground floor, he was about to open the door to the main exit and step out. He stopped himself when instincts acquired, avoiding the Brits over many years took over.

The estate was eerily quiet. Where once there'd been laughter, music and voices, it was as calm as any morgue. Paddy had scoped out the janitor's exit to which he'd been given directions along with the keys to the flat. He took the small side door and ran out swiftly to hide under a walkway thirty feet away, where he stood still as a statue and listened. Out of the corner of his eye, he detected several blurred silhouettes, working in pairs, darting around the vehicles parked at the rear of the building. *Shit*. It was Special Branch. They'd be armed. Motherfuckers! He reached for his Browning but held back.

Running between pillars and posts out of sight under the walkway, Paddy remained undetected. He arrived breathless and exhausted at the base of the adjacent block. About to go on the move again, he stopped when he heard voices and waited. Two men, dressed in civilian clothes but unmistakably pigs, were cursing loudly and walking in his direction. Paddy pressed his back against a pillar and kept out of sight while he listened.

"Typical, ain't it, them ratting on each other? I heard she was Irish."

"As long as the baby's safe," the other man put in, oblivious to Paddy in the shadows a few feet away.

He couldn't think straight. So the useless bitch had called the fucking police! He needed to get far away but couldn't help wondering where the traitorous cunt could've gone.

I'll fucking find you, McKenna. I swear I will! he vowed.

He could hear a convoy of police cars arriving, and officers were waiting to brief the new arrivals in the car park. While they were distracted, Paddy put his head down, pulled up his collar and crept away as quickly as he could in the opposite direction. He was heading for a renowned Republican-friendly pub a mile or two away. He needed to update the OC, and fuck, if he'd ever needed a drink!

****

Chapter Forty-nine

George Edwards loved his job at Hydebank Boys' Home and had settled in very nicely, thank you. Their UK-wide business endeavours were going swimmingly, and they'd been lucky enough to get some fresh stock in. Between him and the House Father, they were making wads of money.

As usual, Dr Harris continued to be a huge liability. Edwards had just thrown him out of his office in a tizzy – it seemed the good doctor had recently discovered Jesus and was looking to repent. The idea went beyond a joke, and Edwards pondered their conversation.

"You've discovered what!" he'd asked in horror and disbelief.

"Jesus. The Church. Forgiveness," Harris had replied in annoyance, perplexed by this rude response.

Edwards got up behind his desk and towered over Harris, who sat wide-eyed like a boy awaiting punishment. His skin appeared drier and more lizard-like than usual.

"And what do this *forgiveness* and *your man Jesus* lark involve then?" Edwards enquired, his questions dripping with malice.

"Repenting, confessing, cleansing one's soul," Harris replied, clearly and firmly, displaying growing confidence; his whole body straightened as he spoke. He wanted forgiveness, to be free from the burden he carried. The knowledge of the harm he'd caused to the numerous men and women he'd neglected in his role as a Police Medical Officer, especially during internment and beyond. Harris also wanted to be free from the taint of the abuse meted out in Hydebank House.

To his astonishment, he had found solace at a friary run by some local monks. They were kind enough to agree that he could stay with them for as long as it took him to repent and heal his soul. His sinning was finally over. The doctor had fought unnatural feelings for years and concealed so many lies.

"You're seriously telling me you think you can walk out of here, just like that, go and sit in some Pope-loving hole to confess everything to those weasel-faced priests? I'm sure they'll love that… Are you out of your fuckin' mind? Wise up!"

Incredulous laughter filled the room. Harris began to shake his head in rebuttal. "No! No, George. I promise I'll say nothing! This is about my repentance only."

Edwards sneered at him in disbelief.

"Aaaah, well, that's good to know. Thank you for that. It'll make me – and I'm sure all our associates – feel sooooooooo much better!" Edwards bellowed, moving uncomfortably close to Harris, who was beginning to realise that coming clean with this bully had not been a smart move. The latest in a long, long line.

"Well, the answer's no, I'm afraid. I won't hear another word of it – you're not going anywhere, let alone moving in with the monks. You'll be staying with us, Dr Harris, so we can keep a close eye on you. And I mean a very close eye. Now get the hell out of my office!"

Harris attempted to object but stopped when Edwards impatiently shoved him out by force and slammed the door behind him. The doctor was quaking. This man truly terrified him.

Back in the office, Edwards made a quick phone call to his friend, the Chief Constable. Bonner had been particularly elusive of late, and after what Harris had shared, Edwards felt the need to talk to him. The doctor knew too much, and the thought of him *confessing* was both nightmarish and comical. He heard the private line ring until the CC answered it personally.

"Bonner."

"It's me."

"What's up?" Bonner asked wearily.

"It's Harris. He's been talking out of place and says he wants out. To lead a clean life. Fat chance of that!"

"Oh, yeah?" Bonner sighed. He knew what Edwards wanted, but he'd enough on his plate dealing with Lemon, Jones and keeping his job. He wouldn't do anything to draw unwanted attention.

"Yeah. So what are you going to do?" Edwards asked edgily.

"Nothing," Bonner clipped back.

"Really?"

"Really," the cop replied. *Here it comes...*

"You do understand the consequences of doing nothing?" Edwards asked pointedly.

"I do, and I'm sorry, but I have enough going on here. Have to go. G'bye," Bonner replied firmly before hanging up. Edwards was left listening to an echoing line. *What*! Was that Bonner he'd spoken to – he'd never sounded so in control. The RUC man had nothing to do with the kiddies and wasn't inclined that way. But he'd benefited financially by agreeing to quash any complaints the mistreated boys made; until now, Edwards felt he'd always held the upper hand in their business dealings.

"Fuck!" he roared, clenching his fists in frustration. It looked like he'd have to deal with the good doctor himself.

Edwards continually gawked at Harris during dinner, eyes boring into him until the doctor felt himself tremble. The boys and even the House Father were reticent, likely sensing Edwards's mood. The room quickly emptied, leaving the two men alone. Edwards walked up to Harris, giving him a cold smile and suggesting they go out.

"Come with me for a drive. We need to clear the air, and we can't do that here." Harris knew the offer wasn't one he could back out of and reluctantly agreed. "Sure."

"Good. I'll see you outside in five."

Harris was terrified as he pulled on his jacket and waited at the front entrance. He hoped and prayed this drive might allow him to talk some sense into Edwards; they could come to an amicable arrangement. Minutes later, he heard whistling as Edwards went around the side of the house and got into his car.

"In you get!" he cried, leaning over and opening the passenger door to the black Datsun hatchback. Harris climbed in, put his seatbelt on – something he always did, having witnessed too many RTA leftovers – and patted down his jacket.

"Where are we going?" he asked uncertainly.

"You'll see," Edwards replied with a tight smile.

Harris sat back in the seat, trying his best to act normal.

Edwards drove towards the outskirts of Belfast. To spare himself the effort of conversation, he played with the car stereo, pressing its various buttons until he was satisfied to hear Madness's 'Driving in My Car'. He laughed to himself while Harris remained silent and apprehensive.

It didn't take long to get to where Edwards wanted to go. The sun was beginning to set. However, enough light was left for the men to see Belfast below them.

Edwards had parked on the edge of a basalt quarry and lake on Black Mountain. Tonight the skyline was dominated by the world-famous Harland & Wolf Shipyard cranes, Samson and Goliath, that reared more than 300 feet above the glowing, twinkling city lights.

"Impressive, eh?" Edwards commented before suddenly turning to Harris and yelling, "Get out!"

Harris found he couldn't move. He immediately recognised the expression on Edwards's face – he'd seen that raw, fanatical hatred and rage in the soulless eyes of killers before this.

The doctor found himself completely paralysed. He'd been playing a dangerous game for years and retained several incriminating photos and correspondence for insurance. He'd also kept a journal safely stored in a safe deposit box and only accessible by his solicitor upon Harris's death.

"Get out!" Edwards screamed, exasperated.

"I... I... I... can't get out. Please, let's talk about this! Don't do this, George. I'm sorry; forget everything I said earlier, please. I beg you!"

By now, Harris was sick with fear. He threatened Edwards with the box's contents, who paid little attention. Instead, he climbed out and lumbered round the front of the Datsun's bonnet to open the passenger door.

"I've got a box with everything in it!" Harris was mumbling. "It's got photos and letters. I'll use it; I swear I will if you don't take me home right now!"

But Edwards couldn't hear him or open the door as Harris had pressed down the lock. The clunking sound it made was like music to his ears. Edwards's contorted face seethed behind the passenger window. Harris's breathing became so rapid that it misted the glass and blocked his view.

"You'd better open this fuckin' door, or I swear to God I *will* kill you!" Edwards yelped, hitting the glass with a fist.

There wasn't a chance in hell Harris would unlock it. He released his seat belt and moved across the vehicle with the gear stick burrowing deep into his back. Edwards continued to bash and thump the window. He suddenly stopped, seconds passed, and then Harris heard and felt an almighty crash coming from the other side of the car. Shards and chunks of glass fell inwards, and hundreds of razor-sharp slivers buried themselves in the doctor's stinging face and hands.

Edwards's hand was soon inside, unlocking and opening the passenger door. Angry as a bear, he caught his breath and waited while watching Harris cower. Adrenaline drove Edwards on. He dragged Harris's scrawny body out of the Datsun, like a drooping rag doll, and lugged him towards the edge of the quarry.

Grasping the doctor's neck with one hand, Edwards snarled menacingly at the terrified man before pushing him out and over the precipice of the dismal black mountainside.

****

Chapter Fifty

"You're fired, woman! Do you hear? I trusted you, and you've told half the world my business. *My private business!* How fuckin' dare you?" Jones had been tipped off by a Londonderry Sentinel Journalist that the Nationalist Derry Journal had sleaze on him and that his PA was the snitch.

Jill Sharkey, Charles Jones's secretary, sat motionless, watching the fat reptilian creep issue another tirade. Over the years, she'd grown so used to them that they no longer affected her. She'd been well prepared for this one. After all, she had told that lovely American reporter everything. She'd been saving up to go to Ibiza, and the newspaperman kindly topped up her fund. However, while lying in bed last night, she'd come up with another idea that'd bring in yet more cash and lots of it.

"Don't you have anything to say?" Jones screamed at the top of his voice. The girl had worked for him for five years and betrayed him. He suddenly saw that Jill was pretty with a nice figure under that prim and proper black-and-white A-line dress. She looked the part with her dark hair tied back in typical secretarial style and round, dark-rimmed glasses. Her lips were thin but highlighted by deep red lipstick. Her eyes were the most striking thing about her. They were dark, fathomless, and today they glowed with anger as she dared to point the finger at him.

"Listen, you pathetic little man," she hissed. "I've bent over backwards for you for years, but watching you grow colder and meaner by the day is too much! You think you're so clever, don't you? Well, let me tell you, boyo, you are not! I've made dated notes of all your shenanigans and taken copies of your private correspondence. Hard evidence, Mr Jones, of all the horrendous, malicious, contemptible things you've done, including killing people and drugging and raping those poor prossies. I could get you sent down for the rest of your life, so *do not test me!*"

Jones was shocked beyond reason. The fuckin' whore had him by the balls. He knew what was coming next, shook his head and sat waiting. Two could play at this game, so he began to laugh aloud – a raucous, hysterical sound that hopefully would confuse her.

Jill knew what he was doing and ignored it. She also knew he was likely trying to dream up some plan to intimidate her, but instead, she remained calm and aloof until he felt awkward.

Like a schoolmistress, Jill put a finger to her lips to quieten him.

"Ssshhhh now, Mr Jones. Your antics won't work with me. I've thought this through carefully, and you can do nothing to hurt or intimidate me."

In all the years she'd worked for him, he'd learnt nothing about her personal life, having never once asked where she lived or about her family and friends. She pointed to a sizeable gilt-framed oil painting of Carrickfergus Castle. They both knew that behind it was concealed a Yale safe.

"There's cash in there and a lot more than usual after that big campaign donation yesterday. I bet it's not all legal tender, but it doesn't matter. I'll help myself in recognition of my long, tedious years here, shall I? Thank you very much. Now, if you'll kindly open it?"

Jones didn't like her condescending attitude – not one bit. He'd likely get his throat cut if the money that belonged to the Ulster Volunteer Force disappeared on his watch! You did not fuck around with these guys; there was £40,000 in that safe. His mind was in knots. If he didn't open it, she'd hand over all the evidence, and he'd go down for life. But if he did, he'd have a hell of a time explaining to the militias that his fucking secretary had stolen their cash. Above all, though, *he did not want to go to jail.*

"Okay," Jones told her reluctantly. Then: "But you've got to give me everything you have, all of it."

"Sorry? I didn't quite get that?" Jill said mockingly, throwing herself into one of his revolving visitors' chairs and playfully swinging it round and round. Jones could kill her right here; he was so furious! He imagined his hands closing around her skinny neck and squeezing it hard…

"I said okay, but I want everything you've got," he repeated in a tone of loathing.

She quickly swung back to face him. "That's okay. I have them here." She produced a couple of bulky envelopes and files from a gigantic black Penney's tote bag and threw them noisily onto his desk. As soon as the bag was empty, she threw it at Jones.

"Well, come on then, sir, do the honours. I've a plane to catch," she told him with a wicked chuckle. *As a safeguard, she'd hidden the best and most incriminating evidence somewhere he'd never find it.*

Jones picked up the bag, and Jill watched him struggle to remove the heavy picture. It was comical when she saw him almost drop it and swear. He finally put the painting down, entered the safe code, and looked back at her.

"Go on then," she said with a steely gaze.

He snorted and mumbled something underwater as he removed enough cash to fill the bag. When he'd finished, he threw it across the room to her. Jill smiled and lifted it, finding it surprisingly heavy.

"It's been a pleasure doing business with you, Mr Jones," she said, promptly leaving the room. Jones never took his eyes off her as she picked up some personal items from her desk in the outer office, including a few photos.

Feeling helpless, he cried after her, "I'll get you for this, you bitch! I swear I will!"

Jill Sharkey kept on walking but raised a single finger in response. *Ibiza, here I come!*

****

That same evening Jones left the RUC black-tie Centenary celebratory dinner at the Grand Central Hotel in Belfast. After the day's antics, he'd overdone it and taken way too many painkillers, leaving him dizzy and nauseous. He was disgusted with the greed of his kick-arse of a secretary, and when he'd opened the envelopes and files after she'd left, he'd found they contained nothing of note. *Sweet fuck all.*

At dinner, he'd tried to put it all to the back of his mind until he could think straight but found that he couldn't. Feeling poorly, he'd left early. As a result, he found himself waiting outside at the top of a flight of worn steps. His car, driven by his new chauffeur and bodyguard, Simon Bond, hadn't arrived. Carroll had been with him for a month, and to Jones's surprise, he liked him. Simon was a man of few words who did as he was told there and then – unlike the many morons Jones had trialled since Lemon's incarceration.

The evening had been a complete shambles as he'd been unfortunate enough to sit next to Chief Constable Bonner. The man was pensive, broody and oddly terse. Jones tried to get more information from him about the murder of Judge Dodds, who'd been shot on his front doorstep earlier that week, but Bonner was reluctant to talk, and Jones found his disobliging mood infuriating. The CC then made the most Goddamn' awful speech before, quivering with embarrassment, he'd returned to say goodbye to the others at his table with some feeble excuse that his wife needed him at home. Jones knew Bonner was lying through his teeth; his wife had left him. He was probably heading off to see the mistress he'd set up in some cottage, although Jones had heard that relationship wasn't going too well either.

It suited him to a tee that the old judge had been conveniently wasted. He was no longer giving value for money anyway. Another willing legal type had recently made it known to Jones that he'd like to take over, and in the end, Dodds's demise suited him perfectly. But Bonner's peculiar behaviour this evening had given him a niggling feeling that all was not right in the Chief Constable's world, and Jones decided he'd make a point of finding out why. The man was a walking time bomb.

Meanwhile, in the Lodge car park, Chief Constable Bonner sat alone in his car, struggling to breathe and with a churning stomach. Somehow, for his sins, he'd ended up sitting next to Jones at dinner, who'd interrogated him about Judge Dodds's murder. Bonner's nerves were still jangling from his nightmarish speech and what was coming. A sudden knock on the door made him jump. Lemon peered in. Bonner rolled down the window enough to be heard.

"All set?" he whispered.

"Aye. I'm here, aren't I?" Lemon replied curtly.

"Yeah, you are, Mark. And remember who got you here. We've made a deal," Bonner reminded him.

Lemon snorted, gurgled and spat revoltingly on the gravel.

"Really!" Bonner shuddered in disgust.

Lemon ignored him and, closer to the window, asked in a low, husky voice, "You've got it then?"

"Yeah," Bonner snapped.

He had taken Lemon out of gaol that afternoon, telling the baffled doctor that, for confidential reasons, he had to personally escort the prisoner to the local RUC police station so he could make a statement about something to do with a ferocious sectarian attack in West Belfast.

The CC opened the car's glove compartment and removed a black package. Inside was the small Browning revolver he'd retrieved from Captain Hickey, who had sliced the Londonderry solicitor's throat instead of sticking to their plan. Bonner wasn't impressed by his improvised tactic. Hickey should have used the gun from the recent PIRA weapons raid so that they'd be implicated in the death.

"Take it. It's loaded."

Lemon snorted and was about to gargle and spit again but stopped as Bonner raised his hand, berating him. "Don't!"

He swallowed and took the small package. "So where's he at?"

Bonner's eyes looked over to the Lodge's entrance and steps. "Over there, waiting for Simon."

Simon Bond was Lemon's older half-brother and a hardened member of the Ulster Defence Association (UDA), a Loyalist paramilitary organisation. Jones was so arrogant that he'd never checked deep enough into his new driver's background to find the link between the two men. Simon had been the only member of Lemon's family to visit him in prison since his wife Mel had told him where to go after his sentencing. The brothers had talked about Lemon getting his revenge on his ex-employer, and it'd been sweet when the RUC man offered to help.

It was soon time. Bonner saw Jones's silhouette impatiently walking back and forth at the top of the Lodge steps.

"Off you go."

Bonner bit his lower lip and felt himself vibrating with fear and nerves. Other than Lemon and Jones from afar, no one saw him drive away.

Back in the car park, Lemon grasped the loaded gun, walked towards the bottom of the stone steps and stopped. He looked up to find Jones marching back and forth, frustrated by the delay and the fact that it was now raining. *Shit!* He heard Lemon's approaching footsteps and, thinking it was Simon, supposed there was something wrong with the car. He squinted as he observed a darkly dressed figure climbing towards him.

Its stance looked familiar; he'd have sworn it was Lemon. He chuckled lightly at the idea and turned back inside for shelter, feeling distinctly unwell. In the distance were the clinking sounds of glasses, loud voices, laughter and music. *Where the hell was Simon?*

The figure drew abreast with him, and Jones found he couldn't see a face under the stranger's fur-trimmed hood. Suddenly fear gripped him, and he took an involuntary step back.

"Mr Jones, sir!" Lemon yelled, stopping him in his tracks.

Jones couldn't believe his ears. *What the heck!* "Lemon, is that really you?" he cried in confusion.

The two men stood face to face, eyes locked. Jones stayed motionless as Lemon pulled his hood down. Jones saw the changes in him caused by incarceration. It looked like the grey-faced man barely contained a wave of anger that struggled to escape. The gravity of Lemon's expression told Jones everything, and dread hit him like a ten-tonne truck as his former bodyguard raised the gun in his hand. He aimed it at Jones's forehead.

"Long time no see, boss," he said in a glacial tone. "You never answered when I wrote and phoned."

Too choked to respond, Jones glared back at him. He knew what Lemon was here to do. He stepped forward, shrugged his shoulders and smiled grimly – an unrepentant, *fuck you, Lemon* smile.

His nonchalance infuriated the other man so much that his hand shook when he fired. The first shot caught Jones in his right shoulder, the second in the pit of his stomach, the third struck his left leg just below the knee, and the last – fortunately for him – whooshed by to graze one scarred, shiny cheekbone.

Straightaway, from the snapping, cracking noises outside, some guests in the Lodge realised there'd been gunshots. They cried out warnings to take cover as panicked cries filled the night, and all hell broke loose.

Lemon ran like a scalded dog to Jones's waiting car. Inside, Simon grinned after watching the fiasco from the safety of the saloon. Lemon screamed with glee and excitement as he threw himself in and slammed the door behind him.

"I got him, Simon! I fucking got him!" Lemon laughed like a hyena as he slapped his brother on the back. Simon joined in. Then, putting his foot down, he barrelled off, the car's tyres screeching and burning as they bounced down the long driveway towards the safe house where they'd lie low for as long as necessary.

"You did good, Mark; you got him rightly!"

****

Bonner watched from afar, relieved beyond telling that it was finally over – he'd finished Jones. He then radioed the local RUC station, informing them there'd been a shooting at the Orange Lodge and to get there fast. He also reported that Lemon had escaped from custody.

His mind raced as he thought of what he had to do next. Recently, he'd secretly met with a Northern Ireland Office senior representative, who'd indirectly and off the record asked for his help. They assured him he could retire with a full pension if this manoeuvre were successful. Bonner saw this as his get-out-of-jail-free card; although it was risky, he didn't hesitate to agree. He welcomed the covert task. For undisclosed reasons, it seemed that young Captain Hickey was now viewed as a loose cannon and an embarrassment to the British. This pleased Bonner no end. After he had introduced Hickey to Jones, the two of them had treated him with contempt and grown as thick as thieves, leaving him sitting on the bench. Well, it was payback time for both of them.

The Chief Constable of the RUC was on his way to Londonderry to secretly meet Provo CO, Cahir O'Connell. Bonner proposed the meeting through Gerard McFarland, the conduit for such unofficial contact. They were meeting in a vicarage in Muff, a small village merely within the Republic's border and not far from the city. As he drove down the A6, Bonner recalled the brief he'd received from his top-ranking contact.

"We know Captain Hickey murdered Brendan Doherty of his own accord and others too – most likely on Charles Jones's direct orders. He, by the way, we're watching very, very closely. Hickey's a lone wolf; he's ignoring orders, not reporting for duty, nor turning up for briefings. The man thinks he's in the Wild West and needs to be dealt with. He's an embarrassment and a liability. Therefore we'd like you to tell Mr O'Connell everything in the hope the Provos will do the necessary."

Bonner strongly suspected that MI5 were behind this and thought their strategy very clever. Getting the Provos to eliminate Hickey would keep the security services clear from any suspicion of dirty tricks. The British Army would be none the wiser if it were made to look as though the young captain had died in the line of duty.

Doherty's death had severely affected the Republicans of Londonderry, who were growing daily more frustrated and angry at the lack of results from the police investigation. Naming Doherty's murderer to them would help keep the peace on the streets while spurring them into retributive action.

Bonner drove towards the border village, listening to the radio and the latest news.

"A prominent Protestant businessman from Belfast, Charles Jones, is the latest shooting victim and has been seriously injured. It's believed that his ex-bodyguard, Mark Carroll, who escaped from custody earlier today, was the assailant and is now on the run along with an unidentified male in a stolen car."

Bonner gulped. *Seriously injured?* Seriously injured damned well wasn't good enough! He wanted that toad dead.

****

Chapter Fifty-one

"I can't leave them alone, Carol, not with my ex stirring up the social and trying to take our Val away. I mean, Mam's coping with this all alone. Maybe it's time for me to go back?" Rob said as the two of them lay side by side in his single bed at Glengowan House. They were breaking the rules of being alone together, no matter whether they were in the same bed.

Upon hearing of Tracey's threats to take Val and the social worker's visit, Rob felt torn between his love for this remarkable woman, who'd helped him, and his concern for his family. His head had cleared entirely. Astonishingly, he'd found kicking the drugs and drinking was much easier when he had a caring, supportive partner to back him up and distract him from any thoughts of relapsing. He attended support meetings and had begun to talk to a therapist, who'd confirmed he had Post Traumatic Stress Disorder (PTSD) – or, as they'd called it in the old days, 'shell shock'. Her diagnosis helped him to see that the trauma of Val's murder and the hatred and bitterness he'd experienced first-hand on the streets of Northern Ireland had played their part in his decision to self-medicate with drink and drugs. By coming to terms with this through therapy, he should hopefully render himself less reliant on harmful substances.

Together they'd put a treatment plan in place. She told him that over the months, they'd talk regularly and suggested he should reconnect with some of the lads who, like him, were now permanently back home and adapting to civvy life. She said that many battle-scarred veterans who'd served twenty or more years found their new way of life sloppy and disorganised. As soldiers, they'd continuously operated under strict discipline and been trained to bottle up their feelings and hide anxiety. In their new civilian status, these men were too proud to admit to their inner struggles and seek help, instead resorting to the temporary oblivion that was readily available at any off-licence or in a plastic baggie bought outside a club or pub. That behaviour left them susceptible to depression, endless nightmares, survivor's guilt and PTSD. It was hugely reassuring to Rob to hear that he was not alone. Other former soldiers thought, acted and felt as he did. But they didn't all have a lover as generous and caring as Carol.

At first, like virgin teenagers, their lovemaking had been awkward and clumsy, but soon it grew carefree and invigorating. Rob felt he'd been given a second chance and had no intention of blowing it.

Carol stroked his forehead and traced a finger along the scar that stretched into his hairline and beyond.

"Does it still hurt?" she asked tenderly.

He smiled sleepily. "Most of the time, more or less. But you've helped heal me, pet, in many ways. I'll never be able to thank you."

She smiled. They had not said they loved each other yet, but they did. She'd never forget when she first saw Rob, so desolate, sick and sad. She smiled again as she thought of how well he'd done and how far he'd come in getting himself back on track. She didn't feel it was down to her but to him. Rob was the one who'd been brave enough to take a leap of faith, and she looked forward to their collective future that now held so much hope.

"What is it?" he asked, noting her smile.

"I'm thinking. You've come so far, and I'm proud of you. But..." Carol stopped, afraid to break the spell and bring them back to reality.

"But what?"

"I think it's time to call your mother and find out what's going on with Val."

Rob was thinking the same but was terrified of making contact. He didn't want to hurt his mam or Val again by neglecting them when they needed his support, but he didn't want to leave Carol behind either.

"You're right, and I've been thinking that myself. It's just... I don't want to leave you. I couldn't cope without you."

Carol sat up in bed and smiled down at him. Rob relished her nakedness; her plump breasts were heavy, and she felt proud when she saw their effect on him. A cheeky smile crossed his face. She kissed him hungrily. Suddenly, an almighty bang on the door was followed by a furious commotion outside the corridor.

"Carol! Are you in there, Carol?" It was Geoff's voice.

"No!" the couple cried, jumping out of bed and wildly searching for their clothes. They didn't get a chance to dress but heard jingling keys and saw the door open to reveal Geoff on the threshold. Carol screamed as she tried vainly to find anything that would shield her from his prying eyes. On the other hand, Rob was livid with the gawking man and ran angrily towards him.

"What the fuck, Geoff!"

Geoff Brady had suspected this affair had been going on for weeks but, until now, couldn't prove it. Everything had been perfect when it was just Carol and him. And then she met this prick. Geoff had had grand plans for her, but this druggie had appeared and ruined everything. It was his turn to be livid.

"You're out of here, mate. Today! I'll give you one hour!"

Carol pulled on a checked shirt of Rob's and cried, "You can't do that, Geoff!"

"Oh, I can, and I have!" he retorted. A small group of other tenants had gathered in the corridor and stood behind him, doing their best to peek at the semi-naked woman and man. Aware of their presence, Geoff angrily waved them away.

"That's enough, all of you! Get back to your rooms."

The gaping men reluctantly disappeared, and Geoff turned back to Carol. His voice softened, and the sadness in his eyes said everything. For him, this was personal.

"You have to go too, Carol."

"I know. I'm sorry, Geoff."

He nodded, his forehead furrowed with deep lines and half-smiled. With his head hanging low, he retreated to his office.

Carol watched him leave. It seemed South Shields was the way ahead.

****

On the journey there with their few belongings, Rob gave a great deal of thought to his future. Geoff had been gentlemanly enough to make things easy for Carol. Although he continued to ignore Rob, he'd taken her aside, told her he'd give her a reference, and kissed her on the cheek.

When Rob phoned his mam to say he was coming home, it'd been like the return of the Prodigal Son – all his sins forgiven. Any signs of anger or disapproval were long gone. He could hear the excitement and relief in Bridie's voice when she took the call he had made from the bus station. There was soon to be a court hearing to determine custody of Val, and he knew he'd need to be on his A-game for that. He knew too that he'd much to make up for at home, especially with his young son. His unease transmitted itself to Carol on the bus ride south.

"Do you think they'll like me?" she asked, her voice full of trepidation at the prospect of meeting Rob's beloved mam and son.

"Don't be silly; they will! I like you, don't I?" he replied playfully.

"Only like?" she jested.

"A big like!" He was unsure how else to word it, shrinking from making a declaration in the middle of a packed bus.

And then Carol did a lovely thing. She stroked his arm and looked deep into his eyes.

"I love you, Robert Sallis," she declared out loud. "And if you *'big like'* me now, I can live with that."

Rob didn't know where to look. This was way more public than he'd have preferred. But ignoring the curious eyes and encouraging nods from passengers, he cupped her face in his hands and answered her in a rich voice of honesty and love.

"And I love you too, Carol Caffrey. So much it frightens the living daylights out of me!"

Then he kissed her, reassuring her that all would be well.

****

Hours later, the Sallis family and Carol sat in Bridie's living room. Although she knew Rob was on his way, she still couldn't believe it when she opened the door, and there he stood.

He looked so fresh and fit, and from the look on his face, her real son was back! She'd warned Val to be on his best behaviour and, bless his cotton socks, so far he had been if a little reserved. But then, that was only to be expected and far better than outright rejection.

Bridie listened as Carol told them about a trip to Loch Lomond when she was a child, fishing with her father, and what a disaster it'd been. Somehow the simple story told in her soft Scottish lilt got Val to giggle, and for that, Bridie was grateful.

He caught his nan's eye and smiled. He seemed happy. He liked this round-faced woman who talked funny; she made him laugh. Val studied Rob. Even though memories of how his dad had been still scared the boy a bit, there was something different about him now. He looked younger and seemed happy.

Once lunch was over, Carol offered to take Val out.

"Would you like to go to the park? Maybe we'll see if we can get a poke too."

"A poke?" he asked, unsure what she meant.

"An ice cream, you silly sausage!" Carol laughed.

She helped him put on his new trainers. Bridie led them to the front door, and Carol held her hand out to Val. The boy hesitated for only a moment. He held onto it tightly, seeing his nan smile when she noticed. The women shared a look of quiet gratification when they said goodbye.

Rob was beginning to clear the dishes, but Bridie told him off and ordered him to sit.

"Jeepers, son, you're looking so much better. I can only think your Da must have heard my prayers and interceded for you. And that wee girl… where the heck did you find her? She's a walking angel. Did you see her with Val?" Bridie's relief at his homecoming was unutterable, and she shed tears of joy.

Rob affectionately wiped them away. He bobbed his head, afraid for a moment that he might cry himself. He flashed her an embarrassed smile, and his voice sounded thick when he spoke.

"She's too good for me, Mam. I know she is."

Bridie rolled her eyes at this. "No, son. No way. She's your Guardian Angel; that's what she is!"

Rob laughed, recalling how he'd thought something similar when he first met Carol. She was indeed his guardian angel, and he knew he'd always need her.

"I'm glad you like her, Mam. That's important to me. I don't know where I'd be today if she hadn't stepped in and saved me."

"It's God's way of looking out for you, son. With a woman like that in our corner, we're going to take Tracey on, and she and Social Services can go straight to hell! Now that you're home, there's no question of the lad leavin' this house. It's his home and yours. No one is going anywhere."

Rob couldn't remember a time when he'd felt so complete. He wasn't just content; he wasn't just satisfied; he wasn't just okay; he was joyous, blissful, exuberant. Happy.

He'd never thought he could feel this way again, not in his wildest dreams. He felt immortal, courageous and brave. He picked up his squealing mam and swung her around before enveloping her in his arms.

"You're right, Mam," he whispered lovingly. "It's only us now, and over my dead body will anyone tear us apart. I've got a lot of making up to do with you and the lad. But remember, Mam, I love you. I love you both with all my heart."

Bridie Sallis felt herself melt into the strong arms of her restored son and willingly surrendered herself to his care. Rob was home, and home for good; everything was going to be okay.

****

Chapter Fifty-two

Caitlin never fully understood why she'd dialled James Henderson's number, remembering it still from the numerous times she'd phoned the house from the factory. In a way, she was glad they'd been interrupted, but she was still left feeling disappointed. The whole idea had been crazy; her emotions were all up in the air. Hearing his voice again caused her immense pain but also revived an exhilaration in her heart that she'd forgotten how to feel. This path was dangerous; the strength of her feelings for James still was frightening. Despite that, she'd let fate decide her future. She'd marry a man who made her feel safe and secure, a man who couldn't hurt her like James. This was all she needed in her life, nothing else.

She and Anne had eaten a quick breakfast and were getting dressed for the hairdressers. Caitlin's eyes surveyed the marshmallow-like, bell-sleeved wedding dress she would wear when they returned. It was a fantastic work of art, and Chris had had no qualms about its cost. She imagined what her family would've thought of it, but if her daddy hadn't died, if her mammy and poor Tina hadn't followed him, she wouldn't be here now in this house. None of this would be happening. She would never have left Derry.

Her nerves jangled, and she fought a cynical inner voice. Was she doing the right thing? Did she *really* love Chris? Did she love him the way she'd loved James? Over the past weeks, these questions had plagued her. She supposed it was in an effort to answer them that she had plucked up the courage to make the call.

Her bedroom door burst wide open, and Anne came in with a radiant smile. She'd just tried on her beautiful, flowing, gunmetal silk bridesmaid's dress for the umpteenth time. She was so excited and felt like a princess in it. A tiny touch of melancholy earlier had made her think of her wedding to Porkie. How pathetically misguided it seemed now – it had been nothing like this. And how awful she'd been to poor Caitlin, making her wear such a lousy homemade bridesmaid's dress!

"Well, me darlin', feelin' any better?" she asked, bearing in mind Caitlin's black mood of earlier.

"Fine, I suppose," her friend replied, bemused.

"Fine. Only fine?" Anne repeated, worried. *Ah, no, here we go again!* "What's going on, Caitlin?"

"Nothing."

"Nothing, hmm?" Anne sat at the bottom of the bed and patted the space beside her. She knew that look.

"Tell me," she sighed, taking a deep breath in preparation for what was coming because something was.

"It's nothing," Caitlin muttered, turning away.

"I don't believe you! Jesus, you look like you're going to your funeral, no matter your wedding! Come on, tell me, please," Anne implored, patting the bed for the second time and motioning her to sit.

Caitlin hated it when Anne read her so well, but then she'd been in her life forever and, at times, was too clever for her own good.

"I called him."

"Who?"

"James."

For a split second, Anne was dumbfounded until she screeched, "No way! The Adonis? Sweet mother of Jesus, you called the Adonis! Why?"

Caitlin nodded guiltily. "I couldn't help it, Anne. I needed to hear his voice one last time," she added, almost in a whisper.

"But, Caitlin, why do that after all this time? You could ruin everything for yourself. Look around you, love!" Anne cried.

"I know, I know!" Caitlin stood up to walk away. *She didn't want to discuss this.*

Anne saw the shutters going down and squeezed her hand. Seeing her friend so unhappy was painful, especially on her wedding day. She knew she needed to tread very carefully.

"I'm sorry for shouting. It was a shock, that's all."

Caitlin tried to formulate an answer, but Anne pressed on, "Well then, what did he have to say?"

Caitlin fell onto the bed and cried, "He wrote me a letter!"

Anne looked confused. "What d'ya mean, a letter? Where is it?"

"Tommy forgot to bring it with him; I've no idea what's in it."

Anne couldn't afford to let Caitlin see her intense relief. To conceal it, she turned her eyes to the floor.

"Sweetheart, it's probably for the best. You don't want to go there; you don't want to go back to that dark place. It's taken you so long to find the one for you, to be happy. Your life is turning into a fairy tale."

She tried to reassure the bride-to-be, "You have a fine, kind-hearted man who loves you, Caitlin, and a fantastic home. You'll never have to worry about the electric running out. Think about that, and you have a wardrobe as good as Princess Di's, for fuck sake!"

Caitlin couldn't dispute what Anne said, feeling selfish and spoilt, yet something wasn't right with her.

"But Chris – is he right for me?"

"The right what?" Anne asked, slightly baffled.

"The right man," her friend replied miserably.

"For fuck sake, Caitlin! Nobody's perfect. Believe me. He's the right man for you to marry! It's pre-wedding nerves; that's all, everyone; everyone gets them. You're bound to be nervous. But listen to what I'm saying. This is serious." Anne paused and lowered her voice. "You've everything you could possibly want, and Chris loves you to death. So please, Caitlin, forget about the Adonis, Derry, the letter… forget all that, please love. This is your wedding day."

****

Gerard McFarland had rung Tommy the previous evening and suggested he stay in London for a few more days. McFarland was awaiting confirmation from his M16 contact that the Brits were ready to reopen negotiations. Tommy agreed; he was feeling poorly and could do with the rest. Up to now, the Brits had remained reticent, and he, like McFarland, was desperate to resurrect some form of dialogue.

It was nearing 9.30 a.m., and, by Christ, he thought it would be a hell of a long day. As usual, Anne Heaney and her unending jovial energy kept him and Caitlin going; she was such great *craic*, a real clown! Between rushing to the hairdresser's, the girls getting their makeup done and playing music much too loud, she'd romped around the house like an overexcited puppy.

Tommy had been warmed and comforted by Chris's words to him last night on the steps of the house as he left for his hotel.

"I'll look after Caitlin, Tommy. I promise she'll want for nothing. I love her." As if closing a deal, the two men had then shaken hands and patted each other on the back.

"Okay, Tommy, got your gear on?" Anne cried merrily, entering the kitchen. She was a sight to see with the most enormous rollers still in her hair and dressed in a long multi-coloured brushed cotton country shirt and house slippers that looked like mice, whiskers and all.

"Look at the sight of you, Anne Heaney!" Tommy cried, though it almost hurt him to laugh.

"Me? I'll be in my finery in two shakes of a lamb's bush! But look at you, all dolled up!"

While he'd first cursed at wearing a morning suit, Tommy admitted he felt grand and dandy in this one. He only wished he could be a bit more robust and energetic; another time, he'd have caused severe damage at the free bar.

"I spruce up all right, don't I?" he asked.

"You do, Tommy, you do!" Anne giggled. She kissed his forehead and whispered, "Let's all have an amazing day and enjoy every minute. Caitlin deserves it. We all deserve a bit of happiness."

"We do that, love."

Tommy hadn't forgotten his gaffe about James Henderson's letter and was annoyed with him for mentioning it to Caitlin on the phone. Whatever was in it would most likely upset her, and Tommy didn't want anything to spoil her well-deserved happiness. He'd decided he'd destroy it as soon as he got home.

****

Chris Pecaro stood before the full-length mirror in his suite. The Goring Hotel was one of his favourites and was centrally placed in the city, off Victoria Street and close to Buckingham Palace. He smiled as he recalled his many discreet *rendezvous* out here, well before Caitlin arrived in his life. Today he was marrying the most wonderful, beautiful, gentle woman he'd ever met. He'd finally found his soul mate and remained convinced he'd get his wife-to-be around to agreeing with him about the baby thing. He'd hold back and see how things went before he finally confessed – the whole idea of a family was out of the question. By then, their lives would have settled and babies apart; Caitlin McLaughlin would have everything and anything money could buy.

****

It was 10.15 a.m. on Tuesday, 20th July 1982, and Penelope Fox was riding her beloved stallion Rochester along the tree-lined South Carriage Drive on the edge of Hyde Park.

This was the largest of London's Royal Parks, but given that it was still early, the whole grassy expanse of it was relatively quiet. Trotting unhurriedly along the sandy track, Pen noticed a smiling woman pushing a Silver Cross pram and a small group of confused Japanese tourists studying maps and looking earnestly around. A jogger ran past as she brought Rochester to a stop. This footpath was her usual route for a ride, and she loved watching the procession of cavalrymen riding past to participate in the Changing of the Guard at the palace whenever she could. Rochester seemed to know that and, empathetic as ever, stood unshakably still against the familiar din of the singing birds, distant bells, dogs barking and faraway police or ambulance sirens. The 350-acre park was a haven for many in the city.

Unsurprisingly, Pen had heard nothing more from her after Mar's recent astonishing announcement, not even a phone call to apologise. It seemed she'd made her choice and, cowardly, disappeared off the face of the earth. Or, most likely, to New Zealand. It hurt still, and Pen couldn't deny it, instead deciding to move on with her own life.

The sun was shining. She was fit, healthy and free to do as she liked. Her future was all worked out. She'd found a perfect site for a stud farm not far from her parent's home in Somerset and, in partnership with her brother Bill had bought the place. When she'd first suggested it, lovely man that he was, he hadn't hesitated; he trusted all his sisters and seemed to be living in a golden bubble of happiness.

Her baby niece Ella, thank God, had been returned safely home, and Bill and Maryann were currently on their way to their country house where, the following weekend, the whole family would celebrate Ella's safe return. Pen couldn't wait!

She'd no regrets about leaving London where, like many others, she'd become a little afraid. There'd been so many Irish terrorist bombings the year before, most of them too close for comfort. There'd been the Territorial Army office in Kensington, then Chelsea Barracks and more. All in all, seven attacks on the heart of London.

She studied a plain, unattractive, six-storey brick building nearby. It was surrounded by a ten-foot-high wall with a steel reinforced gate, and a Union Jack flag flew proudly above it. She caught a slight whiff of dung in the air and heard the sound of whinnying horses. Although this facility looked like a hotel, it was home to the Queen's official bodyguards, the Household Calvary Mounted Regiment.

Every day at the same time, tourists and many others would watch the Changing of the Guard before Buckingham Palace, a ceremony that dates back 360 years.

Today it was the Blues and Royals' turn to participate in it, dressed in their dark blue tunics and white breeches, shiny black boots, red plumes and silver body armour polished to perfection. Consistently immaculate, they always displayed absolute precision in how they sat on their neat, unfazed horses. These were model soldiers, showing no weakness, no fear, only skill and attention to duty. Pen took enormous pleasure in the sight of them. Traditions like this one enhanced her pride in being British.

It wouldn't be long before the parade began, so she decided to take Rochester for a quick gallop and burn off some more of his boundless energy. When she reached the far end of the track, she met Ben, the stable boy, crossing the park; he'd been up overnight with the vet, looking after a mare who'd decided to foal ahead of schedule.

"Hey, Ben. Long night?"

"Yeah, but all good now. Mum and baby are doing well!" He smiled in relief; he'd helped deliver a foal. "I thought I'd go and watch the ceremony." He nodded in the direction of the barracks. "I'm due back at one, and I don't want to go all the way home. I'd likely fall asleep and miss the afternoon shift."

"I'm going over there too," Pen replied enthusiastically. "Do you want to jump up?"

"Nah, miss. Thanks. I'll catch you up."

"Sure. See you there."

"See ya," said the boy with another wave.

Pen turned Rochester around and began to canter; she passed the mother and pram again and noticed more enthusiastic tourists waiting.

When she found her favourite spot, she glanced at her watch; it was close to 10.30 a.m. She looked around, noticed a few parked cars and studied them. She'd need a car when she moved out of town; there'd never been any need to have one in London. She quickly dismissed a Mini and instead considered a lovely blue Austin Morris Marina but decided that, although nice-looking, it was impractical for her new rural lifestyle.

At 10.30 precisely, the gates to the barracks opened, and in two-by-two formation, the parade exited and turned right onto the South Carriage Drive. Each soldier and stallion gleaming in the soft morning light was a magnificent spectacle.

Pen watched in awe until she heard her name being called; she turned to see Ben standing fifty feet behind and waving at her. She smiled and returned the gesture, mouthing that she'd come and join him soon.

In admiration, the onlookers quietened and stood still as the troop of men and horses passed down the curving track towards Hyde Park corner. The thud of hooves, the rustle of leaves and the distant clicking of cameras were all Pen could hear. She glanced at her watch again. It told her it was just after twenty minutes to eleven.

****

Pen never knew what hit her, but many other innocents did, and to their dying day, they'd never forget.

Onlookers heard an indescribably loud noise, along with an almighty flash of brilliant light fading to a scorching amber that disappeared as if in slow motion. The shock wave blew the Austin car, now transformed into a twisted, smoking, tangled mess of metal, up and over the top of the Mini parked behind. Streets away, windows were smashed in. There was an eerie silence as disorientated spectators and shocked soldiers stumbled around in circles.

With ringing ears, some with eardrums punctured by the shock waves, they couldn't hear properly. Any sound seemed vague and distant. They couldn't see much either; the area was filled with a dense cloud of caustic black smoke—the air stank of chemicals and burning flesh. As the light breeze changed direction, the debris and dust dispersed, revealing a scene from hell.

Both sides of the track were awash with blood. Sirens wailed, horses cried out, and men and women, shocked by what had happened, began to scream in horror. Littered around were black, distorted masses of horseflesh scored with running red slashes where four-inch nails, like merciless silver bullets, had ripped into the skin, shredding muscle and bone beneath. Injured soldiers and their mounts had fallen side by side, either dead or dying. Some troopers lay trapped beneath the steeds which had indirectly protected them. Intermittent flashes of clean, unblemished body armour glinted, and shredded red plumes hung in the air as the less badly injured riders rushed to help their comrades.

Ben was safe but stood white-faced and shocked by the appalling sights of slaughter. He held his ears in pain and screamed; there was so much blood, body parts, and the horses… some poor bloody innocent horses, once so brave and beautiful, were now nothing more than dismembered carcasses. It was killing him!

He turned to escape and rushed past a mangled Silver Cross pram, forced to stop when he saw a blonde woman lying face down on the grass. He knelt and turned her over. He saw a slashed and ravaged face with a massive piece of shrapnel embedded in the cheekbone. Ben searched for the baby and saw its bloodied tiny body on the grass a few feet away. It lay very still. He couldn't bear to look more closely at it. Unable to take in any more, he began to cry, not knowing what to do and feeling so bloody helpless. It was then that he suddenly remembered Miss Fox. He had to find her; he couldn't turn his back and leave her here. It didn't take long to locate her, lying underneath Rochester, not far from where he'd seen them a few lifelong moments ago.

"Nooooooooo!" he cried in horror. "Miss, miss!" he yelled. Pen's upper torso was exposed, head tilted back and staring eyes wide open. Her helmet remained in place though askew, and Ben believed he saw her stir briefly. He frantically tried to shake her consciousness, but there was no response. At first glance, she appeared to have suffered no wounds, but as he turned her head to the side, he saw five or six nails embedded in the nape of her neck below the hairline.

His shocked and sickened eyes darted to Rochester – one of his favourite charges – and he saw nail holes puncturing the horse's bleeding skin. The steel nails had found other targets too: the horse's eyes, his muzzle, and peppered along his elongated chestnut neck, reminding Ben of his ma's pin cushion.

Rochester brayed in distress. In a last colossal effort, he endeavoured to lift his head in search of the mistress he loved, but she had gone before him. With a long sigh, he followed her.

****

It was time for them to leave. Tommy's eyes widened on seeing Caitlin reach the bottom of the stairs. *What a sight!* She walked over to him, and he placed his hands on her shoulders. He noticed she wore his sister Majella's silver crucifix.

"Jesus, Caitlin, you're magnificent. I've never seen you look so beautiful," he said shakily.

Her pearl white, raw silk wedding gown had a lace-trimmed bodice with an elegant high neckline. Her hair was curled but tied back from her face under a feathery fringe. An Irish lace veil was attached to a delicate coronet of roses intertwined with ivy and dried shamrocks. A neutral pink lipstick complemented her slate blue eyeshadow and pale skin. She was perfect, and his heart was filled with pride.

"Thanks, Tommy. Thanks for being here. I don't think I could do this without you."

"You know what?" he asked, swallowing his emotion. "Our Majella, your Daddy and Tina would be so proud of you today. Remember, they're here with you, right beside you, watching out for you. I spoke to Martin. He's gutted he can't make it but sends his love. We all want you to be happy, darlin'. Are you?"

She stared at him for a moment, considering his words. "I am Tommy, I promise. And you're right – I can feel them with me. I'll call Martin after."

They heard Anne walking carefully down the hall in the highest pair of grey stilettos Tommy had ever seen. Her efforts were causing her pain, but she looked determined and beautiful. Once again, he felt great pride in these two gutsy Derry girls, and the loving bond between the three of them strengthened. Upon seeing Caitlin, Anne stumbled and quickly thumbed away the tears that threatened to ruin her make-up.

"Gorgeous," she mouthed.

The doorbell rang. They all jumped at the sudden noise and laughed – the bridal cars had arrived. The bride and her bridesmaid picked up their matching bouquets of ivory-white Iceberg roses, green ivy and little sprigs of dried shamrock for luck.

****

London was always busy, and as usual, with the Changing of the Guard and the mid-morning snarl up around Hyde Park and Regents Park, the journey took longer than it should have. The first wedding car, a black Jaguar that briefly reminded Caitlin of James's, sluggishly made its way north to the Town Hall.

"Almost there," the driver said after a while, "the traffic's appalling, as usual, but I've allowed plenty of time, so don't you worry, miss. *'I'll get you to the church on time!'*" He sang the last few words and laughed.

"Thanks," Tommy replied, pulling a funny face back at him. He looked over his shoulder to see Anne alone in the other black Jag.

When they arrived at the Town Hall and prepared to get out, women bystanders stopped in their tracks at the sight of the white-ribboned Jaguar, always intrigued to see a bride. Tommy and Anne helped Caitlin climb out, Anne almost suffocating under the burden of so much raw silk. "Jesus, Mary and Joseph – are you in there, Caitlin!" she cried, and the crowd on the pavement laughed, as did the bride. *Trust Anne!*

They hurriedly made their way towards the Town Hall steps. Caitlin looked up at its Neoclassical stone porch, adorned with the borough's coat of arms and flanked with full-height windows and pilasters to either side. Chris had been spot on yet again; it was the perfect venue.

Anne was flushed and slightly hassled; her leg hurt like hell, but she wasn't giving in to it.

"Did you see the crowd out there? It's like the queue for the Stardust!"

Islington Town Hall was so far from the likes of the disco in the heart of the Bogside that both Tommy and Caitlin nearly wet themselves! *Poor Tommy.*

"Come on, ladies," he whispered, jangling with nerves, "let's make Derry proud. Let's make them all proud," he added with a grin.

With hammering hearts, the trio made their way to the wedding suite. The wedding organiser welcomed them and explained what they needed to do. Within minutes the vast, ornate double doors to the Council Chamber opened, and Caitlin and Tommy walked through, followed by Anne. It was a bright room despite the wooden panelling and large stained-glass windows. There were tiers of horseshoe-shaped seating with red leather cushions, the end of each bench covered in sprays of white flowers. Standing tall and proud, Chris stood next to his substitute best man.

The only thing Caitlin had insisted on was that she should choose the wedding music. It wouldn't be appropriate in the Town Hall to play her father's favourite hymn, 'Here I Am, Lord', so instead, she'd picked one of his favourite ballads, 'Down by the Salley Gardens'.

The walk to her groom's side felt never-ending. Caitlin struggled to contain her tears. She wished her family were there, every single one of them. As always, Tommy sensed her struggle and squeezed her hand.

Chris looked so handsome and happy. With his wide welcoming smile turned on her, filled with love, Caitlin began to feel safe. She was sure she could make him content and learn to love him. It could be a new beginning, and together they'd create a family of their own, far away and safe from the troubling memories of Derry.

Tommy passed Caitlin across to the groom, whispering, "Remember what you said. Please, make her happy."

Chris smiled in agreement, and Caitlin passed her wedding bouquet back to Anne, who winked wickedly at her. Caitlin shook her head and smiled before facing the front as the ceremony began. When it ended, the congregation clapped and cheered, and Chris whispered, "I love you, Mrs Pecaro."

Caitlin gave him a huge smile and replied, "You too."

She quickly turned to face their guests. Everyone looked so happy, as did Chris. She noticed Tommy's wet face and gave him a half-smile. Anne was already in full swing; tears of happiness combined with relief ran down her beautifully made-up face. She rushed to hug Caitlin and then Chris until it was Tommy's turn.

After photographs were taken, the couple eventually reached the top of the Town Hall steps. From there, they became aware of a sudden change in their surroundings. People were huddled together, muttering and mumbling, looking upset and anxious.

"What is it?" Chris asked.

"I don't know," Caitlin replied uneasily. Whatever this was, it wasn't good.

He grabbed her hand and walked down towards one of the small gatherings. "What's happened?" he asked, directing his question to an elegant grey-haired woman with a tear-stained face.

"It's the Household Calvary – hit by another PIRA bomb. I don't know how many dead they've killed horses too! Whatever next?" she cried before turning to seek comfort from a friend.

Caitlin's face drained of blood. Tommy appeared at her other side. He took her hand and squeezed it tight, looking sorrowful. Anne came to join them. All three of them were almost afraid to speak, shocked and ashamed.

Traffic had come to a standstill on Upper Street and the Registrar, running down the steps, approached Chris and Caitlin, looking flustered.

"I've just heard they've cordoned off Hyde Park. Seemingly, it's a bloodbath there! I know you're to have your reception at the Savoy, but you won't get anywhere near it now by road. Come inside, and you can call them yourselves."

Chris quickly looked at Caitlin and shrugged; this wasn't what he'd envisaged for their wedding day. Without warning, their waiting driver opened the Jaguar window and cried, "Listen, everyone, it's on the radio!"

"We have an urgent announcement. At precisely 10:43 a.m., a nail bomb exploded in Hyde Park. It was hidden in the boot of a blue Morris Marina parked on South Carriage Drive and detonated as soldiers of the Household Cavalry, the Queen's official bodyguard regiment, passed by. They were taking part in the daily Changing of the Guard procession from their barracks in Knightsbridge to Horse Guards Parade."

"So far, it appears three soldiers of the Blues and Royals have been killed outright, and another is seriously injured. Further, soldiers, police officers and spectators, including a mother and baby, are also severely wounded. An unidentified horsewoman was also killed; so far, up to seven of the Regiment's horses have died or been seriously injured."

"Explosives experts believe the Provisional IRA is responsible and that someone was most likely present in the park to trigger the bomb remotely. As soon as we have further news, we will update listeners..."

Chapter Fifty-three

Emmett McFadden counted the cash carefully, note by note. He knew exactly how much was in the old Barry's teabag tin. It was enough for his fare to Australia, and he planned to go into Gallagher's Travel and book his ticket the following day. His parents had been visiting Joe and were due back soon. It was time to tell them he was leaving. He'd got all his qualifications and visa, having heard the Aussies were crying out for mechanics in Melbourne, where he'd go first.

Emmett wasn't fearful in the least, he was buzzing with excitement, but his heart was heavy at the thought of leaving his family and Derry. He remembered dreaming of taking Tina McLaughlin and his ma away as a young boy. He was saddened to realise that, after so many years, thoughts of his first love could still hurt. Remembering her cruel fate was always hard for him.

Sitting alone in the kitchen, he finished counting, put the money into an envelope and placed it safely in his pocket. He filled the kettle and glanced at the clock. They should've been back by now, although he'd heard on the radio that there'd been yet another bomb scare on Craigavon Bridge.

He was sure he heard their phone ringing in the back garden shed, where the neighbours were welcome to use it in return for a small cash contribution to the bill. Cursing, he quickly took the kettle off the gas ring and ran to answer it.

"Hello!" Emmett cried breathlessly.

"Ah, Emmett love, it's me!"

He knew something wasn't right from the tone of his ma's voice. "What is it, Mammy? Is it Joe!"

"No, love, it's your Da. He's had some funny turn and collapsed. We had to get the prison doctor to look at him. It turned out it was a panic attack. He's okay. But we missed the bus, and now we're trying to get home. We're in a bar near the prison."

"Jesus, Mammy, a panic attack? Me Da!" Emmett couldn't believe it. Big Charlie McFadden had a *panic attack!*

Maggie hadn't told Emmett yet about his father's deception, she'd been trying to protect him, but after Joe's warning to them, she'd have to. Her head was spinning out of control, and she could hardly comprehend what Emmett told her to do to reach home.

"Mammy! Ma! Are you listening? Get to Belfast, and you can take a bus home from there. Do you have enough money?"

"Just about."

"Okay, call me when you get there and let me know what bus you'll be on. I'll meet you at Foyle Street."

Unseen by her son, Maggie nodded. "Okay, love. See you soon."

About to go, she heard him cry down the line, "Ma! Listen, don't worry, get him home, and everything'll be all right. I promise."

Maggie had no tears left. Life would never be the same for any of them again, and the poor boy still had no idea. "I'll get us home, love. Don't worry."

Looking around the bar with its decorative Union Jacks, Orange Lodge sashes and images of the Royal Family, Maggie felt they needed to get out of there soon. She eyed the bartender, who approached her with a smile.

"Is there any chance I can get a taxi to take us to Belfast bus station, please?" she asked with a dry swallow.

"Aye, love, no bother." The woman and her man who sat in a corner, white-faced and poorly looking, concerned him. "Is he all right?"

Maggie raised her head proudly. "Aye, he's fine, thanks," she replied, forcing a smile.

****

Stepping back into the kitchen, having heard about his father and feeling pretty upset, Emmett was met by an almighty roar hammering through the thin party wall. *Not again!*

Over the past weeks and months, they'd complained to the Housing Executive about their noisy irresponsible neighbours, but with little luck. After half an hour, the battle raged, and Emmett finally lost it and rushed next door. Hammering the letterbox with all his might, his anger was only fuelled when he heard a woman's feral screams.

He knocked again, but no one answered, and with little chance of action left, he bent down to peer through the letterbox. He couldn't see anyone but heard the woman's ear-splitting screams increasing, along with the crying and howling of children. He hoped his other neighbours would react to what was happening, but their doors remained closed. He was genuinely worried now and didn't know what to do. It sounded like the woman was getting a real battering.

In a final bid to get their attention, he banged the door hard.

"Open up! Open this door NOW!"

Nothing. He wondered whether he should put his shoulder to it – that always worked in the films. With relief, he sighted a couple of spotty teenagers dawdling towards him on their BMX bikes and approached them.

"Lads, you wouldn't give me a hand, would you?"

"What's up?" one of them asked, taking a long snort from something he held in a plastic bag and narrowing his eyes suspiciously.

"It's over there." Emmett pointed to the house. "The guy's beatin' the shite out of his wife, and there are children in there as well."

"Ah, Jesus, man, we're not going in there! Don't you know him? He's a nutter, that boyo; I'd stay away from that one!" the other boy told him.

Emmett knew the teenagers were likely right, but he couldn't stand there and do nothing. "Ah, boys, you can't leave me here on me own! Just stand behind me. Let me try one more time."

"Nah, sorry! We're away out of here." At that, the youths stormed off, mumbling about how insane Emmett was to go near that mad dog!

He ran back to the house and looked in at its front window but couldn't see much through the nets. He knocked on the door loudly again and waited for a response. Finally, he had no choice but to go home when the neighbours' house fell silent. There was no point in calling the police, it wasn't done, and they'd be useless anyway, their presence likely leading to a riot.

The whole sorry episode made him even more determined to leave Derry, to begin afresh and live somewhere free from conflict. His frightening experiences with the Unknowns and Liz McKenna still haunted him. The prospect of a calm existence was too tempting to ignore, and Emmett knew that if he wanted that, he needed to get away from this war zone.

****

The morning after Edwards's successful dealings with the good doctor, he called Vinny Kelly into the office. The boy had been on his mind since he'd heard from the House Father about that ridiculous letter. He liked Vinny, and his photographs were still popular; they decided to take him back to Liverpool. Unlike the House Father, who was now off sick with stress, Edwards wasn't prepared to let the boy go anywhere and was ready to challenge any requests from Social Services.

Standing nervously on the threshold, Vinny wore a white T-shirt with a Beachboys US Tour 1982 logo on the front and a pair of dark denim jeans with trainers. He was shaking and sweating with fear.

"Vincent, I want to have a word with you. Take that seat there, the one in the corner." Edwards ordered, his monotone voice oddly eerie. He pointed to the infamous winged chair.

Vinny hated coming into this place, mainly when Edwards addressed him as 'Vincent'. The skin on his arms and neck crawled.

Edwards's smile was too broad, his voice, by contrast, chilly. A presentiment washed over Vinny. Intuitively he was frightened of this man, but today that fear was particularly keen. He noticed Edwards's eyes were cold and full of wickedness. The boy didn't want to sit down but knew from before he'd no choice.

He sat on the chair and protectively crossed his arms and legs. With a loud snigger, Edwards walked over to the door and locked it. He found a tissue in his pocket and stuffed it into the keyhole. Then he crossed the floor and stopped directly before the boy without taking his eyes off him.

"Young Vincent, I have a wee bit of news for you."

Vinny stared at the older man and prayed he was going home! Edwards detected the innocent hope in the child's face and relished demolishing it with one sweeping statement.

"You're not going back to Londonderry."

Vinny's whole world crashed down around him. He jumped off the chair and shielded himself by standing behind it.

"Why not? The McFaddens said I...."

"Stop talking!" Edwards screamed in annoyance. "Screw the McFaddens, Vincent! They've been saying that to get your hopes up, don't you realise that? There's no chance you can go and live in that pit. You're much better off here, son, and to prove it, we're taking you on another wee trip to England. Would you like that? Think about it, Vincent. We're all you have. None of your family gives a rat's arse about you. Look how fast they dumped you in a home. They don't give a shit! You're much better off here with me, your House Father and your wee pal Eddie."

Edwards reached out to stroke the child's smooth face and felt himself growing hard, but Vinny pushed the chair forward and held it out firmly. A sharp pain twinged in his gut, tightened his chest and threatened to overwhelm him. *He wasn't doing this anymore. He couldn't!*

"I'm going home, Mr Edwards! Back to Derry. I don't believe you about the McFaddens, and I'm not going on any trip to England!" he said, shaking his head in refusal.

Without warning, Edwards kicked the chair from the boy's hands, and it crashed sideways onto the floor. He grabbed Vinny by the hair, twisting and yanking his head back at a painful angle. Close to his face, Edwards warned him: "You're going nowhere, wee fella, you hear me? You're going nowhere!"

****

Maggie and Charlie McFadden finally came through their front door before midnight. Charlie had said very little on the long journey home other than that he felt sick. He repeatedly searched Maggie's face for signs of what she was thinking. He knew they couldn't decide anything until Emmett was told about the situation.

Their second son helped them inside, taking their coats and hanging them up. He held a chair back for his ma and looked at his da, full of concern for his condition.

"You okay, Da?"

Charlie nodded without speaking.

As usual, a cup of tea was a necessity. Tension filled the kitchen while the kettle boiled. Charlie felt as if he couldn't breathe. This was all his fault, his responsibility, and he spoke first while still seeking Maggie's approval, though none was given. She stood and rested one hip against the sink.

He coughed awkwardly and stared at the floor while he said, "Emmett, there's something we – I mean, I – need to tell you. Sit down."

He felt the unusual weariness and seriousness in his da's tone and quietly sat. In confusion, he looked at his ma, but she stayed expressionless.

"You know I've been working this past while?" Charlie said.

Emmett nodded. "Yeah, for Rocola. You're lucky 'cos they've laid off a load of people."

Charlie cut in, "I lied."

"Sorry? How do you mean, lied?" Emmett asked in bewilderment. "Sure, you've been doing great, Da, after all our nagging." He laughed nervously.

"It wasn't Rocola I was working."

"Where then?" Once more, Emmett looked at his ma, expecting her to explain; he was confused.

"It was Fort George. I was working as a cleaner for the army," Charlie told him with a deadpan expression. He paused at this point and glanced down, stalling.

Emmett couldn't believe his ears. He shuddered deeply, rocked by disbelief. Charlie McFadden working for the Brits? *Sweet fuck. They were in for it now!*

"The Brits, Da? You've been working for the fuckin' Brits?" he howled.

Maggie snapped, "Don't be using that language to your Father, Emmett."

"But, Ma! Have you not heard what that twerp just said!" Emmett rose and threw his chair aside in anger. He paced up and down the small kitchen as Maggie snapped at him, "Don't talk about him like that. He's still your Father!"

Emmett choked back tears. His da's sudden confession killed him; he couldn't take it in.

"This is un-fuckin'-believable. Why Da?" he appealed. Neither parent answered this until Charlie added plaintively, "There's more."

"More? What could be worse than you working for the fuckin' Brits?"

"Emmett!" Maggie shrilled. "What did I say?" She nodded to Charlie to continue, but he couldn't; he was too distraught.

"He's been warned. He's got to get out fast," Maggie said.

"What? Warned out of Derry!" Emmett wailed. Panic wasn't far away. *This was too much, far too fuckin' much! He'd plans of his own. What about Australia?*

A heavy silence reigned until Emmett took a deep breath and asked, "How many times?"

"Times?" Charlie replied wearily.

"How many times were you warned?"

"Twice. No, three, maybe… I can't remember," Charlie replied, gulping for breath.

Emmett glared at him. "You can't remember? Told you were a marked man, and you kept going? What about us? What about our Joe, after the hell, he's been through!" It suddenly hit him. "Sweet Jesus… he knows! Is that what happened today?"

Maggie snapped out of her dazed state. "Sit down, Emmett. Sit!" she cried, pointing to his empty chair.

Emmett sat, stony-faced and ready. *This better be good.*

"Aye, Joe knows. It was him who told us. That's why your Father had a panic attack. It was too much for him. So now, as a family, we have to decide what to do next," Maggie explained.

"But, Ma, I was going to tell you tonight… I'm going away." Emmett shook his head solemnly. Maggie wasn't surprised by her son's news. She'd found the cash tin and knew he'd been saving up. She'd hoped it was for a new car or the like but understood that, like many local youngsters, Emmett wanted to get away, to build a better life.

"I know," she told him. He noticed the smile lines around her tired eyes.

"You do?" Emmett asked in surprise.

"Remember, love, who made you? I know everything about you," she told him. It was a line she always used whenever they were caught out. "Where are you off to then?"

"Melbourne."

"Aye, that makes sense, far enough away from all this. You go ahead, son. Your Da, Liam and I will be grand, won't we, Charlie?"

Defeated and broken, he stared at her with a face full of sorrow and regret. He'd fucked up. He was an embarrassment as a father and a husband, and shame filled him to the core. All he'd wanted to do was provide for them all. He began to cry silent tears. Maggie finally reached across and took his hand.

"How much time have you got?" Emmett asked them, his stomach churning.

"As soon as," Charlie replied, swiping away tears with the back of his hand.

"Are you staying here, Mammy?"

"Your Da will go first, love, probably over the border. Auntie Trish is too close in Greencastle, so he'll have to go to Cork to our Fiona for a while. It's far enough away. We might have to go to England after that." The very thought of it terrified her. "He's been a total eejit, but he was only trying to bring in a wage. We shouldn't be too angry with him."

"What about all this, Mammy?" Emmett asked, ignoring his mother's comment about his father and referring to the house and furnishings.

"I'll stay here until Liam gets back and then sell everything. You'll go to Australia, poor Joe is going to be holed up for years yet, and your Da, Liam and I will find somewhere – eventually."

She paused, and her eyes dejectedly swept around the kitchen. She thought of all the wonderful years of laughter and tears here. Her heart felt like lead as she remembered their old friends and neighbours, the McLaughlins. Caitlin was now away in London, getting married. They'd been invited but couldn't afford to travel. Like the McLaughlins, the McFaddens had joined the long list of families ruined by the conflict.

"We'll have to start again. We've no choice. What's that old saying? Every moment is a new beginning. Something like that." Maggie half-laughed and pulled at her son's arm. "It'll be okay, I promise. Have I ever let you down?"

"I won't go, Mammy. I'll stay here with you. I've got my savings. That'll help," Emmett replied half-heartedly. The disappointment and shock of the news had destroyed him, but he couldn't leave his family in the lurch. It was the least he could do. Joe had kept his father alive.

Maggie opened her arms in invitation, and Emmett fell into them. It'd been long since they'd hugged, and he embraced her hard.

"I don't think so, son, but if I could, I love you more for making such an offer. No, you have to go, Emmett. I won't tell you again. It'll be okay. Trust me."

He pulled away and fixed his eyes on hers. "Are you sure?" Maggie nodded. "Then only if I can give some money. That should help, at least for a bit."

Maggie smiled. She loved this lad so much and would miss him beyond words. Suddenly the commotion began next door again, and Emmett heard his mother swear for the first time!

"They're about the only fuckin' thing I won't miss about this place!"

****

Chapter Fifty-four

After Chris spoke to the Savoy, who warned them of the situation in Central London with staff unable to get to the hotel since the city had come to a standstill, they'd had no choice but to postpone the reception.

With the wedding celebrations prematurely over, the subdued guests started to make their way home; the news was too horrific for celebrations.

Caitlin, Chris, Tommy and Ann returned to the townhouse in silence. Chris attempted to cheer them up and celebrate with a glass of champagne, but none of the Irish detail could contemplate a drink. Instead, they sat glued to the television, from which they learnt of a second devastating attack in Regents Park when a bandstand exploded, killing six military band members and causing many casualties and a further fatality.

The bus journey back to Derry had been nightmarish, and Tommy swore he'd never repeat it, but then it was unlikely he'd have to. He'd promised Caitlin he'd visit the doctor as soon as he got back, and unsurprisingly the diagnosis wasn't good.

"It's your prostate, Tommy. It's in a bad way. Your PSA levels are through the roof. It appears you've left it too late, my friend – it's only a matter of time now – but we'll make you as comfortable as we can."

Dr McKay explained the ins and outs of what Tommy should expect over the coming weeks, not months. He wasn't quite sure how he felt when he left the surgery. He wished he'd brought Kathy with him as he'd half-listened to what the old doc said, but he wasn't yet able to tell her – no one knew.

He didn't only feel sick from his prostate; his soul felt sick too. After the dastardly bombings, it'd been made very clear to McFarland, who'd been so close to restarting talks with the Brits, that he should basically *fuck off!* The citizens of London and the world hadn't begun to recover from the traumatic incidents, nor were they likely to. What stung so many were the terrible images of the butchered horses. The Provos had kept this operation so close to their chest that the security services had heard no word of it, and now the pressure was on. Much-needed Provo funding from the US dried up due to the carnage.

To top it all, reporters sniffed out the connection between the kidnapped baby rescued from the PIRA and the horsewoman killed in the Hyde Park bombing, who had been her aunt.

James called Tommy as soon as he heard he was back. At first, Tommy was frosty, but hearing James's genuine concern for his safety assured him that all was fine, and his anger lessened. They talked a lot about the park bombings, and then James mentioned he'd been working with Bill Fox, the father of the kidnapped baby.

"He's a good guy, Tommy. It's beyond words what happened – that poor sick baby snatched away and then Bill's sister dying so tragically. I can't begin to imagine how his family are feeling."

"The poor wee critter, and aye, it was sad about the aunt," Tommy replied, waiting for the next question and likely the reason for James's call. It didn't take long.

"I hear you forgot the letter?"

Tommy sighed, fell into his chair, and shook his head; he didn't need this! He could either lie or tell the truth, but as a dead man walking, he'd nothing to lose and felt he should be honest.

"Yeah, James, I did. And I don't plan to send it on."

James dropped his head in defeat. Any other hope of getting near Caitlin had ended. Tommy heard his disappointment and pointedly told him: "Listen to me, son, Caitlin's taken a vow. She's happy now. Maybe God's telling you to let her go. She's married, you're still legally married with a young family to think of, and Caitlin will never come home to Derry. Not now, not ever! It makes no sense to drag all that back up again."

Tommy heard James groan before he replied miserably, "You're right; I know you're right. Best left alone."

"Good lad. That's the best way," Tommy sighed.

To defuse the tension, he mentioned a newspaper article in the *Derry Journal* about Rocola. "It seems like retribution is in the air now that our friend Mr Jones is on the front page again. He's a cat with nine lives, that one."

"You've no idea, Tommy. Likely you'll know his ex-bodyguard tried to take him down. It's a shame he missed that black heart by a mere fraction! Barter tells me they've loads on Jones now, including messing us up with a fake order, although we can't legally do anything about it. Nevertheless, they'll likely charge him with tax evasion until they can build a stronger case. Bonner's involved in it all somehow. They're dropping like flies."

"Aye, so I heard. There's something dodgy about that Chief Constable. Sorry, James, I know you were a friend of George Shalham's, but many believe the RUC is shambolic and collusive."

"I'm sure they're not all bad, Tommy. A few rotten apples perhaps, but I suppose it doesn't look good with a man like Bonner being the Chief Constable," James said, a little defensively, remembering how determined upon peace poor George Shalham had been.

Tommy wasn't getting into a debate about the RUC; he was too tired. He brought the call to a close. "Listen, I probably won't be seeing you for a while, you've likely guessed I've got a bit of a health problem, so I'll say this one more time. Let Caitlin go and get on with your own life. You've two beautiful children – enjoy them while they're young. They grow up too fast, believe me!"

James desperately wanted to talk more about Caitlin but could tell Tommy was tired. When he'd heard about the London bombings, he'd been frightened senseless until he knew she was okay. Selfishly, he'd hoped they'd stopped the wedding, but it seemed not. Drunk and crying, Marleen called him to say that Pen was the horsewoman killed in Hyde Park. James was sorry to hear that, and more so when he realised that Bill Fox was her brother.

"Will you be okay, Tommy?" James asked him in concern.

"Nothing I can't handle, son. Don't worry. As I said, let her go and look after you and your own. 'Bye-bye now."

"'Bye, Tommy. You take care," James said fondly, unaware they were speaking for the last time.

****

Paddy Gillispie sat in a dark corner of a small freehold on the outskirts of Ned's Point in County Donegal. Fury with Liz McKenna and her double-crossing tactics still raged within him. He detested touts but found himself back in Ireland with his tail between his legs, ready to face the music with the Leadership, thanks to a traitor in their midst. It was ironic, but he and Brian Monaghan had been brought to Derry 'specially to catch grasses, and now Paddy found *himself* grassed up.

The long journey home from London had been arduous, thanks to the heavy police presence at ports and other terminals and blanket media coverage of the return of Ella and the events in the London parks. The authorities only knew that a Provo cell had kidnapped the child. Little else. It appeared they'd not caught McKenna, though when they did, Paddy knew she'd open like a flower.

He got the Toyota as far as Liverpool, where he burnt it out, then hid in a cheap, rundown B&B. As planned, he shaved off most of his thick curling hair, sideburns and beard, bought a pair of thick black-rimmed glasses from a Chinese bric-a-brac stall, and dyed any remaining hair blond. He took some new photos and picked up an under-the-counter passport before catching a ferry to the Isle of Man, where he moved around and slept rough for a few nights before getting the midnight ferry back to Dublin.

Successfully through the border checks, doubled up with extra Gardai, Paddy went straight to the safe house, where he contacted the

OC and briefed him on his whereabouts and status. In return, a clipped command instructed him to head to Ned's Point outside Buncrana and await further orders.

It took Paddy nearly three days to reach his destination, on short journeys hidden in numerous car boots and ultimately concealed amongst frozen pig carcasses in the back of a refrigerated lorry. He had never known cold like it; his whole body ached, and he was dog-tired.

They were expecting the OC that night, and Paddy's host, a burly 1950s IRA volunteer and farmer, kept close. O'Connell was late, but the patient farmer was courteous as he passed Paddy another hot whiskey, noting that his comrade still trembled from the cold.

A while later, car headlights lit up the bachelor's living room that looked like a woman hadn't set foot over its threshold in years. "That's you then," the farmer said, buttoning up a navy blue boiler suit over a scraggy woollen jumper and jeans.

Paddy shook the stocky man's hand. "Thanks for everything," he said gratefully. With a wave of dismissal and a murmured, "No bother," the farmer made himself scarce.

Reminiscent of a Tasmanian devil, Cahir O'Connell lunged into the parlour and slapped Paddy heartily on the back. "Fuck me, I didn't recognise you there for a sec – will you look at you?" He moved nearer to the peat fire. "Ye'd never believe it's nearly feckin' August. It'd freeze the bollocks off you out there!"

"Don't talk to me about freezin' bollocks!" Paddy wisecracked with a shiver, recalling the long journey shared with the frozen pork. "You on your own, sir?" he asked in surprise – the OC usually had a bodyguard.

"Aye, it's me lonesome today. I'll sit, shall I?" the OC asked, keeping his black leather coat on and, without waiting, stole Paddy's still-warm chair and finished off his hot whiskey.

"Ah, lovely," he said, savouring the hot drink before studying Paddy. He shook his head in disbelief. "I can't get over the way you look. You're a changed man."

O'Connell rubbed his hands together and stared into the hypnotising flames. "Now that's a lovely sight there, Paddy. You can't beat the smell of peat." He'd always loved an open fire, bringing back memories of his granny's cottage in Malin Head.

The OC's attempts to fight the fallout from the baby's kidnapping with the Provo Leadership had fallen on stony ground. The volunteers involved had reported to him. Therefore he must carry the can.

O'Connell hated being in the spotlight and decided politics wasn't for him. Too many knew he'd blood on his hands, so he could never stand. If Paddy Gillispie ostensibly kept on the straight and narrow after this final task, he could have a political career in the future. His involvement in the Fox kidnap was known to only a handful, and he'd always been careful to keep word of his other ruthless operations on a strictly need to know. However, many had suspected his involvement in murky dealings. He was gifted with a healthy amount of that self-belief most politicians possess and was a natural charmer when he chose to be. But more importantly, he was utterly loyal and could be managed efficiently from the wings.

O'Connell's voice grew low and severe. "Right, Paddy, I want to hear every word of what went wrong in England. I want to know minute by minute what occurred and what happened with McKenna especially." He sat back in the chair and folded his arms.

Paddy told him everything from start to finish, including his sub-zero journey to Buncrana. He gathered more turf and threw it on the fire, creating sparks and a warm glow.

Despite the all-ports alert, the OC was secretly impressed by how Gillispie had managed to get home. It appeared London hadn't been his fault for two reasons. Monaghan should have sussed out the baby's illness as part of his preparation, and McKenna had done for the op by calling in the cops. The only good thing about it was that she'd saved the baby's life. If the kid had died, it would've been a total PR wipe-out!

Paddy finished, and the OC raised his eyebrows and pursed his lips, wondering how he'd send word of all this to the Leadership. He rubbed his hands, held them out to the fire, stared into the dancing flames, and explained the next move.

"Do you understand what's likely to happen when the Brits lift McKenna? Because it will happen eventually, trust me. She has no family or friends in England and can't come back here. She'll likely tell them all she knows to get herself a deal, and this country is swarming with pigs and Brits nowadays, so we're giving you one last assignment. After that, we'll put you on a plane to Boston or the like. You can stay there for a while until things quieten. We've bigger plans in play for you."

The idea of Boston appealed to Paddy, and he didn't object.

"There's plenty of support there; we'll get you a new ID – give you some dough to set you up," the OC finished.

Paddy felt he was getting off lightly, having expected much worse. He sighed with relief but remained intrigued about his final task.

"That's fair enough, sir. Will ye keep an eye out for my sis Dolores in Armagh?"

"Absolutely! She's a proud volunteer, one of the best," the OC replied, nodding his head enthusiastically.

"She is," Paddy agreed. And braver and stronger by far than he was, not that he'd admit as much to the OC.

"What's the plan for my final op, then?"

"I've instructed Monaghan to return from Belfast, and I want you two together on this one."

"That's grand," Paddy promptly replied. It'd be good to see Brian again, allowing them to rekindle their friendship.

"You've heard of Brendan Doherty, the solicitor? Poor bastard who nearly got decapitated," the OC barked.

"Half the country knows about it, sir," Paddy replied.

"Yeah, well. He was a good man – a true Republican." O'Connell had been especially fond of Doherty and knew better than most what the man had done for Derry's Catholic citizens.

"And?" Paddy asked hurriedly.

The OC couldn't share how he knew who'd murdered Doherty, but he'd devised a classic ruse for revenge on the perpetrator. In two nights, their target would be waiting at a boathouse by the River Foyle near Termonbacca, a Carmelite retreat outside Derry.

O'Connell coughed, pulled out a photograph and passed it over to Paddy, who viewed a black-and-white image of a good-looking British Army captain posing in full ceremonial dress. He looked like a cocky bastard with his perfect white put-on grin.

"Who's he?"

"Alan Hickey. He's the fucker who did Doherty, and there's more. He was in on that young Gaelic team massacre a few years back, and a couple of fellas were shot dead in West Belfast for no reason other than being Catholic. This Loyalist-loving boyo here played a part in those deaths personally."

Paddy remembered them well and cocked his head. "Go on."

"He's a fuckin' maverick, a loose cannon, and I want you and Monaghan to make him disappear. You're going fishing, Paddy, so don't screw this up. You want to make it to America, don't you?"

O'Connell's loaded tone sounded borderline threatening. It unsettled Paddy, who sat studying the photograph. "Where's Brian?" he asked.

"He's at a safe house in Shantallow. You haven't seen him for a while, have you? I heard you'd a domestic. Come to think of it, he was off our radar there for a while too, trouble at home apparently."

Unexpectedly O'Connell turned authoritarian. "I want youse to fuckin' forget all that playground squabbling, Paddy, and make this job swift and clean? *You hear me?*"

The atmosphere in the room felt hazardous as O'Connell's cold eyes bored into Paddy's. This change of conduct revealed the dark side of the OC that Paddy had heard about but had never personally witnessed before.

"Do I make myself clear?" he pressed.

"Aye, I'll sort it," Paddy answered nervously, unusually spooked.

A few moments passed in silence until O'Connell pulled himself together, smacked him on the back, and laughed. "You get this right, and before you know it, mucker, you'll be drinking a pint in the Black Rose, singing your fuckin' head off! Remember, swift and clean, Paddy, swift and clean!"

"I know, I hear you," Paddy replied, unaccountably depressed. They might say they had big plans for him, but he was back to being a killer, at least for this final time.

****

Paddy trekked across Sheriff's Mountain high above Derry in darkness the following night.

Brian, waiting for him, sat alone in a dimly lit kitchen that smelt of cabbage and bacon. Used to having 'company', the host family had wisely made themselves scarce and sat in the front room watching loud TV. He'd made himself a lousy cup of tea with dried milk; he hated the stuff, but there was no milk in the near-empty fridge. He took a sip, gagged and threw it down the dish-laden sink.

Without warning, the back door opened, and Brian turned round, ready for action. A blond, crop-haired, bespectacled man stepped inside, smiling widely. *Who the fuck...?*

"Welcome back to the Maiden City," Paddy said teasingly. He loved his new look's effect on people; even Monaghan was shocked and didn't recognise him at first.

"Fuck me, is that you, Paddy? You scared the crap out of me! Jesus, you look so different," he cried, drawing closer to examine his comrade. He couldn't believe the change. True, Paddy had lost weight... but his hair! Brian doubted whether Paddy's mother would recognise him now. But it was good to see him.

Paddy closed the door behind him, elbowed Brian and laughed heartily. "Aye, it's me, ye stupid git! I've not changed that much, have I?"

Brian couldn't get over it. "Bloody heck, Paddy, it's amazin'!" Any hint of their past falling out was behind them.

****

Hours later, the two men were still sitting in the kitchen, catching up on the kidnap and planning their forthcoming op. As Paddy struggled to understand Liz McKenna's betrayal, Brian attempted to soothe his fury.

"I don't think the girl had a choice, Paddy. After Hyde Park, the last thing we needed was a dead baby hitting the red tops. You saw how people reacted to the deaths of horses… imagine if a Provo-abducted baby died? There'd be hell to pay."

Paddy sneered, "That wain wasn't going to die because of us! It was going to cry itself to fuckin' death. All it did was yam, yam and yam, and then it took some sort of turn. Now that *was* scary! I thought me head was going to burst from its constant yowling."

Brian knew Paddy only joked but shook his head gravely. "You didn't see it in the news then?"

Paddy slowly placed his mug down and shook his head. "See what? Jesus, we're never out of the papers, but I haven't had much time to sit down with them!"

"The wee one was sick – I mean, really sick. She had asthma. I didn't know; it never came up when I looked into the Foxes' background. No one knew, only her immediate family. Finally, they put out that she could die of an attack if she took one. It was on the radio, the TV, the whole shebang, that day McKenna did a runner. She must've heard the news. That's probably why she skedaddled."

Paddy couldn't believe it. "Nah, that can't be right?" He shook his head.

Brian tried to make him see sense. "It can, Paddy, and it is. Think about it. You weren't picked up getting across from England. I know you'd your new passport, and you look right different, but they would've got you if McKenna had grassed to them. They would've known your contacts and would've lifted you by now." Brian had reluctant admiration for the girl's course of action.

Paddy sighed and pursed his lips. "Ye think?"

"Aye, Paddy, I do think. You're sitting here with me the night because of her. For so long as Liz is free, you're safe. Better hope she stays that way."

"Shit," Paddy replied, bewildered by the thought of it. Perhaps the girl was as loyal and clever as she'd first appeared. Brian was likely right; if the baby had died, it would've been lethal to the cause. A deeply buried part of him acknowledged that he hadn't been very diligent about following the news on that last day or since. And he hadn't made things easy for a volunteer new to the stresses of a live op while all the time that wain had been seriously ill. Maybe McKenna did the right thing?

"So tell me, what's up?" Brian asked, forcing him to ponder the enigma of Liz McKenna another time.

****

Setting Hickey up had turned out to be a piece of piss for Bonner. The army captain met him in a local leisure centre in Antrim, where the cop passed him a birthday-wrapped small box and envelope. The box held a confiscated Provo pistol, and Hickey quickly opened the envelope to find it contained a newspaper clipping and a man's photograph. In neat, small handwriting, Hickey saw a name, a time and a place within its margin.

The CC enlightened him on what he said was Jones's instructions from his hospital bed. Hickey then enquired about the businessman's condition.

"He's been very fortunate," said Bonner through gritted teeth. "It'll likely be months until he's back on his feet, so he's asked me to take over." *A blatant lie.* Bonner hadn't been near Jones and was more than livid that the swine survived.

Hickey was perturbed by Bonner's assertion that Jones placed so much trust in him. It niggled at him. It didn't sit right after Jones's disdain for the cop. No matter, he'd take great delight in carrying out this hit against the cream of the crop and deal with Bonner later.

Hickey scanned the newspaper clipping of his target: OC Cahir O'Connell of the Provisional Irish Republican Army. *Bingo!*

****

The afternoon of the meet, Brian sat in the Rainbow Café. He always found it bizarre that two of the most active operational Provos could sit in plain sight opposite one of the largest RUC police stations in the province, Strand Road Barracks.

Paddy visibly enjoyed his new persona as he joked with and teased Siobhan, the owner. Brian returned to his paper for a while but looked up and saw the waitress whispering in his friend's ear. To Brian's surprise, her words seemed to take Paddy aback and confuse him. He thought for a moment, whispered something to her, and Siobhan nodded in agreement.

Returning to the booth, Brian asked what had occurred. "Nothing," Paddy snapped, attempting to shut him down.

"You're sure?" Brian asked, unconvinced.

"Yeah. I'm sure."

Brian left it alone, folded his paper and looked over at the heavily guarded RUC station. Razor wire topped a ten-foot reinforced steel fence set above a stone wall. He thought of the poor buggers locked up in there over the years, who had been subjected to merciless hidings.

Siobhan approached them and offered Brian more tea, saying, "Mr Monaghan?"

Brian nodded and mopped up the tea she spilt onto the table. Her hand seemed less steady than usual. He thanked her nevertheless, and she retreated behind the counter.

He leaned over the table and whispered, "Is she okay? She doesn't seem right."

Paddy urged him closer with a finger and lowered his voice. "You see the lovely Siobhan there? She's one of our best plants. Think about it. Here she is, serving all those RUC fellas across the road, bringing them their sandwiches and such into rooms full of maps and files, all 'cos the fuckers can't eat anywhere safely on the West Bank. For years. You, Mr Monaghan, have no idea," Paddy informed him before gulping down his tea.

He was, in fact, worried; Siobhan had said she wanted to meet him later in private and appeared to be upset about whatever was on her mind.

In a sympathetic tone, Paddy continued, "She's tired, Brian. The poor woman is dog-tired, strung out and forever living on her nerves with what she's doing."

Brian could never have imagined an ageing waitress secretly working for the Provos for years, but when he thought about it, it was genius!

****

Around 5.30 p.m., Paddy was back in the Rainbow, sitting in its spotless stainless-steel kitchen opposite Siobhan. At her insistence, he'd come alone. She'd changed out of her pink and white uniform and pinny, and it felt slightly weird to see her in everyday clothes.

Nevertheless, she'd only managed to pull the rug from under his feet. Distraught and with his head in his hands, he found himself momentarily unable to speak.

Siobhan grabbed his elbow and squeezed. "I'm sorry, love, but I'm one hundred per cent sure it's him. I've gone over it again and again in me head. I've been watching and listening every time I've been in that pit since. Jesus, Paddy, they'd gone out to get a quick fag, and I saw me chance! There were loads of files lying open. I couldn't resist it, could I? That's when I saw it. One of those blue MI5 files stamped 'Pending'. Well, I opened it quickly, and there were photos of him, stuff about his sisters and his name all scored out and something like 'Cawley' written over it instead."

She paused before tightening the final screw in the informant's coffin. "I saw some sort of signed confession too… then, Jesus, Paddy, they nearly caught me at it, and I dropped a cup of tea on the floor to distract them." She finished, "Brian Monaghan's the grass you're all looking for. I'm so sorry."

Paddy couldn't reply, still hoping against hope that she'd tell him it was all a mistake. She read his mind.

"No, son, no mistake. It's definitely him. He's the one we've been looking for."

Paddy smiled sorrowfully. He thanked her and left to meet his friend Brian Monaghan aka Cawley.

****

It was drizzling just before ten that evening when Hickey finally arrived. It'd taken him slightly longer to drive to the bloody meeting point than he'd envisaged. At one stage, he'd got lost going down the narrow, winding tree-lined lanes past some religious-looking building swamped with statues of saints and finally reaching the decrepit boathouse. He was pleased that he'd left early. He was always meticulous about time-keeping – it allowed him to prepare mentally and find himself good cover.

For once, Bonner had produced the goods. While it was well known the OC loved fishing, no more than a handful of his closest aides knew he regularly sat by the River Foyle late at night so that he could think.

Hickey wondered how he should do it. Bullet? Or a knife, perhaps, nice and clean like that muppet of a lawyer? He found an excellent hiding spot behind some evergreens not far from the boathouse and threw himself down. He knew the OC would have a bodyguard, so Hickey decided to use the gun with its silencer on the bodyguard from behind. He'd then use the knife on the OC. With all the time in the world, he'd wait and allow the men to set themselves up, settle down and relax before making his move.

****

Disguised as a fisherman, Brian moaned, "What the heck does he have in these bags?" His eyes darted around the woods to find the likely spot where their target would be hiding. He and Paddy wore long dark green waterproof jackets with their hoods pulled up and tied tightly beneath their chins.

"It's not far," Paddy intoned with a heavy heart; O'Connell had given him precise directions. A little later, Paddy watched Brian carry the fishing rods, bags and pieces of equipment and dump them in the boathouse. There wasn't much in it, a couple of rickety old chairs and some worn netting. A blue-and-white rowing boat that'd seen better days barely stayed afloat in the river alongside.

Paddy sighed heavily; he still couldn't believe it, but believe it, he must. Siobhan was a veteran spy; she wouldn't get something so important wrong. There was only one course of action, but Paddy struggled with it; loving Brian like a brother, he worried he wouldn't be able to do it. He needed Brian's help and decided they'd talk after.

Brian had noticed Paddy had been quiet, disturbingly quiet, all night and was concerned. He'd been in such good form the previous night and earlier with Siobhan. He wondered what'd happened to turn his friend silent and brooding. He wouldn't be worried about the Englishman. He was army-trained, whereas they were seasoned street fighters. The officer didn't stand a chance.

****

Hidden amongst the foliage, Hickey realised the men were planning to fish from a dock at the far side of the boathouse, not along the river as he'd assumed. He watched them set their equipment down. He smirked; two sitting ducks would be easy enough to handle, but he couldn't see who was who. Needing to get closer, he crept along the tree line.

"Any sign?" Paddy asked Brian in an undertone, pretending to play with a fishing reel.

"Nothing. I'm going to take a leak. I can feel him; he's out there somewhere. I'll take the torch."

"Right, be careful," Paddy replied without thinking.

Brian gave him a smile that tore at his heart. *What was it they had over you, Brian? You, of all people!* He remembered the years they'd spent together; they'd been through so much. What the fuck had the Brits done to turn such a good man? Once his friend was out of sight, Paddy released a deep, uncontrolled groan.

Brian stopped and looked back, thinking he'd heard something. He peered through some branches and saw Paddy bending over as if in pain. Brian grew concerned and was about to turn back when he saw his comrade pick up a rod and walk to the far end of the boathouse. *He was fine.* Brian moved on towards a thicket of trees. Annoyed with his bulky waterproof hood, he opened it and pulled it down.

On high alert, he pretended to take a leak inside the wood. He whistled, appearing relaxed, but instinctively knew he was being watched. Hickey wasn't so much of a cad that he'd shoot a man when his trousers were halfway down his legs. He waited.

Brian slyly removed a handgun he'd tucked down the front of his boxers. Meanwhile, Hickey crept behind and prepared to cock his pistol, but it was too late. Brian spun round, and Hickey found himself facing the barrel of a gun. Brian pointed the torch at the Brit's face and swore. *Shit!* He then shone the light on his own face, allowing Hickey to see him.

"I don't believe this!" hissed the Brit, recognising Brian. This man had saved his life, getting him out of that sticky situation in The Shamrock, and had posed no threat to him when Hickey intercepted him after the meet with Doherty. Now he was waving a loaded gun in Hickey's face! Time for him to come up with some proper answers.

"Well?" Hickey hissed.

"Well, what?" Brian replied.

"Why did you stop that crowd from killing me in Belfast? Are you on our side?"

"No. Family, watching out for my girls." Brian whispered miserably, lowering his gun.

Reluctantly Hickey followed suit and, slightly confused, asked. "Family? Then why are you here?"

"To kill you."

Hickey gasped. Bonner had set him up; he'd walked straight into a trap.

"Ditto," he said despondently.

Brian's face tensed. "Then do it! Do what you've come here for!" Suddenly, he began to cry, leaving Hickey stunned. "You bastards have had me by the balls for years, using my family, blackmailing me, turning me into a fuckin' tout! So do it!" Brian screamed at the top of his lungs.

At this point, Paddy stepped out of the woods, having heard his comrade's angry words that confirmed what Siobhan had told him.

In bewilderment, Brian looked at Paddy and saw his friend's shattered expression. *He'd heard it all!* Brian walked towards him, attempting to explain, but Paddy shrank back in horror and disbelief.

It was the final straw for Brian. He had to end the endless pressure and concealment from the men whose cause he respected and had tried to serve. With him gone, his sisters would be safe, he realised bitterly.

He raised his gun to the side of his temple. "I'm so sorry, Paddy," he said and fired.

"No… God, no!" he yelled as Brian's body crashed to the leaf-strewn ground. Paddy ran over but was stopped in his tracks as something whined close to his head and stung his cheekbone. A second bullet nipped his wrist, and he dropped his gun. *Shit!*

Hickey, who had run for cover, maintained a steady firing rate. Paddy couldn't see him but scampered for the thickest cover as fast as he could, zig-zagging back to the boathouse. A spray of bullets chased him, splintering trees, bushes, and undergrowth. One finally caught him on his inner thigh, and he fell. The burning pain was excruciating as his leg became a lead weight. With every last ounce of strength, he dragged himself to the questionable safety of the boathouse.

****

His breathing grew ragged, and beads of sweat ran down his face. Blood flowed down his leg. He felt weak and nauseous. His stomach twisted. Paddy's eyelids grew heavy, consciousness ebbing, and his whole body trembled and shivered. He was so fuckin' cold… he almost thought he was back in the refrigerated lorry again. He forced himself to focus, slid off his sweatshirt, and tied one arm as tight as he could above the wound in his thigh. He had to get to the deck and find another gun in the fishing bag. His blood rushed, and his heart felt it would burst as he hauled himself over.

Rushed footsteps were coming through the trees as Paddy scrabbled through the bag. He finally found the piece but struggled to load it with blood trickling down his wrist. He could hear branches cracking nearby in the wood. *Christ!* His fingers were clumsy, and he loaded it as fast as his uninjured hand would allow.

Hickey was incensed by the setup. Bonner was to blame, and there'd be a reckoning. He'd been surprised when the big man had aimed at him. Although the guy had saved his life in the Provo bar, Hickey would've shot him tonight, asset or not, for pulling a gun on him but had been beaten to it by his suicide. As for the other man, Hickey knew he'd caught at least one bullet.

There was no point in him hiding, Hickey thought; there was nowhere for him to go. He checked his weapon and, brave and unstoppable, stepped onto the deck like a superhero. But nothing happened; there was no one there.

The only noise was the fast-flowing river, the wind and heavy rain pounding against the wooden deck. Raindrops sprayed into Hickey's eyes and clouded his vision. As he wiped them away with the back of one hand, Paddy, hiding behind one of the decrepit doors, took his chance and struck the Brit with a large rock to the back of the head.

The man cried out and groped for something to hold onto but failed, falling painfully onto his knees and flat out while the searing pain in his skull robbed him of breath.

Paddy, by then barely standing himself, kicked Hickey's ribs one, two, three and then, exhausted, a fourth time. It was a sloppy, careless fight as both men struggled to summon what little strength they could.

As the officer attempted to get back up, Paddy searched for the bloodied stone, swung it behind him, then whacked the prostrate man's head once more, convinced he heard the skull crack like an egg.

Paddy slumped to the deck beside him, staring through the hammering rain at the black sky above. He threw up from shock and pain. Jesus, Brian was dead, and he'd been a tout… Wiping his mouth and turning to look at his victim, he knew from the blood and brains surrounding the man's shattered head that he was dead. Rolling onto his side and utilising every last bit of energy he had, Paddy forced Hickey's body into the swiftly moving current of the swollen river.

Then, howling with grief, he began to cry. Suffocating anguish convulsed his whole body. *Brian!*

****

Although their wedding day hadn't been all they'd hoped for, Mrs Christopher Pecaro lay happy and content on a soft sunbed by an azure blue sparkling swimming pool in a hotel in Positano.

It was a beautiful, luxurious place, but at times she found it challenging to handle Chris's angry tirades when he listened to reports from home on the BBC World Service. As yet, they'd caught no one for the London bombings or Ella's kidnap. With her Irish blood, Caitlin felt very uneasy about the tone of the reporting and the way all her countrymen were banded together in the public perception. So far, she hadn't dared to suggest they should talk about having a family, though Chris had promised they would while they were on honeymoon. Regardless, she decided she must look to the future. She would concentrate on bringing joy, light and hope into her so far tumultuous life. One day she'd have those babies!

She felt Chris kiss her hand and heard him murmur, "I love you." This time, without hesitation, she replied, "I love you too."

To be continued...

"Hope is being able to see that there is Light despite all the darkness."
Desmond Tutu

The Importance of Book Reviews

Book reviews are much more important than you might think, especially for self-published authors. At times, self-publishing can seem like a free-for-all – anyone can do it, put a book on Amazon and hope for the best ☹

Nonetheless, I've worked particularly hard to make my writing professional and enjoyable to read and having seen the reviews for *Turmoil* and *Darkness* so far, I might just be doing that!

Book reviews can take many forms, be either brief or long, include a critique or perhaps a summary – though no spoilers, please. It doesn't matter what form you use, it's a review.

The benefits of reviews to both author and reader include:

Saves Time, Decreases Risk to Reader

- Reviews make books a known quantity. They help you become familiar in advance with what a book is about, prepare you for what you will find in it and offer you a greater chance of connecting with a particular title, even before you read the first page!

Greater Visibility, Greater Chance of the Stones Corner Series Reaching a Wider Readership

- Book reviews give books greater visibility and a better chance of reaching a wider audience.

- On some websites, books that have been multiply reviewed are more likely to be shown to prospective readers and buyers than books with few or no reviews.
- Book reviews also help to bring titles to the attention of book clubs, bookstores and blogging communities.

Your reviews can help my books reach new readers.

So, please, take a few moments to leave a review for *Turmoil, Darkness* and *Light* on either:

https://www.amazon.co.uk/
https://www.goodreads.com/

Summary of Main Characters and Locations:

The McLaughlin Family, 30 Blamfield Street, Derry	Patrick (father), Majella (mother), Martin (eldest), Caitlin and Tina (youngest)
The McFadden Family, 29 Blamfield Street, Derry	Charlie (father), Maggie (mother), Joe (eldest), Emmett and Liam (youngest)
The Henderson Family, Derry	James Jnr (father) Marleen nee Fry (wife), Charlotte and Paul James aka PJ, (twins)
	James Snr (father), Catherine (mother)
	Roger (uncle), Jocelyn (aunt)
Tommy O'Reilly, Derry	Kathy (daughter), Granny O'Reilly (mother) Majella McLaughlin (sister)
Robert Sallis (Rob), ex-British army, South Shields, England	Bridie (mother), Val (son); Val Holmes (best friend) Tracey (ex-girlfriend/mother to Val)
Charles Jones Esq, Belfast	No family, Jill Sharkey (PA), Mark Carroll (Lemon/ex-body guard)
Anne Heaney, Derry	Matt Friel (boyfriend), Sean (son from previous marriage) and Caitlin's best friend
Patrick (Paddy) Gillispie, Derry (Belfast)	Dolores (twin)
Brian Monaghan, Derry (Belfast)	Teresa (wife)
Elizabeth (Liz) McKenna, Derry	George Edwards (step-father)

Chief Constable Henry Bonner, Belfast	Wife unknown
William Barter, Journalist, USA	Family unknown
Christopher (Chris) Pecaro, London	Potential Investor in Rocola
William (Bill) and Maryann Fox, Somerset, London	Ella (daughter), Sarah, Penelope and Emma (sisters to William)
Vincent Kelly, East Belfast	No family, Eddie Lafferty (friend) and Liam McFadden (best friend)
Alan Hickey, Army Intelligence Officer	Family unknown